JAMES DEEGAN MC spent five years in the Parachute Regiment, and seventeen years in the SAS.

He served for most of that time in a Sabre Squadron, from Trooper to Squadron Sergeant Major, and saw almost continuous service on operations in Northern Ireland, the Balkans, Africa, Iraq, Afghanistan, and elsewhere. He fought in both Gulf Wars, and was on both occasions amongst the first Coalition soldiers to cross the border into Iraq. He was twice decorated for gallantry and, on his retirement from the Special Air Service, as a Regimental Sergeant Major, he was described by his commanding officer as 'one of the most operationally-experienced SAS men of his era'.

He now works in the security industry, in some of the world's most hostile and challenging environments.

James Deegan

# Once a Pilgrim

ONE PLACE. MANY STORIES

HQ
An imprint of HarperCollins*Publishers* Ltd.
1 London Bridge Street
London SE1 9GF

This edition 2018

1

First published in Great Britain by
HQ, an imprint of HarperCollins*Publishers* Ltd. 2018

ISBN: HB 9780008229474
TBP: 9780008229481

TO ALL THE BRAVE MEN I HAVE KNOWN WHO WILL NOT SEE OLD
AGE. THEY ACCEPTED THE RISKS, STEPPED INTO THE BREACH, AND
PAID THE ULTIMATE PRICE.

*UTRINQUE PARATUS*

*WHO DARES WINS*

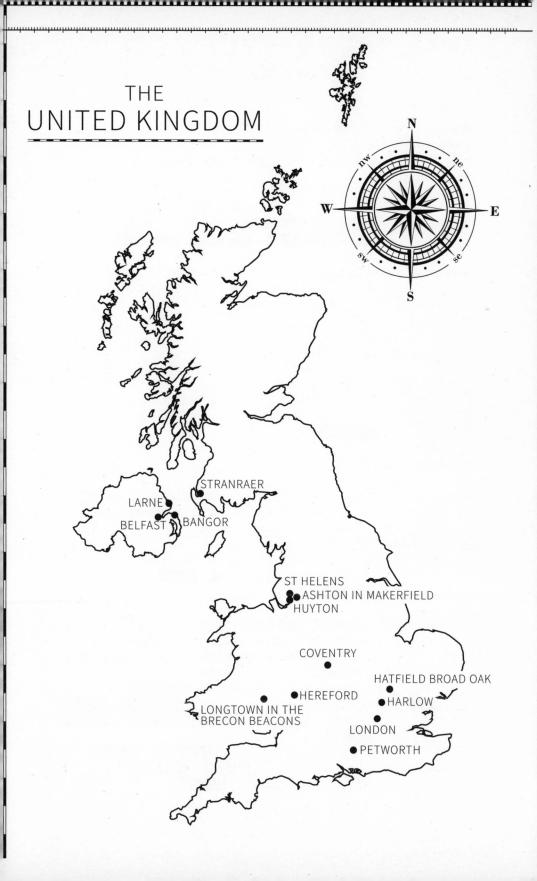

# THE
# UNITED KINGDOM

STRANRAER

LARNE
BELFAST BANGOR

ST HELENS
ASHTON IN MAKERFIELD
HUYTON

COVENTRY

HATFIELD BROAD OAK
HEREFORD
HARLOW
LONGTOWN IN THE
BRECON BEACONS
LONDON
PETWORTH

## John Carr - CV

**Personal**

| | |
|---|---|
| **Born:** | Edinburgh, Midlothian |
| **Parents:** | Father - James John Carr (deceased) |
| | Mother - Mary Margaret Carr |
| **Siblings:** | Brother - Alex Mark Carr (younger) KIA Afghanistan 2006 |
| | Sister - Louise Mary Carr (older) |
| **Addresses:** | ███████, ████████, Hereford, Herefordshire |
| | ████████████, █████████ ███████, London |

**Physical Description**

| | |
|---|---|
| **Height:** | 6ft 2in (187cm) |
| **Weight:** | 15st 6lb (95.5 kg) |
| **Hair:** | Dark |
| **Eyes:** | Blue |

**Distinguishing marks:**

Extensive tattoos to upper body (chest and back) and arms

2.5in (6.35cm) inverted semicircular scar to chin (grenade shrapnel from action in ████████)

**Military Career**

**Units :**     Third Battalion The Parachute Regiment
22nd Special Air Service Regiment

**Secondments:**

Special Reconnaissance Regiment
Operational Detachment ██████ ██████████

**Operational Theatres deployed:**

Northern Ireland multiple deployments
Iraq - two Gulf Wars and Counter-Insurgency campaign
Afghanistan - Operation ████████
Balkans - Bosnia, Kosovo, ████████, ██████.
Africa - Kenya, ████████, ████████, ████████, ████████.
Middle East - Yemen, ████████, ████████.
Latin America - ████████, ████████.
Far East - Brunei, ████████.

**Specialist Infiltration skills:** Mobility/Air
**Specialist Military skills:**
        Sniper
        Demolitions
        Medic
        Communications
        Jungle Warfare Instructor
        Counter Insurgency Expert
        Close-Quarter Battle
        Hostage Negotiator
        JTAC
        Mortars
        Surveillance – Technical and Physical

**Languages:**   Spanish – advanced
        Serbo Croat – advanced
        Arabic – fluent

**Specialist skills:** Helicopter Pilot (civilian)

**Honours and Awards:**
        MBE – Northern Ireland
        Military Cross – awarded for gallantry in
        ███████████
        Bar to Military Cross – awarded for gallantry in ███████████
        Mention in Despatches – Classified Area

**Foreign award:** Silver Star (US) – awarded for gallantry in ████.

**Security Clearances Held:** Top Secret

**Total length of Military Service:** 22 years

**Retiring Rank:** Warrant Officer Class 2 (Squadron Sergeant Major)

**Current Occupation:** Head of UK Security to Konstantin Avilov

**Personal data:**
**Status:**   Divorced
**Children:**   Son – George (serving soldier Parachute Regiment)
        Daughter – Alice (first year of A levels)
**Hobbies:**   Mixed Martial Arts

*We are the Pilgrims, master; we shall go*
*Always a little further; it may be*
*Beyond that last blue mountain barred with snow*
*Across that angry or that glimmering sea*

From *The Story of Hassan of Baghdad and How He Came to
Make the Golden Journey to Samarkand* (1913)
JAMES ELROY FLECKER (1884–1915)

These words are inscribed on the clock tower at Stirling Lines,
Hereford, along with the names of those members of the
Special Air Service who have fallen whilst serving.

# PART ONE

# BAGHDAD, IRAQ

# I.

SERGEANT MAJOR John Carr stood in the low light, fighting unfamiliar emotions and watching his blokes go through their final equipment checks.

Even at this hour, the air was brutally hot and humid, and it stank of open sewers, old garbage fires, and diesel fumes from the idling vehicles.

Foul in his nostrils as it was, he inhaled deeply: to Carr, it smelled like nothing on earth. He was going to miss it.

Tonight would see yet another operation against yet another high value target – this one a man codenamed 'Joker'.

Joker: Sufyan bin Ahmed, a former colonel in Saddam Hussein's Republican Guard and now the leader of The Obedient Servants, a vicious Al Qaeda-in-Iraq cell responsible for multiple atrocities and deaths.

Another night, another nasty bastard.

The men of 22 SAS and Task Force Dagger had been at this for a long time now, year after year spent hunting and killing the murderous jihadists who had turned Iraq into a charnel house, slick with blood. Most of the action took place close enough to smell the other man's breath, and sweat, and fear, in dark, dank rooms in backstreet houses and compounds, where the enemy holed up to make his stand.

With this tour drawing to its end, Carr's Squadron had been lucky, with only a couple of soldiers wounded and none killed. They were facing a foe who prayed for his own, glorious death, and that presented a very particular challenge. But it was one which the men from Hereford were more than equipped to meet: their phenomenal skill at close-quarter battle, and their proficiency in the art of room combat, had changed the course of the campaign, and the flow of volunteers was drying up. The streets of the Iraqi capital might be teeming with those who loudly proclaimed their desire for martyrdom; few actually stepped up.

Squadron Quarter Master Sergeant Geordie Skelton wandered over, one giant fist wrapped around a hot brew, despite the thirty-five degree heat.

He and John Carr had passed Selection together, and had gone on to serve in every theatre to which the SAS had been committed during the nineteen years they had spent at the tip of the spear. Carr would have stepped through the gates of hell with Geordie by his side, and the feeling was mutual.

'What's on your mind, buddy?' said Skelton, slurping tea.

'Getting out,' said Carr, quietly. Absent-mindedly, he rubbed his chin, rough with stubble, and felt the livid, crescent moon scar under his lower lip. A few yards away, a couple of young troopers cracked up at something a third had said. He envied them: they had years of service ahead of them. 'Knowing I'll never do this again,' he said. 'Knowing it's all over.'

'Fuck me,' said Skelton, with a laugh. 'That's another day. Let's get this one done first, eh?'

'Yeah, you're right,' said Carr. 'Feeling sorry for myself. Give us a swig of that brew.'

Skelton handed over the mug, and Carr took a big mouthful of the strong, sweet tea before handing it back.

'Knowing my luck I'll get clipped tonight,' he said, with a rueful half-grin.

'Howay, man,' said Skelton. 'What the fuck's up with you? Twenty years of dickheads shooting at you, and you've never had a scratch, bar that fucking Action Man scar on your chin. And even that's just made yous a fanny magnet. Your luck, you'd jump into a barrel of shite and come out clean.'

'Aye,' said Carr. 'I'm only kidding. If either of *us* get clipped it's all went south, that's for sure.'

That was true: at their level of seniority, John Carr and Geordie Skelton would not even be entering the target building. Grizzled old men like them would hang around at the back with the Squadron HQ element, directing the whole thing, while the young guys did the business.

The building in question was a pale grey, two-storey villa to the south of Masafi Street, in the hard-core Sunni suburb of Dora, on the southern bank of the meandering Tigris. Two hours ago, Carr had delivered the briefing – the last he would ever give – and had watched the blokes poring over the aerial photographs of the area, until every man-jack of them knew the place intimately. Each of the multiple assault teams had gone over its individual tasks, step-by-step, ensuring that they knew exactly which rooms each of them would clear, who would go through which door, what their limit of exploitation would be…

Nothing was left to chance: that was the only way to make sure – or as sure as possible – that you walked back out of the room you'd breached.

As ever, the intelligence picture was imperfect. The informant – who had been promised a lot of US dollars, a new ID and six seats on a US Air Force Globemaster out of Baghdad for himself and his family – was confident that Joker would be at the premises this evening, preparing a giant improvised explosive device for an attack on civilians in the central Shia district of Sadr City. What he could not say for sure was how many of Joker's lieutenants and underlings would be there.

Carr thought back to the conversation he'd had with the spook who had provided the intelligence for tonight's target.

'We want them alive,' the spook had said, looking down his nose at the thickset Scot – a difficult thing to do, given that Carr was a good six inches taller than he. 'Especially Joker.'

Carr had shrugged. 'Is that so?' he'd said, with a smile. 'You cannae even tell me what we're up against.'

'It's very important,' the intelligence officer had said.

'Really?' Carr had said. 'Well, you'll get him in whatever state he comes out of that building.'

And he'd stared directly into the eyes of the spook, until the man had been forced to look away. 'But we need...' he'd said, almost plaintively.

'What you *need* is to know what it's like to step into a room where there's an armed man trying to kill you. When you know that, then you'll understand why that's not an order I'll be giving my men.'

Truth was, Carr didn't have a whole lot of respect for the intelligence community: a first in Politics from Cambridge and a nice, soft pair of hands were not much use out here in the nightmarish killing zones of Baghdad, and this particular miscreant was even worse than most of them. Carr had taken an instant dislike to the superior little fucker – not that the answer would have been any different with a spook he did like.

'One chance,' he'd said, finally. 'He'll get one fucking chance, and that's if he's lying face down on the floor when my guys go in. If not, you get him in whatever state he comes out.'

Geordie Skelton threw away the dregs of his tea.

'Look on the bright side,' he said, to Carr. 'The Squadron'll run a damned sight better once I'm in charge.'

Carr chuckled: Skelton was due to replace him as Sergeant Major at the end of the tour.

'I might come back and see how you're getting on,' he said. 'If I fancy a laugh.'

He looked at his watch.

01:15 hrs.

Fifteen minutes until they rolled out of the gate of the FOB on the southern outskirts of Baghdad, which was home to TF Dagger.

'Time to go, Geordie,' he said. 'Mount up.'

Geordie Skelton grinned and stepped up into his vehicle, which would bring up the rear of the mobile column. Carr walked down the line, telling each vehicle commander in turn to mount up, until he reached the front. The plan called for Carr to lead the blokes to the lay-up position, from where the Squadron would move the final couple of hundred metres onto the target on foot. He would remain at the rear with Geordie and his driver, the OC, a signaller and his own driver, a young Brummie trooper called 'Wayne' Rooney.

Rooney had joined the Squadron from The Rifles six months earlier, and he was already a promising blade. He'd looked momentarily downcast when Carr had told him he was missing out on the assault.

'Everyone has to step out to work with the HQ now and then, Wayne,' Carr had said. 'Your turn tonight.'

Rooney was already in his seat, and Carr winked at him as he climbed aboard.

'Alright, son,' he said. 'Ready to roll?'

'Yes, sir,' said Rooney, not yet comfortable with calling his Sergeant Major by his first name. The informality of the SAS, when compared with the line infantry, could be disconcerting at first.

Carr thought about correcting him but decided against, on the basis that it might worsen the young trooper's discomfort. Instead, he smiled, strapped on his Kevlar helmet, and grabbed his Diemaco C7 – a Special Forces M4 variant fitted with a heavy duty barrel, night-sight, and a flash suppressor.

The vehicle moved forward, and each vehicle behind followed on.

The time to target was twenty minutes.

They picked their way north, past shuttered shops, burned-out cars, and fire-gutted houses. Before the war, Dora had been a predominantly Assyrian Christian neighbourhood, but in the chaos of the early occupation the lunatic fringe had moved in and begun a programme of religious cleansing. It seemed like every third house was daubed with symbols which had been used to identify their occupants as Shia, or Christian, or Mandaeists – whatever *they* were.

The streets were deserted – you had to be crazy to be out and about at this time of night. But that meant that anyone on the streets *was* crazy, so the men manned their vehicle-mounted weapons and scanned the route for enemy activity as they progressed to the target area.

As they passed the bloated corpse of a donkey, Carr looked at his map with the route marked on it.

'Next left, Wayne,' he said, glancing at the young Brummie.

'Yes, sir,' said Rooney.

'For fuck's sake,' said Carr, under his breath. He shook his head and grinned: it was too far back to remember, but he'd probably been just as bad himself as a new trooper.

Twenty minutes after leaving the FOB, the vehicles pulled over and went static at the LUP.

The teams all dismounted and shook out into the order of march, ready to move towards the target, each man going down on one knee and scanning the immediate area for any threat, the pitch black turning green in their night vision.

Carr walked over to Geordie and the Squadron Commander for a final brief.

Everything was good, no issues.

Carr keyed his radio mike, and sent one transmission. 'All teams, move to final assault positions.'

The men started to go forwards slowly towards the target. It was only two hundred metres, but it took a full ten minutes, moving quietly, carefully: they'd been in Dora enough times to know that the locals would react aggressively as soon as they worked out what was going on. Every man in the area owned a gun, and most would relish the chance to have a pop. They'd all wake up as soon as the explosive charges effected the breaches, but there was no sense in giving them a head start.

Eventually, the assault teams were at their final positions, and awaiting the radio transmission for the show to commence.

Carr carried out a check on the comms to confirm that everyone was ready to go.

All team commanders confirmed.

Carr gave the OC – Evan Forrest – a thumbs-up.

Forrest keyed the pressel on his radio and uttered the words which had launched a thousand assaults.

'Standby, standby… Go!'

There were two deafening explosions, instantly followed by the wailing of car alarms activated by the pressure wave from the breach charges, and the assault teams were in.

From where Carr stood, he could hear the immediate crackle of small arms fire coming from inside the villa.

He fought the temptation to ask questions on the radio, to find out what was going on; the teams had to be allowed to get on with their task with no interruption.

Instead, he turned to speak to Evan Forrest, and it was at that moment that gunfire erupted from a building directly opposite the target.

It was wild and high, and the assault team at whom it was directed were able to take cover inside the walled compound of the grey villa.

Carr watched as they began returning fire.

'Fucking amateur,' said Geordie, and he was right – the gunman had fired two long bursts, the first of which had illuminated his position in one of the upstairs rooms, the second of which confirmed he had not changed his position.

But this was still very much not ideal: a number of Carr's men were now engaged in a firefight inside *and* outside the target.

He made a quick decision. The team outside was Delta 18 Charlie, led by Steve Smith. Steve was a good man, and full of balls, and that meant that in a matter of moments he'd be over the wall and rushing across the street to take out the shooter.

That was not the best way to deal with this threat.

Carr keyed his mike. 'Steve, it's John,' he said, calmly. 'Stay put, mate, and keep suppressing that house. We're in a blind spot to them so I'm going in round the back. Okay?'

Smith's reply came back a moment later. 'Okay, John, got it. I think there's at least three shooters in there.'

'Noted, mate,' said Carr. 'Moving shortly.'

He turned to the small group he was with. 'Right,' he said. 'Evan, you stay here with the scaley and Jedd, okay? Me, Wayne and Geordie are going to take them fuckers out.'

The OC nodded.

'You watch your back round here, Evan,' said Carr. 'Geordie, ready? Wayne, ready?'

Rooney nodded. 'Ready, John,' he said, the effort to use Carr's first name written all over his face.

Carr grinned. 'Good man. Right, let's go.' He pressed his transmit button. 'Moving, Steve.'

Smith acknowledged.

Carr led Geordie Skelton and Wayne Rooney into the alley behind the shooters' house, until they were level with it. As they reached a rear gate, in the shadow of an eight-foot back wall, he stopped.

A sound, from the other side of the wall – low voices, and the click-clack of weapons being cocked.

Carr raised his hand to stop Geordie, and put his finger to his lips. Wayne immediately took a knee and turned to cover their rear.

Carr moved forward and looked through the gate.

He saw four men, one of them placing an RPG7 warhead into its launcher, the others peering cautiously around the side of the building towards the target house where the assault teams were still engaged.

Carr looked back towards Geordie.

Gave a thumbs down – enemy – and held up four fingers.

Geordie nodded.

Carr removed a fragmentation grenade from his assault vest and showed it to Geordie, who nodded back and immediately brought up his weapon to cover him. Noiselessly, Carr removed the pin and casually lobbed the grenade over the wall, and moved back into cover.

In the darkness, and amidst the cacophony from the firefight, the men neither saw nor heard the grenade land.

Three seconds later it detonated, partially eviscerating the three to the side and leaving them moaning and writhing on the ground. Carr stepped through the gate, followed closely by Geordie. The RPG man turned, seeing only black shapes – though Carr saw him well enough, and saw his look of utter surprise – and opened his mouth to say something.

Carr placed the barrel of his weapon into the centre of the man's face and squeezed the trigger. The muzzle flash illuminated his head as it exploded from the impact of the high velocity round, and Carr was turning and moving before the body hit the floor.

Geordie took care of the three on the ground and then they moved quickly to the back door of the house, ready to make entry.

As they reached it, a burst of gunfire erupted from the window above, followed by shouting.

Carr turned: Wayne Rooney had been following them through the gate, and had taken rounds directly into the chest and face; his body armour had absorbed the impact to his chest, but a round had just clipped his right temple. It might have been survivable, ironically, if it hadn't been for his helmet. As it was, the bullet had bounced around inside the Kevlar, ricocheting through his brain and making mincemeat of it. An inch to the left and things would have been different.

★

But shit happens.

The temptation was to run to help him, but that would have been suicidal, and pointless: Carr knew the young trooper was dead before he hit the ground.

The only thing to do now was get into the house and kill everyone inside.

Cursing, he opened the door.

He and Geordie stepped into a darkened kitchen, and paused to listen. They could hear some movement upstairs, but nothing in the immediate vicinity. While Geordie covered an open doorway which led into a hall, Carr keyed his mike and transmitted. 'Steve, it's John. We're in the downstairs of the house. Make sure no-one fires into the downstairs, okay?'

He listened for a response.

*Nothing.*

He repeated the transmission.

This time it was acknowledged.

With rounds smacking into the upper floor, and rapid AK fire being returned, the two men quickly cleared the lower floor of the building.

Carr got on the net again. 'Steve,' he said, 'Downstairs clear. We're moving upstairs. Stop firing.'

'Okay, John.'

Carefully, John Carr and Geordie Skelton headed up the marble staircase. They cleared the rear rooms of the house – whoever had shot Wayne Rooney had obviously returned to the front – and came to the final two doors, which faced the target building.

Both doors were closed.

Carr pointed at the first and held up one finger.

Geordie understood that he was going to be the first through the door.

He nodded and took up position.

Carr pressed the door handle and pushed it open.

Geordie stepped through.

Directly in front of him, an insurgent began to turn, lifting an AK47 and swinging it around.

Geordie fired two quick shots into his face, and the man was punched backwards and straight out of the open window.

To the right, a second insurgent turned to engage the SAS man, who beat him to the shot and pulled his trigger…

*Nothing.*

It couldn't have happened at a worse time.

'Shit,' screamed Geordie. '*Stoppage!*'

He began to drop into the kneeling position, reaching for his pistol, knowing that he would not have time to draw it and take out the threat, knowing also that Carr would hear and respond.

The big Tynesider felt the impact of the round in his mid-thigh at the same moment that he heard the report of Carr's weapon sounding over his head.

The shooter was flung backwards against the wall; just to make sure, Carr stepped forward, put the barrel of his weapon to the man's forehead, and shot him again.

Then he turned to Geordie. 'You okay?' he said.

'What do you fucking *think*?' said Skelton, through gritted teeth. 'I've been fucking *shot*, you daft twat. Fuck *me*, it hurts.'

'It's only a flesh wound, you big girl,' said Carr, with a sniff. 'Sort your weapon out.'

Geordie nodded, cleared the stoppage, and stuck in a new magazine.

It was as the mag was slapped home that Carr looked down, and immediately saw that it was far from a flesh wound.

Geordie's leg was sticking out at an unnatural angle, indicating that the round had hit bone; Carr knew that he could bleed out quickly from a shot to the femur, especially if the femoral artery was damaged.

'Oh, bollocks,' he said. 'Right, Geordie. I'm going to pull you over to the wall over there and prop you up. Keep an eye on the doorway, okay?'

Another nod.

Sweating, Carr dragged Skelton the ten or twelve feet over to the side of the room. It was a bastard – he weighed more than 270lbs with all his kit, and he couldn't help much, and Carr felt horribly vulnerable, especially when he had to turn his back to the door to sit him up.

Once that was done, Carr pulled the tourniquet from his chest rig.

'Keep watching that fucking door,' he said, feeling for the entry point on Geordie's leg.

He found it, and then located the exit wound on the back of the thigh. It was large, and wet with blood, and full of bone splinters.

*Shit*, he thought. But at least the artery appeared to be intact.

'Okay, mate,' he said. 'It's fine. I'm going to put this on, yeah? It's going to hurt a bit.'

Carr applied the tourniquet and pulled it tight.

Geordie let out a low moan of animal pain; he was a hard man, and Carr knew he must be in something near agony.

'That's done, mate,' he said, wiping his bloodied hands on his combats. 'Now listen, I need to go and clear that last room. Anyone but me comes through that door, you kill them. Got it?'

'I'm coming,' said Geordie. 'You can't do it by yourself.'

He tried to stand, but fell back down.

'Ah, shit,' he said. 'That *does* fucking hurt. Give me a hand up.'

'Don't be stupid,' said Carr. 'Stay here.'

Geordie gave him a thumbs-up with his left hand, his right wrapped round the pistol grip of his Diemaco, which was aimed at the doorway.

Carr smiled, returned the thumbs-up, and stepped out and back into the hallway.

Looking at the door to the last room, readying himself to step through that breach.

And then the handle started to move, and the door began to open.

Carr moved to the wall, flush to the door, and took aim.

A bloodied hand gripped the side of the door recess, and then a man of sixty or so stepped out, unarmed, hands cradling his belly. His white shirt was stained red with blood from a gunshot wound to the stomach, and when he looked at Carr the Scot saw shock but no fear in his eyes.

He smiled at Carr and nodded – as if he was acknowledging a stranger in the street, on a nice summer's day. But then another man, much younger, stepped out behind him.

The second man looked at Carr for a split second, yelled 'Allahu akhbar!' and raised his hand.

Carr was diving back into Geordie's room when the suicide vest detonated, and the force seemed to propel him even quicker.

Momentarily stunned, he came to a few moments later, lying in a heap in the floor, his ears ringing, covered in plaster and dust, and coughing and choking.

From outside, somewhere across the street, he could hear a voice shouting, 'John! John!'

He sat up and looked around himself.

His hearing became clearer, and he realised that the shouting was coming from Geordie.

'Jesus man,' said Skelton, his own pain momentarily forgotten. 'Fuck me. You okay?'

Carr patted himself down, and stood up. 'Mother*fucker*,' he said. 'That was close.'

He could feel the heat before he saw the flames.

'Geordie,' he shouted. 'We've got to get out. The place is on fire. I'm gonnae have to help you up. It's going to hurt, bud.'

Skelton shot him a withering look. 'Just get on with it,' he said. 'It's not like I can fucking hang around, is it?'

Carr keyed his radio. 'Steve, house clear. We're coming out the front. Get some guys over here to pick up Wayne, he's down at the back.'

He helped Geordie to his feet, and they made their way quickly down the stairs, the injured man hopping on his good leg and cursing as he went; the flames were confined to the top floor, close to where the guy had detonated, but still the heat drove them on.

Outside, the assault teams had cleared the grey villa, and they were now starting to regroup, ready to move out.

In the distance, one or two shadowy figures were flitting across the road – locals, roused by the firefight.

As yet they'd not been contacted.

But it was only a matter of time.

They needed to get moving.

Geordie was starting to falter, the adrenalin waning.

Carr laid him on the ground, as gently as he could.

'Medic!' he shouted. 'Medic! Quick!'

One of the team medics rushed over and took in the situation. 'Has he had morphine, John?'

'No mate, nothing. The tourniquet's only been on couple of minutes. Soon as you get a drip in him, get him back to the vehicles and call into the Ops room. Casualty requiring immediate surgery, get the medevac stood by at the FOB.'

For a moment, he'd considered bringing the medevac into

Dora, but he didn't think the injury was life-threatening, and he wasn't going to risk a heli and its crew, even for his best mate.

With Geordie handed over, he looked at his watch: from the first explosion until now, only six minutes had elapsed.

He jogged over to the OC. Forrest was standing talking to the primary assault team leader, and Carr picked up the tail end of the conversation.

'Definitely dead?' Forrest was saying.

'That's right, boss.'

'Fuck me. We're going to be popular now.' He looked at Carr. 'Did you hear that? Joker's dead.'

'Yeah,' said Carr. 'Good news.'

'It's not fucking good news, John.'

'Hey, boss,' said Carr. 'We've got Wayne down round the back there, and Geordie's took a bad one to the leg. So you're right, it's not good that he's dead. It's fucking great. Now, we need to get the fuck back to the FOB.'

# 2.

SIX MONTHS LATER – nineteen years after he'd passed Selection and walked into Stirling Lines in Hereford for the first time as a young blade – it was all over.

Carr had spent the time since getting back from that last tour on gardening leave, getting ready to leave the Army.

It wasn't easy – the military was all he'd known since his early adulthood – and his marriage was collapsing. Not many lasted in his line of work: the longest period he and Stella had spent together since he'd joined the Regiment was three weeks, and being thrown together – with all the comedown of a demanding trip to Iraq, and the emotion of leaving... They weren't at daggers drawn, but she didn't know him anymore, and he didn't know her, and neither of them cared too much. She was talking about taking the kids back home to Bangor, the County Down town where they'd met and courted. He wasn't too keen on that – his little girl, in particular, was happy and settled in a good little school near Hereford – but he wasn't sure he had the strength to fight her.

At least he had a decent job lined up – security manager with an oil company in Southern Iraq. Eight hundred quid a day, month on, month off. He might finally buy himself a decent car.

He'd spent a fair while with Geordie – that round in Dora had shattered the SQMS's femur, and after three operations and a lot of metalwork he'd been left with a nice limp and a good line in bitter, melodramatic asides. The SAS never medically discharges any man against his will – there's always a desk job needs doing somewhere – but Skelton had put his own papers in. If he was never going to make sergeant major, and clearly he wasn't now, then what was the point?

'Probably for the best,' Carr had said, deadpan, as he sat in his mate's hospital room. 'You'd only have ruined the Squadron, anyway.'

The last thing he'd done in uniform was to attend the funeral of Wayne Rooney. It always upset him to see a flag-draped coffin, adorned with a beige beret, and it was even worse when the guy in question was young.

Rooney had been just twenty-four, and engaged to his childhood sweetheart.

But Carr took comfort in the fact that the men who wore that beret accepted the risk that came with it.

He'd been very glad to know Paul – the dead man's real Christian name – he told the young man's mother and fiancée, as the wake got going.

Glad, too – he didn't add – that his days of visiting grieving families were over.

And now here he was, sitting in front of the Commanding Officer in Hereford for his farewell chat.

It was a bittersweet moment.

Carr and Mark Topham had been around each other for almost every year of the Scot's Special Forces career, and they liked and respected each other, despite coming from very different backgrounds.

Topham had been born into privilege – big house, expensive school, his father a High Court judge – whereas Carr had grown up sharing a bedroom with his brother in a council tenement in Niddrie, the grey, miserable, shitey, arse-end of Edinburgh.

A welder, his dad, and his mum a school cleaning lady. Hard-working, good and decent people – his mother, in particular, had been a regular at Craigmillar Park Church just across the way – but there'd never been much in the way of luxury. If his dad was scratching around for work, and he often was, then some weeks there'd not been much in the way of food, either.

Mark Topham's school friends were all stockbrokers or lawyers or businessmen; off the top of his head, Carr could name half a dozen pals from his own early years who were dead from heroin, or booze, or from looking at the wrong guy in the wrong way in the wrong pub. His best pal from junior school, Kenny Shaw, was currently doing a twenty stretch in Saughton for killing a guy in some stupid gang feud, and Carr knew that he could very easily have ended up alongside him. The very day he'd gone down to the Armed Forces Careers Office in Edinburgh – a fresh-faced teenager, in love with the idea of soldiering – a local ne'er-do-well had collared him outside the chippy and offered him twenty quid to keep a shotgun under his bed for a couple of weeks.

He'd been tempted, as well: he'd never seen twenty quid in his life. But he'd walked away from it – partly because it just felt wrong, mostly not wanting to upset his mum – and every day he gave thanks for that. The Army had given him discipline and focus, and turned him into a man.

And now, all those years later, he looked across the desk at Topham, waiting for him to try and twist his arm.

He wasn't disappointed.

'You know it's not too late to change your mind, John,' he said. 'What would it take to keep you? Realistically?'

'I'd like to be an operator in a Sabre Squadron again,' said Carr, knowing he had more chance of levitating. Experience and know-how took you a long way, but there was no substitute for the strength and fitness and aggression that a younger man could bring.

'Yes,' said Topham, making a church steeple out of his fingers and smiling ruefully. 'I thought you'd say that. But that's the one thing we can't do. Not even for Mad John, I'm sorry to say.'

Carr smiled despite himself at the nickname, which had followed him round the Regiment for the last fifteen years.

'Of course you cannae,' he said. 'But you asked. What else is there? Become an officer? No offence, Mark, but that's not me.'

'This has been your life for nearly twenty years. Are you sure you want to walk away from it all?'

Carr looked at the CO for a moment. 'No, I'm sure I *don't* want to. I fucking hate the idea. But it comes to us all, and this is my time. I'm going to walk to the main gate, hand in my pass, and it's all behind me.'

'I respect that. It's a shame, but I respect it.'

Carr smiled. 'Not to mention, I've been offered a job I can't refuse. Twenty years living in shitholes, getting shot at, blown up, eating compo... It's time to enjoy life. It disnae last forever. I want the cash.'

'You tight Jock bastard,' said Topham, shaking his head and grinning.

Carr laughed. 'Me, a tight Jock bastard? Here's you with your stately home, and your polo ponies.'

'Fair one,' said Topham, with another rueful expression.

'Boss, trust me, I hate it more than you do, but it's just time to go. At least I can walk out the gate with my head held high, and think about all the guys we knew who didn't have that option. I beat the clock. Ask young Rooney if he wants to walk out the Camp again. Ask Pete Squire, or Jonny Lawton, or Rick Jones. Ask any of them.'

'True. A lot of good men on that clock.'

'Too many.'

Mark Topham stared out of the window at a cloudless blue sky. The thump of a helicopter landing on the field outside bounced through the glass.

'Well, you can't say I didn't try,' he said, with a resigned smile. 'You've had a citation submitted for the night in Dora, by the way.'

Carr raised his eyebrows. 'Just doing my job,' he said. 'It's not about the medals.'

'Sell it to Ashcroft, then. But joking aside, well done. Richly deserved.'

'Thanks boss. Means a lot.'

Topham stood up, and Carr followed suit.

The 22 CO held out a hand. 'I can honestly say, John, that it has been an enormous pleasure and a singular privilege to serve with you. You're always welcome here. Godspeed.'

A slight lump in his throat, and his eyes stinging a little, Carr nodded.

'Aye,' was all he could manage.

He strode out of the Commanding Officer's room into the corridor and towards the exit to the Regimental Headquarters building, where he walked, head down, straight into a tall, slender man in the corridor – a man whose angular appearance belied his considerable tenacity, courage, and intellect.

Major General Guy de Vere, Director Special Forces, who had arrived a few minutes earlier on the helicopter, for a planning meeting with Mark Topham.

'Christ, John, you nearly took me out,' said de Vere, when he saw who it was. 'I understand you're leaving us?'

'Yeah, that's me, boss,' said Carr, shaking the outstretched hand. 'I'm out the door. Civvie street.'

'Mark couldn't persuade you?'

'Nah. Sorry.'

De Vere shook his head. 'Oh, well,' he said. '*Amicitiae nostrae memoriam* something-*sempi*-something *fore*.'

'I'll be honest with you, boss,' said Carr. 'I havnae a clue what you just said there.'

'Cicero,' said de Vere. '*I hope the memory of our friendship lasts forever.*'

'Jesus,' said Carr. 'I'm not *dying*, you know. I only live down the road.'

Guy de Vere smiled broadly and clapped Carr on the shoulder.

'Tell you what, John,' he said, 'we've come a fucking long way since that night in the Clonards, haven't we?'

# PART TWO

# BELFAST, NORTHERN IRELAND
# TWENTY YEARS EARLIER

# 3.

LANCE CORPORAL JOHN CARR hefted his rifle in his left hand and looked across the vehicle yard at the young officer.

'Jesus,' murmured Carr. 'I reckon your missus shaves more often than he does.'

Next to him, Corporal Mick 'Scouse' Parry chuckled. 'You cheeky bastard,' he said. 'Fair one, mind.'

A thin, pink dawn was just catching the top of the Black Mountain on the edge of west Belfast, but the inside of Fort Whiterock was still lit by orange sodium. In the glare of one of the lights, the second lieutenant – who was very tall and very slender – was struggling to lay out the unwieldy tribal map on the bonnet of his Snatch Land Rover.

'He's in my wagon, is he?' said Carr, with a thin smile. 'I think I'll stick the lanky streak of piss up on top cover. See what he's made of. Hopefully he'll get a pissy nappy in the face.'

'Character-building,' said Parry, with an approving look.

The officer finally succeeded in smoothing down the map, and now he made a show of studying it.

'Look at him,' said Carr, shaking his head. 'The height of the bastard, he'll make a fucking good target. Mind you, he's a thin cunt. They'll hardly see him if he turns sideways.'

Scouse Parry chuckled again.

Off to the left, near the main gate and in the shadow of the base's massive walls, a group of soldiers – members of 7 Platoon, C Company of the 3rd Battalion of the Parachute Regiment – stood around, stamping their feet against the cold, breath forming clouds, waiting on the order to load their weapons.

Two Snatch Land Rovers and a grey armoured RUC Hotspur idled in the background, blue diesel exhaust drifting slowly over the white-frosted tarmac.

Two policemen leaned against their wagon, carbines slung round necks, smoking cigarettes and talking quietly about a young WPC one of them had his eye on.

Occasional laughter erupted from the soldiers; one started coughing violently and cursed and threw away a butt.

It was going to be a long day: patrolling and setting up VCPs in Ballymurphy, Andersonstown, and Turf Lodge till long after dark, and finishing with a shift change for the RUC at Springfield Road, before a return to the relative safety of Whiterock.

All in the shadow of the Provisional IRA's murderous bombers and gunmen.

'I'll go over and have a word,' said Carr. 'Wind him up a bit.'

'Go easy on him,' said Parry, with a smile. 'Five minutes.'

Carr strolled across the asphalt to where 2Lt Guy de Vere was bent over the map, trying to cram the different areas of the city – shaded orange for the Protestant sectors, green for the Catholic – into his memory.

'You alright there, boss?' said Carr.

De Vere turned to look at him. He felt oddly intimidated by the hard-faced Scottish NCO, despite being several years older and senior in rank. He couldn't decide whether it was down to Carr's undeniable physical presence – he had a Desperate Dan jaw, broad shoulders and merciless eyes – or his brooding silence. The man had barely said a word to him before now, and what he did say was said in such a thick accent that subtitles would have been useful.

At least the blokes seemed to understand what he wanted.

'Fine, thanks, corporal,' he said. 'I was just having a last minute refresher.'

Carr's face was an expressionless mask, his mouth hidden by a drooping, bandito moustache of the sort the men seemed to favour.

'Good idea,' he said. 'Mean fucking streets out there.'

'Yes,' said Guy de Vere, slightly nervously.

A month earlier, the Paras had lost three A Coy men to a remote-controlled bomb hidden in a ruined cottage down near Mayobridge: the city just beyond the gates was every bit as hostile.

De Vere was fresh out of the box, new in the battalion, and in the Province, and today's was his first patrol, on his first tour. He was nominally in charge, but really his role was to watch everything that Scouse Parry and John Carr did and said, and learn.

Not all that long ago, he'd been enjoying a lucrative career as an investment banker in Hong Kong. But, vaguely unsatisfied with life, he'd chucked all that in to come home and do something more meaningful with his life – a decision which had left his Toms shaking their heads in wonderment when they'd found out about it.

Half an hour earlier, Carr had seen de Vere take a wander up into one of the sangars overlooking the streets outside, and he tried to imagine what the officer was thinking.

Probably:

*Last year I was earning six figures and living the dream.*

*Now I'm in a shithole where half the population wants to take my bastard head off.*

*What the fuck have I done?*

'Boss, you're doing top cover,' said Carr. 'It'll give you a better look around so's you can understand the Area of Operations.'

*Plus, it'll do you some fucking good to go through what the lowest, youngest, newest crow in the multiple goes through,* he thought.

De Vere nodded. He didn't fancy top cover one bit – you spent the whole day exposed, on offer to whoever wanted to have a pop – but he didn't show it.

'Right you are, lance corporal,' he said.

'Main thing is, keep your eyes peeled for that RPG cunt down on Kennedy Way,' said Carr. 'He's an ex-French Foreign Legionnaire. Knows what he's about.'

De Vere nodded again: he'd had that worrying piece of information stuck into his head a few times in a series of scary briefings.

'If he gets one off and it hits the wagon, that'll seriously ruin your day,' said the Scot, with a cheerful grin. 'You'll be lucky if it only takes your legs off.'

De Vere pushed his shoulders back. He thought for a moment about the journey up from Palace Barracks the previous evening. That had been bad enough, and it had been in the back of a Saracen, a purpose-built armoured vehicle with sixteen mil of steel protecting him. Hot, and claustrophobic, but at the end of the day sixteen mil was sixteen fucking mil. The Snatch was a lot more vulnerable.

'I'll keep my eyes peeled, corporal,' he said. 'Don't you worry about that.'

'Good,' said Carr. He looked at the second lieutenant more closely. 'You okay, boss?' he said. 'You look a bit white.'

'I'm fine, Lance Corporal Carr.'

Carr felt for him, momentarily. He remembered his own first time out of the gate: he was a fighter by nature, but even his arse had been going a little.

'Listen,' he said, leaning in closer and lowering his voice. 'Everyone shits themselves the first time. The trick is, dinnae let the blokes see.' He looked over at the Toms. 'It'll be fine. The RA have got snipers, but they're shite. I've never heard of anyone being hit in a moving vehicle. And that cunt with the RPG?' He looked at the young officer's rifle. 'You see the fucker, just give him the good news with that.'

He threw back his head and laughed, and at that de Vere felt a weight lift off his shoulders. He looked at Carr: at a shade over six feet tall, and thick-set and hard-eyed, he held his loaded 6.5kg SA80 rifle like it was a toy, and wore his parachute smock folded back at the sides in a style the men favoured. His helmet was covered in camouflage scrim held in place with a thick black rubber band. All in all, he looked very 'ally' – the current Para Reg slang for cool.

'Thanks, Carr,' he said. 'Much appreciated.'

'Nae problem, boss. Just another day. It gets a lot easier after this one.'

'John,' shouted Scouse Parry, from across the yard. 'Get ready to roll.'

'Aye, Scouse,' yelled Carr. 'Two minutes.' Then he looked at the soldiers. 'You lot!' he barked, in his thick Edinburgh growl. 'Let's start fucking sparking! First three to the loading bay!'

Three Toms made their way over and stood pointing their weapons casually into the bay.

'Load!' said Carr.

The soldiers went slickly through the drill, checking their safeties, inserting a magazine, securing their pouches, hands gripping front stocks.

'Make ready!'

The sound of three SA80s being cocked, racking a live round into the chamber. Three sets of eyes and thumbs re-checking three safety catches.

'Mount up!'

They stepped away from the loading bay and walked to their vehicle.

'Next group. Come on, get a frigging move on!' snapped

Carr. He looked over at de Vere. 'Then it's you and me, boss!' he shouted, in a voice that almost sounded like an order. 'Let's get weaving. No time to think about your girlfriend.'

'I don't have a girlfriend, lance corporal,' said de Vere, his voice higher and reedier than normal.

He realised immediately that he had responded too quickly, too sharply.

He hadn't meant it, but stress does funny things to people.

'Boyfriend then, is it, boss?' said Carr, with a broad grin. 'I mean, equal opportunities and all that. And you being a public schoolboy.'

From across the yard, Carr heard Scouse Parry cackle.

He saw de Vere open his mouth to speak, and then shut it, and force a grin.

*Good boy*, he thought. *You're learning.*

A moment later, Carr and de Vere made their own weapons ready, and Parry walked over.

'My vehicle first then, boss,' said Parry, to de Vere. 'Then the RUC, then you and Carr. Eyes on stalks, eh?'

Parry walked off to the front Land Rover, whistling tunelessly, nodding at the RUC and chivvying his driver and Toms aboard.

Carr watched Guy de Vere bend his tall frame to get up on top and then climbed into his own vehicle.

He looked at his driver, a young Cornish private called Shaun Morris.

'This new rupert's shitting himself, Shaun,' he said, with a chuckle. 'Long way from the playing fields of Eton.'

'Where's that?' said Morris.

'Never mind,' said Carr.

Up ahead, Parry was running through a final check, making sure everyone was on-board.

Then he looked toward the men manning the gate.

'Get it open,' he shouted, and stepped into the vehicle, shutting the armoured door behind him.

And then his driver put the vehicle into gear, and they all headed out through the gates.

# 4.

IT'S A BIG THING, to kill a man in cold blood.

So Gerard Casey had slept badly in the little back bedroom in the terraced house in Lenadoon Avenue, a mile or two distant from Whiterock.

He'd woken up at 5am in the middle of some kind of sweating nightmare, and since then he'd been sitting on the edge of his bed, watching the red digits on his clock radio move slowly onwards.

Nearly six now.

He sparked up another Red Band and grimaced as he sucked down a lungful of cheap, bitter smoke.

Right leg jiggling on the frayed carpet.

*Sure, you'll be fucking fine, Gerry*, Sean had said, a day or two earlier. *The first time's the hardest. But after that it gets easy.*

His older brother, 'Sick Sean' Casey. An Active Service Unit member, a soldier in A Company in the 1st Battalion of the Provisional IRA's grandly-titled 'Belfast Brigade', and a proven and tested killer.

Gerard stared at the U2 poster hiding the peeling woodchip paper on the wall opposite.

Bono, in that fucking silly hat and them fucking silly shades.

*I can't close my eyes and make it go away, either.*

Guts churning, he stubbed the fag out in the loaded Harp ashtray on his little bedside table and stood up, pulling the grey kecks out of his arse.

Went to his chest of drawers and took out a pair of jeans.

He looked down at his hands. They were shaking slightly.

'Get a grip,' he said to himself. 'Fucking twelve hours yet.'

He put the jeans back and selected another, older pair.

He'd be burning every scrap of clothing on his body later on, and he didn't want to be getting rid of his only pair of 501s.

The old Wranglers, they could go.

He bent down, stepped into them, and pulled on a plain black T-shirt.

Looked out his bedroom window.

Four days to Christmas, and there were trees and lights in half the front windows in the street.

Across the rooftops he could see the raised security tower of Woodbourne police station.

Things had been different in the area since the Paras had taken over. Those bastards didn't fuck around, and God help you if a patrol caught you late at night. They'd kicked the shit out of one of the main players the other week, put him in hospital good and proper. Then they'd spray-painted the wall of his house with 3 PARA WE OWN THE NIGHT.

The police had done fuck all about it, even though an official assault complaint had been put in.

The peelers laughed about it, so they did. He'd heard talk of it in the Davitts.

Treat us like second-class citizens, so they fucking do.

He looked at the tower and shivered, and for a moment he had an eerie feeling that he was being watched.

He shook his head.

Paranoia.

Better get used to that, Gerry.

He was brought back to reality with the banging of a fist on the front door.

A second later, another bang.

Louder this time.

'Would you ever piss off!' yelled Gerard's mother, from her pit down the landing.

'It's alright, ma,' shouted Gerard. 'It's just Sean.'

His mother said something muffled and angry, the hangover making her head thump, but Gerard had already cracked open his window.

'Stop banging the fucking door,' he hissed. 'I'll be down in a minute.'

In the dawn-dark street below stood Sean, hopping from foot to foot, blowing on his hands, dressed for the cold.

Sean was Gerard's way in to the RA.

His recruiting sergeant.

He wanted it, did Gerry. He wanted to be a Republican foot soldier, like Sean.

He wanted the respect, the attention, the name.

The women.

Who hardly gave him a second glance, now, but would be all over him like a rash once he made his bones.

But he also knew that he was crossing a line.

Right here, right now, he was just another wee civvie standing in his back bedroom.

By the time he was back in this room tonight he'd have crossed over into another world, a world from which there was no way back.

He felt anxious.

The paranoia was back.

# 5.

AT EXACTLY THE MOMENT that Gerard Casey opened his window, another alarm clock sounded.

This one was on a cheap Formica bedside table, next to the head of a young man in a very similar bedroom, in an all-but identical terraced house, about five miles distant as the crow flies.

Only five miles, but Northland Street was a world away from Lenadoon Avenue. It might as well have been a different country, and in a way it was: to get there, you'd to wade through rivers of blood.

The young man in Northland Street – William 'Billy' Jones – opened one eye, clicked off the alarm clock, and groaned.

He was glad of the money that came with his recent promotion, but he missed the extra couple of hours' kip.

Rubbing the sleep out of his eyes, he half-rolled, half-fell out of bed and onto his knees.

From there, he stood up and stumbled into the bathroom for a piss, and then stumbled back to his bedroom to pull on his uniform.

Black trousers, white shirt.

He fished a badge saying 'Assistant Manager' from his trouser pocket, and pinned it on his chest.

Stifling a yawn, he crept slowly downstairs to the kitchen, trying to be as quiet as possible.

His da' would have been out with the boys until the wee small hours, and he was not a man to annoy when he was hungover, his da'.

Not a man to annoy at *any* time: Billy Jones Senior was a leading commander in the Ulster Volunteer Force, and a violent man with a hair-trigger temper and a light-heavyweight's physique. He wasn't shy of using his hands, even now his son was twenty.

Billy Senior was a dyed-in-the-wool bigot, for whom the only good Catholic was a dead one. Billy Junior bore no such hatred. He'd flatly refused to get involved with the UVF, and Billy Senior had made it quite clear that he despised the boy for it. He was a coward, a traitor, a taig-lover…

*Christ.* Billy Junior smiled guiltily to himself as he reached up for the cornflakes. *If only the old bastard knew.*

He was seeing a Catholic girl, a pretty wee thing called Colleen who worked in the bar. They'd had to keep the whole thing secret – his da' would kill him if he found out, definitely kick him out the house, and hers wouldn't take it much better. The sooner the two of them could save up the money to get the fuck out of this Godforsaken city, and move in somewhere together… London, maybe. Maybe the States. Somewhere that it didn't matter whether or not you believed in the Virgin Mary, or thought the sun shone out of King Billy's arse, or cared what football team anyone supported.

Colleen had hinted that she wanted to get married, settle down, have kiddies.

He imagined a big family wedding.

His old man would go proper mental.

*A fucking papist wedding in a fucking Fenian church?*

Red-faced, veins bulging, steroid-popping eyeballs sweeping over everyone in the other pews.

And then the reception… Billy Senior and his brothers on the lager and scotch, her da' and his brothers on the Guinness and vodka chasers…

*Fuck me, but it would be a bloodbath.*

Nah, they'd be living together. Somewhere a very long way away.

Hey, maybe they'd get wed in Vegas? Just the two of them.

An Elvis wedding.

He grinned, put his bowl in the sink and slipped on his favourite red adidas jacket.

Upstairs, he could hear the old man snoring.

He'd see Colleen tonight when their shifts overlapped.

Not for long. Just a kiss and a wee cuddle.

Five minutes alone.

Go back later to walk her home.

It wasn't much, but it was better than nothing.

And it wouldn't always be like this.

# 6.

BILLY HAD LET himself in at the front of Robinson's just after eight.

Switched on the lights and the heating.

Ran his hand down the length of the dark wood bar to check it wasn't sticky and breathed in the mixture of stale fags, spilt beer, and Pledge spray polish.

He walked to the office at the back of the pub.

Looked at the notebook to see if the night manager had left anything.

They were running short of Carling Black Label.

One of the bar staff had given her notice, but temporary cover was being arranged – one of the lads, his younger sister had done a bit of bar work before.

All good. No problems.

Humming tunelessly to himself, he went into the kitchen and from there down into the cellar to double check the lager stocks.

At just after nine o'clock, he went back to the front door to let in Stephen and Laura, the cook and barmaid who were on that morning.

'Alright guys?' he said, with a broad smile. 'Is it cold enough for ye, is it?'

For a moment, he stood in the doorway, smelling the frosty air, and looking up and down the street.

His last morning on earth, and he had no idea.

# 7.

LATE MORNING, and the Paras and their RUC colleagues were pulled up in the middle of Ballygomartin Road, right on the western edge of the city, putting in a VCP.

John Carr had finally allowed 2Lt de Vere to come down from top cover, and now the two men were standing side-by-side.

De Vere was standing to Carr's left, watching him out of the corner of his eye, and mimicking his stance and movements, sometimes consciously, sometimes without even knowing he was doing it.

Carr in turn had been watching the young officer all morning, assessing him, looking for weaknesses.

He was no-one's idea of a class warrior – though his father was a staunch Communist – but he was only human, and he defied any working class Scotsman not to get a wee bit ticked off by the chinless Old Etonians the Army kept putting in charge.

But it was like anything: some were shite and some were okay, and, to be fair to the beanpole next to him, this one didn't seem too bad.

Completely fucking clueless, obviously, but there were just a few signs that he might have the makings.

For starters, he'd stayed up top throughout without even the hint of a complaint, and when they'd gone down Kennedy Way he'd got a proper game face on, his rifle into his shoulder, covering his arcs. True, he hadn't had any filthy nappies lobbed at him, but there'd been a few stones thrown and more than a few insults shouted in his direction, especially when they'd been down by the Bombay Street peace line early doors, and he'd taken it all in his stride, unflinchingly. Carr had known plenty of new ruperts who'd shown a lot less backbone.

They'd been doing VCPs for four hours now, give or take, and had pulled over plenty of cars. Sometimes the vehicles were searched, and sometimes the drivers just got spoken to for a few moments and then waved on. Carr could see that the apparent randomness of it was confusing de Vere, but at least he had the honesty and good sense to realise that he was out of his depth. Credit to him, he was doing his best human sponge act, trying to soak up the signs and tells and little indicators that Carr, Parry and the police officers were working on.

Their vehicle was in the middle of the current checkpoint, pushed out into the opposite side of the road to create a chicane between the police Hotspur to the front and Mick Parry's Land Rover to the rear.

The traffic was light, and in a lull Carr turned to look at de Vere.

'Alright, then, boss?' he said, surprising the officer. 'Coping, are we?'

'Just about, corporal,' said de Vere, gripping his SA80 a little tighter. 'Thank you.'

'We got shot at down here last week,' said Carr, casually. He nodded at a distant block of flats. 'Fella with an Armalite had a pop from over there.'

De Vere followed his gaze.

'Missed the top of Keogh's head by three or four inches,' said Carr, deadpan. 'Now, someone as tall as you...'

De Vere looked at him, careful to stand at his full height.

'I don't...' he started to say, but Carr cut him off.

'Customer coming, boss,' said Carr. 'We havenae time to stand here gossiping.'

An old purple Morris Marina up ahead was being flagged down by the RUC, and its driver was pulling over as directed – a sensible move, with the eyes and rifles of several stony-faced members of the 3 Para multiple trained on him. Enough people had been shot for driving through checkpoints that you had to be off your face on drugs or drink, or deeply stupid, or a member of PIRA with weapons on board and no other options, to try it.

Carr waited until the car had come to a halt and the driver had switched off the engine and was showing his hands.

He looked at de Vere. 'This one's an old hand, boss,' he said. 'Conor Gilfillan. Bomb-maker. He'll have nothing on him, but we should fuck him about a bit. You can have a word. Off you go.'

De Vere swallowed hard. 'Right-ho,' he said, and walked over to the Marina, making a wind-your-window-down motion with his hand.

He leaned in and looked at Gilfillan, a weaselly-faced little man with piggy eyes and several day's growth.

'Can I ask where you're going please, sir?' said de Vere. 'And I'd like to have a look in your boot if I may?'

Gilfillan stared at him with ill-disguised contempt. 'Sure, this is a free country, is it not?' he said. 'What fucking business is it of yours where I'm going?'

Carr leaned in past de Vere and rammed his gloved hand between Gilfillan's legs.

Grabbed his balls, and squeezed.

Hard.

'Answer the officer's question, you RA cunt,' he said, applying yet more pressure.

The bomb-maker's eyes were almost popping out of his head, and both his hands were on Carr's wrist, trying in vain to pull him away.

'Jesus,' he said. 'Fuck.'

Half an hour later, a chastened Gilfillan was finally allowed on his way, after apologising to Guy de Vere for his rudeness and watching the Paras conduct a thorough but fruitless search of his vehicle.

'Never mind *May I look in your boot please, sir*, boss,' said Carr, phlegmatically, as he watched the Marina disappear. 'That's how you handle cunts like him. You're never going to make a friend of the fucker, so why bother trying?'

De Vere nodded.

Just then, a woman pushing a toddler in a buggy walked past.

She didn't break stride, or look at them, but out of the corner of her mouth she said, 'You look after yourselves, lads. It's a good job you're doing.'

Carr watched the young second lieutenant follow her with his eyes, and then the look of surprise which came over his face.

'What?' said Carr, eyebrows raised. 'You think they all hate us?'

'No,' said de Vere. 'Obviously not, but...'

'We get a lot of that,' said Carr, turning to look down the road, eyes sweeping for threats. 'Most people here are no different to most people anywhere. They just want to live their lives, and they know us and the RUC's the only thing stopping a massacre.'

'Would it be that bad?'

Carr looked at him with a face which said, *Are you serious?*

'It'd be a bloodbath, boss,' he said. 'There's not many of the bastards, but they're some of the most evil people you'll ever meet. On both sides.' He paused, narrowing his eyes for a few moments at an old Ford Granada which was approaching, and then relaxing. 'But don't you worry. You'll find all this out for yourself.'

# 8.

MIDDAY. SICK SEAN and Gerard were sitting around the Casey family kitchen table with Ciaran O'Brien, a thickset man who smelt of sweat and old beer.

The third team member, O'Brien was another hardened Republican from a long line of hardened Republicans stretching back to the 1600s, the Eleven Years' War, and beyond.

It was a way of life for some people.

The three of them spoke in hushed voices, as if the breadbin might be bugged.

Which, actually, it might be. You literally never knew, until the fuckers kicked the door in one day and dragged you away.

The hard work, the reconnaissance and the planning, had been done.

The weapons had been removed from the cache in Milltown Cemetery off the Falls by the hide custodian the previous night. He'd stripped, oiled and reassembled them, and moved them into a temporary location in the Poleglass, over Derriaghy way.

The final weapons-move to the forming-up point – McKill's, a well-known Republican bar on the Suffolk Road, out on the south-western outskirts of the city – would not take place until just before the Active Service Unit arrived to collect them. The less time the guns were in play, the better. To be caught with them was effectively a death sentence: many a good man had been killed by those murdering Brit bastards, even when he'd known the game was up and was trying to surrender.

They'd collect their vehicle at McKill's, too. A red Ford Sierra – the most common car, and the most common colour of that car, in the city. Stolen to order three weeks earlier, hidden away and fitted with ringer plates that went to an identical vehicle, so that it would at least pass any casual check by the peelers.

If any of them got a little more nosey, all bets were off.

Gerard Casey couldn't sit still.

He stood up and went out into the back garden to smoke the last of his twenty Red Band.

'That's a filthy habit,' said Sick Sean, after him. 'It'll kill you.'

He burst out laughing, but he was half serious: Sean Casey was a muscle nut gym monkey who lived on grilled chicken, salad, and handfuls of parabolin, winstrol, halotestin, and whatever other anabolic steroids he could get his hands on. Plus an occasional amphet sharpener.

'Is he gonna be alright?' said Ciaran O'Brien. 'Your wee man?'

He pronounced it 'marn'.

'He'll be fine,' said Sean, dismissively. 'It's a piece of piss.'

They sat in easy silence for a few moments. The kitchen smelled of the stale chip pan, and O'Brien's Blue Stratos aftershave. The only sound was the relentless tick of the plastic clock on the wall behind Sick Sean's head.

Ma Casey stuck her head in and said she was off to the Co-Op.

Sean frowned and nodded curtly.

She meant the pub. An hour or so, and she'd be drunk; two hours, and she'd be oblivious.

Gerard came back into the warmth of the kitchen, rubbing his freezing hands together.

'Let's have another go through the plan,' said Sean.

'I know the plan,' said his younger brother, sharply.

'I didn't fucking ask if you knew it, boy,' spat Sean. His body had tightened and his fists were suddenly bunched. 'I said *let's go through the fucking plan.*'

Gerard stopped in his tracks. When his brother was in this mood, you didn't push his buttons unless you liked hospital food.

'Listen, Gerard,' said Sean. His voice was a little calmer, but his teeth were gritted. 'Sitting here and talking about it, that's the easy bit. The *next* easiest bit is killing the fucker. D'you know the hard bit?'

Gerard nodded.

'The hard bit's not getting fucking caught and spending the next thirty years in Long Kesh. So let's *go over the fucking plan one more fucking time.*'

The younger man nodded again, a mental image of Billy Jones Jnr entering his head. The three of them had spent hours and hours over the last two months in surveilling their target, and by now he knew Billy's face and his movements better than the back of his own hand. A week earlier, he'd even stood at the bar in Robinson's and made sure to be served by Billy, so that he could see his face right up close, and really know the detail.

He'd looked into the lad's eyes, and had seen his own reflection.

Seemed a nice enough guy, no different to himself.

*Don't think like that.*

'He leaves Robinson's at the end of his shift between six and six-thirty,' he said. 'He takes about ten minutes to get to the car park.'

'What's he wearing?'

'Black trousers, white shirt, and he always has that red adi jacket on.'

'Car's he driving?'

'Dark green Austin Allegro. W reg.'

'Where will we be parked?'

'Behind his vehicle – not directly behind, but somewhere we

can cover all approaches, and enough distance so's I've time to react when we see him.'

'Good,' said Sick Sean, unclenching his fists and relaxing slightly. 'Okay, we see him walking up. What then?'

'When he's near the driver's door, I get out the car, walk straight towards him. Ciaran gets out and covers my back with his AK. You get ready to start the engine.'

'You missed something.'

Gerard Casey thought for a moment. Then he said, 'Sorry. When we see him we all pull our balaclavas down.'

'Bingo. Carry on.'

'I walk straight to him, slow and steady, take my time, no running. I get to just beyond arms' length, and stop before I fire. I put two rounds in the middle of his back. When he goes to the ground I put the barrel to his head and put another round into him. Then I turn around and walk back to the car, with the gun down by my side.'

Sean nodded. 'You never run,' he said. '*Never*. Nice and steady. Remember that. Okay?'

Gerard nodded. 'I get in the car, and Ciaran gets in after me. Then we drive slowly out the car park and head back.'

'Balaclava?'

'We lift them when we're in the car and away from the area.'

'Some hero gets in your way on the way back to the car?'

Gerard Casey hesitated. Had they discussed that possibility? He couldn't remember.

'What you going to do, son? Fucking *think*.'

'Show them the pistol and tell them to fuck off.'

Sick Sean shook his head. 'You kill them, Gerard,' he said, emphatically. 'Stone cold. Man, woman or child, I don't give a shit. Got it? I'm not doing that kind of time for no-one, understand?'

Gerard nodded.

'We're going to give his old man an early Christmas present, alright,' said O'Brien, with a big grin.

'He's definitely not a player?' said Gerard.

'No,' barked Sean, 'but that doesn't fucking matter. Don't go fucking thinking about it too much. He's guilty by association.'

There was a heavy silence in the kitchen.

A dog barked outside.

Gerard Casey got up and patted his pocket.

'I need to go and get some more fags,' he said. 'I'll be back in half an hour.'

'Fifteen minutes,' said Sean. 'And Ciaran's going with you.'

'Why?'

'Because I fucking say so, that's why. This is a military operation, and we have procedures. I'm not having you phoning your handler and warning off the Special Branch.'

Gerard gawped at him. Eventually he blurted out, 'I'm no fucking tout.'

'I know you're not, son,' said Sean, flatly. 'It was a joke. If you was, sure you'd be dead by now, brother or not. Now go and get your fags, and then we'll go over the plan again.'

# 9.

LESS THAN HALF a mile away, LCpl John Carr's Land Rover led the three-vehicle Parachute Regiment/RUC patrol in through the big steel gates to Woodbourne police station, and parked up.

It was just before 13:00hrs, and within a matter of minutes the ravenous Toms were wolfing down police canteen sausage and chips, full of cackling and abuse.

Lt Guy de Vere carried his metal tray to the table and sat down opposite Scouse Parry and John Carr.

'Not the sort of scoff you're used to in the Officers' Mess, boss,' said Parry, shovelling a forkful of chips into his face, and winking at Carr. 'But I bet you're hungry.'

Carr chuckled. 'Aye,' he said. 'All that nervous energy, eh, Scouse?'

De Vere smiled: after a morning in their company, he was just starting to get used to the soldiers' gentle piss-taking.

'I was more scared of Private Keogh's driving than the PIRA,' he said, cutting into a fat sausage.

'Fucking hell, boss,' said Keogh, next to him. 'I'm the best driver in the battalion!'

The other driver – Morris – shouted something abusive from the other end of the table. They all dissolved into raucous laughter, and de Vere started eating.

When they'd all finished, Parry disappeared off and John Carr wandered over to the hatch and fetched them both a huge mug of steaming tea.

'We've got five minutes, boss,' he said. 'Get your laughing gear round that.'

'Thanks, Corp'l Carr.'

They sat there, the tall, blond, well-bred Englishman and the dark, hard-faced Scot from the sprawling Edinburgh council estate: wildly different in many ways, but brought together by the uniform and pride in their work.

Carr watched him sip the hot, sweet tea. He looked knackered, but then the special stresses and strains of walking the streets of Belfast in a British Army uniform did take it out of you, and it was worse when you were the FNG and trying to catch up. Young Guy de Vere would have learned more in this half-day than in his entire Army career to date. The episode with Conor Gilfillan... they didn't teach you stuff like that at Sandhurst, thought Carr.

It was as though de Vere had read his thoughts.

'At least there'll be no junior Gilfillans,' he said. 'After what you did to his bollocks.'

Carr grinned. 'There's about a dozen of the little fuckers already, sadly,' he said. 'But the greasy wanker will remember you, alright, boss. Nasty wee shite.'

'All those tricolour-painted kerbstones and murals,' he said, leaning back and looking at Carr. 'And the graffiti. *Fuck the Brits. Troops Out*. It's not the most salubrious city, is it?'

'Come again?' said Carr.

'Belfast. It's a bit rough.'

Carr picked at his teeth with a match. 'Where are you from?' he said.

'Marlborough,' said de Vere. 'Well, a village not far from. My family has a farm there.'

'Nice part of the world,' said Carr, laconically. 'I can see why you'd think Belfast was not very salubrious.' He picked a bit of sausage out of his teeth, looked at it and put it back in his mouth. 'But Belfast is better than where I'm from. See these semi-detacheds and nice rows of terraces?' he said. 'We dinnae have too many of them. Where I'm from, it's all fucking tenements.' He chuckled. 'And we dinnae have the polis and the Army keeping order, neither. It's dog eat fuckin' dog.'

He watched in amusement as de Vere blushed slightly.

'So where are you from?' said the young officer.

'Niddrie, boss. East Edinburgh.'

'I don't think I know it.'

'You wouldnae. Shitehole. Good for heroin, stabbings, single mums, and dogshite. That's about it.'

'Family all up there?'

'Yeah.'

'Girlfriend?'

'Nah. I mean, I've got a bird, like, but I met her over here.'

'Planning to get married?'

'To Stella?' Carr laughed, and then was serious. 'Tell you the truth, I've not thought about it.'

'Father in the Army?'

'In the war. But he left as soon as he could, like. He didnae like being fucked about by posh English bastards. No offence.'

It was de Vere's turn to laugh. 'I'm certainly English,' he said, 'and some might say I was posh, but my parents were married and I promise not to fuck you about any more than I absolutely have to.' He paused for a moment. 'So what made you join?'

Carr thought for a moment. 'Always wanted to be a soldier,' he said. 'Since I was a boy.' He grinned. 'I like a good scrap, boss, and there's no better way to get yourself into a scrap than join the Paras.'

'And what are your plans?'

'Selection.'

'The SAS?'

'Aye. I'm down for the next course.'

'Good luck.'

'No such thing. Hard work and mental strength, that's what'll get me through.'

De Vere polished off his tea and looked round the room.

His eye fell on Mick Parry, deep in conversation with the two RUC men.

'Corporal Parry seems an impressive guy,' he said.

'Sound as a pound,' said Carr. 'Hard fucker, like. But fair. The blokes love him. Officers, not so much.'

De Vere nodded.

'Brave, as well,' said Carr. 'Where we met Gilfillan, down on Ballygomartin? We were there three weeks back. Friday night. Drizzly, it was. Road was wet. Fucking joyriders come down there at seventy, maybe eighty. Stolen XR2i.'

He paused.

'You know we lost one of the guys to a joyrider at the start of the tour? Never stopped. Hit him on the white line in Andytown. Good mate of mine. Fucking tragic.'

De Vere said, 'Yes, I know about the incident.'

'Ever since that, the blokes are fucking twitchy about joyriders,' said Carr. 'And the joyriders know it. So this XR2i comes down the road, sees us, and the driver jams on the anchors. Greasy road, shit tyres, the driver was only fifteen. No idea how to get out of the skid. He rolled the car and it hit a lamp-post fifty metres from our position. Set on fire. The lad was fucked up and dead, but there was three other kids trapped in the car – his mate and two wee girls. Mick run straight up the road and dragged them kids out of that car. Knowing it could have gone up at any minute. Or that some PIRA wanker might see him and have a pop.' Carr finished his own drink. 'He should get an award for it, really.'

'And what…' said the young lieutenant, but he was interrupted by the tramp of Mick Parry's German para boots on the green lino.

'Right, John,' he said, to Carr. 'Time to get the lads sparking.' He looked at the lieutenant. 'You too, boss. Can't sit around all day chin-wagging with this idle fucker.'

# 10.

AT AROUND THAT moment, a call was being made from a secure line at 10 Downing Street in London.

The man making the call was a major in the Royal Anglians who was on military liaison attachment to Mrs Thatcher's personal staff.

The man receiving the call was the 3 Para adjutant in Belfast.

The call was to confirm final arrangements for an event which the two men had been discussing over the previous three days – an unannounced flying visit to Belfast by the PM.

The previous Thursday, gunmen from the Provisional IRA's Belfast Brigade had shot three off-duty RUC men in a pub off the Shankill Road, killing two and seriously injuring the third. It came hot on the heels of the deaths of three members of the Parachute Regiment in the Mayobridge bombing, and together they demanded a political response.

At some time after 6pm that evening, Mrs Thatcher would be flying in for a secret visit to Knock, to meet grieving family members, and to rally the troops.

A pre-Christmas morale booster.

And, because of that, the city would be crawling with extra Army patrols, cars full of Special Branch, undercover members of 14th Intelligence Company – the surveillance specialists known as 'the Det', whose job it was to infiltrate both the Republican and Loyalist communities – and various other watchers, followers and shooters.

# II.

AT A QUARTER-TO-FIVE, as the winter darkness fell, the Casey brothers and Ciaran O'Brien finally left the house in Lenadoon Avenue.

Gerard felt simultaneously light and heavy, terrified and excited.

It was weird how the other two looked so relaxed; he tried to copy them.

Well-practised in counter-surveillance, they moved on foot – you spotted a tail much quicker that way – and headed across Lenadoon Park, a nice, wide-open space with enough ambient light to see if you were being followed. They walked out onto Derryveagh Drive, and then down to the Suffolk Road, which was long and straight enough to give good views in either direction.

They turned north.

Almost immediately, Sean said, 'Shit!' and dropped his head into his collar.

On the opposite side of the road, a joint Army–RUC mobile patrol was approaching, moving between one exercise in fucking up people's lives and another. The front driver slowed, and the top-cover in the tail vehicle gave them a long stare, his SA80 rifle held at the ready. A tall, slim officer, he was new in the Province, but he was a diligent man, and he'd spent hours poring over mugshots of the main players. He might well have recognised

Sean Casey and Ciaran O'Brien, had the light been better, and that would have been enough to get them a tug. Worse still for the IRA team, the soldiers were Paras, which quite possibly meant hours of being pissed about, and the job off for that night.

But in the gloaming and the drizzle the top-cover couldn't make them out, and the Land Rovers rumbled and trundled on their way.

A few minutes later, the three of them walked in to McKill's. It was early and empty, and the barman was polishing glasses. One man sat nursing a pint at a table by the wall – a low-level player who nodded respectfully to Sean and Ciaran. Gerard Casey, his stomach light and queasy, threw a strained half-smile at the barman, and got a quizzical look in return before the fellow went back to his polishing; something was clearly up, but he knew better than to see or ask anything.

They headed straight through to the office at the rear of the building.

The door was locked.

Sean rapped on the flaking green paint with his knuckles.

It was opened – slightly, at first, then wide – by a dark-haired man in his mid-thirties who was wearing dungarees and a thick jumper.

Gerard realised to his surprise that he knew the guy – his name was Martin Thompson, and he coached a kids' Sunday football team down on the Rec there.

Gerard had had *no* idea that he was a member of the RA.

The cell structure, in action.

They stepped past Thompson, and the door was locked behind them.

The room was empty apart from an old table, a few chairs, a sports holdall, and a telephone.

Sitting on the table was another man, late twenties, a ginger bog brush on his head, and a face full of freckles – Brian 'Freckles' Keogh, Gerard knew *his* rep alright.

Next to Freckles was what Gerard recognised in the glare of the single bare lightbulb as a folding stock AK47, with two of its distinctive curved magazines lying beside it. There were also two pistols – he couldn't have named them, but one was a modern-looking thing and the other an old revolver. Next to the revolver was a mug which bore the Celtic FC crest and contained a magazine for the automatic and six rounds for the revolver.

He realised with a jolt that both of the men were wearing pink washing-up gloves. In his state of controlled panic, the incongruity made him want to giggle, but he fought it back and kept his silence.

'Alright, fellas,' said Thompson.

'Alright, Tommo,' said Sean.

He nodded at Freckles.

'Evening, Freck.'

'Ready?' said Freckles.

'As always.'

Martin Thompson picked up the holdall and opened it. 'Here's your change of clothes for later,' he said, indicating a Tesco carrier bag. 'And you'll need these.'

He picked out three other carrier bags and handed them over. Each contained a pair of pink Marigolds, still in their plastic packets, and three new balaclavas.

'You know the drill,' said Martin. 'Get yourselves gloved up before you touch the weapons.'

Each of the three pulled on a pair of the gloves.

'Over the bottom of your sleeves,' said Sick Sean to his brother, holding out a wrist. 'Like I showed you.'

Once the gloves were on and the sleeves tucked in, Freckles produced a roll of duct tape and went from one to the other, taping the gloves in place.

'That's great, Sean,' said Gerard, as casually as he could. He felt oddly talkative, and blurted out, 'Feels a bit weird.'

His voice sounded as though it was coming out of someone

else's mouth, and for some reason a vision came to his mind: a trip to Barry's in Portrush… What had he been? Seven? Eight? He'd got on the roller coaster, full of bravado, and then they'd locked the lap belt on, and there was no way off, and he'd pure near shit himself, and there was nothing to do but sit there and go with it and hope it wasn't going to be too bad and just wait until it was all over *because you can't get off can't get off can't get off*

'You'll get used to it,' said Ciaran O'Brien, calmly. 'It'll keep the forensics off your hands. Unless you like the look of the H Blocks?'

The two new men chuckled. 'Ah, leave him be,' said Martin.

*Nothing to do but go with it, and hope it's not too bad.*

Satisfied, Freckles stood to one side and the three men walked to the table. O'Brien picked up the AK, cleared it, then loaded a magazine and made it ready. He put the spare magazine into the inside pocket of his leather jacket. Gerard went to pick up the semi-automatic – it was a 9mm Browning Hi-Power – but Sean slapped his hand away. 'Fuck off, that's mine,' he said, grabbing it, loading it and putting it into his waistband.

Gerard Casey picked up the revolver, and looked at it in disbelief.

It was a late-model Webley, liberated from an unfortunate British Army officer at some point in the previous half century.

Its wooden handle polished smooth by many hands.

Bad hands.

'This looks like a fucking antique, so it does,' he said. 'You sure it'll be okay?'

'Better than an automatic,' said his brother. 'No chance of it jamming. Sure, it'll blow that prod fucker's brains out, I know that much. Make a hell of a fucking bang.'

O'Brien smiled wolfishly. 'And a hell of a fucking hole in his head,' he said. He pushed the Celtic mug across the old table. 'You'd better load it.'

'Is that all the bullets I get?'

'If you need any more than that you're a dead man,' said O'Brien, flatly. 'We'll not be hanging around.'

Gerard Casey broke the pistol open and emptied the half-dozen shiny .38 brass cartridges into his gloved palm.

Trying and failing to hide the shaking of his hands, he slotted them slowly into the cylinder.

'Where's the car?' said Sick Sean.

Martin picked up the phone and dialled a number; it rang once and was immediately answered.

'Car,' he said, and put the phone down. He turned to the three. 'Be out front in five minutes, boys.'

Gerard looked at the pistol in his hands, and then slipped it into his waist band. He stared at the floor, not wanting to look around.

There was a knock on the door and then a voice through the wood: 'Car's out front, Marty.'

Gerard brought his head up.

Sean was staring straight into his eyes, and now he smiled.

'Showtime,' he said, his grin widening into a leer.

Gerard shivered. He had never until that moment realised just how evil his brother looked.

But there was no going back now.

# I2.

AT 18:00HRS, THE PARAS had conducted the shift change for the RUC crew, and now they were sitting in Springfield Road police station, drinking yet another round of Tetley teas.

Second lieutenant Guy de Vere reckoned he'd drunk half a dozen cups already that day, and not out of the dainty little Royal Doulton china teacups that his mother liked, but out of big black plastic Army mugs which each held about a pint. It was playing hell with his bladder.

Around him, the men were relaxing in the smoky warmth.

Mick Parry, an unlit B&H fag in one corner of his mouth, was telling one of the older Toms a filthy story about a girl he knew back in Wavertree.

Keogh and Morris were sucking Fox's Glacier Mints and bickering good-naturedly over who was the better driver.

John Carr had his head buried deep in a dog-eared book.

'What are you reading?' said de Vere.

Carr held it up. '*Chickenhawk*,' he said. 'Robert Mason.'

'The Vietnam book?' said de Vere, unable to keep the note of surprise out of his voice.

Carr looked at him. 'I might never have went to Eton, boss,' he said. 'But they do teach us to read, you know.'

'I didn't mean it like that,' said de Vere. 'And I didn't go to Eton myself, either.'

'Not posh enough?' said Carr, with a grin. 'The OC won't let you in the Mess if he finds out.'

'You read a lot of military history?'

'A fair bit, aye.'

Pte Keogh leaned over. 'Guess his favourite song, boss,' he said.

'No idea,' said de Vere.

'*Dancing Queen*,' said Keogh, with a cackle. 'By Abba.'

Carr grinned. 'That's a fucking good track, right enough,' he said. 'But let's get one thing straight. My favourite song is actually *Love Will Tear Us Apart*.'

'Joy Division?' shouted one of the Toms, from across the room. 'Bunch of poofs.'

'Bollocks,' said Carr. 'It's a fucking classic. Ian Curtis, a man gone too early. Brilliant band.'

'I don't think I...' de Vere started to say, but Carr was away, singing the first few lines of the song.

'Jesus,' said Scouse. 'Cover your ears, lads, what the fuck is that? Sounds like a ladyboy in distress.'

'Get to fuck, Scouse,' said Carr. 'You know the birds love my singing. Gagging for it, once I start.'

'Maybe that fat NAAFI bird up in Whiterock, mate, but no-one else,' said Parry. 'Oh yeah, that other fat bird in Palace Barracks.'

'They all need loving, Scouse,' said Carr. 'And don't get jealous. I've got a *Readers' Wives* you can borrow later.'

'Fuck off, you jock bastard!' said Mick Parry, and the rest of the room fell apart.

De Vere smiled to himself: this was evidently a tight-knit bunch of blokes, high on morale and led by a pair of excellent NCOs. He'd begun the day feeling like the proverbial fish out of water but, to his amazement, he was already starting to feel accepted. In turn that felt like an enormous privilege.

He looked at his watch: 18:15hrs.

They were done for the day, bar the drive back to Whiterock, and he was just starting to think about getting back to his room, and writing that letter to his father to let him know how his first day had gone, when an RUC inspector stuck his head in and beckoned Parry outside.

A minute or two later, the Liverpudlian corporal returned.

'Okay, guys, listen in,' he said, looking at the blokes. 'Get your kit on, and let's get out to the vehicles. We're not done yet after all.'

He came over to Carr and de Vere.

'John, boss, they want us to do some extra VCPs in the Clonards,' he said, with the air of a man who was entirely used to being fucked about by the Army, and could take more of it than they could ever dish out. 'Down in the Lower Falls area. We're gonna be out a bit later than we thought.'

'Right-ho, Corp'l Parry,' said the young officer, standing up. 'Any specific reason?'

'There's something big going on, but they don't share shit like that with the likes of us, do they? The RUC crew don't know, neither.'

'Thanks, Parry,' said de Vere. He hesitated for a moment, and then dropped his voice and leaned in slightly. 'It's been a good day. You've been a great support.'

'It's not over yet, boss,' said the corporal, with a broad smile. 'Trust me, this bollocks can go on all night.'

Outside, the Toms were already waiting patiently next to the vehicles.

'Listen in,' barked Parry, and proceeded to give them a quick brief, pointing on his map to where they would set up the first VCP.

They would leave the RUC station and head along the Springfield Road into Kashmir Road, then right into Clonard

Gardens, and finally into Clonard Street, facing towards the Falls Road.

They'd put the VCP in at the junction with Ross Mill Avenue and Clonard Street – a chokepoint that everyone had to pass through, if they were trying to cut out the Falls so as to avoid the nearby RUC station.

At 18:35hrs the vehicles rolled out of Springfield Road.

Five minutes later they were set up in the Clonards, and the VCP was operating.

# 13.

THE IRA HIT TEAM found a space in the row behind the Allegro, about six cars along to the right of the driver's side and sitting between two other cars so that they would be shielded from Billy Jones's view as he walked to the car.

The car park was poorly-illuminated, and the route to his vehicle kept him away from theirs, so there was no chance of him seeing them and spooking.

It was perfect, near-as.

Sick Sean Casey killed the engine and the lights, but left the key in the ignition. He rubbed his head – it was itchy under the hot, rolled-up balaclava – and took the pistol from his waistband. He hid it under his right leg, where he could get at it quick if needs be.

In the rear, Ciaran O'Brien absently patted the AK, which was lying on the seat next to him under a dark towel.

Gerard held the Webley up, staring at it in the low, orange light from the nearest lamp.

'Put that fucking thing down, Gerard,' hissed Sean.

If a chance RUC patrol or – God forbid – an undercover SAS team rolled into the carpark, just as Gerard was waving his frigging gun around like he'd just won it at the fair, the last thing the three of them would see was muzzle flash. Those fuckers were out there every day and every night, and if they saw a pistol in your hand it was game over.

No warning, no surrendering.

No second chances.

*Murdering bastards.* He looked out of the window and sighed. *Be glad when this is fucking done.*

Gerard slipped the revolver under his right leg like he'd seen his brother do and sat there, fingers *rat-a-tat-tat* drumming on his thighs.

Ten or fifteen minutes, and they would be moving.

This was the vulnerable time, the sitting and the waiting.

He leaned forward and clicked the radio on – quietly, quietly.

Some old song he didn't know.

Something about fear, and guilt, and a fire.

He grimaced and clicked it off again.

'Hey, leave it on,' said O'Brien, leaning forward. 'That's *Funeral Pyre*. It's a fucking good song. The Jam, was it? I remember when it come out.'

He whistled a bar or two of the tune.

Gerard Casey switched the radio back on, and said nothing.

*Twenty years old, and about to make his name…*

O'Brien grinned.

To be fair, he thought, he'd probably been like that the first time himself.

*Actually, no, I fucking wasn't. But my first really* was *a piece of piss. That fucking tout, strapped to the chair in that barn, crying and begging. With my old man watching.*

It was eight or nine years ago now, but he remembered it well: the cold steel of the pistol in his hand, the muzzle to the guy's elbows, then his knees, then his ankles.

Finally his temple.

Once the order was given, O'Brien had been careful to show no weakness, and no hesitation, even though he knew the guy, and his sons.

All the time, his da' watching, expressionless: he could never have shown the old bastard up.

He leaned forward and squeezed Gerard's shoulder.

'You'll be alright, Gerry,' he said. 'We'll be in The Volunteer tonight and I reckon that Roslyn McCabe'll have her knickers at her ankles for you, once she knows.'

Gerard looked over his shoulder and tried to smile. 'You reckon?' he said.

'Definitely,' said Sean. 'Sure, I've fucked her sister, and the young one's no better. Tiocfaidh ár lá, son. Now keep your eyes on that car.'

# 14.

A LITTLE OVER A MILE due west, the Paras and their RUC attachment had plotted up in Clonard Street.

But whatever it was that had forced them to stay out later than expected, it hadn't reached the Clonards.

They'd been in place for approximately fifteen minutes, but the area was as quiet as the grave.

So far they'd only had to deal with five or six cars.

Some had turned into Clonard Street and then into Odessa, blatantly avoiding the checkpoint, and, as he and John Carr stood beside the open door of Parry's vehicle, a red Renault Trafic van did just that.

'Doesn't necessarily mean fuck all,' said the corporal, out of the side of his mouth, from the vehicle commander's seat. 'All sorts of reasons people don't want to get fucked about, boss. Might just want to get home quicker.'

Not for the first time that day, de Vere reflected on an unfortunate fact about the work they were doing.

Yes, they were making life harder for bad men. But they were making life harder for good men, too.

'Not too static, boss,' said Carr, and wandered off to the side of the road.

Stamping his feet in his boots to get some blood back into

them, de Vere crossed to the opposite pavement, and took a moment to look around himself. He could just about make out his men in various doorways up and down the street, rifles at the ready, covering the VCP and the approaches. The dark made him uneasy: even now, a man might be hidden in some shadow with an Armalite into his shoulder.

But he knew that he was going to have to live with it.

Back in the middle of the road, the two RUC officers were leaning against their vehicle, their weapons held very casually, smoking.

Carr wandered over and nodded in the direction of the coppers.

'They'll probably get it if it's coming, boss,' he said, quietly. 'Look at that one tabbing away. The end of his fag's standing out like a bulldog's bollocks, right in the middle of his swede. Plus their drills are shit. Standing out in the open, not moving around.' He shook his head. 'I suppose you cannae blame them, in a way. Same shit, day in, day out, year after year. Maybe anyone'd get complacent. Got to take your hat off to them, really. When they go home at night this disnae stop.'

Carr walked on, and de Vere watched the RUC men. It was true: the tips of their cigarettes were like bright red bullseyes in the dark street. He knew that many of the PIRA players regarded the local police as the true, traitorous enemy, the Brits being not much more than an inconvenience who would fuck off once the local opposition was scattered and broken.

*Rather them than me*, he thought, and immediately felt ashamed of himself.

Shaking that off, he stifled a yawn. He ached for the comfort, if you could call it that, of his room in Whiterock.

A hot shower, something to eat. His bed.

Maybe they'd finish before too long?

It was very quiet. He hoped so.

Not that it had been all that bad a day. The nervousness he'd felt that morning was gone.

Carr had been right: it was getting easier.

*Good man, Carr.*

The sort of man the British Army lived and died on.

# 15.

NOT LONG AFTER six-thirty, Billy Jones Jnr handed over to the evening manager at Robinson's, ran him through the stock-take and the till, and managed to have a few minutes in the back office with Colleen before he said goodbye.

Eventually, he walked her back to the bar, pulling on his adidas jacket, and put his foot on the brass rail.

'It's gonna get messy tonight,' he said, raising his voice over the hubbub.

The place was already buzzing with several raucous Christmas office parties.

Girls with Santa hats on their heads, knocking back Malibu and Coke.

Lads with pints in hands and wandering eyes.

Wham! on the speakers.

*Last Christmas.*

A heart, given to someone special.

'Shall I pick yous up at midnight, darlin'?' he said.

'Aye,' said Colleen, with a cheeky grin and a twinkle in her eye. 'Don't be late, 'cos I have something for you.'

He blushed – *stop blushing you eejit* – and said, 'Really?'

'Uh huh,' she said. 'And I think you'll like it.'

'I'll not be late then,' he said, with a big smile.

A man appeared at his elbow waving a tenner, so Colleen broke off.

Billy zipped up his jacket and walked out of the pub, the smile still plastered across his face.

She was a rare one, alright. He couldn't wait for midnight.

Five minutes later, hands thrust into his pockets against the cold, he reached the car park.

Jangling his keys.

He shivered. He knew the car would be bitterly cold inside – the heater was crap, the seats were plastic. Probably have to scrape the ice off first.

Still, only ten minutes and he'd be home and in front of the gas fire for his beans on toast or fish fingers and chips, or whatever his ma had in mind. Then he'd…

He became dimly aware of footsteps behind him, light and quick, and then – before he could turn to look – two things happened simultaneously.

There was a thump in his back – it felt like he'd been hit with a sledgehammer – and a deafening sound.

He knew right enough that it was gunfire – you didn't spend twenty years in Belfast without recognising *that* sound – but he was confused because it sounded so *close*.

Shots always rang out somewhere *over there*, half a mile away. Not right next to you.

*Didn't they?*

He realised that he was being pushed forwards, and then it happened again – the thump, the noise – and he staggered, felt the strength go from his legs.

There was pain too, now – real pain in his back, searing heat and stabbing sensations – and he couldn't breathe, like he'd been badly winded.

He collapsed onto his knees.

Tried to stand up but couldn't.

His head was spinning.

He fell forwards.

Somehow, he realised, he was now flat on the ground, his face pressed against the cold, wet tarmac.

Confusing.

*What's… How…?*

The last thing that Billy Jones Jnr felt was something hot being pressed into the soft flesh behind his left ear.

Then nothing.

# 16.

THE RED SIERRA nosed its way back towards the Falls Road.

At first, no-one said a word.

Gerard Casey was trembling with adrenalin, and an odd mixture of pride and shame, of happiness and grief.

He'd just killed an innocent young man, only a year older than himself.

So what the fuck did that make him?

But then, this was war, and he'd done it for the cause.

That, and Roslyn McCabe, and her knickers round her ankles…

Their route had taken them back along Great Victoria Street, passing by Robinson's, and now they were in the evening traffic, heading north to join the Falls from the Divis Street end, well away from Springfield Road RUC.

Travelling slowly in the bumper-to-bumper flow, fighting the urge to overtake somehow, or turn off and take a quicker route.

In the cold night air, the sound of the three shots would have travelled a fair way.

Someone might already be kneeling over Billy Jones' body.

Someone might have seen the red Sierra leaving the car park straight after the hit.

You just never knew how quick that someone could call in its description, or how quick the police and the Brits could react.

Their focus now was on ditching the car and getting it alight as soon as they were on safe ground.

A patch of scrubland off Glen Street.

The two gallon can of four-star in the boot, and a match.

Then pile into McKill's.

Get the weapons back to Martin and Brian.

Strip.

Hand over their clothes for burning.

Dress.

Then off to The Volunteer, and a nice cold Guinness, and then...

Outside, it was sleeting and Baltic cold, but inside the vehicle heating was turned down low.

If the car misted up a little, so much the better.

Sick Sean driving slowly, not wanting to attract any undue attention, just another guy going about his business.

A big, fuck-off grin on his face.

Occasionally looking at Gerard.

Who was the first to speak.

'Christ,' he said. '*Christ!*'

'Fucking outstanding,' said Ciaran O'Brien, from the back seat. 'Fucking brilliant!'

'I told you the wee man would be fine,' said Sean, over his shoulder. 'It's in the blood. He's a stone-cold killer. Did you see the way the big sack of shite went down?'

'I did,' said Ciaran, from the back. 'A good operation, Gerard. Well done. Proud of you, son. No hesitation. Straight in there. UP THE RA!'

He shouted the last, and punched the seat in glee as the car turned left into the Falls, moving with the ebb and flow of the traffic.

'He was the same age as me, near enough,' said Gerard, half to himself.

'He had it coming,' said O'Brien. He clapped Sean on the shoulder, and hooted in delight. 'Billy Jones' fucking son! What a fucking result!'

'Yeah, his old man's going to go fucking bananas when he finds out,' said Sean.

'He'll…' said Ciaran.

Then, suddenly alert: 'What's that? Is that a siren?'

It was. In the distance.

*Sirens*, plural.

'Ach, it's miles away,' said Sean, after a moment.

But it was a timely reminder to them all.

*Keep focused.*

*Don't relax.*

They were still in play, and any number of people in this miserable, benighted city would kill them on sight, if they got the chance.

The UDA. The UVF. The UDR. The RUC.

Even INLA, if the mood took them.

And of course the fucking SAS, or 'the men in cars' from the Det, 14th Int Coy, who were often mistaken by their targets for the boys from Hereford.

They were fiendishly good at what they did.

Sure, them bastards could be behind them right now.

Or ahead.

Or both.

Just waiting for a radio message to take down three men in a red Sierra.

Sean glanced nervously in his mirror.

'Keep your eyes on the road, Sean,' said Ciaran O'Brien from the back seat. 'You look out for checkpoints, let me worry about who's following us.'

Gerard Casey now slumped in his seat.

All that nervous energy gone.

The car drew level with Leeson Street.

The traffic was slow.

*Must be the lights at Springfield Road Falls junction.*

*That's all it is.*

*We'll be on our way in a jiffy.*

But fate was not on their side.

Unbeknown to them, Margaret Thatcher had landed at Aldergrove forty-five minutes earlier, and the security services were on high alert: twice the normal number of regular Army, twice the RUC presence, not to mention spooks, undercover SF and various others.

And just then the red Sierra rolled to a stop behind a bus – right under a fucking streetlamp, of all things.

# 17.

SICK SEAN CASEY looked out of his window and met the eyes of a man behind the wheel of a car stuck in traffic on the opposite side of the road.

Six feet away.

No, four.

Lit up by the same streetlamp, and the lights from the car behind the IRA team.

*Big guy, probably six-two, moustache. Scruffy bastard.*

Sean Casey habitually noted faces; he had a good memory for them which had helped keep him alive, until now.

He didn't know this guy.

But there was *something* about him – for all that his gaze was casual – and Casey sensed it straight away.

And he felt his guts lurch.

'Your man there…' he said softly, almost to himself.

Moustache's shirt and pully and jacket looked like an Oxfam scarecrow's hand-me-downs, and his hair was collar-length and unkempt.

But it was all *too* carefully done – too *studied*.

It looked like an act, and it didn't hide his bearing, which was fit, and strong, and confident.

*Military.*

Sick Sean would never know it, but he was spot on.

The man was a lance-jack in 3 Para Close Observation Platoon, dressed in civvies and driving an admin vehicle from a resupply visit to his mates at Springfield Road RUC, where they were pulling extra hours for the visit of the Iron Lady.

Bastard fate had brought Sick Sean and the man with the moustache together, separated only by a few millimetres of glass and a white line.

Moustache's passenger and vehicle commander were idly looking out of their own windows in the opposite direction from the stolen vehicle, visually covering their arcs while stopped, oblivious for now as to who was on their right.

But Moustache was suddenly wide awake, eyes narrowed, trying to place the face, flicking into the rear of the Sierra.

*That guy looks familiar. Who the...?*

Sick Sean could almost see his cogs turning, his mind's eye flicking through mugshots and briefings.

Then he saw it click into place.

*Sean Casey.*

*Sick Sean Casey.*

At that point, Moustache should have yawned and broken his stare — he'd had it hammered into him enough times by the SAS instructors at Hythe and Lydd — but even the best of men can fall victim to the shock of the moment.

Instead, he turned to the vehicle commander.

'That's that cunt Sean Casey, opposite,' he said, under his breath. 'And it might be Ciaran O'Brien in the back.'

The commander snapped his head around and locked eyes with O'Brien.

'We're made,' said Sean, a flustered edge to his voice. 'The fucking SAS!'

The soldier said something to his passenger, and reached down.

That was enough for O'Brien. A split second later, he brought up his AK47 and opened fire from the back seat.

The blinding muzzle flash lit up the interior of the vehicle, but it was the noise which really shocked Gerard Casey. It was thunderous, the pressure from the long burst resonating through the car and erupting out of the destroyed window.

In his panic, O'Brien fired off almost a full magazine. They were unaimed shots, the weapon jumping around in his grip, but even so it was a minor miracle that only one round found its target. That round took the COP lance-corporal in his right shoulder, split and scored and shattered its way down his humerus, and exited near his elbow, putting him completely out of the game.

O'Brien was shouting, 'Drive! Drive! Drive!' but Casey was already on his way.

Gunning the engine, swerving round the bus, battering and scraping his way past the traffic behind the Army car.

The carburettor sucking in air.

Behind them, the COP vehicle commander had stepped out onto the tarmac, his Heckler and Koch MP5K raised.

He fired two short, aimed bursts into the rear of the moving vehicle, which was now ahead of the bus and accelerating away, sliding left and right, wheels squealing.

The back window frosted from the impact of the rounds, but, with civilians in cars and on foot, he was forced to hold his fire as the Sierra got beyond thirty metres.

But one of his rounds had done its job.

It had entered the rear right side of Ciaran O'Brien's neck and had exited the front left side, opening the jugular vein as it passed through flesh and muscle, blood and matter spraying over Sean and Gerard. O'Brien was thrown forward and released the AK, and it clattered and slid past the gearstick and into the front passenger footwell at Gerard Casey's feet.

Sick Sean screamed through the traffic and turned right through a gap into Clonard Street, his mind whirling with the noise and smell of shooting and sudden fear.

'Fuck, fuck, fuck!' yelled Gerard, scrabbling on the floor for the Webley which had been jolted from his grasp, and ignoring the AK.

He looked over his shoulder at O'Brien. Both his hands were trying to stem the flow of blood from the gaping hole in his neck and he was gasping for air, drowning in his own blood.

Nothing would save him.

Narrowly missing a car coming out of the Clonards, Sean Casey gritted his teeth and put his foot further down, desperate to put as much distance as possible, as quickly as possible, between himself and the soldiers, so that they could torch the car and fuck off.

They might have made it, too, but for the fact that a mixed RUC/Army VCP had been set up at the far end of Clonard Gardens.

The sound of the gunfire was masked and confused by the ambient noise, but several of the soldiers and their RUC colleagues had instantly turned their heads in the direction of the Falls.

Then the screaming pitch of the Sierra's engine confirmed that something was going down.

And now they saw the car race into the Clonards.

'Army!' shouted Gerard.

His brother had already seen them, and was yanking the wheel right into Odessa Street. But even as he began the turn, he knew he was in trouble. The Ford wasn't designed to take ninety degree corners on slick, sleety roads at approaching fifty miles per hour, and as it screeched and skidded over the wet tarmac the tyres lost their grip.

The car careened into a parked truck, bounced back out into the street, and clipped the kerb on the opposite side.

Now completely out of control, it mounted the pavement

and smashed through the low wall in front of one of the squat, red-brick terraced houses, burying its bonnet in a bay window.

There it sat for a few moments, engine revving madly in neutral, until Sean Casey leaned forward and switched it off.

Ciaran O'Brien had been thrown forward between the front seats. He lay still and silent, blood pulsing from his neck in ever-smaller spurts.

'Come on, Gerry,' said Sean, scrabbling and reaching into the front foot well where the AK had ended up. 'We've got to get out of here.'

'What about Ciaran?'

'Fuck him, he's dead.'

'We need to torch the car! That's the plan!'

'No time. Fucking come on!'

Sean Casey pushed open the driver's door – it was buckled, so it wasn't easy – and staggered out of the wreckage.

As he stood up, two things happened.

The first was that the front door of the neighbouring house opened, and a young woman appeared.

The second was that several of the soldiers from the VCP sprinted around the corner and started towards them.

'In there!' shouted Sean to his younger brother, pointing at the open doorway.

But Gerard stood motionless, pistol still in his hand, half-raised.

In one weird moment of clarity, he thought to himself: *This is karma. I should not have murdered Billy Jones.*

Sean stared back at the soldiers.

This was not happening. This was not how it was meant to fucking be.

He'd only ever killed unarmed men – up close, taking pleasure in it, laughing about it later. The kudos it brought him. The pints in the bar. Being *someone*. Bigger, harder men scared to meet his eye, for fear of what he and his pals might do to them.

This was very different.

He raised the AK.

Suddenly, it seemed to weigh a ton.

The muzzle danced.

He couldn't hold it level.

In the small part of his brain that was still thinking rationally, he heard himself say, *Why's it so heavy?*

Somewhere, he heard the snap of a round from Mick Parry's SA80 pass close to his head, and then the whine of the ricochet.

He could see another soldier in combats...

*And why the fuck do they wear camouflage in a city?*

...standing, rifle raised.

Taking aim.

*He's fucking shooting at me!*

He pulled the AK trigger.

Four shots, all way too high, and in that half-second the magazine ran dry.

He pulled it again.

*Heard the dead man's click.*

Started to shout, 'No, wait!'

John Carr stood ramrod straight, SA80 aimed, like he was on the range at Sennybridge.

In the split second before he gently squeezed the trigger, he recognised the man in his sights from one of the many briefings he'd attended.

*Sick Sean.*

An evil man.

Christmas and his birthday, rolled into one.

Casey's brain was telling him to get down, but he was paralysed by fear, the same fear which now emptied his bladder.

Carr's round took him just below the nose on his upper lip, snapping his head back like he'd been smashed in the face with a steam hammer. It left only a small, cauterised entry wound, but erupted out of the back of his skull, taking teeth and brains and blood with it.

Stone dead, he hit the ground, the AK flying from his grasp and clattering to the pavement feet away.

Almost simultaneously, a shot from Mick Parry hit Gerard Casey in the shoulder, spinning him round and back and down to the ground.

He lay there, winded, yelping, for a moment or two, staring at the body of his older brother.

Then, horrified, and powered by adrenalin and terror, he scrambled to his feet, leaving the Webley on the pavement.

Bent double, not stopping to look at Sean, he half-rolled, half-fell past the screaming woman and into her house.

He was standing, wild-eyed in the living room, bright red blood pulsing from his wound, his brain overloaded with information and questions, when two soldiers burst in.

Mick Parry and John Carr.

The three men stood looking at each other, panting – for a half-second, no more.

Then Carr stepped forward and stabbed Gerard Casey's cheek with the barrel of his rifle, as if it was bayonet practice, breaking his cheekbone and putting him straight down onto the brown carpet.

The soldiers stood over the young shooter, rifles pointed at his chest.

Blood was still streaming from his wound; it would later transpire his carotid and subclavian arteries had been nicked by the SA80 round.

His eyes were vague and unfocused.

Parry bent down and slapped his face. 'Wakey wakey,' he said, with a grin. 'It's Para Reg time!'

Gerard Casey groaned.

'We've just killed your mate,' said Parry. 'Shot the wanker in the face.'

'My brother,' moaned the stricken man. 'No.'

He half-coughed, half-sobbed. A guttural sound.

'Ambulance,' he said, thickly. 'Please. It hurts.'

He closed his eyes, and a vivid image swam through his mind of Sean's head disintegrating.

He vomited and started choking on the bitter bile.

The housewife had come in, hand to her mouth in horror, and now she raised the receiver on the telephone.

'You put that fucker down,' said Parry, getting up and pushing her roughly into the darkened kitchen.

Carr got down, his left knee in Gerard Casey's blood, and pulled a first field dressing from his webbing.

Ripped open the boiler suit and tore the sodden T-shirt underneath it apart.

The wound was pulsing red.

He lifted the injured man slightly and felt at the back.

No exit wound.

Young Casey's eyes were starting to roll back in his head, and his breathing was becoming laboured and irregular.

Carr was applying the field dressing onto the wound on his collarbone when Parry reappeared.

'What the fuck are you doing?' he said. 'We're not saving this cunt's life, John.'

'We're better than them,' said Carr, through gritted teeth. 'He needs an ambulance.'

'Fuck that,' said Parry. He squatted down next to Casey, pulled off the dressing and threw it across the room. 'Three of my mates were killed at Mayobridge the other day by your mob, pal,' he said to the groaning man. 'Young lads, blown to pieces by cowards. If you think I'm calling yous a fucking ambo you must be confusing me with somebody who gives a shit.'

The blood was spurting more slowly, now, so Parry pressed his hand on Casey's chest, making it flow quicker.

'How does that feel?' he said. 'Does it sting a bit?'

'He's going tae bleed out, Mick,' said Carr.

'Yeah,' said Parry. 'That's the general idea.'

Just then, they heard a stifled sob behind them, and turned to see the homeowner standing in the kitchen doorway, hands over her mouth.

'Get her back through there, and tell her to fucking stay there,' said Parry, to Carr. 'Then get outside and tell the boss I'm giving this wanker first aid.'

Carr hesitated for a moment.

Then ushered the sobbing woman out of the room and into her kitchen, and left the house to do as he was told.

An ambulance was finally called ten minutes later.

By that time, Gerard Casey was unconscious.

By the time it arrived he was dead.

# 18.

BILLY JONES SENIOR sat in the Long Bar on the Shankill Road, surrounded by a gang of his shaven-headed cronies.

The TV in the top corner of the pub was on about some shooting in central Belfast, but he paid it no particular mind. He was sipping his whisky chaser and trying to decide between another pint of Carling or a move on to Strongbow, when two uniformed RUC men walked in, faces nervous, flat caps in their hands.

Someone walked hurriedly out of the bar, head down, and through the open doorway Billy briefly saw flashing blue lights and the camouflaged tunics of a group of soldiers.

The RUC men's eyes swept the room and settled on him.

They walked towards his table.

'Evening, Billy,' said one of them, respectfully. 'We've been trying to get hold of you. Can we have a word in private, please?'

Billy Jones looked up at them with the dead gaze of a reptile. 'Anything you want to say to me you can say in front of the boys,' he said. 'We've no secrets here.'

'Only, we tried your house, Billy,' said the officer. 'Couldn't get an answer, couldn't find your wife, so... Well, we thought you'd be in here.'

'Spying on me, is it?' he said with a mocking grin, and a suck on his teeth. He shook his head, almost sadly. 'You fucking peeler bastards.'

'Billy, I really think it would be best in private.'

'Spit it out.'

The two officers looked at each other. The one doing the talking sighed.

'Okay,' he said. 'Have it your way. It's about your son. Billy Junior.' His eyes flicked up at the TV, which was showing a car park, now brightly lit and crawling with police. 'He's the one that was killed tonight.'

Billy looked at him. Not a flicker of emotion.

He casually picked up his Bells and threw it back.

'Is that yous?' he said, with a grimace at the heat of the spirit. 'Are yous done?'

'Aye.'

'Then get the fuck out,' he shouted. 'Go on. Fuck off!'

'We're sorry, Mr Jones, our condolences, we...'

'Fuck *off*, you fucking *wankers*!'

The two constables turned on their heels and walked away, heads down, hands resting lightly on their sidearms, Billy Jones' eyes burning into their backs.

When the door was shut, the men at the table exchanged looks.

'Billy,' said one. 'I'm sorry. He was a good kid.'

Billy Jones Senior looked at him in disgust. 'You what? He was a fucking embarrassment, so he was, and you know it. If you can't speak the fucking *truth* to me, you're no fucking *good* to me. You can get the fuck out as well.'

'Yes, Billy,' said the man, and hurried out without finishing his drink or putting on his coat.

Jones looked up at the bar. A man in a blue Rangers shirt put down his pint, walked casually over, and bent his head.

'You and Tam McDonald,' whispered Billy Jones Senior, hoarsely. 'You get fucking out there tonight and kill two fucking Catholics. Any fuckers, I don't care, but it better be on the news first thing in the morning. Cut their throats.'

The man nodded, and walked out of the bar leaving half a pint on the counter.

Billy sat back, looked at his cronies and belched. 'I reckon I'll go on the Strongbow now, boys,' he said. 'Davey, you're in the chair.'

# 19.

PAT CASEY SAT IN HIS usual seat in the corner of The Volunteer on the Falls Road and tried to look vaguely interested as another greasy sycophant paid his respects and offered to buy him a pint.

The eldest of the three Casey brothers, it was common knowledge that Patrick was a senior figure in the Belfast Brigade command structure.

This being one of Belfast PIRA's favourite pubs, there wasn't a man alive could drink the beer Pat Casey was offered on an average night.

There probably wasn't the beer in the bar to make good on all the offers.

He waved the guy away with a half-smile, keeping his eye on wee Roslyn McCabe as she sat at the bar sucking down something with a pink umbrella in it.

Fuck, but she was a great wee ride, all legs and arse in that tight little white miniskirt.

She smiled at him, and he just stared back at her.

He'd fucked her in the alley round the back of the bar last week, and he'd a mind to do it again tonight.

*See how things go, eh.*

*Dirty wee whore. Not marrying material, but...*

Pat Casey's status might have been common knowledge, but proving who he was and what he'd done, to the satisfaction of a court, was a very different matter. He was a clever man who'd never been caught and who seldom got his hands dirty these days. Not that he was frightened to: he'd done his time as a foot soldier, and had earned the nickname 'The Brain Surgeon' for his close quarter assassinations.

Breathing down your neck, only ever one round to the head – that was how he liked it.

But that was in the past. Violence was a big tool in the box, but the real means to the Republican end was political, not military. Pat had the gift of the gab, he could turn on the charm if required, and he had no criminal record. Those in the highest echelons had identified him as a good man to have in place when the bloodshed eventually forced the hands of the Brits.

He tore his gaze away from Roslyn's legs and looked at his watch. Sean and Gerry should have been here by now, but they were probably taking it nice and careful. He felt a slight sense of unease, but pushed it away. Sure, they'd be in any minute, and he'd be toasting them with the rest of the fellas.

He thought about his brothers.

Sean was an experienced lad but too hot-headed and unpredictable, and Pat had little doubt that one day he'd make a martyr of himself.

But Gerry – Gerry was smart, and cautious.

A bit young, was all. All he needed was experience. Once he had that, the youngest of the three Casey brothers looked to Pat to have the potential to become a significant player.

Pat had personally sanctioned the 1st Battalion operation on Billy Jones Jnr. This was west Belfast, not the Wild West – you didn't just rock up and kill people willy-nilly, there were procedures and rules, and a strict code of conduct. Junior men thought up jobs and brought them to the table. Senior men turned most of them down as impractical, or too dangerous, or too expensive, and gave a few the green light. Sean had brought up Billy and suggested Gerry as the shooter, and, after a little thought, Pat had agreed to the killing.

It went without saying that he'd have much preferred to have hit Billy Senior, but that cunt was too wily to get caught out. Young Billy would fit fine, would send the right message to the prod bastards.

And then, as he'd been driven over to The Volunteer a couple of hours earlier, the BBC radio news bulletin had been full of a shooting in the city centre near the Europa.

An unidentified male killed by unknown assassins.

Of course, he'd known what the *craic* was, and he'd felt elated.

He was looking forward to shaking young Gerry's hand, and seeing the surprise and pride on his face. It wasn't common practice for senior figures to go round back-slapping the ASU members, and it would all have to be very unofficial, but, sure, this was his younger brother. To congratulate him in person, and bring him into the Brigade... Well, it was a good day for the Casey family.

He threw back half his pint and winked at Rosyln. She tried her best to look demure, but she didn't have it in her. Later...

He noticed the clock over the bar behind the young woman.

Now they *were* late.

What the hell were they playing at?

His eye wandered round the bar, and it landed on the TV in the opposite corner.

And he went cold all over.

A reporter was standing in the darkness of the Lower Falls, his camera crew's lights showing a red Ford Sierra.

Crashed into a wall.

'Jimmy,' shouted Pat, looking briefly at the barman. 'Shut the fucking music off and turn that up, will you.'

The barman complied as if his life depended on the speed of his movements.

'On the record, the police are staying tight-lipped,' the reporter was saying, 'but they believe the men may have carried out that earlier shooting in the city centre. It was on their way back into west Belfast that they were identified by an Army patrol. They ended up here in the Clonards, where all three men were killed by the security forces. At this stage…'

Pat Casey stood up, knocking over the remains of his pint, and the chair he'd been sitting on.

He shook his head, feeling nauseous.

*Surely fucking not.*

Not bothering to put on his coat, he hurried from the bar, which was suddenly quiet, a sea of eyes and gaping mouths.

He passed out onto the street, through the security cage placed there to delay unwanted visitors, and straight towards his waiting driver. The engine was running by the time he reached the car.

'The Clonards, Paulie,' he said.

'What is it, Pat?' said the driver.

'I think my brothers are dead. And Ciaran O'Brien. Murdering Brit bastards.'

'Mother of God, Pat,' said Paulie, crossing himself. 'I am so fucking sorry.'

'Just drive.'

# 20.

THE CLONARDS WAS CLOSED off by a number of Army and RUC vehicles.

Blue strobe lighting bounced off the houses.

Soldiers, rifles at the ready, stood on a cordon and watched a large crowd of locals from dark eyes under helmets.

There were shouts of abuse, and every now and then someone lobbed a stone from the back of the crowd.

Pat Casey got out of the car and approached the police cordon. He could see forensic officers in white suits clearing the area.

He approached the first RUC man he saw and said, 'Who's in fucking charge? Get him over here.'

The constable walked over to a detective inspector and pointed back towards Pat.

The DI walked casually over. 'Good evening, Mr Casey,' he said, with a broad smile. 'And how can I help you?'

'Someone told me that's my brothers dead there,' spat Pat. 'I want to fucking know.'

'That's interesting, Mr Casey,' said the detective. 'No names have been released yet, so why would you think it might be your brothers?'

'Don't get fucking smart with me, you bastard. I want to know.'

The DI looked at him for a moment. Then he said, 'Sure, why don't you come with me, Mr Casey?'

He lifted the tape, and Pat ducked under.

The two men walked to the wrecked Sierra.

'I don't know if you recognise this man?' said the detective, when they reached the vehicle.

Sean Casey lay on the ground, his ruined head in a pool of blood and pulp, sightless eyes staring into the drizzle of the night.

'Fuck me,' said Pat Casey.

'Can you positively identify this individual as your brother, Mr Casey?'

'You know full well that's Sean, you fucking cunt.'

'Oh, dear,' said the detective inspector, allowing a look of great sorrow to settle on his face. 'May I say on behalf of the *Royal* Ulster Constabulary that I am terribly sorry for your loss, sir.'

'Where's Gerry?'

'Ah, yes. We do have two more bodies. If you could help us with identification that would be grand.'

'Show me, you bastard.'

The inspector shone his torch into the car. Ciaran O'Brien's bloodstained corpse lay wedged between the front seats.

'Now, is that your Gerard?'

Pat Casey looked at the police officer. 'If you don't stop fucking me around, I swear...'

'Please calm down, Mr Casey,' said the inspector, 'or I shall have to have you arrested. We do have one further individual dead in that house there, but I'm afraid I can't let you go in there because it's a potential crime scene. If you'd like to hang around the body will be moved shortly, so you can see it then.'

'You fucking...' said Casey. 'Someone'll pay for this.'

The detective smirked. 'It does look as though someone's already paid for something tonight, Pat.'

Casey put his face close to the police officer's. 'What did you say?' he growled.

The detective stared back at him, poker-faced. He was a veteran of nearly twenty years of this shit, and he was not easily intimidated. When he'd woken up that morning his life had been in danger, and when he went to sleep that night nothing would have changed. He'd lost several colleagues to the likes of Casey, and would quite cheerfully have pulled out his sidearm and shot him in the face there and then.

'What did I say?' he said. 'What I said, Pat, was that Gerard died crying and begging for his life. Three-nil to the Parachute Regiment, I believe. I'm going to have a few drams the night toasting this lot into hell. Now, fuck off out my sight. And pass my condolences to your mother. When the old cow's sober, mind.'

Pat tried to stare him down, but the policeman just winked at him.

'You're a dead man walking.'

'We're all dead, Pat, even you. It's just the *when* bit that we don't know.' He chuckled. 'Ask your brothers.'

'You're a dead man. Whoever did this is a dead man. As long as I live.'

'You take care now, Pat, you hear?' said the detective. 'Your poor ma wouldn't want to lose all her boys in one night, would she?'

Casey turned on his heel and walked away, passing within twenty feet of Mick Parry and John Carr, who were now part of the cordon securing the area.

Back in his car, he looked at Paulie the driver.

'They're all dead,' he said. 'Sean, Ciaran, Gerard. All of them head-jobbed. Fucking murdered by the SAS.'

'Scum, Pat,' said Paulie. 'Scum. They don't play by the rules. It's that shoot-to-kill, that's what it is fucking is. That bitch Thatcher. It's her death squads.'

96

Pat Casey clenched his fists so hard that his nails nearly drew blood from his palms.

'As God is my fucking witness,' he said, 'I swear I'll find the fuckers that did this. If it takes me fifty years I will have their fucking lives.'

PART THREE

LONDON
MODERN DAY

# 21.

JOHN CARR WOKE up with a thick head, a pretty blonde he didn't know, and a bad feeling about the day ahead.

The clock radio said it was just after 5am, and he knew it had been gone 2am when he'd finally got to sleep, thanks to the attentions of the girl snoring gently next to him.

He lay there for a moment, silently cursing. Perhaps the only thing he regretted about his time in the SAS was that it had ruined his sleep patterns. Years of raids carried out in the wee small hours will do that to you.

Still, he'd always been able to function on not much kip. Plenty of times he'd not slept for a couple of days straight: if you thought about it like that, three hours was luxury.

He turned on his bedside light and looked at the blonde.

Early twenties and very fit, but not quite so hot with her hair everywhere, her mouth slack and a line of crusted drool snaking its way down onto the pillow.

What was her name?

*Emily?*

*Emma?*

*Elizabeth?*

Something beginning with E, he was sure of that, but he was fucked if he could get any further than that.

He could just about remember her coming on to him at the bar over in Fulham.

About ten-ish, when he'd been about eight pints deep.

It had been Guy de Vere's annual birthday bash – always a big night, and a good chance to catch up with one or two blokes he'd not seen for a while.

He hadn't gone there looking for a woman – there were enough women in his life as it was, and they complicated things: he liked simplicity, and routine, and order.

But somehow they always seemed to find him.

He moved slightly, and she stirred.

'Morning, John,' she said, opening two enormous blue eyes and looking very directly at him. Her voice was clearest cut glass crystal, roughened slightly by the Marlboro Lights she'd been smoking all night. She gave a sleepy smile, and then looked at him reproachfully. 'You really are a very naughty boy.'

'Am I?' he said.

'Bringing me here, doing all those unspeakable things to me, when you hardly know me and you're old enough to be my father.' She yawned. 'I'm not that sort of girl.'

'I think you are. And I'm not old enough to be your father.'

'You're not far off.' She rubbed her eyes and ran a forefinger over his chest and up onto his chin. 'Who did this to you?' she said, tracing the upside-down crescent of the scar below his mouth.

'A guy,' said Carr.

'How?'

'He threw a grenade into a room I was in.'

'What terrible manners.'

'It was a bit cheeky.'

'What happened to him?'

Carr looked at her, sideways. '*I* happened to him,' he said.

The girl chuckled. It was a breathy, filthy sound, and Carr felt his heartbeat quicken a little.

'Where was it?' she said.

'That's classified,' he said. 'Sorry, love.'

She chuckled again. 'You don't even know my name, do you?' she said.

*Eeny meeny miny moe.*

'Emma.'

'Uh huh.' Her hand was off his chin now, and was resting on his pectoral muscles.

He tensed them slightly in response: no point doing all that work at the gym if you didn't get the pay-off.

She laughed, reading him like a cheap paperback.

'I have to be honest, John,' she said. 'I don't normally go for men with tattoos. But you can be my bit of rough.'

Carr looked at her sideways again, an eyebrow raised. 'Is that so?' he said, with a slight grin.

'I'll have to housetrain you, of course,' she said. She pointed to one of the designs. It showed a winged figure holding two swords. 'What's this one?'

'St Michael,' said Carr. 'Patron Saint of the Airborne.'

'Really? How fascinating.'

He rolled out of bed, naked, and walked to the bedroom door.

Her eyes followed him, taking in the artwork covering his upper arms and back. To her eye, it meant nothing; to Carr, each tattoo told a personal story, of death, and sin, and other regrets.

'Must have cost you the earth,' she called after him. 'Nice arse, by the way.'

He heard her dissolve into giggles as he padded out into the hallway.

A quick piss, and he was in the shower.

She joined him a few moments later, and they did it all over again under the hot water.

Later, in the kitchen, he made her a cappuccino and himself a mug of strong tea, and stood there looking out of the window.

Chewing paracetamol for his head, wondering why he felt uneasy.

Below him, Primrose Hill looked a picture in the dawn light, the bare branches of the trees picked out by a rare hoar frost.

The girl stood next to him, swamped by his ivory bathrobe, warming her hands on the coffee cup.

'I'm going to have to go to work in my going-out clothes, thanks to you,' she said. 'I'd borrow a shirt, but I think you'd get three of me in one of yours.'

'Sorry,' he said.

'Is there a Mrs John?'

'Used to be.'

'Oh?'

'Divorced a while back. We drifted apart.'

'Oh. Children?'

'Boy and a girl.'

'Tell me more.'

'George is in the Army, Alice is in her first year of A levels.'

The girl snuck an arm around his waist. 'And is there a woman in your life?'

'Women,' he said. 'Plural.'

'Well, that's not very gentlemanly, is it?' she said, with a smirk.

'I never said I was a gentleman. I'm not into being tied down. Tried it once.'

'I'd like to see you again.'

He turned to look at her, eyebrow raised. 'Of course you would, darlin',' he said. 'You don't see this walking down the street every day, do you?'

She laughed. 'I like a man with confidence.'

'I was taking the piss,' he said. 'A bit.'

She put the coffee cup down, and went to get dressed.

When she came back he was still standing, looking out of the window.

'I've written my name and number down on your pad,' she said, handing it to him, and grinning. 'And where did you get fucking *Emma* from?'

He looked at the notepad.

Her name was scrawled above a mobile number.

It said 'Antonia de Vere'.

He looked up at her, staring closely now, the realisation slowly dawning.

Regimental balls and summer barbecues and Hereford parties over the years...

Everyone bringing their families.

Wives, sons.

*And daughters.*

Oh, shit.

'Yes,' she said, giggling. 'I didn't think you recognised me. But then I suppose I am all grown up, now.' She leaned forward and kissed him lightly on the cheek. 'Don't worry,' she whispered, into his ear. 'I won't tell daddy if you won't.'

And with that she was gone.

# 22.

AS CARR SCREWED up the piece of paper with Antonia de Vere's name and number on it, and dropped it in the bin, his mobile rang.

Alice: his seventeen-year-old daughter, calling from school, before first lesson.

She was in the lower sixth at Cheltenham Ladies' College, something he could never quite say without laughing – or *larfing*, as Alice would have put it, now that the faint Norn Iron twang she'd inherited from her mother had been educated out of her. Half of her friends were foreign royalty or the offspring of hedge fundies and supermodels: no-one else there with mongrel Niddrie and Bangor blood, that was for sure.

'Hi, sweetheart,' he said. 'How much?'

'Come on, daddy,' said Alice, exasperated. 'I don't only phone about money, you know.'

'I know, darling. But how much?'

She chuckled. 'I need fifteen hundred pounds, dad,' she said. 'Someone's dropped out of the ski trip and my name's next on the list.'

'Oh aye?'

'You knew all this.'

'When?'

'First week of Easter. Matilda and India are going.'

'Easter? Shouldn't you be revising for your end-of-year exams?'

'All under control, dad.'

It probably was, too. Alice had inherited his own mania for organisation, and was always on top of her schoolwork.

'Fifteen hundred quid, though? Are you going skiing or buying the mountain?'

He and his ex-wife had struggled financially in the very early days of their marriage, a young trooper's wages not being all that great, but it was a long time since Alice had wanted for anything, and he was keen that she should know the value of money.

And, to be fair, fifteen hundred quid was fifteen hundred quid. A bright girl, she'd won a scholarship to Cheltenham from her prep school near Hereford, but the fees were still murderous and he was glad of the cash he'd salted away in his eighteen months on the Baghdad–Kabul circuit, and the six figures he now earned as head of London security for the Russian billionaire Konstantin Avilov.

He smiled to himself.

*Standing here in his handmade, fifty grand, Smallbone of Devizes kitchen, thinking about fucking school fees.*

His old man's red-under-the-bed head would have exploded if he'd lived to see it.

'What does your mum think?'

'She said it's up to you. Pleeeaaase.'

'When are you next over seeing your mum?'

'I'm flying over next Friday for the weekend.'

He was silent for a moment.

'Dad? You still there?'

'Just messing with you. Email me the payment details.'

There was a loud squeal on the other end of the phone.

'I'll be checking with your mum, though.'

'You do that, dad. Got to go now, bye!'

Carr looked at his phone and shook his head in amusement.

Then clicked through and dialled Stella, his ex-wife, at her home in Crawfordsburn, a few miles outside Bangor.

Their divorce had been amicable enough, not least because they'd both been determined to stay civil for the sake of the kids, and they got on better now than they had for most of their time together. He couldn't quite remember why they'd ever got married – it was a long time ago, and he was certainly very different to the boy he'd been back then – but she was a good person. Most importantly, as far as he was concerned, she was a very good mum.

She answered almost immediately, and she knew exactly why he was calling.

'I've said it's up to you,' she said, laughing. 'I know you'll have said yes, mind. She can twist you round her little finger, that girl.'

'It's not cheap,' he said.

'Sure, you're rolling in it, so you are,' said Stella. 'Careful of them moths when you open your wallet.'

'As long as you're happy?'

'She's only young once.'

'True.' He scratched his stubble. 'Has she mentioned that boy recently?'

'Which boy?'

'The lad she was talking about who she met in Cheltenham at her friend's eighteenth.'

'Nick? Aye, she has.'

'Is he her boyfriend?'

'Ach, I think they're just pals.'

'Because I want to know what his plans are.'

There was a peal of laughter down the phone.

'His *plans*? Sure, I'd say they're the same as your plans was when we started courting, John Carr,' said Stella.

'They'd better not be. She's too young for anything serious.'

'Is she now? She'll be fifty years of age and Prince Charming will come calling for her, and you'll be there on your Zimmer frame telling him to piss off,' said Stella. 'No-one will ever be good enough for your wee girl.'

'I'm not…' said Carr.

'John, you've to face facts. Kids grow up. Look at George, in the Paras. I believe they even let him hold a gun, sometimes.'

Carr had to smile.

'Fair enough,' he said. 'But keep an eye on her. How's things with you, otherwise?'

'Can't complain,' she said. 'House feels empty sometimes with just me and David rattling around in it, but his work's going well and I keep myself busy. Sure, you should come over some time. It'd be nice to see you.'

'I might do that, Stel,' said Carr. 'Listen, I'd better be off. Take care of yourself, yes?'

He ended the call, and looked at his watch.

Five to nine.

Time for the gym.

He grabbed his kit and left the flat.

When he reached the bottom of the stairs he bumped into his neighbour, a young estate agent called Daisy, who was just leaving the ground floor flat she shared with her boyfriend.

She looked very tidy in her tight grey suit – curves in all the right places, he'd always thought.

'Morning, Dais,' he said. 'You look knackered.'

'Thanks,' she said. 'Someone kept me awake half the night.' She looked at him, pointedly, and grinned. 'Who was the lucky girl this time?'

'Sorry, Dais,' said Carr, and felt himself flush slightly. 'I thought we were quiet.'

'I'll forgive you if you buy me dinner at the weekend,' she said. 'James is away on a stag do.'

Her eyes stayed on John Carr's just a beat longer than necessary, and then she said, 'Christ, I'm going to be late for work.'

'After you,' he said, opening the communal front door.

He stood and watched her wiggle away in her tight skirt.

And grinned.

And thought about Friday.

# 23.

AS JOHN CARR watched Daisy wiggle away, four men were sitting around a beige table in a grey conference room at the Police Service of Northern Ireland's headquarters in Knock, Belfast.

Charles Hope, assistant chief constable of the PSNI, and the man in overall command of the force's criminal investigations division, sat below a large abstract painting.

On Hope's left was Gary Baxter, deputy director of the Public Prosecution Service for Northern Ireland and widely tipped as a future UK DPP.

On Hope's right was Conor Maguire, civilian head of the PSNI 'media directorate'. Maguire had spent his twenties as a Sinn Fein member, and had flirted with PIRA itself, though he'd had neither the stomach nor the balls for the dirty work. Back in the RUC days, the only way he'd have got inside Knock was in handcuffs: now he was one of many who had been appointed to significant roles in the transition from the old force to the new, as part of the plan to bring the Province's Republicans onside.

Facing them was Detective Superintendent Kevin Murphy. Murphy had joined the RUC in the mid-1980s, a rare Roman Catholic in those days, and had spent most of his career in the Branch. He was closing in on three decades of cheap suits, bad coffee, and strip-lit offices, of bombs, bullets, and bullshit, but the finishing tape was in sight. His brother ran a fishing business in the Yukon, and he'd asked Kev to join him as a fly-fishing instructor for the summer. Four months to go, and then he was on a flight to Calgary. A hop to Whitehorse, then two hours' drive north on the Klondike Highway, and he'd be in a log cabin, with all this nonsense behind him. He could almost taste the salmon.

But desperate as he was to leave the depravity and death behind, Kevin Murphy was a conscientious police officer, and it was that dedication which brought him to this meeting room early on a cold February morning.

A constable put down a tray of bottled mineral water, coffee and biscuits, and left.

ACC Charles Hope cleared his throat. 'Right, gents,' he said. 'Let's get straight into it. Detective Superintendent Murphy, the floor is yours.'

'Thank you, sir,' said Murphy. 'The purpose of this morning is to bring Mr Maguire up to speed on an operational issue that may attract significant media and political attention.'

The media man narrowed his eyes and put down the pen he'd been clicking.

'And, Mr Maguire,' said Murphy, 'I must stress that none of what I'm about to tell you can leave this room.'

Maguire's face darkened a little, but he nodded. 'Fine,' he said.

'As you know, my team works on major cold cases from the Troubles,' said Murphy.

And, God knew, there were enough of them. Hundreds of serious unsolved crimes, from murder to punishment-rape and torture, to kidnapping and armed robbery. The RUC had usually known exactly who'd committed these offences, but getting the evidence to secure convictions had often been impossible. When the reward for talking to the police was a 10mm masonry drill bit through every major joint, followed by a 9mm round in the forehead, witnesses tended to forget important details.

'We've been investigating the murder in 1984 of a young UDR soldier taken from his home in Newry at night, and found dead on the border two days later,' he said. 'It's common knowledge that the man who killed him was a fellow by the name of Sean Casey, brother of MLA Patrick Casey.'

Conor Maguire leaned forward, pushing his spectacles up on the bridge of his nose with a fat forefinger.

'Sean Casey was a very violent man,' said Murphy, 'known as "Sick Sean", though not to his face. I suppose you mind your ps and qs with a man who enjoys torturing people to death, especially if he's PIRA royalty. Which he was. His father, his uncle, his brothers, all players. And I include Pat Casey in that.'

'Never proven,' said Conor Maguire.

'All sort of things are never proven,' said Murphy. 'Pat Casey put at least a dozen men in the ground, take my word for it.'

'He's a member of the Assembly,' said Maguire. 'You should watch what you say.'

'I assume I'm amongst friends and can speak freely?' said Kevin Murphy. He looked at the media man for a few moments, and then continued. 'Anyway, Sean Casey was put before the courts twice but he was untouchable.' He sipped his water. 'Now, Casey's been dead some years, but one of his pals from those days has decided to co-operate.'

'Who's that?' said Maguire, sharply.

'I'm sure you understand that I can't share the identity of witnesses.'

The man in question was in the end stages of terminal liver cancer, and had decided to make peace with his conscience. But releasing his name into the wild... well, he wouldn't be dying from the cancer, that was for sure.

'Word gets around,' said Murphy, 'and once you start turning over rocks, memories get stirred, and other fruit falls from the tree. Two days ago a woman attended the PSNI station at Strandtown and spoke to the desk sergeant concerning another matter, which occurred on the evening of Thursday, December 21, 1989.'

'Which was?' said Conor Maguire.

The detective perched a pair of reading glasses on his nose and opened his file. 'Getting old,' he said, with an apologetic grin. 'That matter was the death of Sean Casey's younger brother.'

# 24.

THE OTHERS LISTENED as Kevin Murphy outlined the events of that day, finishing with the moment when the woman had been bundled back into her kitchen by John Carr, on the orders of Mick Parry.

He was expecting a reaction, and he got it.

'Jesus Christ,' said Conor Maguire. 'That's not how I've heard it.'

'No,' said Murphy, drily. 'I imagine not.'

The legend – told late at night even now, in the right clubs and pubs – was that the three men had died heroically. Depending on *how* late it was, and how drunk the storyteller, it had taken anywhere between thirty and fifty Brit soldiers to kill them, and only then after they'd shot dead an entire SAS team, with the whole thing hushed up to avoid embarrassing Margaret Thatcher.

'I've heard the same stories,' said the detective. 'Truth is, O'Brien opened fire on the COP vehicle and wounded one fellow. Sean Casey only got off four shots, which went into the bedroom of a little girl opposite and took out her My Little Pony collection. Gerard never fired his weapon at the soldiers at all.'

'All this stuff about pressing his chest so he bled out, and refusing to call an ambulance,' said Maguire. 'Are you saying we have *evidence* that Gerry Casey – Pat Casey's brother – was murdered by the British Army?'

'That's a matter for Mr Baxter, whom I briefed yesterday evening,' said Murphy. 'He's the lawyer, after all.'

Gary Baxter took a sip of water and paused. 'No,' he said. 'It's not murder. The shootings of O'Brien and both Casey brothers were themselves lawful. They were armed men posing a threat to life. Gerard Casey needs a little thought, because he survived that initial shot for a while.'

'Exactly,' said Maguire. 'The chest? The ambulance?'

'As for the chest,' said Baxter, 'the soldiers claimed they were trying to perform CPR and an attempt was made to apply a first field dressing – one was seized which was covered in Mr Casey's blood.'

'*Mr* Casey?' said Murphy, sharply. 'He'd just murdered an unarmed twenty-year-old man, let's not forget.'

'He might have been unarmed,' said Conor Maguire, 'but his family were terrorists, through and through. His father was a leading UVF man, lived and died by the sword.'

Which was true enough: Billy Jones Senior had himself been assassinated during the war that had erupted after his son's killing.

'Whatever, I suspect that that explanation would still hold,' said Gary Baxter. 'And, anyway, the key issue, both for that and the ambulance, is causation. As I understand it, the post mortem found that Gerard Casey was doomed by the initial shot?'

Kevin Murphy looked at his file. 'Both his carotid and subclavian arteries were breached,' he said. 'The coroner heard from a cardio-vascular specialist, fellow called Briggs. He said, quote, "If this had happened in my operating theatre Gerard Casey would still have died".'

Baxter sat back in his chair, and looked at ACC Charles Hope. 'Well, that probably nails it, then,' he said. 'We should seek counsel's advice, but it's going nowhere. The soldiers may or may not have acted as we might wish. But murder? I doubt it.'

The room was silent for a few beats. Then Conor Maguire said, 'What about stopping the woman from calling an ambulance?'

'Both soldiers said that the ambulance was requested through the military communications net,' said Murphy. 'But there's the fog of war. They had dead terrorists and for all they knew others who were injured and potentially other shooters. They were trying to do CPR, a crowd was already gathering outside. Yes, they stopped the woman picking up the phone, but that was SOP. They didn't know who she might be calling. Everything went through the Ops room. The Duty Watchkeeper got a radio message at about 7.20pm and relayed that to the ambo immediately.'

'But surely they could have been quicker?'

'Perhaps. But it would be very hard to prove.'

'What can you tell us about this new witness?' said ACC Hope.

'She's a Roman Catholic,' said Murphy, 'but she has no known connection to Sinn Fein, or any Republican terrorist organisation. Nothing of concern in her background.'

'Criminal record?'

'No. She works in the accounts department of a small business off the Falls. Widowed, but her husband had no connections. He died in a straightforward road traffic accident six years ago.'

'So why's she come forward now?'

Murphy shrugged. 'We haven't interviewed her properly yet. She told the desk sergeant she'd heard someone mention Sean Casey's name, and it brought the whole thing back. It's usually because they've had something on their mind and they want to get it off their chest.'

'And what about bringing the soldiers in?' said Hope.

Gary Baxter pursed his lips. 'I think an arrest would probably be justified, in the light of these allegations,' he said. 'We could see what they have to say. You never know.'

'They'll lawyer up and go no comment,' said Murphy. 'Would you fancy going up to Maghaberry with the blood of two Caseys on *your* hands? It's just one witness's word against the two of theirs.'

'Who were the soldiers, as a matter of interest?' said Conor Maguire.

Murphy nodded. 'I was just going to come on to them,' he said.

# 25.

KEVIN MURPHY ADJUSTED his reading glasses, and looked at his notes.

'Michael John Parry, born Toxteth in Liverpool. Father was a docker. Joined the Third Battalion of the Parachute Regiment, 3 Para, as a seventeen-year-old. Mentioned in Dispatches for actions at Mount Longdon in the Falklands. Travelled to Northern Ireland for their residential tour in early 1989, by which time he was a corporal.'

He looked at the three men opposite him. 'I remember that period well myself,' he said. '3 Para ended up losing seven men. Two in a drowning, five to PIRA actions. One of them was a young private called Murray who was tortured to his death after a honeytrap girl lured him out to west Belfast. Most unpleasant. Anyway, he left the Army in 1998 at the rank of sergeant. Currently employed as a delivery driver for Parcelforce in Huyton, near Liverpool. Married, two grown-up daughters. No criminal record apart from a couple of minor pub fights as a young squaddie.'

'And the other one?' said Hope.

Murphy reached for his water and took a good swallow. 'Yes, John Carr's a wee bit more interesting,' he said. 'Born in Niddrie, south-east Edinburgh. Parents were decent, hard-working people.

Joined 3 Para at seventeen and was a lance corporal when he arrived here in 1989.'

He paused for a moment. 'I must stress the need for confidentiality here,' he said. 'In January 1990 he left Northern Ireland and went back to the mainland to attempt selection for the Special Air Service. Passed that course in the summer and went straight out to the first Gulf War with 22 SAS. He spent the next nineteen years in the Regiment. You name it, he's done it. Fair bit of time over here, plus Afghanistan, Iraq, Africa… Twice decorated for gallantry. Known at Hereford as "Mad John", which tells its own story.'

'Also out of the Army now?' said Charles Hope.

'He retired from the SAS and the military at the rank of Sergeant Major. Did a year or so as a security manager with an oil company down near Basra, then a bit of private security work in Baghdad and Kabul, and now works as head of UK security for a guy called Konstantin Avilov, one of those ex-KGB billionaires that grow on trees in London. Carr reports in to Avilov's head of security, a former Russian Foreign Intelligence Service spook by the name of Oleg Kovalev.'

'Personal life?' said Hope.

'He met and married a girl from Bangor when he was here. Two children, divorced when he left the Army, and the ex moved back over here. He's been a bit of a dabbler in the stock market. Whispers of insider trading, but nothing's ever been proved. He owns a big house in Hereford, and apparently has the use of a nice flat somewhere in north London.'

'Does anyone remember working with him?' said Maguire.

'I actually have a vague memory of the guy myself,' said Murphy, 'but his last sustained period in Northern Ireland was as part of a joint police–Army team tasked against the South Armagh sniper in the nineties. Most people will have moved on.'

'What was he like?'

Murphy shrugged. 'It's a long time ago,' he said.

'Okay,' said the ACC. He turned to Conor Maguire. 'My main concern, if there's no charges to be brought, is dealing with the inevitable media shitstorm,' he said. 'There's a further complicating factor, too. Kevin?'

'The Army patrol that day was nominally led by a young second lieutenant who had only arrived in battalion a week earlier, and in Northern Ireland a day or two before. He was out on familiarisation, being babysat till he learned the ropes, so Parry was effectively in charge.'

'Significance?' said Maguire.

'That second lieutenant is now Lieutenant-General Guy de Vere, ex-Director Special Forces, now Commander Field Army. Basically, the British Army's 2IC, and a decent bet for the top job sometime in the next three or four years.'

Charles Hope looked at Maguire. 'So you see the issue. Between that and Pat Casey and the SAS, the media'll have a field day,' he said. 'Not to mention Sinn Fein, and others. We must avoid any suspicion of cover-up or whitewash. No rioting. No political fall-out. So what's our PR strategy?'

There was a long silence, while Conor Maguire thought.

'Well, you can guess my personal position,' he said, eventually. 'The first thing we should do is make full disclosure to Pat Casey and his mother, and assure them that we'll assist the family in any civil action. Parallel with that, we should formally announce that we're re-opening the case, and then we should investigate it thoroughly, and let the courts decide.'

'That sounds awfully like throwing two innocent men to the wolves,' said Kevin Murphy.

'What?' said Maguire, mockingly. 'Do you not have faith in our own officers and the courts?'

'The punishment is the process. Their names and addresses will be revealed. Their lives could be endangered. Their families' lives. All in the name of a PR exercise.'

'The British Army has done a lot of very bad things to my people in Northern Ireland.'

'If you want to get into that,' said Murphy, 'your people have done a few bad things themselves. I knew the fellows who recovered the body of the UDR reservist that Sean Casey tortured to death. They didn't sleep for weeks. I saw plenty of similar things myself. Let me tell you, him and Ciaran O'Brien...'

'Whoah, gents,' said Charles Hope, palms raised. 'Let's just take the heat out of this. Right, here's our actions. Gary, can you speak to counsel and get me a formal advice? Kevin, can you visit the new witness in person and stress the importance of her speaking to no-one about this until we've concluded our enquiry? Conor, can you work up a full strategy document for me, starting with a statement that's ready to go in case it all blows?' He sat back. 'I think that's it, for now. Christ, I sometimes wish I'd stayed at the Met.'

# 26.

KEVIN MURPHY WALKED out of that meeting and down the corridor to the lift.

Whistling.

Nonchalant.

Got into the lift.

Travelled to the basement.

Got out, walked down the corridor.

Stopped in front of a window marked 'PROPERTY STORE'.

'How's it going, Rob?' he said to the civilian employee on the other side of the glass, a former RUC man of the old school who'd been invalided out, after a car bomb blew off his foot, and re-employed on contract. They went back years.

Rob put down his paper.

'How the devil are you, Kev?' he said, with a big grin.

'Not so bad...' began Murphy.

After a few minutes of small talk, he said, casually, 'So, I need to get into the store to have a look at something from one of the cold cases we're looking at.'

'No problem, pal,' said Rob, clicking on his computer keyboard. 'What is it?'

'I need to book out some exhibits relating to the Crown and McIntyre.'

*Tap tap tap* on Rob's keyboard.

Murphy was uncomfortably aware of the little CCTV camera watching him.

But he had a legit reason to be here, and as long as he was careful…

'Sorted, Kev,' said Rob. 'Just sign when you come back out?'

'Surely,' said Murphy.

The door to the property store buzzed and opened, and he walked in.

He headed straight for the relevant section, but once he was out of sight of Rob, and the cameras, he stopped.

Picked a shelf.

Rooted quickly through the first box.

Then the second.

The fifth looked promising – a box of stuff recovered from a local fence who'd been charged with burglary and handling.

Found what he was after in a matter of moments.

Not crucial to establishing the guy's guilt, so no harm would be done.

Perfect.

Put it in his pocket, collected his exhibits, and walked back to Rob to sign out.

# 27.

JOHN CARR GOT back from the gym at a shade after midday with a good endorphin buzz on, and arms and legs that felt like lead and were burning with lactic acid.

He wasn't a phys nut, or a born gym monkey like some of the lads in the Regiment had been, but he stayed in shape because it was good for business, in all sorts of ways.

He lifted weights – a lot of them – three times a week, and ran seven miles on the other four days. When time allowed he fitted in a fifteen-mile swim or a hundred miles on the static bike, to keep his CV in good order. He topped it all off with training and fights at a mixed martial arts club in Kentish Town at least once a fortnight.

As a result, he wasn't all that far off the shape he'd been at his physical peak.

But, fucking hell, it took a lot more work to stay there than it had in his twenties.

He stripped off his kit, dumped it for his cleaner to deal with, and padded naked into his bathroom.

He weighed himself – at ninety-six kilos, a shade over fifteen stone, and eight per cent body fat, he was happy enough – and went for a long, hot shower.

After that, he knocked up some chicken pasta and a protein

shake, and when he'd finished those he made himself a cup of tea and went to sit in his living room to sort out some admin.

A few bills and a bit of junk mail.

A letter from the Regiment inviting him to a Clock Tower Fund supper – guest speaker, ex-DSF Guy de Vere. Which made Carr wince, and think of Antonia de Vere, and carefully, guiltily, slide the letter back into its envelope.

Another, this one from the fixtures secretary of the Regimental rugby club inviting him to play in a vets' team against the Royal Navy. That one he put to one side: in his day, Carr had been the SAS representative side's first XV blindside, and he missed the fun of smashing people on the pitch and getting pissed with them after the match. A chance to turn out and batter the matelots was not to be missed.

A couple of begging letters from military charities which he supported.

All good.

Then he took out his notepad.

His day job was to handle the UK security for Konstantin Avilov, a one-time KGB officer who had mysteriously acquired vast, worldwide interests in oil, mining, and information technology – perhaps not entirely coincidentally after his friend and mentor Vladimir Putin had become president of Russia in 2000. Avilov had trained under Putin at the old Kaluga facility, had spent a decade as his right-hand man, and had helped his boss to seize power in the maelstrom that had followed Boris Yeltsin's resignation. He'd been handsomely rewarded for his loyalty and support, and now he was handsomely rewarding John Carr for his.

It was a simple enough job – Avilov was in London roughly two weeks a month, for business meetings and to party, and Carr and his London team received him and his travelling security, kept them alive – because there were real and present threats to him, as there seemed to be to many of these oligarchs – and then sent them on their way when they were finished doing whatever they were doing.

Two weeks later, rinse and repeat.

For that, Carr was paid six figures – nowhere near what he could earn in the world's various blood-soaked sandpits, true, but London was short on rocket-propelled grenades and long on nightlife, and he also received handsome expenses, six-monthly bonuses, and the use of this three-bed flat in Primrose Hill and a very nice burgundy BMW X6. Carr was actually more of a biker – he owned a Triumph Thunderbird Storm, which he loved to thrash up and down the motorway when he got the chance – but on cold winter's days like today, he had to admit, the Beamer was very pleasant.

The reason for the notepad was to sketch out a plan for the boss's next visit, in a week's time. He was coming over to complete some business purchase or other – Carr didn't know the details, and didn't want to know them – and would then spend a week in his flat at Chelsea Harbour, cutting a swathe through the capital's best restaurants, bars and call-girls.

He had just drawn up the itinerary and started selecting the team when his mobile vibrated on the coffee table in front of him.

A text.

He didn't recognise the number.

'Hello John,' said the message. 'Please call me to discuss something that you need to know about.'

'Hmm,' he said to himself.

He wasn't a man to rush things.

Maybe he'd call later, maybe he wouldn't.

But he was certainly intrigued.

And that bad feeling from earlier in the morning was back, grumbling in his belly.

He put the phone back on the table and went back to his planning.

# 28.

SEVERAL HUNDRED MILES away, a man in a black jacket walked into The Volunteer on the Falls Road in Belfast.

In the bad old days – or the good old days, it depended – the man would never have been able to meet his contact like this.

Back then, the 'Vollie' had been a favourite boozer among Belfast PIRA men, and when you walked through the door you did so under the assumption that you were being watched by the men in cars, or one of their associated groups.

Even if those evil fuckers were taking a day off, or following a more important target – sure, they couldn't follow yous *all*, now could they? – the rumour was that they had a permanent eye-in-the-sky watching the front door of the bar, and a dozen other Provo hangouts. The Army Air Corps seemed to have a helicopter over the city all day and all night, the whop-whop of distant rotors punctuating any silence; aboard were supposedly operators using stand-off surveillance gear that let them recognise you from their aerial platform far away across town, *and* read the headlines on your copy of *An Phoblacht*, *and* count the change in your pocket.

So the rumour went.

But that was all in the past. Tony Blair, the Ceasefires, General John de Chastelain and all that… Now the SAS and most of the spooks had moved on, with bigger fish to fry – the kind of fish who wouldn't be seen dead drinking Guinness in the Vollie, or anywhere else – and most of the time no-one was watching the front door, or much cared who was inside, or what was being discussed.

Sure, some of the bhoys still used it, but now it was mostly just a place to drink stout, tell tall tales, and watch the Celtic game.

But, even so, the man in the black jacket ducked his head into his upturned coat collar as he walked in.

The man he had come to see – known as 'Freckles', for obvious reasons – was sitting at a table beneath a signed Kerry GAA shirt once worn by Seamus Moynihan, All Stars Footballer of the Year in 2000.

Mid to late fifties. Pale, thinning ginger hair, a faded black Thin Lizzy T-shirt stretched tight over his pot belly.

Nursing a whiskey – Kavanagh Single Malt – on the rocks.

The Dubliners were on the sound system, Luke Kelly singing about Derry, the armoured cars and the bombed-out bars.

The lunchtime crowd was sparse – just a few lads here and there, chatting to orange-coloured girls, the irony, and a bored barman flicking through an old copy of *Loaded*.

Black Jacket bought a pint of lager and sat down at the table. 'Bout ye, big lad?' he said.

'Ach, full o' the blade,' said Freckles, rubbing his eyes and pulling a face that said the exact opposite. 'Róisín's pissed half the time and pissed off the rest. Stacey's lost her job at Specsavers. Johnny's still Johnny. So it's all good. You sure you weren't followed, coming here?'

'Sure, it's a free country, isn't it?' said Black Jacket. 'And I'm allowed a lunch hour. I'm just visiting an old school pal for a drink, so I am. Anyway, there isn't the manpower, even if they wanted to.'

He took a big glug of Harp and belched.

'So what can I do you for?' said Freckles.

'What if I told you that I know where to find the men who killed Sean and Gerard Casey and Ciaran O'Brien?'

There was a long pause. Then Freckles sat back in his chair.

'Christ,' he said. 'That's been a long old time. It was them Para bastards, wasn't it?'

'It was.'

'And you know who it was?'

'Their names, home addresses, current jobs, the lot.'

Freckles took a sip of his whiskey. 'Are you suggesting... what *are* yous suggesting?'

'I'm suggesting someone might like to pay they two fellas a wee visit and introduce them to Mr Nemesis.'

'Come again?'

'Fuck's sake,' said Black Jacket, rolling his eyes. 'I'm suggesting someone might like to go over there and kill the fuckers.'

Freckles was silent for a moment. Then he said, 'Are yous wearing a fucking wire? You trying to get me lifted?'

'No, I am *not*, you melter,' hissed Black Jacket, indignantly. 'You fucking catch yourself on.' He glanced over at the door marked *Gents*. 'You can take me in there and pat me fucking down if you like. I'm handing you two of the bastards on a fucking plate here. You cheeky fecker.'

'Alright,' said Freckles, looking around the bar. 'Keep your fucking hair on. And careful who yous call a melter.'

'Sorry.'

'And a cheeky fecker.'

'Sorry.'

'Right. So who are they?'

'Michael Parry and John Carr. Parry's a delivery driver now in the north of England. Carr works in private security for some Russian in London. He was in the SAS after the Paras, and all.'

'An SAS man?' Freckles sat forward slightly.

130

'That's right.'

'Christ. We might like to have a look at that. That'd be fucking beezer, right enough.'

'Aye, that's what I've been trying to fucking say to ye,' said the man in the black jacket. Still shaking his head, he downed his pint and stood up. 'Listen, you ask them and get back to me. It'd be nice to get the bastards back for Gib and Loughgall, eh?'

# 29.

AT FOUR O'CLOCK, Carr's mobile rang.

He put down the book he was reading – an old Len Deighton WWII thriller, *Bomber* – and picked up the phone.

And frowned.

Oleg Kovalev – Konstantin Avilov's head of security and, therefore, John Carr's immediate boss.

A good guy, but he didn't make too many social calls.

Carr had plans for the evening – a curvy little redhead from the gym, she'd been flirting with him for weeks and he'd finally given in – but he had a funny feeling in his gut that he wouldn't be meeting up with her, after all.

Sighing, he answered the call.

'Carr.'

'Johnny, is me,' said the Russian. 'Listen, something has come up. You know Konstantin was in Amsterdam today?'

'Aye.'

'Okay, he's flying to London tonight, instead of Moscow. For business meeting.'

'Tonight?' said Carr.

'Today, actually. We at Schiphol now. Just about to fly. Konstantin would like you to meet us at City Airport at five-thirty. We do the business at Dorchester Hotel. Then we go out on the town. You come too. Okay?'

Carr breathed deeply, and closed his eyes.

A long, long time ago, hard, wise men had burned the famous 'seven Ps' into his brain: Prior Preparation and Planning Prevents Piss Poor Performance.

Leave nothing to chance.

Have a plan.

Have a fall-back plan.

And know them both, inside out, upside down, and back to front.

It was hard to plan for things which were sprung on you, and he didn't like the sound of a night on the town, either. His job was to protect the Russian, not to fanny about the place telling the guy war stories and sharing three hundred pound bottles of champagne with him. Just lately, Avilov had been finding excuses to drop in like this, and it was clear to Carr that he was crossing the line between adviser and friend, between bodyguard and drinking buddy.

Probably a good thing for Carr's future prospects, but it made life hard.

'Listen, Oleg,' said Carr. 'You guys need to understand. It's hard for me to keep Konstantin in one piece if I can't plan ahead properly. It's even harder if he wants me to go on the piss with him. Don't get me wrong. I like the guy, he's a good bloke, but I have to keep that distance. It's how it works.'

Oleg chuckled. '*Good bloke*,' he said. 'I like this. Look, I know, Johnny, I understand. What I can say? He thinks you're good bloke also. Plus, you don't speak Russian, so he can talk freely.'

'Who else is coming over?'

'Only me. And just one car, please. Boss wants to feel free.'

'I don't like that,' said Carr.

He liked to have a minimum of four on the job – two operators plus two drivers in two vehicles. And all of them trained and licensed close-protection officers, strictly ex-Paras and Marines – he'd have preferred ex-Hereford men, but they were way too pricey for UK work. It wasn't fancy or complicated, just basic, belt-and-braces stuff, but it could be the difference between a good day and a very bad one.

Oleg snorted. 'You worry too much. Is low-key meeting. No-one knows he is coming. We fly in, driver collects us, we have the meeting, we have some fun. Just some dinner, some drinks, maybe some girls. No risk. No problems.'

'It just sounds light on bodies to me, Oleg,' he said.

'Relax. Is just a flying visit. Hush-hush. No problems.'

Carr sat back in his chair and thought for a moment.

He wasn't best pleased, but then what gets people killed are patterns.

*Patterns.*

You get up at six every day, leave your house at seven, drive the same route to work, park in the same car park, stop for your daily coffee in the same Starbucks… if the *barista* knows you, if he knows you like your skinny latte extra hot, in a takeaway cup even though you drink it inside, and knows that you spend fifteen minutes reading the sports pages before you walk the last three hundred yards to the office… Well, if someone wants to get to you, you're already a dead man.

If you know you're under threat, you don't set patterns.

You keep knowledge of your movements to a minimum, you buy your coffee at a different place every morning, and you don't schedule appointments a week ahead.

And Avilov really did have enemies. There was permanent background chatter about contracts being taken out on him; Carr had no way of knowing how serious that chatter was, but he did know that two of Avilov's business associates had been murdered in the last couple of years, so he had to assume that it was grounded in reality.

He liked Avilov well enough, the job was easy, and the money was fine.

But if your principal won't take advice then you have two choices: quit, or make the best of a bad job.

So: was it quitting time?

Some level of risk is unavoidable – that's just life. The trick is not to make it easy for the bastards.

That was Carr's mantra.

But deep down, he knew that one random, unplanned visit to London was probably safe enough.

*It's not Libya*, he thought. *I can live with it.*

He sighed.

Looked at his watch.

Better ring the curvy little redhead and give her the bad news.

'Okay,' he said. 'I'll be there. Five-thirty at City, you say?'

'Yes. We're taxi-ing to the runway now. You must get your skate on. Is this the word, skate?'

'*Skates*,' said Carr. 'I need to get my skates on.'

'Crazy,' laughed Oleg. 'Get skates on. You English, you funny, funny people.'

'I'm Scottish.'

'Is same thing,' said Oleg, dismissively.

# 30.

A MAN WITH greying black hair, thick spectacles, and thread veins on his broken nose which spoke of too many late nights in too many rough bars sat in the Beehive on the Falls Road, nursing his first pint of the evening, thinking.

Many moons ago, the life of the man with the broken nose had become inextricably linked with those of two British soldiers.

He'd all but cast them from his thoughts, but now – suddenly, unexpectedly – they had stepped back into them.

*Parry.*

*Carr.*

How to deal with them?

The place was alive with eyes, so he needed to tread carefully.

Do the right thing.

More importantly, be *seen* to do the right thing.

He looked up.

Sitting across the table from him was a woman.

She looked scared half to death, but the dominoes players on either side were scrutinising their pieces with extraordinary care and attention.

See no evil, hear no evil, speak no evil. It paid to be a wise monkey at times.

'Marie, is it?' he said. 'Marie Hughes?'

She nodded.

'So tell me what you told the police.'

Marie Hughes did as she was told, the man listening impassively.

When she had finished, he said, 'So you're saying they didn't call my brother an ambulance?'

'Yes.'

'That they deliberately made him suffer and die?'

'Aye.'

He sat back and thought for a few moments. Then he said, 'Listen, sweetheart, you've nothing to fear from us. But I don't want you speaking to the peelers from now on, okay? Newspapers, too, if they come knocking. We want to control this information, so you don't speak to anyone without my say-so. Especially not the police. Got it?'

She nodded again.

'Not a word.'

'Not a word,' she said.

'Good. Now, Danny here is going to drive you home and give you some money for your trouble,' said the Irishman. 'And yous'll keep your bake shut. This meeting never happened. Understand?'

'Uh huh.'

'Are you sure?'

'I'm sure.'

The man nodded towards the door. 'On your way, then.'

After she had gone, another man came over from the bar and took her place.

'What d'ye reckon then, Pat?' he said, to the man with the broken nose.

Pat Casey – or, to give him his full title, MLA Patrick Casey, current member of the Northern Irish Assembly for Drugannon Moor, and former 2IC of the Belfast Brigade of the Provisional IRA – finished his Guinness, and then set the glass on the table.

Said curtly to a man with a fistful of dommies at the table to his right, 'Freddie, set me up another o' them.'

# 31.

JOHN CARR COULDN'T settle.

Konstantin Avilov's private aircraft – a gaudy, gold-painted, £30 million Sukhoi Superjet 100-95 SSJ, with its own roster of foxy Eastern European stewardesses and former Russian air force pilots – had arrived bang on time, and now they were in the bar at the Dorchester.

Which was starting to fill up with rich pissheads.

Over to Carr's right, with his back to the wall, Konstantin Avilov was sitting at a table, deep in conversation with another crook from the old days of the Soviet empire.

The only words Carr could make out were '*Da*' and '*Niet*', but it all seemed friendly enough, with lots of raucous laughter, nodding, and gesticulating.

Their business had been concluded an hour ago in the guy's suite, and this was just the drink to seal the deal.

The deal no doubt meant that someone, somewhere, was getting screwed, and that Avilov and his pal were making another little fortune for themselves, but Carr's interests were more prosaic: was anyone in this room intending to harm Konstantin Avilov? The pissheads were noisy, unpredictable bastards, the kind of crowd among which someone more sinister could hide.

A few feet away, Oleg Kovalev was in a hushed discussion with the other guy's top security bod.

That looked friendly, too.

Clearly, they thought everything was under control.

If Carr had been the sort of man to relax at times like this, he might even have relaxed.

But he didn't relax very often, and he never relaxed at times like this unless every living soul in the room was covered by a man he trusted, and the room itself was covered, and the building, and the approach and departure routes.

Relaxation was what got you fired.

At *best*.

At worst, it got you killed.

Behind the bar, some old geezer was mixing up another bunch of cocktails.

Out of the window, he saw a tourist bus pull up in the Park Lane traffic. The tour guide was saying something over the loudspeaker; flashbulbs were firing in the evening dark.

Just then, Konstantin Avilov stood up, beaming, and shook the hand of his buddy.

'Is good deal for you, good deal also for me, Georgiy,' he said, in English. 'We make lots of money, everybody happy.' He looked over at Carr. 'John, come over here, please. I want you meet my friend.'

Carr got up, swept the room, and walked over.

The other Russian had that flat, wide, hard face, born of winter on the steppes.

Six foot tall, powerfully built – early sixties, but still physically tough for all that.

Narrow eyes.

*Killer's eyes.*

What looked to Carr like many years in the Red Army under his belt.

'Is my friend, Georgiy Krupin,' said Avilov. 'Georgiy meet John, John meet Georgiy. Georgiy was Colonel in our Spetznaz. You know Spetznaz, John? Better than SAS.'

Carr smiled and shook Krupin's outstretched hand. 'I dinnae know about that,' he said.

'I don't know either,' said Krupin, with a self-deprecating grin, and excellent English. 'I have to admit, I always feared that the Special Air Service had the… what's the phrase? Had the *edge* over us. Numerically, we were stronger, of that I am sure. But you guys paved the way for all special forces everywhere. It's a pleasure to meet you.'

'Likewise, Colonel,' said Carr.

'I understand from Konstantin that you served for nearly twenty years?' said the Russian, pulling his cuffs down and adjusting his tie. 'You were in Afghanistan?'

'Yes,' said Carr. 'Manhunting.'

Krupin blew out his cheeks. 'A hellish place,' he said. 'We were glad to get out. I lost many good men there.'

'We lost a few ourselves.'

'So I understand,' said Krupin. 'But it was a failure of your politics, not your soldiers. You have good men, but you fight with one hand tied behind your backs by the *devochki* in Washington and London. *Slabaki* who never saw even one single punch thrown in their entire lives. The Apache, the Spectre, night vision 2.0… *Bozhe moy*! With western military hardware like this and Russian leadership, we would kill every last one of those goatfuckers, eh?'

'Enough,' said Avilov. 'Is vodka time!'

# 32.

THEY LEFT THE DORCHESTER and Mr Spetznaz at nine. The driver – Terry Cooper, an ex-Para, the brother of a former 22 comrade of Carr's, and a man with a decade in Met Counter Terrorism under his belt – was waiting outside in one of Avilov's armoured Range Rovers.

He took them straight to some sort of fusion restaurant in Mayfair, where Avilov was greeted like a favourite son – he knew the owner, a Ukrainian gangster – and the three men were fed yellowtail tuna and Wagyu steaks, and had £200-a-glass scotch poured down their throats.

At least, Oleg Kovalev and Konstantin Avilov had scotch poured down their throats; Carr accepted one drink and left it untouched.

Eventually Avilov noticed.

'John,' he said, his voice steady and clear. Among his many talents was one for holding his booze. 'John, why you not drink with me?'

'You know the score, boss,' said John. 'I'm working. I don't drink on the job.'

All those years in the Army had stamped a mark on him which said Duty first, fun second.

'Bah,' scoffed Avilov. 'What you protecting me? Oleg is here. Anyway, nobody here want to hurt Konstantin. Is fine. Have a drink!'

'I'd rather not,' said Carr. 'Thank you, though.'

'Oleg is drinking.'

'This isn't Oleg's town. I'll drink if I'm in Moscow, but not here.'

Oleg Kovalev beamed at Carr, and said something in Russian to the boss man. They both laughed.

'Oleg says you are better man than him,' said Avilov. 'I don't know. You both great men for me. You don't want to drink, I respect that, John.'

'You can show it by paying me properly, then,' said Carr, grinning.

The two Russians erupted in laughter, and beckoned over more whisky.

'So, tell me about Afghanistan,' said Avilov.

Monday it might have been, but for the super-rich every day is a Friday.

It had all the makings of a long night.

# 33.

THEY MOVED ON from the Mayfair restaurant at 11pm and climbed into the Range Rover to travel to a private members' club in Dean Street, Soho.

It was only a mile or so, but at Carr's request Terry made it five miles by taking a very circuitous route, and they arrived just after 11.30pm.

Soho was rammed, and buzzing with people and cars and bikes and cabs.

A second Range Rover – the second Range Rover John Carr had wanted – might have noticed the motorcycle which pulled up further down the road.

But good as they were, Carr and Terry Cooper alone stood no realistic chance of spotting it.

# 34.

TWO HUNDRED MILES NORTH, in the saloon bar of the Wheatsheaf in Westfield Street in St Helens, a fifty-three-year-old man was finishing off the last dregs of a pint of Carlsberg.

It had been a long day for Mick Parry, driving round his hundred square mile beat, dropping off tat from Amazon to lonely housewives, eBay obsessives and small businesses, but he'd enjoyed his game of darts and a chinwag with a few of the lads, and now it was time for bed.

'That's me, fellas,' he said. 'Better get back before I get a bollocking.'

He nodded his goodnight amid a chorus of good-natured jibes and chuckles, and stepped out into the orange glare of another Merseyside night.

He shivered at the cold, blowing a cloud of steamy breath as he did so, and smiled to himself.

'Christ, you're going soft, Michael,' he said to no-one.

Soft he'd never be, but it was true that he wasn't the man he'd once been. The only mark of that man from the past was the Parachute Regiment cap badge which had been inked onto his right shoulder in Aldershot thirty-five years earlier, and which was currently hidden under a T-shirt, a fleece and a thick black donkey jacket.

He pulled on a beanie hat and started walking.

# 35.

PATRICK BEARNÁRD CASEY finished off his fifth or sixth Bushmills chaser and jerked his head in the direction of the door.

'Let's you and me go for a wee dander, Freckles,' he said.

Outside, on the Falls Road, the night air was every bit as cold and damp as it was in St Helens, and both men pulled their coats tight around them.

They strolled in slow silence down the empty street for a minute or two.

Then Casey said, 'Let me ask you a question, Freck. If two of your brothers had been murdered in cold blood, and one day someone knocks on your door and says, *Here they are...* What would you do about it?'

'Sure, I'd kill the fuckers. No, wait. I'd *torture* the fuckers, *then* kill them.'

'Yes,' said Pat Casey, reflectively. 'I think you would.' He kicked an empty Coke can along the pavement, and it skittered and bobbled into the gutter. 'What would you think of me if I did nothing about it?'

'Truthfully?'

'Truthfully.'

'I'd think you'd gone soft. I mean, I'm sure you'd have your reasons, but...'

'Nah. You'd be right, big man. You'd be right.'

They walked on in silence, until they reached the Falls Park.

'Jesus, it's cold,' said Casey.

They turned into the park, found a bench, and sat down on the damp wood.

After a few moments staring into the inky black, Casey said, 'I'm not putting this to the Army Council. This isn't official, it's personal.'

'Are you sure that's wise?' said Freckles. 'If it gets out that you've done something like this off your own bat...'

'Fuck them,' said Casey, dismissively.

Freckled nodded.

'It's a big job, mind,' said Casey. 'Over the water, as well. We need someone we can trust. Someone proven. Someone reliable. Most important of all, someone who can keep his gub shut if it all goes tits up.'

'I'd say Johnny Kerrigan,' said Freckles, 'but he's in jail. Next best thing is Dessie Callaghan.'

Casey looked at him. 'Persuade me.'

'We need someone with balls, right? Dessie has balls to spare. The only thing he's scared of is us.'

'Okay. Go on'

'He knows his way around a weapon. He done that gubby OIRA fucker from Limavady who was causing all that shite, *and* he done that tout over Whiterock way. There's two just off the top of me nut.'

'They was a few years ago now.'

'Aye, but he *did* them. Never hesitated. Credit in the bank.'

'True enough.'

'And like you said, you need someone who can keep his trap shut. You can trust Dessie there. He done time for that peeler, didn't he?'

'Which peeler?'

'The off-duty one the boys kicked to death in the city centre? They seen him out on the piss, Pat Mulcahy's lad started on him, and it got out of hand. Mulcahy did most of it, and he got away scot free. Dessie done half a six for it, and he never said nothing to nobody.'

Pat Casey pushed out his lower lip in thought. 'Fair point, I suppose,' he said.

'I think Dessie might be your man,' said Freckles.

Pat Casey was silent for a while.

Then he said, 'Unless we contract it out? Some Eastern European. A Turk.'

'I don't think that's a good idea. You want to keep this close.'

'Aye, you're right,' said Casey. He stood up. 'Alright. Dessie it is. Can you have him brought to one o' the safe houses? And let's do it tomorrow morning before I change my mind.' He pulled his coat tighter around himself and shivered. 'Right, that's me away. Night, pal.'

# 36.

IT WAS JUST AFTER 3am when Avilov called it a night and left the club in Soho.

He and Oleg Kovalev, slightly unsteady on their feet, walking either side of a leggy Czech girl, who was wearing an electric blue minidress and six-inch heels.

The girl giggling and saying something in her own language which the two men seemed to understand, and to appreciate.

Carr let them get a good few paces ahead, staying in the shadow of the door, the better to maintain situational awareness.

It was that, and the fact that he was stone cold sober, that saved their lives.

Except the girl's.

Even at that time of the morning Dean Street was still busy, and Carr's eyes were everywhere.

The first thing he noticed was three pretty young women, short dresses, low-cut, waiting for a cab or a lift home. Carr liked pretty women in short, low-cut dresses as much as the next man, maybe more, but he was disciplined in all matters: they passed in and out of his optic nerve in half a heartbeat.

The second thing he noticed was a stationary motorcycle, engine running, rider watching him, fifty yards up the street.

*Courier?*

*No, no couriers about at this time of night.*

Simultaneously with *that* thought, he noticed a third thing – a man in his early thirties breaking away from the wall a few metres the other side of the club door.

Short, dark hair.

Fit-looking.

Jaw clenched.

Dark, medium-length peewee jacket.

Black leather gloves.

Trying and failing to look casual.

Eyes focused like lasers on Konstantin Avilov.

Walking way too purposefully.

John Carr had seen this man and men like him in many shapes and guises and in many places over the years: he had worked with them, against them, *been* one of them.

And he knew exactly what this was, like he knew that the end of the day brought darkness.

This was Death.

*How the fuck did he know we were here?* he thought, before it left his consciousness and was filed in the box marked 'Later'.

The assassin drew level with Carr and passed him, eyes still locked on Avilov.

As Carr peeled away from the door, the man came to a halt six feet from the boss and his party – the three of them still utterly oblivious.

Oddly, they were lucky that he was a professional.

Amateurs do strange and unpredictable things, but this guy was following a strict choreography, a series of dance steps drilled into him at some unknown academy by expert tutors, all designed to ensure that roughly 7.5 grammes of lead would leave the muzzle of his pistol at some 400 metres per second and bury itself in the back of Konstantin Avilov's head.

Carr, now two yards behind the man, watched him begin to

adopt a classical combat shooter's stance, his feet going firm and slightly apart, left just ahead of the right. At the same moment, he swept the corner of his jacket away to expose the pistol in his waistband, bending slightly backwards to ensure that the weapon would be released unhindered.

In half a second, the pistol was drawn, and the heel of his right hand was pushed straight forward into the waiting palm of his left, forming a perfect triangle.

And the muzzle was rising.

*Quickly.*

Carr's brain was now divided and running at two speeds.

One side was yelling *Fuck how the hell did I get into this shit I don't get paid enough I don't want to be here...*

The other side was utterly calm, and was firing off a lightning series of automated responses, instructing his limbs as to how to deal with this situation.

A lifetime of experience, distilled into its essence; years of training boiled down into a second, a second-and-a-half tops.

The two Russians and the Czech girl had reached the four-by-four, and Oleg was opening the rear door.

The barrel was now at forty-five degrees and sweeping upwards... but then there was a moment's pause – a slight break in the movement.

When he performed his own microdetailed after-action review later on, Carr would realise that this fleeting delay was a 'tell' – trained as this guy clearly was, this was his first cold-blood hit. No-one finds it easy the first time, and there is often that momentary hesitation.

Added to which, the killer had made a basic mistake.

*Target fixation.*

He hadn't considered any threats to himself.

Specifically, he had not considered the threat posed by John Carr, who was now on his right shoulder – the worst position, from the killer's point of view, if he wanted to remain in control of his weapon, and of the situation.

A multitude of things happened almost simultaneously.

Carr grabbed the killer's wrist with his left hand as his right closed around the barrel of the pistol, taking control of it and forcing it inward and downward.

At the same time, he was shouting a warning to Oleg.

Oleg Kovalev looked over his shoulder, saw the threat and reacted instantly, grabbing Avilov and protecting the boss with his own body. Later, in that after-action review, Carr would admit that he was impressed by this.

A true bullet-catcher is hard to find. That *is* loyalty.

Two panicked shots rang out, skipping off the pavement in front of them, the noise of the second dissipating as Carr's hand closed firmly on the barrel.

Using the leverage from his grasp of the wrist, he twisted the weapon violently. The man's index finger, still trapped within the trigger guard, splintered under the pressure.

His wrist was next to break.

He released the pistol with a primeval scream.

Carr had pivoted in front of him, and now he had the weapon in his own right hand. For half a moment, he thought about turning the fucker inside out with two rounds to the chest.

Instead, he smashed the steel as hard as he could into the bridge of the guy's nose.

The cartilage broke, blood exploding from it, and the man instinctively put his hands up to protect his destroyed face.

And now he was on his knees and vomiting. Carr brought the pistol down as hard as he could on the back of his skull and sent him into darkness.

The whole incident had taken only three or four seconds.

Somewhere up the street, a motorcycle engine was gunned, and the killer's ride was away and gone.

Carr turned around.

The Czech girl was lying dead in the street, one of the rounds having ricocheted off the pavement and taken her at the top of the neck.

The second had hit Oleg Kovalev in the centre of his lower back and knocked him and Avilov to the ground. The Aspetto Kevlar vest which Oleg was wearing underneath his pale blue Stefano Ricci blazer was state-of-the-art thin, but fortunately for him it had done its job. He'd be left with a bruise, and £5,000 out of pocket for a new Ricci jacket, but at least he'd walk into the shop to buy it, not be wheeled in.

He and Avilov – now very sober indeed – were getting up off the floor. Carr sprinted over and bodily pushed both men into the rear of the Range Rover. Then he dived in through the open passenger seat door, and the vehicle was suddenly charging up the street – Carr yelling 'Go go go Terry!' and still holding the pistol – before he'd even shut the door.

They were already halfway down Dean Street, and now the driver roared into Old Compton Street, and then down Frith Street, going against the one-way sign.

Luckily, it was empty of other cars, a minicab or two apart, and the driver nudged 80mph as he approached the junction with Bateman Street.

At which point he jammed on the brakes, and screamed left.

'Stop please, Terry,' said Carr, and the SUV slid to a halt.

Carr got out.

Stood, head cocked on one side.

Listened. Looked.

*Nothing.*

No-one was following them.

No sign of the motorcycle.

No follow-up hit.

A few late night drinkers staring at him, open-mouthed.

Nothing else.

'Wankers,' he spat.

He got back into the vehicle and looked into the rear.

'You okay?' he said to Oleg.

'I love Kevlar,' said the Russian, with a fierce smile.

Carr showed him the pistol. 'MP-443 Grach,' he said. 'They must be stupid to use something this exotic.' Then he looked at the boss. 'Two choices, Konstantin,' he said. 'I get out and go back to wait for the police and Terry gets you out of here, or we *all* go back and get to the shooter before the police, or before anyone comes back for him. Choose.'

'What you think, John?' said Avilov.

Whisky, champagne, vodka, sake, more vodka, and he was as level and sober as a confirmed teetotaller: amazing what that sort of adrenalin jolt can do for you, especially when combined with a Russian liver.

'I think we should go back and get anything we can out of him before the cops show up,' said Carr. 'We can't obstruct the cops, we can't take anything away, but I'd like to know who the fuck he is right now.'

Avilov leaned forward. 'Go back,' he said to the driver.

Terry gunned the motor, turned left illegally back into Dean Street and swerved to miss a black cab coming the other way.

They arrived back outside the club exactly one-and-a-half minutes after they had left it.

The three young women in party dresses stood there, open-mouthed, at the sight of the two bodies on the pavement.

A couple of doormen had put the Czech girl into the recovery position, and were on the verge of realising the futility of that act – they were kneeling in at least two pints of her blood.

A man whom Carr recognised as the club sommelier was bent over the shooter, feeling his neck for a pulse.

This time, both Carr and Oleg Kovalev got out of the Range Rover.

They listened.

A distant police siren.

They looked.

The street was deserted. Another black cab drove slowly past, the driver gawping. No other traffic.

'Sixty seconds,' Carr said to Kovalev. 'Then the police will be here. Remember, there are cameras all up and down the street.'

Kovalev nodded.

'Make way please,' said Carr, his voice full of authority. 'This man's a doctor.' He grabbed the sommelier by the arm, hoisted him up and sent him spinning back towards the club. 'Get in there and call the police!'

The man scurried back inside.

That was the first part of the job done.

The second part was to draw attention away from Oleg.

'Oh my God!' he yelled, pushing the two doormen aside and kneeling down by the dead Czech girl. 'Sarah! She's fucking dead!'

He picked her up bodily, her blood and spinal fluid spilling over his shirt.

Her mouth lolled open, eyes stared sightlessly into his.

'Have you called the police?' he screamed at the doormen and the three young women who were watching, horrified. 'She's been shot in the head! Call the police! Call the fucking police!'

His estimate of the police response time was almost perfect: two cars, one of them a red Trojan armed response vehicle, raced into the street just over one minute later.

Three armed officers carrying MP5s were straight out and quickly covering the scene, and the uniforms from the panda were ordering everyone to 'STAY WHERE YOU ARE!'

Five minutes later, the scene was swarming with hi-vis jackets and blue-and-white tape.

# 37.

THE SHOOTER, GROGGY and groaning, was taken off to hospital under armed guard in an ambulance, and Carr waited his turn to be interviewed.

Despite the mess he'd made of the guy, he was absolutely confident that he'd used reasonable force, but it looked a lot better to stick around and co-operate than to make the Old Bill come and find him.

Some time around 4am, a detective constable identified himself, took Carr's details and said, 'So you're the security guy for the Russian chap?'

'Yes. One of.'

'And you disarmed the shooter?'

'I did.'

'That was some good work.'

'Just lucky, I guess.'

'Do you know what happened to the weapon? Only we can't find it?'

'I do. It's in my boss's vehicle, locked in the safe.'

'Technically, that means you've committed the offence of possession of a firearm,' said the DC.

'I look forward to you explaining to the CPS that they need to charge me,' said Carr, 'when I've prevented at least one murder, and probably more, and retained a firearm for the sole purpose of handing it to the police rather than allowing it to be picked up and recycled into the London underworld.'

'I'm not saying we'll charge you. But we can't have civilians who are unfamiliar with firearms wandering around with automatic pistols.'

'I'm not unfamiliar with firearms.'

'Ex-Army?'

'Yes.'

'I was in myself. Signals. You?'

'3 Para, then 22.'

'22? You mean Hereford?' The copper sat back on his heels a bit.

'Yes.'

'Ah. That changes things. How long?'

'Nineteen years.'

'Right,' said the officer. 'You *are* familiar with firearms, then. How did you handle the weapon?'

'I took it off him by the barrel and then I held it by the grip. My prints will be all over it, except on the trigger.'

'I need to seize it, please.'

'Sure,' said Carr, with a grin. 'You didn't think I wanted to keep it, did you?'

They walked to the Range Rover, and the driver opened the safe in the boot.

'I've made it safe,' said Carr.

The DC nodded in appreciation, picked it up using a pen and dropped it into a clear plastic evidence bag. 'What is it?' he said. 'Glock?'

'Nah,' said Carr. 'Grach PYa. Eighteen-round magazine, 9mm, semi-auto, very accurate to fifty metres in the right hands. Issued to a number of Russian military and police units, including some special forces.'

The copper nodded in appreciation. 'I wonder how many of these Grachs are knocking around?' he said.

'Who knows?' said Carr, with a shrug. 'SO15 might be able to give you some idea. My guess would be not too many. Nice weapon, designed to replace the Makarov, but it never really caught on. I dare say you could get hold of a box of them in the Balkans. You can get anything you want over there.'

'Did you speak to him?'

'Didn't say a word. I disarmed him, put him out of the game, and we left, in case of any follow-up hit. As soon as we were clear we weren't being followed we came back. We only went round the corner – check the CCTV, it'll show we were gone for a minute, two at most. When we got back, I concentrated on the girl and my colleague put the shooter into the recovery position to wait for you guys.'

'Right.' The police officer looked intently at Carr for a moment. Then he said, 'Well, I need to take a full statement, and I need to get this thing' – he held up the pistol – 'to forensics. Why don't I give you a lift to the nick? It'll be more comfortable there, and I can do a proper interview.'

'Am I under arrest?'

'No. Entirely voluntary.'

'Fine,' said Carr. 'I'll want a lawyer, though.'

'Will the duty solicitor do?

'Yes.'

'Let's get going, then.'

They headed to Charing Cross nick, where the officer got Carr a cup of tea and the duty solicitor, a tidy young brunette in a figure-hugging blouse.

Once she had confirmed that he wasn't being arrested, and demanded and received an assurance that he was not suspected of committing any offence, the interview started.

It was a boring process, thoroughly carried out, and it was 9am before he was shown the door.

On the steps outside, under the mock-Grecian portico, he looked at the lawyer.

'Where do we go from here?' he said.

'Well, I expect they'll have charged the gunman by now,' she said, looking Carr up and down, and clearly liking what she saw. 'You may be needed to make a further statement, and if so the police will be in touch direct. You'll certainly be needed at the Old Bailey in three or four months' time. Given the people involved, and your own unusual background, you might want to make an application to give evidence behind a screen. If you need me to deal with that you can give me a call.'

'Nah, I'll not need a screen.'

'Well, here's my card anyway,' she said, smiling innocently. 'You never know – something else might come up that you need me to handle for you.'

Carr grinned. 'Do you sleep with all your clients?'

'Very few of them, actually.'

'Maybe I'll give you a bell,' said Carr.

'I look forward to it.'

She put her hand on his chest, and ran it left to right across his pecs.

'By the way,' she said. 'It might be worth changing your shirt.'

He looked down: clothes were a weakness of Carr's, and one of the few things he didn't mind spending cash on. He was wearing a light blue Paul Smith shirt which had cost him £175. It was ruined, stained with the dead girl's blood.

'Ah, fuck,' he said.

'Naughty boy,' said the lawyer, with a tut. 'Such language.'

She shook her head and disappeared back inside. Carr watched her backside appreciatively, and then stepped into the street to find a cab.

A taxi pulled up a few moments later, and he headed for Chelsea Harbour, where Avilov owned a two-thousand square foot apartment overlooking the Thames, bought in 2005 for a couple of million quid and now worth several times the original purchase price.

He was lucky like that.

When Carr was buzzed in, he found his boss and Oleg sitting opposite each other on two white leather sofas.

Both men looked grim-faced.

'Get back okay?' said Carr.

'Half hour ago,' said Oleg. 'They still interview you, so we come.'

Avilov had stood up, and now he extended his hand to Carr.

'You save my life today, John,' he said, rubbing a bruise on his temple. 'You hurt my head when you push me into car, but this I can forgive.' He smiled weakly. 'You save my life. We are brothers now. Forever.'

'That's nice to know,' said Carr. 'Maybe they'll come after me too, now. Being as I'm family and all.'

The Russian laughed. 'I think they want only me.'

'Who are "they"?'

'I get only a little information out of the guy,' said Oleg Kovalev, with a shrug. 'Give me one hour with him and I get everything, but one minute… It's not enough. He speak with Kharkiv accent, he has tattoo on right arm here.' He indicated his wrist. 'Skull with beret and crossed knives.'

'Spetznaz?' said Carr.

Kovalev nodded. 'Spetznaz,' he said.

'Sent by the guy from the Dorchester?' said Carr. 'He's ex-Spetznaz.'

Avilov sighed. 'No. Is *crazy* if it is him. We just did deal, good deal for both of us. You know me, John, I make lot of enemies in my life. But he is not one of them. Is probably just… What is word?'

'Coincidence?'

'Da, coincidence. Lots of Spetznaz leave Army, need work. I have ex-Spetznaz working for me, myself.'

'Most important thing,' said Oleg, 'is now we know there is serious problem. Death threats, everyone has them. But this guy was really trying to kill Konstantin. This afternoon, Konstantin flies back to Moscow, stays there for a while. I stay here, and you and I look at all our UK contacts. Who knew Konstantin was in London, how they find out where he was.' He paused and looked directly at John Carr. 'The driver?'

'Nah, it's not the driver,' said Carr. 'I can vouch for Terry personally. Forget that. But it could be the car. I'll have it checked for a tracker.'

'Good idea,' said Oleg. 'Who else knew?'

Carr thought for a moment. On Avilov's insistence, he hadn't called in extra personnel.

'No-one,' he said. 'Where's Kharkiv?'

'Kharkiv?'

'You said the guy had a Kharkiv accent.'

'Ah. Is in far-eastern Ukraine. On Russian border.'

'Who owns the restaurant we were at last night?'

Oleg Kovalev and Konstantin Avilov looked at each other, and then back at Carr.

'Ukrainians,' said Oleg.

'Maybe start there, then?' said Carr.

There was a silence, and Oleg said, 'Also, I have the shooter's mobile.'

'The number?'

'His phone.'

'His *actual* phone? Why the fuck did he have that on him?'

Oleg shrugged. 'I guess he thought he was safe,' he said. 'I took it from him outside the club, posted it through shop door. My friend collect it this morning. This friend, he has some special skills. He is cracking it now.'

'You mad bastard. You'll be on CCTV. They're bound to come for you.'

Oleg chuckled. 'I was very careful. Cameras will show nothing. If police suspect me...' He spread his hands. 'What they find? I don't have phone no more. Maybe we find information from it. Maybe then I am *not* mad bastard?'

# 38.

TO THE UNTRAINED eye, Amcomri Street was just like any other dreary residential road in any British town.

But the large, pro-Republican mural painted onto the gable end wall of a house at one end – and the other murals in surrounding streets, and the tricolours hanging from many of the houses – left no room for doubt: this was the pulsing heart of west Belfast's nationalist movement.

Amcomri Street had been named after The American Committee for Relief in Ireland, a charity set up on the other side of the Atlantic in the 1920s to funnel cash to people who'd suffered hardship during the Irish War of Independence. The street itself had been built with some of that money, and a meeting was currently taking place in one of the cramped houses within it.

The electoral roll said that the house was home to Peadar and Constanza Mulligan. They paid their bills on time, and never caused anyone any bother, but then they were never – ever – at home. If anyone knocked on a neighbour's door, the neighbour would have said that Mr and Mrs Mulligan were away seeing relatives in Australia, or touring Europe, or enjoying the cruise of a lifetime… Wherever they were, they were away for the foreseeable future, enjoying their richly-deserved retirement.

None of that was true, of course. The neighbours were hard-core

Republicans, and Peadar and Constanza Mulligan didn't actually exist, and never had done: their 'home' was one of a number of PIRA safe houses, kept on after the worst of the Troubles was over, because you never knew when they might start up again.

There were five men in the living room of the little terraced house.

The first was there to sweep for bugs and provide security.

The second was Black Jacket, the man who had met Freckles in the bar down the road the day before.

The third was Freckles.

The fourth was MLA Pat Casey, presently cleaning the grease off his thick black specs.

The fifth was Desmond 'Dessie' Callaghan, a six-foot two-inch, part-time doorman and IRA enforcer, with a broken nose and narrow eyes. A veteran of the Belfast Brigade since 1990, he had got in on the final days of the Troubles, but there had been less call for his undoubted skills in recent years.

'Of course you can rely on me, Pat,' Dessie was saying, indignantly. 'When have I ever let anyone fucking down?'

'Watch your tone, Dessie,' said Security. 'Remember who it is you're talking to, now.'

'I'm sorry, Ryan,' said Dessie. 'But fucking hell.'

He scratched his crewcut, looking distinctly unhappy.

'I'm serious,' said Casey. 'If I give you this job it never comes back to me. Understood?'

'I don't know how you can even fucking ask me that,' said Dessie.

'I said is that *understood*? Because if it does come back to me I'll have you fed into a woodchipper, feet first, slowly.'

'It won't. If it goes wrong, it's on my back. I know that. I'm a fucking volunteer, Pat, I understand.'

Casey looked at Black Jacket. 'Do you recognise this fella, Dessie?' he said.

Dessie followed his eyes. The man in the black jacket was fat and scared – he had a damp upper lip and trembling hands.

*Way out of his depth*, he thought. *Not a fucking player.*

He took an instant dislike to the Jacket.

'I dunno. I might have seen him around. Why?'

'Never mind why. You've never seen him before and you'll never see him again, got it? He's going to fill yous in on the job and then we'll talk about it.'

Dessie nodded.

'Tell him about the targets,' said Casey.

Black Jacket nodded, and started talking.

Callaghan's eyes widened slightly as he listened, and by the end his heart was pumping, good and proper.

'This is a big job,' said Casey, softening his tone. 'No-one's to know about it. Not your woman, your ma, your best pal. No-one. It's not official. It's not sanctioned. It's personal. For me. What do you reckon? Can you do it?'

Dessie looked at him.

Inside, his mind was racing.

Pull this off, and he'd be a legend; he'd never need to buy a pint again, and everyone who mattered would know what he'd done.

But he was determined to retain a professional detachment.

'Pat, you've been a leader to us,' he said, 'and it'd be an honour and a pleasure to do this for you. But even if it wasn't for you, I'd still be in. Won't be a problem as long as it's planned right.'

'Good man,' said Casey.

He nodded to the Jacket, who produced a photocopied page from the Merseyside *A-Z* – no-one would be using the internet to research this job.

'The obvious thing is to do Parry first and Carr second,' he said. 'Carr's the better target, but he's going to sound more alarm bells because of who and what he is. An ex-SAS man who works for a Russian billionaire… That'll be all over the papers, and that would bring a lot of heat we don't want. Agreed?'

'Agreed,' said Casey.

'So, Michael Parry's a Parcelforce driver, these days,' said the man with the black jacket. 'Works out of the depot in Huyton, on Merseyside, half an hour away from where he lives, which is *here*, in Dawson Avenue, bottom end of St Helens. Council estate, two or three miles from the police station. Shares the house with his wife, who's called Sharon, and a daughter in her twenties. The neighbours are elderly on both sides. The house is a mile from the A58, and then it's three or four miles south to the M62, so that's an obvious route away.'

Dessie Callaghan studied the map, and then looked up at the Jacket.

The Jacket looked away, unwilling to meet his gaze.

'So I shoot the fucker in his house and get on my toes,' said Dessie. 'Is that your plan?'

Black Jacket cleared his throat nervously. 'Well, I…'

Dessie pulled a scornful face. 'Do ye want to have me pinched, do ye? People don't use firearms over the water. It'd bring all sorts of shite down on my head. They'll flood the area. Detectives, TV appeals… I'd never get anywhere near the second man.' He shook his head. 'Nah. I'll do the fucker up close, with a knife. He's a Parcelforce driver, is he? I'll get to him while he's out making his deliveries. I'll make it look like a robbery gone wrong.'

'Good thinking,' said Black Jacket.

Dessie raised his eyebrows. 'Thanks a lot,' he said. 'You cheeky fucker. Do we know what hours he works?'

'Not yet, but we will by the weekend. Hoping we'll have a current photo, as well.'

'What about the other fella? The SAS wanker?'

'John Carr. He has a house in Hereford but he spends most of his time in a flat in Primrose Hill in North London. He's younger than Parry, so he'll be quicker and more alert, but he won't be armed so he'll be no trouble.'

Dessie looked at him again. 'That's easy for you to say, pal,' he said, sharply. 'Sure, you'll be sat on your fat arse watching *The X Factor* while I'm at work, will you not?'

'It's a figure of speech, is all, Dessie,' said Black Jacket. 'Don't take it the wrong way.'

'I don't take nothing the wrong way,' said Dessie, coldly. 'Anyone live with him?'

'No,' said Black Jacket. 'Divorced.'

'Are they still in contact with each other, these two bastards?'

'Not as far as we know.'

'Anything else you don't know?' said Dessie.

He was glowering at the other man, now.

'Look, don't get me wrong here,' said Black Jacket, hastily. 'I'm doing the best to bring you what information I can,' he said, looking to Pat Casey for support. 'If you want me to leave, I'm gone.'

Casey cleared his throat, and raised his hand to calm the situation.

'What we have here, Dessie,' he said, 'is a great opportunity to avenge three volunteers. My two brothers and Ciaran O'Brien died that day at the hands of these two. We can make them pay for that. We can also make Carr pay for Seán Savage and Danny McCann and Mairéad Farrell, and the poor lads at Loughgall, too. No-one here is taking the piss. We're all on the same side. Soldiers like you need intelligence to help you carry out your missions, and people like your man here are just there to provide you with what you need.'

Dessie sat back in his chair, brooding.

Eventually, his face lightened. 'Aye,' he said. 'Fair enough. My da' was a good pal of Ciaran O'Brien's. I'll do Parry first, and then Carr. That fucker, if I get the chance I'll bind him up and take my time with him first. If not, I'll shoot him but I'll make sure he knows it's coming and why. I reckon I can be done and away back over here before they can react.'

'Sounds good,' said Pat Casey.

'First thing is how to get over there without them noticing,' said Dessie. 'How's about I fly to France and hire a car in a false name? Then...'

For the first time Freckles spoke up. 'What the fuck are you on about?' he said, dismissively. 'What d'ye think this is, a fucking TV show? Take the Larne ferry. You don't need to show a passport nor nothing. Go over as a foot passenger, there's a bus to Stranraer. Once you're in Stranraer, someone can meet you with a car. Why make it harder than it needs to be?'

Dessie Callaghan looked at him, and then looked away. After a few moments, he said, 'Aye, that would work. Okay. I can do the job and then get back before anyone knows. I'll need a clean car in Scotland, clean weapons, and a routine for the both of them... Where they live, what their daily movements are.' He smiled. 'And I will need them current photos. Don't want to be killing the wrong Brits, do I?'

'That can all be arranged,' said Casey. 'Freckles?'

'Just say the word. I'll get Flan on the car. Mickey can sort the weapons from the Kosovans in Coventry. Give us twenty-four hours for that.'

'Good,' said Pat Casey. 'Well, that's settled, then. Unless there's anything else?'

The man in the black jacket cleared his throat, nervously.

'There was one thing, Pat,' he said. 'I know where the SAS man's family is, if it's any use. His ex-wife's originally from Bangor, but they got divorced a wee while back, and she moved back. They've a couple of kids.'

Pat Casey looked at Freckles.

'Interesting,' said Freckles. 'Might be good leverage. You never know.'

'Where's she live?' said Casey.

'At Crawfordsburn,' said Black Jacket. 'With her new fella.'

Pat Casey leaned back in his chair.

'We should find out a little more about them,' he said. 'Send someone round, Freck. No-one linked to me, and tell him to be careful.' He looked at the man in the black jacket. 'That's good work. Well done.'

The man coloured in pleasure at the praise.

Casey turned his gaze on Dessie Callaghan, and now he spoke firmly. 'Okay, we're done here,' he said. 'I repeat, Dessie, this cannot come back to me. *Ever.* Under *any* circumstances. Understand?'

Dessie returned his stare. 'I understand yous all right, Pat,' he said. 'Sure, I'm just a volunteer, avenging three volunteers. I know my place.'

# 39.

JOHN CARR AND Terry Cooper took Konstantin Avilov and Oleg Kovalev back to City Airport, waited while the tycoon boarded his Sukhoi – after he'd hugged Carr and kissed him on both cheeks – and watched it depart.

Oleg said his goodbyes and took a cab into the city, and Carr and Cooper walked back to the Range Rover.

On the way, Carr said, 'You did well last night, Terry. Apart from parking half a mile from the club door.'

'Yeah,' said the Londoner. 'Sorry about that. That Merc blocked me out. Scary times, eh?'

'Aye, right enough,' said Carr. 'When you drop this off at the garage, I want you to sweep it for bugs and trackers. Just in case.'

'Makes sense,' said Cooper. 'The boss doesn't think…?'

'Och, no,' said Carr. 'No, not at all. But if there isnae a bug, we've got a lot of thinking to do. Presumably you've been doing all the usual counter-surveillance stuff?'

Cooper's Special Branch years had made him expert both at tailing people and at avoiding being tailed.

'Yep,' he said. 'Always. And you saw the routes I took last night. If we were followed, they were bloody good.'

Carr nodded, thoughtfully. 'Yes, I...' he began, but then his mobile vibrated in his pocket.

Another text, from that anonymous sender.

*'Did you get my text John?'* it said. *'Do get in touch.'*

# 40.

ACROSS THE IRISH SEA, a man sat on a sofa, brooding.

For once in his life, he just wasn't sure what to do.

He tried to think it through.

Make the call, his handler would take the necessary action, Dessie would be pinched, and the two men would live.

But the circle of knowledge was very small, and there was the risk – however tiny – that it would come back to him. He'd headed things like that off before, and he was confident he could do it again. But you never knew.

Alternatively, don't make the call, let Dessie go, and allow fate to play out.

It wasn't like those two didn't deserve it, after all.

But if his handler found out he'd known…

His thumb hovered over the keys on his phone.

*And hovered.*

# 41.

IT WAS ALL GOING off on *Emmerdale*, so Frances Delahunty wasn't best pleased when the phone rang.

Tutting, she muted the TV and picked it up.

'Hello?' she said, in broadest Dublin.

A familiar voice spoke.

'*Who?* Right... Well, he's in the bat' dere at the minute, so... Alright, alright, will you settle? I'll fetch him out. Would you hauld on.'

Shaking her head and muttering, she trudged upstairs with the cordless phone, and along the landing to the bathroom.

'Mickey,' she said, putting her ear to the door. 'It's for you.'

'Who is it?' came her husband's muffled voice.

'It's Freckles.'

A sound of splashing and cursing.

Then, 'Sure, am I not having a fucking bat', here? Can it not wait?'

'Can it not wait?' said Frances Delahunty into the phone.

Then, 'No, he says it cannot wait, and you're to get your fecking arse out of that water right now.'

More muffled cursing.

'I'll leave the phone by the door here.'

She placed it on the floor and then, shaking her head and tutting some more, she hurried back downstairs.

Where Charity Dingle was behaving like a mare in the Woolpack, as usual.

'Sure, that's typical,' said Frances, to herself. '*Typical.*'

# 42.

THE FOLLOWING MORNING, Mick Parry arrived at work in his blue VW Passat.

He'd been tailed from the moment he left his house until a half-mile earlier, when the follow car had broken off after alerting the man with the long lens camera.

Parry's employer provided a staff car park, and the car park was conveniently overlooked by a small stand of trees on a hill a quarter of a mile to the north. As the former paratrooper got out of his vehicle and leaned back in to collect his sandwiches, the man with the camera – dressed in dark trousers and an old Army surplus camouflage smock, and standing behind a large beech tree in the copse – fired off thirty or forty frames.

Parry disappeared into the main building, and the cameraman looked down at the screen on the back of his Nikon.

*Perfect.*

Five or six very clear shots showing Parry's face.

He put the camera in his bag, and trudged back through the copse to the lane below.

There was an internet café in Burnley, an hour to the north-east. He'd crop and upload the clearest two or three images into a draft post on a new blog which had been created the day before.

Later that day, someone in Rosnaree, just south of the border in Co. Meath, would log in to the blog, using a VPN to hide his location.

He would print off the photos of Parry, along with images of his house, and his car.

Then the draft post would be deleted, along with the whole blog, and the paper versions driven north across the border for whoever it was who needed them.

The man in the lane whistled tunelessly to himself as he got into his car.

A little Five Live, or maybe some Radio Two, and the journey would pass in no time.

# 43.

DETECTIVE SUPERINTENDENT KEVIN Murphy had only just sat down at his desk in PSNI headquarters when there was a knock at his door.

Detective Sergeant Nigel Johnson – a very good friend, and a highly trusted operator in his part of the Historical Enquiries Team – stuck his head in.

'Morning, boss,' he said. 'I've just had confirmation from Five that they'll see us next week on the Bernie MacMurray case.'

A few months earlier, they had discovered that MI5 was sitting on old telephone intercepts which might help clear up a murder from thirty years ago. The spooks – keen as ever to protect their sources – had at first denied any knowledge of the transcripts, but they had now at least admitted their existence, and were prepared to discuss a limited release.

'Thames House,' said Johnson. 'Next Friday, 10am.'

'So that's what… a week today?'

'Aye. I'll sort flights for the day before.'

'Grand,' said Kevin Murphy. 'I doubt we'll get anywhere, but it's a start.' He looked at his watch. 'I'll just get myself a cup of coffee and then we can get out and see the woman in the Sean Casey–British soldiers enquiry.'

An hour later, Kevin Murphy and Nigel Johnson arrived in the car park of a small office complex where the Divis met the Falls, five minutes from the Bobby Sands mural on the side wall of Sinn Fein's HQ in Sevastopol Street. There were still plenty of Republican headcases, active 'Continuity IRA' terrorists, and people who just plain despised the polis in the area, so they'd travelled in an unmarked car crewed by two uniformed policemen, with Glocks on their hips and rifles in the boot, and followed by a second vehicle with two more cops aboard. Murphy was glad of the back-up.

He and Nigel Johnson left the uniformed officers in the vehicles and made their way to reception.

The receptionist, a pinched-faced woman in her fifties with a badge on her left breast which said 'Aoife O'Mahoney', looked at their warrant cards with undisguised hostility.

'Yes?' she said. 'What d'yous want?'

Murphy beamed at her. Thirty years of bitterness and antagonism, and this stuff just washed off him now.

'I'd like to see Marie Hughes, please,' he said.

'What about?'

'Police business. Can you get her for me, please?'

'She's busy.'

Murphy smiled. 'Not any more,' he said.

The woman looked as though she was about to respond, but instead she picked up her phone and dialled a number.

Marie Hughes arrived in reception a few moments later.

A nervous-looking woman, she was wringing her hands and would not meet the eyes of the two officers.

Kevin Murphy introduced himself, and then turned to the receptionist. 'Would you have a wee room when I can talk to Mrs Hughes in private?' he said. 'I'd be ever so grateful.'

Grudgingly, the woman opened the door and showed them through into the office.

'You can talk here,' she said, indicating an orange sofa next to a watercooler.

'I really would prefer to talk in private,' said the detective. 'No offence.'

But Marie Hughes spoke up. 'It's fine,' she said. 'Aoife's a friend. And I've not much to say, anyway.'

Murphy nodded. 'Okay,' he said. 'As I said on the phone, I just wanted to go through the statement you made the other day about the death of Sean Casey?'

'I don't want to say nothing,' said Marie Hughes.

Murphy raised his eyebrows. 'Oh?' he said. 'How do you mean?'

'I don't want to talk about it.'

Murphy and Johnson exchanged looks.

The senior officer opened his case and handed her a couple of sheets of paper. 'Is this the statement you made?'

Marie Hughes refused to look at the document.

'Do you want to retract it?'

'I don't know. Yes.'

'Is everything okay, Marie?'

'I'm just confused.'

Kevin Murphy sat back.

People were always retracting statements, or not showing up to court, or changing their evidence in the dock, and who could blame them? He well remembered one particular case, where a man who'd helped officers to arrest a gang of IRA blaggers had been taken out and crucified with tent pegs – literally, half-inch diameter steel rods, hammered through his shins and arms. After a lengthy spell in hospital, and the loss of his left leg from the knee down, the man had remembered that he hadn't seen the robbery take place after all, and the blaggers had walked away laughing.

All it took was for a couple of bhoys to pay someone a visit, and pretty much any case could collapse.

'Okay, Marie,' he said. 'Listen, I grew up in this city, and I've been a policeman here for a long time now. I've seen it all, don't you worry about that. People change their minds, and I don't condemn anyone for doing it. I don't have to walk in your shoes, do I?'

'No.'

'So I'm going to give you a wee while to think about it. In the meantime, I do have to ask you one question, formally. Is that okay?'

'Yes.'

'Have you been told not to talk to us?'

She hesitated. Then said, 'No.'

Murphy leaned forward. There was no point at all in trying to put pressure on this woman, even if he'd wanted to.

'Okay, Marie,' he said. 'Well, I think we've gone as far as we can for now. Thank you for your time. Here's my card so you know how to get hold of me if you want to.'

'Okay. Thank you.'

He and Nigel Johnson both stood up, and shook her hand in turn, and the receptionist opened the door and showed them out, scowling.

In the car on the way back to the PSNI HQ, Johnson said, 'Who's got at her?'

'Strange, isn't it?' said Murphy. 'The Brits? They don't know about it, and if they did they wouldn't put the arm on her.'

'Republicans?'

'Aye. But why? You'd think they'd want to shout it from the rooftops.' He sighed. 'To be honest,' he said, eventually, 'I don't really care. There's no case to answer, and we'd only have wasted weeks on it. It's not like we've nothing else to work on.' He paused for a moment. 'We've done our best. Sinn Fein can't say we've covered anything up.'

By the time they were back at the office, they'd almost put it out of their minds.

And that would have been that, except for the fact that Aoife O'Mahoney went home that night and mentioned to her husband

Joe that the peelers had been in talking to Marie Hughes about the death of Sean Casey, and Joe O'Mahoney mentioned it to a couple of the lads down the club that night, and those lads mentioned it to others, and before you knew it it had reached the ears of Pat Casey.

And Pat Casey was not best pleased.

Sure, had he not *expressly* told that stupid woman not to talk to the peelers?

And, if she couldn't follow a simple fucking instruction, then how could he be sure she'd not talk about her meeting with him in the Beehive?

And if she talked about that...

A horrifying thought struck him.

*What if she already had?*

Cursing, he reached for the phone.

# 44.

A COUPLE OF DAYS after he'd photographed Mick Parry in Huyton, the same man parked up in a street in Primrose Hill, north London.

This time he was in a scruffy white Renault van, which had only three hubcaps, a rack of paint-splattered ladders on the roof, and a magnetic vinyl sign on the side, which gave the name and number of a bogus building firm. On the dashboard was a yellow hard hat, a copy of *The Sun* and a Thermos flask.

No-one gave it a second glance in this part of London, where everyone was always in a desperate hurry to get somewhere, and every other house had builders beavering away on loft conversions or extensions to take advantage of the upward spiral of property prices.

But if they *had* looked at it they might have noticed that the rear windows had been silvered over.

The man was sitting in the back of the van, on a wooden chair, looking out of those silvered windows. At his feet was the camera with the long lens. In his hand was a Motorola walkie-talkie, of the sort that you can buy for thirty quid in any electronics shop.

And just now it crackled into life.

'On his way,' was all it said. 'Jeans, blue shirt, brown jumper.'

The man put down the walkie-talkie and picked up the camera and waited.

Fifty metres away, a man in jeans and a brown sweater appeared between two parked cars, waited for a gap in the traffic, and then crossed the road at an easy jog.

Camera guy zoomed in.

Black hair, combed back in a slight quiff.

Fit and strong-looking, big shoulders and arms.

Eyes that were busy, and a big fuck-off scar on his chin.

The sort of face to make you think twice.

*John Carr.*

'I'm glad *I* haven't got to take the fucker on,' murmured the man to himself, as he pressed the button.

The camera clicked thirty times before the target reached the opposite side of the road and disappeared around the corner.

The man in the back of the van stood up, crouching, and climbed past a curtain into the front seat. He put the camera on the floor and picked up the copy of the *Sun*. Two minutes later, another man opened the passenger door and climbed in.

'Get him?' said the new man.

'Perfect.'

He started the van and waited for someone to let him out.

An hour or so to get the pictures placed where they wanted them on the internet, and then it would be time to head back home.

# 45.

A DAY OR TWO LATER, John Carr's ex-wife was putting out her bins before driving off to work when the old lady next door popped her head out of her front door.

'Morning, Stella,' she called. 'I've been hoping to catch you.' She came out of her door and hurried over in her slippers and housecoat. 'There was a fella in the close yesterday, acting funny. I seen him walk by your place a couple of times. He didn't know I was watching. I was behind me nets.'

Stella stopped dragging her bin and stared at the old lady.

'That's interesting, Rose,' she said. 'What was he about, d'you think?'

'I couldn't rightly tell you,' said Rose. 'I was watching the birds on the feeder and I seen him walk by the once. Then he come back. Then he done it all over again. He had his head down, in his jacket, like, but he was looking at your place, alright. I mean, I thought he might be a burglar.'

A slight feeling of unease came over Stella – a once-familiar feeling that she'd almost forgotten.

When she'd been with John, a stranger nosing about the place would have raised alarm bells, red flags and klaxons; all British soldiers were targets, and there were no targets bigger than the SAS.

But with the worst of the Troubles finished, and her second husband being a financial adviser at a bank over in Belfast – a little dull, compared to John, to tell the truth, but far more domesticated – such concerns had long ago melted away.

'Strange,' she said. 'Why would he be interested in our house?'

Thinking, *It's probably nothing. Rose is mad as a box of frogs, after all, and nosey to boot. Too much time on her hands, and...*

And then it occurred to her: George.

Could it be that someone had discovered that her son was in the Parachute Regiment?

Only the SAS themselves were more hated in Republican circles, and Stella was obsessively careful about his persec – to the point where only her own parents, her husband, and Alice knew what George did.

His aunt and uncle, the neighbours, even his school friends… they all thought he'd gone travelling.

But no matter how careful you were, you could never be sure.

She put her hand to her throat, feeling a cold chill come over her.

'Did you get a good look at him, Rose?' she said.

'I didn't recognise him, that's for sure,' said the old lady. 'I'd say he was about your age. Dark hair. Normal size. When he walked past the second time I come out me house and watched him walk down there.' She nodded in to the middle distance. 'He got in a blue car and just drove off.'

'Don't suppose you got the number?' said Stella.

'With my eyes?' said Rose, chuckling.

'Could you say what kind of car it was?'

'Blue, love. That's about it.'

Stella dragged the bin into position and fished out her car keys.

'Well, thanks Rose. If you see him again, try and get the registration number. Or call the police.'

'Aye, I'll do that,' said the old lady. 'Anyway, I thought I'd tell yous. I'm away back in afore I catch me death.'

She turned and shuffled back inside, and Stella walked to her car.

For the first time in years, she had a quick look under it, and then she got in and set off for work.

She thought about the mystery man in the blue car all the way to the Ulster Hospital at Dundonald, where she was a ward sister in the maternity unit, and when she got there she phoned John Carr.

# 46.

AT ALMOST THE moment Stella called her ex-husband, a man drove Dessie Callaghan into the Asda car park in Larne in an old Renault Laguna, switched off the engine and looked at his passenger.

'Good luck,' said the man, putting his hand out.

'Ah, fuck that, Kev,' said Dessie, cheerfully. 'I've got fate and the centuries on my side.' He chuckled. 'Not to mention, they won't see me coming. Beidh ár lá linn!'

'Beidh ár lá linn,' said Kev, quietly. 'You take care of yourself over there.'

'Listen, I know it's an older brother's job to worry,' said Dessie, 'but you don't need to. I won't say it'll be a piece of piss, but I'll be back next week and they'll be pouring drink down my neck in every bar from here to Bantry Bay.'

'Australia?'

'Cork, you dickhead.'

With that, he reached into the inside pocket of his Stone Island parka and took out a tweed cap. He pulled it on and down low over his eyes, picked up the adidas holdall in the footwell, pushed the door open, and sauntered off.

Halfway through the ten-minute walk to the ferry terminal, he put on a pair of shades and a scarf which covered the lower part of his face; it was a cold enough and bright enough morning that no-one would have thought that odd.

At the terminal he bought himself a ticket on that morning's 10.30am sailing – for cash, not the cheapest way of doing it, but it left no electronic trail – and waited for the word to board P&O's *European Highlander.*

A couple of minutes later, that announcement came over the tinny loudspeaker.

He strolled up the gangplank and made his way to the bar, where he bought himself a pint before heading out on deck.

Despite the sunshine, it was empty save for an old Catholic priest who was leaning on the guardrail.

Callaghan stood next to the Father, towering over him, and together they watched the Northern Irish coast slowly give way to the grey sea.

'So what takes you over, son?' said the priest, at length. 'Is it business, is it?'

Dessie shifted on his feet, a little uneasily. He'd left the church behind many years ago, but its hold was hard to shake. He'd never quite rid himself of the feeling that Jesus, Mary and, fuck it, Joseph too were just over his shoulder, watching his every move.

'Something like that, Father,' said Dessie. 'Just a bit of work I have with my cousin in Glasgow. Yourself?'

'Visiting my sister in Edinburgh,' said the priest. 'She has the cancer, poor thing. She's not long.'

'Shit, father,' said Dessie. 'That's a motherfucker.'

'Well, I wouldn't put it quite like that,' said the priest, with an amiable smile, 'but I share your sentiment.' He looked out to sea one final time, and nodded. Then he turned to Dessie. 'Well,' he said, 'I hope your job goes well. Now I must be away inside, it's cold enough out here to freeze the cassocks off me.'

Dessie watched him go, and sipped his pint, and he was still standing there when the ship docked in Scotland.

At Cairnryan he boarded a bus for the ten-minute drive round Loch Ryan, to Stranraer.

187

When he got off the bus he walked on fifty yards to The Arches, a little tea shop where he'd been told to meet his contact.

It was warm in the tea shop, and steamy from the hot water urn, and it smelled of bacon and cakes.

He found an empty table – actually, they were all empty, bar one, at which sat two old ladies, gossiping and cackling – and ordered himself a ham-and-cheese toastie and a glass of Coke.

As he waited for those to arrive, he picked up a dog-eared copy of the local paper and started thumbing through, one eye on the door.

He checked his watch now and then, and when his toastie arrived he ate it with some impatience – he expected to be treated with respect, and that meant punctuality.

By the time the café door opened, with a tinkle, he was not in the best possible mood, but he kept it in check because he knew it was more important than usual not to draw attention to himself.

'Sorry I'm late,' said his contact, a middle-aged Scot in a thick Arran sweater. 'We had a burst pipe at home this morning, of all things. I didn't have a number for you so I couldnae call.'

The apology mollified Callaghan a little, and he held out his hand to indicate that the man should sit down.

The Scotsman made nervous small talk, while Dessie finished his toastie and his Coke, and then the man slid an envelope containing a set of keys across the table. He unfolded a hand-drawn map, and swivelled it to face Dessie.

'Car's what your people asked for,' said the Scot. 'A dark-coloured Mondeo in good nick. Just serviced, 13 plate, forty-odd thousand miles on the clock. Sound as a pound. Won't attract any attention at all.'

Dessie nodded.

The man pointed at the map.

'It's parked up down by the college,' he said, tracing a route with his finger. 'Out of here. First left, few hundred yards down there.'

Dessie nodded. 'Simple enough,' he said. 'How do I get down south?'

'I programmed the satnav to take you as far as Gretna,' said the man, with a sideways look at him. 'Left is north, right is south. I dinnae want to know any more than that.'

Dessie looked at him, contemptuously.

'No offence,' said the Scotsman, hastily. 'There's a full tank, it's registered tae a Roger Milner at an address in Birmingham. That's on a piece of paper in the glovebox. Genuine address, genuine name. He's a salesman for Dulux paint, if you need to tell anyone. Nothing outstanding on the guy or the vehicle. Both clean as a whistle.'

'How long will it take me to reach Gretna?' said Callaghan.

'Och, a couple of hours. It's a hundred miles, near as damnit.'

Callaghan said nothing, just stared at the man, enjoying his growing discomfort.

Eventually, the Scot said, 'I'll be seeing you, then. Good luck.'

And with that, he stood up, picked up the hand-drawn map from the table, and left.

Callaghan waited for five minutes, and then did likewise.

Outside, he followed the Scotsman's directions and soon found himself in Academy Street, where the Mondeo was parked up a stone's throw from Dumfries and Galloway College. He leered at a passing trio of female students, and then opened the Ford's back door, threw his bag onto the seat, and climbed into the front.

He arranged the seat and mirrors to his liking, and then turned the ignition key, started the engine, and the satnav, and set off.

He drove carefully, at two or three miles an hour either side of the speed limit, using his mirrors and indicators a lot and observing lane discipline – he didn't want to get pulled over for anything.

As he drove east down the A75, he admired the countryside and hummed a repetitive bar from *Flower of Scotland*, his mind getting into gear for the challenge ahead.

# 47.

CARR WASN'T TROUBLED by the call from Stella – his ex-wife had always been a worrier, and he took half of what she said with a pinch of salt and discarded the rest – but it didn't hurt to take sensible precautions.

So he'd emailed George to give him a heads-up, just in case he was over in Bangor any time soon.

Unusually, George had come back almost immediately: he wasn't in Northern Ireland for the foreseeable future, because he was off to the States on a freefall parachute course and adventure training, and then off to Kenya for a couple of months with 3 Para on exercise, and then…

Then he was thinking about Selection.

Carr was just writing out a long and detailed explanation of why he should wait another year – a message he knew his stubborn, hard-headed son would ignore – when the door buzzer sounded.

He got up and looked at the video screen.

*Oleg Kovalev.*

He buzzed the Russian in, and he appeared at the internal door a moment or two later. He was limping slightly, and he grimaced as he shook Carr's hand.

'Thank God for Kevlar, eh, Johnny?' he said. 'Four, five days, but still, it hurts. Like being punched in kidneys by very big man, many times.'

'Tell me about it,' said Carr, with a wry chuckle. He could still remember the shock and temporary sense of bewilderment from where a sniper's Dragunov round had hit him in the chest plate and put him on his arse in Baghdad one night in 2008. 'Just thank your lucky stars it wasn't three inches lower.'

The Russian nodded in agreement.

'We have a drink?' he said.

Carr raised his eyebrows. 'Bit early, isn't it?'

'Never too early.'

'If you say so,' said Carr. 'What d'you fancy?'

The Russian nodded. 'A scotch, if you have one?' he said.

'If I *have one*?' said Carr, grinning. 'I'll give you something that'll knock your Russki socks off, pal.'

He padded into his kitchen, reached into a cupboard, and took down a bottle. He poured two generous measures and added a little mineral water.

'Try that,' he said. 'Chivas Regal Royal Salute. Thirty year old.'

Oleg took a sip and nodded in appreciation. 'It's good,' he said. 'I mean, is not vodka, but I can drink it.'

Carr laughed. 'You any further on with the shooter?' he said, walking through into the living room and sitting on one of the two sofas.

Kovalev sat down opposite him. 'A little,' he said. 'I made some calls. Name is Sasha Yurchenko. Is thirty-three years old, married man, no kids, originally from Merefa, which is thirty kays from Kharkiv. Kharkiv is east Ukraine, right on border. So maybe you right about Ukrainians. He was corporal in 3rd Guards Spetsnaz Brigade, based at Tolyatti. Was involved in second Chechnya war, which was some very heavy shit. *Very* heavy. Left Spetznaz two years ago, went into private security. Like you.'

The Russian sipped his whisky.

'Why did he leave the Army?' said Carr.

'Time was up,' said Oleg. 'Could have signed on for another

five years, but Russian Army is not like British Army. Shit money, shit equipment, nobody cares about you.'

'Sounds *exactly* like the British Army,' said Carr.

Oleg grinned. 'Maybe,' he said. 'Anyway, he can make more money outside, have better life.'

'Who was he working for?'

'Officially, day job was working for Russian bank in London. Unofficially, this is big question. Sixty-four dollars.'

'Sixty-four *thousand* dollars,' said Carr. 'Anything from his phone?'

'Not yet. I hope soon, but is hard to crack.'

'Have the police spoken to Sasha yet?'

'No. He was in…' He clicked his fingers. 'What is word? Yes, *induced*. Was in induced coma for three days for brain swelling. Is awake now but eating through tube. Doctors wait for his swelling to go down. Police will talk to him tomorrow. You did proper job on him, John.'

'We aim to please,' said Carr. 'I wonder what they'll get out of him.'

'Nothing,' said the Russian, dismissively. 'Back home, he will be singing like canary in one half-hour. Here, no.' Oleg put on a weak, pleading voice. 'Police will just ask him, *"Please can you tell us who you are working for?"'* He says nothing, goes to prison, does his time.'

'He'll get thirty years,' said Carr. 'Will he do that long?'

'Of course. He is Spetznaz. His wife will be paid, his mother will be paid, one day he will go home.'

'How about the motorcyclist?'

'If they know about him, so far British police don't find him.'

'So what do you think?'

Oleg knocked back the last of the whisky, and pulled a face. 'Well,' he said. 'I…'

And then his mobile rang.

He picked it up and spoke in Russian.

His face gradually broke into a smile, and eventually he was chuckling.

He ended the call and looked at Carr.

'My friend,' he said, 'has opened Sasha's phone.'

# 48.

THE WINTRY SUN had long set over Coventry by the time Dessie Callaghan pulled into a grubby street lined with terraces of run-down houses.

He trawled slowly down the road until he found the correct house, which was signified by the number '46' daubed on the low front wall in thick white paint.

There was a space a few yards further down, so he parked up, retrieved his bag from the back, and walked to the front door.

His knock was answered by a bleached-blonde in her thirties.

'Yes?' she said, in a voice that was half-way between the industrial English midlands and somewhere in eastern Europe. 'Can I help you?'

'I'm here to see Walter,' said Callaghan, using the phrase he had memorised. 'He said he might have a dog he wanted to sell.'

The woman looked up and down the street, and then opened the door. 'You come in, please,' she said.

She showed Callaghan to a tatty sofa in the cramped front room, and disappeared upstairs.

He sat and waited, literally twiddling his thumbs, and looking around the room. He was just wondering what kind of people would put a brown sofa and brown cushions in a room with brown wallpaper and a brown carpet, when the living room door opened and a solid, mean-looking fucker in a purple tracksuit, with pitted olive skin and a suedehead, walked in.

Dessie stood up, and they shook hands.

*Christ, he had some grip.*

'Peter?' said the man, in the same accent as that of the woman.

'That's right,' said Callaghan.

'My name is Walter,' said the man, whose name was actually Gjergj Leka.

He looked jovial enough, but he also looked like he'd cut your throat for a pastime.

That made two of them, thought Dessie.

'Is that so?' he said. 'You have something for me?'

'Yes. I was expecting you. Follow me, please.'

They walked up the stairs, and Gjergj led him into the back bedroom.

On the bed was a Co-Op carrier bag.

Gjergj picked it up, reached in and handed over a small leather sheath with a black handle protruding from one end.

Dessie took it and withdrew the knife.

To his surprise, the blade was not shiny and silver, but matt black.

'Kizlyar Korshun,' said Gjergj, proudly. 'Very strong. Used by FSB.'

Dessie nodded, never having heard of the Russian internal security service before.

He hefted it in his hand: it had a nice weight, and the double-edged blade was extremely sharp.

'Feels good,' he said.

Gjergj handed over a small box.

'Glock 17,' he said. 'Brand new, was never fired before. Totally clean. Two magazines, seventeen bullets each. One box fifty bullets.'

'May I?' said Callaghan.

'Of course.'

He took the pistol out of the box. It was cold, and solid.

'A beautiful thing, Peter,' said Gjergj, like he'd designed and built the fucker himself. 'Is accurate to fifty metres.'

'I'll be a lot closer than that if it comes to it,' said Callaghan, with a wolfish grin.

An hour after he had arrived in Coventry, he was on his way again, picking his way back north to the M6 through the late evening traffic.

This time he was singing to himself, and tapping out a ska beat on the wheel with his thumbs.

'This town,' he kept intoning, in a cod Jamaican accent, 'aaahh–aaahh, is comin' like a ghost town.'

# 49.

OLEG KOVALEV WAS back at Carr's flat very early the following morning, his face alive with glee.

'Come with me, Johnny,' he said, rubbing his hands together. 'I have something to show you.'

Outside, it was another beautiful winter's day, crisp and clear, and the Russian's breath trailed behind him in the still air as Carr followed him to his pearlescent white Range Rover – a five-litre V8 monster, with Overfinch carbon-fibre body-styling, calfskin leather seats, and more wood than you'd find in a small forest.

Nothing if not big-time, Oleg.

'Where we off?' said Carr, as he slid into the passenger seat.

'Boss's place in countryside,' said the Russian, with a sideways look.

Avilov's private estate near Petworth in Sussex – a huge Georgian mansion with fifty-odd rooms full of gold leaf, electronics and bling, set in 150 acres of parkland.

'What for?' said Carr.

'Some people the boss wants you to meet.'

'Who?'

'One of them is Mr Dima Goncharenko, owner of Konstantin's favourite Mayfair restaurant,' said Kovalev. 'Other is a friend of Dima, name is Andriy Dzyuba.'

'Why?'

'You know why, John.'

'Stop the car,' said Carr. 'I don't know what the fuck you've got planned, you crazy Russian bastard, but I've got an idea.'

'Please,' said Oleg. 'Come with me. When we get there, you talk to Konstantin. After that, you leave. Not a problem for you, I promise.'

Carr looked at him, weighing the decision.

In the end, he decided to go with it, for now.

'You'd better not be fucking with me,' he said.

Oleg shook his head.

He was silent for a few moments, and then he said, 'Glovebox. Confidential files from Metropolitan Police and Sluzhba Bezpeky Ukrayiny. You know? Ukrainian internal security service?'

Carr nodded. He considered asking Oleg how he'd managed to get hold of Met and SBU intelligence, but he wouldn't get an answer, so why bother? He was an old KGB/FIS hand: the Russian spooks had their ways, and that was that.

He reached into the glovebox and took out a thin manila folder.

Started reading.

It showed that the two men concerned were both thoroughbred vermin.

They had come to Britain as part of the Ukrainian diaspora, and – on the surface – were legitimate businessmen. Dima Goncharenko – the older of the two – owned the restaurant in which they had eaten the other night, along with a portfolio of flats and houses in north and west London. Andriy Dzyuba, his right-hand man, ran a large door security firm in the city.

But behind the scenes, Goncharenko was a rapist and racketeer who had trafficked women, arms and drugs across Europe. Dzyuba handled their heroin operation. He'd taken on and defeated various groups of Turks, Kurds and Snakehead Chinese in setting it up, which told you something. He had also served four years in a

British jail for beating a high class prostitute so badly that she had lost an eye. The girl had later committed suicide after being told that she would be further disfigured with acid for giving evidence against him. She'd been from Edinburgh, as it happened, which endeared Andriy Dzyuba even less to Carr.

'You know this Goncharenko,' said Oleg, when Carr had finished reading. 'He is the employer of Sasha the gunman. We know this.'

'How?' said Carr.

'Sasha's phone,' said Oleg. 'You know my friend cracked it? Sasha was in touch with Goncharenko few times.'

'That's careless.'

'Is *very* careless. Maybe Sasha thought he would kill us all and walk away, no problems. If you didn't save us, maybe he is right.'

'Why would Goncharenko want to kill Konstantin?'

'For money,' said Oleg. 'Look, he is gangster, yes? First in Ukraine, now London. Trust me, John, he has killed many people. To have Konstantin Avilov killed is not problem for him. Just another body. Plus also, you and me, he doesn't want witnesses. No way he would let us live if he can kill us. '

Carr thought about that for a moment: he decided that Kovalev was probably right.

'So who paid him?' he said, eventually.

'That's what we find out.'

# 50.

MICK PARRY'S PARCELFORCE van left the Huyton depot at just after 7.30am, and headed north on the A58 to Ashton-in-Makerfield, to make the first of its drops for the day.

Parry had a stonking headache – he'd been out for a few beers with an old Army mate the night before, and 'a few' had turned into 'a lot'.

It had led to a major bollocking from his wife: he hadn't got home until gone midnight, with Stevie in tow, and they'd both been completely banjaxed.

So he drove cautiously; he strongly suspected that he was still over the limit, and he didn't want to attract any police attention.

He'd never been trained in counter-surveillance, and he had no reason to be concerned that anyone might be following him, and in any event his van didn't have a rear view mirror, so he didn't notice the black Ford Mondeo which had been parked down the road from the depot, and was following him now, three or four cars back.

Dessie had carried out a recce of Parry's home the previous evening, and had nearly taken him out as he staggered home from the pub, but he'd had another guy with him – a big fella, looked handy – and they'd disappeared inside while a taxi was called to take the mate home.

A proficient burglar, Callaghan had briefly considered a change of plans, and breaking in, once Parry and his missus were alone. It appealed to his sense of the dramatic, but he'd decided against, not because he didn't want to kill the woman – he was perfectly happy to kill her, too – but because two people murdered in their beds was a much bigger story than a robbery gone wrong, and he didn't want the heat that those headlines would bring.

No: Robbery gone wrong. That was still the way to play it.

The hardest thing had been establishing which of the many vans leaving the depot was being driven by Parry, and even on a busy industrial estate he couldn't spend too many mornings just plotted up, waiting, without people starting to notice him.

That meant he was doing it today, as soon as the moment was right.

For now, he bided his time, tucked in well out of sight in a line of morning traffic.

# 51.

IT WAS COLD and damp – when was it not cold and damp in Belfast? – and the sun was barely visible through the grey morning clouds.

The old man was an early riser, a legacy of forty years carrying hods and mixing muck on building sites, and the streets outside were empty and quiet.

He opened his door to let the dog out into the front garden.

In the near distance, the Black Mountain loomed over the streets of the Turf Lodge.

The dog had done its business, and he was about to walk back into the house when he noticed something lying on the small square of grass in the centre of the cul-de-sac.

Something pale and long which he couldn't make out.

'What's that there?' he said to himself, and went back inside to fetch his glasses.

He found them by the toaster, slipped on his wife's pink house-coat and a pair of slippers, and walked back out and along the garden path to the gate, and started across the road.

The little dog ran ahead of him, but it stopped a few feet from the object and started to bark.

And it was at that moment that the old man started to feel sick.

Because now he could make out what it was that was lying on the grass.

It was the semi-naked body of a woman.

It was not the first body he had seen, but it was a while since the bad old days.

'Jesus,' he whispered, crossed himself reflexively. 'Jesus, Mary and Joseph.'

He walked a step or two nearer.

She was lying face down in the dew, in a crucifix position, beaten black and blue and then shot in each ankle, each knee and each elbow.

Only then had she been released from pain by the coup de grâce – a bullet to the back of the head.

Whoever had done it – and the old man had lived long enough to know that it had been an IRA punishment squad – had clearly been sending a message: *We're still here, and you don't want to fuck with us.*

They'd afforded her the small dignity of allowing her to keep her underwear on.

The old man hesitated.

The last thing he wanted to do – the *very* last thing – was to get involved, but the local kiddies would be walking past on their way to school in the next half-hour or so, and he couldn't let them see this.

He took off the housecoat, laid it over the body and, head down, hurried back inside to call the confidential hotline.

At about the same moment, on a patch of waste ground in Andersonstown, a guy in his late teens – name of Tomas Kelly – was stepping from the white van which had been stolen the day before and used by the interrogation team.

He had done as instructed and kicked the body out in the Turf well before dawn, but it had not sat well with him. In fact, he felt sick to his stomach: the woman had been not far shy of his grandmother's age, and the sound of her screams, mixed with her begging and protestations of innocence, and the laughter of the two men who had tortured her... He knew that it would haunt him.

Still, he shouldn't have joined if he couldn't deal with this kind of shit: she was a tout, they'd said, and that was how you dealt with touts.

He opened the back of the van and looked at the bloodstained interior. On the floor were two fuel cans. He unscrewed the lids of each and liberally splashed petrol over the inside of the vehicle. Then he picked up a milk bottle with a petrol-soaked rag sticking out of the top.

He retreated twenty feet, lit the rag and threw it at the van.

The whole thing went up with a *whoof* and then quickly settled back down to a steady blaze.

He felt the heat, and watched the flames for a few seconds, and then he turned on his heel and walked away.

# 52.

IT TOOK ALMOST two hours, but eventually Oleg Kovalev turned into the driveway of Konstantin Avilov's place in Petworth.

The security team at the gate verified them and opened the gates, and Oleg crunched on down the half-mile driveway to the main house.

He drove round the house and parked up at the large row of garages which housed Avilov's collection of classic cars.

A couple of Russian security guys were standing outside the garage at the extreme left, and now one of them disappeared inside.

A moment later, he returned with Konstantin Avilov himself.

'John,' he said, holding out a hand and smiling fondly. 'Good to see you. I want to show you something.'

Carr and Oleg followed Avilov back inside the garage.

Several more of his Russian security detail were standing around, sleeves rolled up. One or two were breathing hard, as though they'd just been working out.

Two men were suspended by their wrists from the ceiling in the centre of the garage, their bare feet a few inches above the floor.

Which was spattered with blood and vomit.

One of the men was either unconscious or dead.

The other Carr recognised – which wasn't easy, given that his face was a puffy mass of cuts and welts and bruises.

A pink snot bubble popped.

He was still in the land of the living.

'You remember this guy?' said Avilov. 'Runs the restaurant in Mayfair.'

He walked up to the man, who flinched.

'Dima, I want you to tell my friend John what you just told me,' he said.

Dima Goncharenko looked at Carr through one swollen eye – the other was shut – and whispered something.

'I cannae hear you, pal,' said Carr.

With a supreme effort, the Ukrainian raised his voice.

'We arranged the hit on Mr Avilov,' he said. 'On behalf of a man in Russia called Vitaly Vasiliev. He paid us thirty thousand pounds. We agreed five thousand with Sasha.'

'You see, John,' said Avilov. 'Not even a proper price for me. Very insulting. What else?'

'Vitaly was very angry that the hit failed. I was supposed to find another man to kill Konstantin, also Oleg, also you.'

Carr looked at him. 'That's just fucking bad manners,' he said. 'Mind, you wouldn't be the first to try.'

'Sorry,' said Dima. 'I promise… We will go to Russia and kill Vitaly instead.'

Avilov chuckled. 'I trust you, of course,' he said.

Carr hardly heard them. He was too busy computing what level of shit they were all now in, and how best to get out of it.

The Russians were being unbelievably casual about all of this: it could only be that they'd grown used to getting their own way in Moscow.

Over there, rich men could put a stop to police investigations with a simple phone call – and that was the sort of luxury that could make the best of guys sloppy.

Whereas, over here…

He turned to Avilov. 'Listen, boss,' he said. 'And listen well, yes? I'm not squeamish, and I havenae any moral problem with fucking people up, as long as they deserve it. And this pair truly deserve it. But this is fucking amateur hour. You're playing with fire, here, and you're in danger of getting very badly burned. I don't know what you're planning to do with these cunts – and I do not want you to fucking tell me, ever – but look at the floor. Have you never heard of polythene sheeting? I know you don't rate our police very highly, but they're shit hot on forensics. All that blood...' He paused, and shook his head in disbelief. 'Jesus. If you have what you need then, whatever you're going to do, do it quickly. Then this place needs bleaching and steam-cleaning.'

'Please,' said Dima Goncharenko, his eyes widening. 'No...'

Avilov looked at Carr, slightly taken aback, his brow darkening.

'Let's talk outside, John,' he said.

They walked out of the garage, the Ukrainian shouting hoarsely behind them, and shut the door.

'And the bleach and steam-cleaning is just a quick fix,' said Carr. 'You need to have this floor taken up and relaid as soon as you can get a contractor in. Like, tomorrow. Pour a couple of litres of oil on the floor and have the guys smack it about with hammers so that it *looks* like it needs replacing, too. The builders probably won't get nosey, but you never know.'

He looked at the two Russians, and sighed.

'I'm going to speak frankly, Konstantin,' he said. 'If you don't like it, fire me now. But please listen. You're in the shit here, even if you can't see it, and the reason you're in the shit is because you didn't take my advice in the first place. I told you to take your security seriously, and you didn't. Remember?'

The Russian nodded.

'This isn't Russia, boss,' said Carr. 'I know guys like you can do whatever the fuck you like over there, within reason, but this is England. You havenae got the British government onside, and you cannae pay the Met police off. If they're onto you, you won't be able to bribe your way out of it, not with a million pounds. Not with a billion.'

'*If*, Johnny,' said Oleg. 'How they get onto us?'

Carr nodded towards the garage. 'How did you get hold of them?' he said.

'Two of my guys picked them up last night. Dima outside his restaurant. The other at his flat.'

'How do you know they weren't seen? What about CCTV?'

'They're professionals,' said Oleg.

'I'm sure they are,' said Carr. 'But the best people make mistakes, get caught out.' He paused. 'How did they get them here?'

'Transit van,' said Oleg.

'So let me paint a picture for you,' said Carr. 'Tonight your man there is not going to turn up at the restaurant. Okay, maybe he misses the odd night. But two nights? With no phone call? Sooner or later, someone's going to wonder where he is. It's going to get out. Maybe via the rumour mill. Maybe someone just calls the police – one of the legit employees at the restaurant, say. Either way, it will get to them, and the police will be very interested. Don't forget, they know *exactly* who and what this Dima guy really is. So they'll do the cameras, and they're going to see two men carrying something into a Transit van somewhere in Mayfair.'

He looked at them.

Both had their eyes fixed on him.

He had their full attention now, that was for sure.

'Have you heard of ANPR?'

Oleg nodded, and then looked away, embarrassed at his own carelessness.

Avilov shook his head.

'All the major roads in the UK are covered by cameras that record the traffic. Chances are they'll follow that van all the way out to somewhere near here. And then they're going to start wondering who has property out this way, and they'll be especially interested in talking to anyone with a name that ends in *ov* or *ski*.'

'So what you suggesting?' said Avilov.

'Where are the two guys who brought them here?'

Oleg nodded at the men standing outside the garage.

'Okay. These guys need to take their phones a long way away and destroy them. The SIMs, too. Cell site analysis will show them there and here. That's some bad juju, Oleg, you know that.'

Oleg Kovalev nodded. 'Yeah,' he said. 'You're right, Johnny. *Fuck*.'

'Then get them on the next flight out of here to Moscow. Like, this afternoon. Tonight at the latest. We have to work on the basis that the police may be looking for them right now. Unlikely, sure, but do you want to risk the rest of your life in prison on that chance? Once they're in Moscow, they're gone and they won't be coming back to give evidence against you, me or anyone else. If the Met try to extradite them, you can have a word with Mr Putin, right?'

Konstantin nodded.

Turned to the two men, and barked something in Russian.

They looked startled.

One shouted a question back, and got a mouthful from Oleg.

They hurried off to a Volvo which was parked near the main house, got in and drove away.

'Where's the van?'

'Behind the garages,' said Oleg.

'Show me,' said Carr.

They walked around the building.

'Right,' said Carr, looking at the blue Transit. 'This needs to be burned, then crushed. You must know someone in scrap metal? Someone discreet?'

Oleg nodded.

'Get it done today,' said Carr. 'Get someone reliable and loyal to drive it there and oversee the whole thing.'

Covering his hand with his sleeve, he opened the vehicle's passenger door.

'See that?' he said, pointing to the inside of the frame. 'That's the VIN plate. Unique to the vehicle. It needs to come off and disappear before it gets crushed.'

'Okay,' said Oleg.

Carr popped the bonnet.

Pointed to the offside wheel arch. 'It's there, too,' he said. 'Make sure that gets removed with an angle grinder.'

'Okay.'

'I'm serious.'

'I know. I will make sure they remove it.'

'The engine number is here.' Carr pointed to the centre of the engine block. 'Same with that.'

'Okay,' said Oleg.

'Before it leaves here, do a thorough decontamination – nothing in the glove box, no papers, no receipts lying around. Give the obvious surfaces a wipe down, too.'

'Of course.'

'One last thing. Tell your guy to remove the licence plates once he gets to the yard. And he brings them back here, and he hands them to you in person.'

'I will tell him.'

'Then you burn those plates.'

'Okay.'

'Then he fucks off to Russia as well.'

'Okay.'

'Make sure he does all this. Don't let him get lazy.'

'I swear, Johnny.'

There was an uncomfortable silence for a moment or two.

Carr broke it by saying, 'So, am I fired or what?'

Konstantin Avilov patted him on the arm.

'Never, John. I told you before, you saved my life. Me and Oleg, we are your brothers.'

He fished in his pocket.

Pulled out a set of car keys.

'I ask Oleg to bring you here today for two reasons,' he said. 'First, I wanted you to hear what Dima had to say. That is over. We never speak of those two *mertvets* again, and we will never hear from them again, either. In future, I take your advice much more seriously.'

He handed over the keys. 'Second reason, I bought you a new toy,' he said.

Carr took the keys and pressed the fob.

The door to a garage three or four down opened noiselessly.

Inside was a black Porsche Cayenne Turbo S.

'Paperwork inside, John,' said Avilov. 'Also another little gift.'

'Cheque for fifty grand, Johnny,' said Oleg, out of the corner of his mouth.

Avilov said something to him in Russian, mock-angry.

Oleg chuckled. 'Boss is cross with me – wanted it to be surprise,' he said, with a smile.

'Just a bonus, John,' said Avilov. 'Also, twenty per cent pay rise from now.'

Carr looked at the Porsche, and then back at the Russians. 'I would say no need, boss,' he said, with a grin. 'But I'm Scottish, so cheers.'

'Now go, Johnny,' said Oleg. 'Before you see something you don't want to see.'

# 53.

AT SOME POINT during the day, Dessie Callaghan had realised that his plan to kill Mick Parry and make it look like a robbery wasn't going to work.

The bastard never left the vehicle except to deliver parcels to homes or businesses, and there were always people around.

So at about 3pm Dessie jacked it in and drove over to St Helens, where he plotted up in a café on the other side of town from Parry's house, for a bite to eat and to think about a new strategy.

Eventually, and reluctantly, he came to the conclusion that the only option he had was to park near the house and hope to follow him if he went out. He didn't like it, at all, but at least it was the middle of February, so it would be dark; as long as he sat out of any street lights, chances were he could go unnoticed.

And indeed he did, which is how – to Dessie's delight – he found himself watching Mick Parry leave home at 9pm that evening, heading off for a quick jar at his local.

Sending up a quick prayer of thanks for British squaddies and their never-ending thirst for alcohol, Callaghan pulled his tweed cap down tight on his head, ran the scarf around his face, and let himself out of the Mondeo.

He gave Parry a good twenty yards, and kept light on his feet as he tailed him ten minutes up the road to a boozer in Mill Lane called The Wheatsheaf.

He debated following the ex-Para bastard inside, just for shits and giggles, but decided against – the place was bound to have CCTV, and while the scarf held up in the cold night air he would have to remove it inside.

Instead, he doubled back and moved his car into Gerards Lane, a long, straightish road – just a cut-through, no housing, he was happy to see – down which Parry would surely walk home.

Driving as slowly as he could without drawing attention to himself, he checked carefully for any cameras.

There were none, that he could see, so he did a three-pointer and parked up beneath a long line of trees, next to a low stone wall.

Perfect: he was in near pitch-black, but his quarry would be illuminated by a streetlight further up, near a railway bridge.

He turned off the motor and his lights, and listened to the engine tick its heat away in the silence.

He opened the glove box and took out a pair of soft leather gloves.

Put them on, reached under the seat for the matt black knife, and placed it on the passenger seat.

It was only then that he realised the strange synchronicity: he was here in Gerards Lane to avenge the death, among others, of a lad called Gerard.

Had to mean someone up there was watching out for him, right?

He smiled at that, and began drumming lightly on the steering wheel.

*In, out and away.*

This bastard would never know what had hit him.

So Dessie spent the next hour and a half huddled low in his seat, daydreaming, watching the odd car drive by, and humming to himself, alternating between rebel songs and old SLF and Undertones tunes from his early teens.

Then, at a quarter to eleven, his man came round the corner into the otherwise deserted street.

Parry had been under strict instructions from his wife not to turn up in the same state as he had the previous night, and she had meant it; ex-Para or no, he was not going to argue the toss.

She'd only allowed him to go out because it was darts night, so he'd slowly nursed a mere three pints and had left the pub not long after the match was over.

That meant that he was pretty much sober, and that his adrenalin levels were already slightly raised.

His route took him straight past the Mondeo, but he didn't notice it until he was nearly upon it.

He saw the driver's door open, and a man step out, but he didn't pay much attention to the guy until he got right up close and realised that the bloke was looking straight at him.

Then he paid attention.

Mondeo Man was about his height, and stocky, and a good bit younger, and he looked handy, under the coat and the scarf: the street was lonely, and dark, and, instinctively, Parry balled his fists inside his jacket pockets.

As he drew close, to Mick Parry's surprise, the man spoke to him.

'Evening, Mick,' he said.

*What's that accent?* thought Parry. *Sounds familiar.*

'Alright, mate,' he said. 'How's it goin'?'

Still thinking, *Do I know you? The voice... I know the voice.*

'Sure, it's going grand, big man,' said Mondeo Man, now standing directly in front of Parry, blocking his way.

Parry thinking, *This is a bit weird. I must know the bloke but...*

And then the man pulled his hand out of his pocket and punched Mick Parry in the chest.

At least, Parry thought it was a punch.

'That's for Ciaran O'Brien and the Casey brothers,' said the man, though Parry never heard it – or, if he did, it didn't register.

'What the fuck...?' he started to say, but then the man punched him again, this time in the neck, and Parry felt the strength ebb from his legs.

He stumbled forward, and as he did so he swung a haymaker right.

In his youth, Parry had been the 3 Para light-heavyweight champion, and had boxed for the Army. Some had suggested, quietly, that he ought to leave the forces and have a crack at the pro game, but he loved soldiering and beer too much for that. He'd had a decent chin and a reasonable defence, but his method had been based squarely on attack, and on the dynamite bombs he'd thrown to blast his opponents out of the ring.

Even in his dying moments, fat and unfit, he still packed a hell of a punch.

His fist smashed Dessie Callaghan flush in the face, re-breaking his broken nose, loosening two front teeth, and knocking him spark out.

The momentum of throwing and receiving the punch sent both men sprawling over the low stone wall and into the thick of the undergrowth on the other side.

A few moments later, Callaghan sat up, covered in dirt and twigs, cursing.

He was slightly befuddled at first, but his head quickly cleared.

He fumbled for his phone and turned on its torch.

Next to him, a scarlet bloodstain seeping across his chest, was Mick Parry.

His eyes were open.

He looked surprised.

He looked *dead*, is what he looked.

Callaghan tried to get up and promptly fell down again, like a baby giraffe in an ice rink.

He tried again, and this time he made it to an upright position.

He put his hand up to his nose and winced.

'Ouch, ye *fucker*,' he said to himself.

He found the knife and slotted it into its sheath. Then, blinking and pulling on the low branches, he hauled himself out of the trees and over the wall, and stumbled the few yards to his car.

He scrabbled with the door and collapsed inside, and somehow he managed to start the engine and drive away.

Any watching police officer would have pulled him over immediately as drunk, but there were no cops about.

So, cursing at the stabbing, electric-shock sensation in his head, Dessie Callaghan got the hell out of St Helens.

# 54.

MICK PARRY'S WIFE finally gave up and went to bed at midnight.

To say she was not best pleased was an understatement.

To say she was not entirely surprised, ditto.

Sharon Parry had been married to Mick since just after he'd passed P Company, so she was more than used to him promising to be home on time and then coming in late, three sheets to the wind.

Four or five sheets, sometimes.

Then he'd spend the next hour or so either hunting for food and eating it in front of bad telly, with the volume near maximum, or lying next to her in bed, telling her how much he loved her, and giving her great, big, slobbery kisses.

Before falling asleep draped across her like a dead weight.

Snoring like a warthog.

She wouldn't change much about the big, daft, old bastard, but this...

She sighed. However you cut it, it spelled a bad night's sleep, and she had a particularly big day ahead of her tomorrow.

Lots going on at work, and then a trip to the wedding dress shop for a fitting with Michaela, their youngest.

Only a couple of months until the wedding, and then she and Mick would be on their own.

Free, at last! They'd been saving for a holiday to Florida, and she literally could not wait.

She smiled, and then she frowned again.

Love him though she did, he was late, and she'd warned him not to be, and she had explained why not.

She wrote a note, in capital letters, and left it on the stairs: 'YOU CAN SLEEP ON THE SETTEE TONIGHT MICHAEL PARRY x'

Then she turned in.

In the morning, she came downstairs and found the note where she'd left it.

The sofa was undisturbed, and there was no sign of her bear-like husband, groaning, over a cup of tea.

'Have you seen your dad?' she said to Michaela, who was eating cornflakes in front of the TV.

'No, why?'

'No reason. He must have stayed round at Dave's. Probably couldn't face me. I told him not to be late.'

'Oh, aye, I saw the note,' said Michaela, with a chuckle. 'I feel sorry for Dave's wife.'

Sharon looked out of the window, fighting an uneasy feeling.

But then Mick was Mick.

More than once in their married life he'd not come back from a night out, calling her apologetically from some mate's house in some town miles away with no idea how he'd got there.

He'd slowed down a lot these days, but anything was still possible.

Then again...

'I bet he's got a lift,' she said.

He sometimes cadged a lift into work with one of the other lads – especially if he'd had a skinful.

*What with the drink-drive laws, and that.*

She called his mobile, but it was switched off.

She called his mate Dave, got no answer, and left a message.

Then she tried to put the nagging worry out of her mind and get ready for work.

# 55.

AT FOUR O'CLOCK that afternoon, a five-year-old boy walked slowly and carefully along the stone wall in Gerards Lane in St Helens, holding his mum's hand to stop himself falling over into the undergrowth on the other side.

The boy's mum was pushing a buggy carrying his little sister with her free hand. She was tired of dawdling, and she was just about to get the boy down from the wall so that they could speed up, when he suddenly stopped.

She turned to look at him.

'Come on, Ahmed,' she said, with a snap that she instantly regretted. 'Your dad'll be home for his tea in a bit.'

But he didn't move. He just pointed into the bushes below, and said, 'There's a man.'

'You what?'

'There's a man,' he said, pointing. 'In there.'

'What do you mean?' said his mum, turning the buggy and walking back to him. 'There's no man in there.'

Then she looked over the low wall, and had to put her hand over her mouth to stop herself screaming.

Within five minutes the police were there; within a further fifteen minutes, a doctor had been called to certify death, the road closed, the scene cordoned off, and officers were being drafted in from all over the force area to start house-to-house enquiries.

The body was identified as that of a local man called Michael Parry shortly before six o'clock – at about the same time as blood samples recovered from Parry's right fist had arrived in a lab for analysis.

By 8pm, the blood had been confirmed as belonging to one Desmond Michael Callaghan.

Forty-four years of age, said the Police National Computer.

Last entered address – Mica Drive, Belfast.

Juvenile convictions for shoplifting, assault, resisting arrest.

Adult convictions for grievous bodily harm and the manslaughter of an RUC constable.

*Suspected member of the PIRA's Belfast Brigade.*

The officer reading the information stopped at that and read it again.

Then he picked up a phone.

# 56.

BY THE TIME his name popped up, Dessie Callaghan was a couple of hundred miles away on the Essex–Hertfordshire border – lost, hungry, tired, and pissed off at the incessant throbbing in the front of his face.

At least he knew the Mondeo was safe.

Sure, a national alert would have been put out if they'd had the make or the plate, and he'd passed several cop cars *en route* without any of them turning a hair.

Even so, he'd cut across country to get south, keeping off the motorways and A roads to avoid the ANPR system, and driving slow to avoid triggering any speed cameras. He wanted to make it as hard as possible for anyone to pick a pattern, even if it meant a journey of three or four hours had taken twice that.

He'd also taken the SIM card and battery out of his mobile, though he was itching to stick them back in and call the fat four-eyed bastard back home who'd got him into all this trouble. When he got back – *if* he got back, he didn't like to tempt fate – that cocky wee bastard was going to meet up with Dessie and his baseball bat, and it wasn't going to be pleasant.

Well, not for the fat four-eyed bastard, anyway.

Currently, it was dark, and drizzling, and he was heading along an overgrown lane in the arse end of Hertfordshire somewhere near Bishop's Stortford.

Thanks to that bastard Parry and that lucky punch, he'd had no sort of sleep the previous night – he'd pulled over in a layby and maybe got half an hour, split into ten minute bursts – and he was gagging for a bed.

Then a sign: 'Stansted 1', and a little aeroplane motif.

Stansted Airport.

Airports had hotels.

And airport hotels had a lot of transient trade.

Transient trade meant anonymity.

He turned right, and a few minutes later he was driving into the terminal area.

But as he did so, it occurred to him that airports were also crawling with peelers.

Unsure of his next move, he drove around a roundabout three times and then headed back out, following signs to the A120.

Maybe he'd be better off in a little B&B somewhere in the sticks?

Another roundabout, a left and then a right, and he found himself travelling along another country lane, towards a village called Hatfield Broad Oak.

On the left as he drove in was a farmhouse with a small sign which said 'Bed and Breakfast'.

He slowed down and stopped, considering the pros and cons.

On the down side, the people who ran the place were more likely to remember him than the staff of an airport hotel with three hundred rooms.

On the up side, they were more likely to take cash, and he didn't want to leave any sort of trail.

He started the engine back up and turned into the driveway.

# 57.

DETECTIVE SUPERINTENDENT KEVIN Murphy was in his office the following morning, just signing off the latest inputs to the file on another old IRA murder, and thinking about organising a cab to the airport – he and Nigel Johnson were flying to London that afternoon, for their meeting with MI5 the following day – when there was a knock on his door, and a face appeared.

'Ah,' said Murphy. 'The man himself.'

'Can I have a word, boss?' said Johnson.

'Sure,' said Murphy, shaking his head sadly. 'I was just looking at this O'Hara nonsense. Fancy stoving in your own brother-in-law's head with a lump of concrete over a minor slight on a night out. These meatheads.'

'Aye,' said Johnson. 'Nutters, the lot of them. Anyway, listen. There's been a bit of a development in the Gerard Casey thing.'

Murphy raised his eyebrows and sighed. '*Ohhh, the hokey cokey,*' he said, sing-song style. 'She's decided she wants to talk again, has she?'

'No, it's not that,' said Johnson, coming into the room and shutting the door behind him. 'One of the two guys involved has been murdered on the mainland.'

Murphy's mouth dropped open and he sat up straight. 'One of the two ex-soldiers? Which one?'

'Michael Parry. He was stabbed to death in St Helens the night before last. They found his body late yesterday.'

'My goodness.'

'That's not all. Merseyside are looking for one of ours for it. I was just down in main CID and there was a couple of TIU lads in there gubbing off about it, so I had a wee listen-in.'

'TIU' was the Terrorism Investigation Unit, part of the force's Serious Crime Branch.

'Who's in the frame?'

'Dessie Callaghan. Big, hard bastard. Flat nose. We had him for the manslaughter of Joey Carlton – that off-duty RUC constable who got beaten to death outside the Duke of York. Must be fifteen years back, now. Dessie got six years for it. Poor Joey's blood was all over his trainers and jeans.'

Murphy sat back in his chair, and took off his reading specs. 'Aye, I know the fellow,' he said. 'How do they know it's him?'

'DNA. Looks like your man Parry got off a punch as he went down. The dickhead's blood was splattered all over his fist.'

Murphy nodded. 'Where is he now?'

'On his toes.'

'Have they put anything out over there?'

'Press-wise? Not yet. As far as I could tell from earwigging, Downing Street's involved. I suppose the political ramifications are pretty big. Sounds like the local peelers are presenting it as a random mugging that got out of hand. They haven't named Dessie as a suspect, or put any pictures out, but obviously behind the scenes there's a lot of work going on to find the daft fucker.'

'Did you mention our interest?'

'Not yet. Thought I'd tell you first.'

'Someone's been flapping their gums,' said the senior detective. 'It has to be linked.'

'Any idea who?'

Murphy looked at him for a moment. 'No,' he said.

'If it's a leak, are we thinking the other soldier's at risk?'

'Aye, he could well be. Can you inform the Met and get them to go round?'

'I will that.'

'Obviously, we'll need to give him our own warning as well.' Murphy looked at his watch. 'Can you type one up? We're on the one o'clock flight. You and I can deliver it. I'll speak to the boss.'

'Okay.'

'And can you make a list of everyone who knew, from Charlie Hope to the fellow who delivered the coffee at that meeting I had?'

'Will do.'

'Thanks Johnno.'

The detective sergeant left, and Murphy thought for a moment.

Then he turned to his computer, called up the summary file for the original investigation into the 1989 incident, and clicked from there to some intelligence documents.

# 58.

KEVIN MURPHY SAT at his desk, trying to work out what had just happened.

Logically, the hit must have been ordered by Patrick Casey.

Sean and Gerard had been killed in the incident involving Parry.

Who *else* was linked to them *and* had the standing to call it?

Fat chance of proving it.

Fat chance, even when Pat had just been a PIRA scrote.

But now he was a member of the Assembly…

Kevin Murphy opened Casey's intelligence file.

Started reading.

First, the incident itself.

Casey had turned up at the scene, drunk, and had made threats to an RUC inspector on the cordon…

Reading that made Murphy smile.

*Eddie Jessop, it had been, and he could just imagine how Eddie had dealt with Pat Casey.*

But then he stopped smiling and made a quick note to contact Eddie, at his magnificent retirement hacienda up there in Castlerock, Co. Londonderry, and make him aware of these developments.

Maybe ask him how serious he thought Casey had been.

He read on.

'CASEY also issued threats to the life of whoever was responsible for the deaths of his brothers,' read Jessop's log. 'Quote: "Whoever did this is a dead man. As long as I live."'

*Whoever did this.*

*As long as I live.*

Well, it was good enough for Murphy, if not for a court; certainly, it was good enough to speak to the boys in TIU and get them to send a couple of lads down to interview Casey, ask him his movements, put the frighteners on.

He laughed, a short, bitter laugh.

*Put the frighteners on? Who was he kidding?*

Casey was big enough and ugly enough and long enough in the tooth to know that they'd have nothing on him unless people spoke, and people wouldn't speak.

Not even Dessie, if they found him.

But then, Casey certainly wouldn't have made the initial call to Dessie himself.

So who had?

In ten minutes, he'd eliminated a dozen men and drawn up a list of three possibles.

Paulie McMahon. Long-time bodyguard and driver for Casey, still very loyal to his old boss.

Con McLaughlin. Belfast PIRA's main day-to-day link to the South Armagh bhoys, by dint of marriage to the snaggletooth sister of one of that bunch of maniacs.

Brian 'Freckles' Keogh. The RA's Belfast armourer from the late 1970s until the final ceasefire.

Murphy sat back.

Could be any of those three.

# 59.

KEVIN MURPHY SMILED at ACC Charles Hope's secretary and said, 'Okay to go in, Sally?'

'Aye, Kevin, he's expecting you,' said Sally.

'That's grand.'

He knocked once on the door and opened it.

Hope was sitting at his desk reading a report. He pushed it away and sat back in his chair when he saw Murphy.

'Morning, Kevin,' he said. 'How can I help?'

'Morning, sir,' said Murphy. 'Have you heard about Dessie Callaghan?'

'The moron who got into a fight on the mainland yesterday evening? Yes, it was raised at the morning briefing. TIU are looking into it − apparently he's got some sort of Republican connections.'

'Did you hear the victim's name, sir?'

Charles Hope looked at him blankly. 'I suppose so. Probably. Why?'

'It wasn't a fight. It was a hit. The fellow who died was Michael Parry.'

'Parry. Is that…?'

'Aye, one of the two soldiers we were discussing the other day.'

Hope stood up, hands on his hips. 'Christ,' he said. 'Are you sure? I mean, how do you know it's a hit?'

'Okay, I don't *know*,' said Murphy, 'but Callaghan's a long-time member of the RA and a confidante of three people I know who are close to Pat Casey. It just looks like too much of a coincidence otherwise.'

'Shit. Pat Casey? We can't start making allegations like that without some very good evidence indeed.'

'No, I understand that sir. This is just me talking to you.'

'Have you told TIU?'

No, I only heard about it myself twenty minutes ago. I thought I'd come to you first.'

'Fuck. We must have a leak.'

'You think?'

If Hope recognised the sarcasm, he ignored it. 'What about the other soldier?'

'I'm getting contact details for him. We're asking the Met to go round and warn him.'

'Good.'

'We'll need to deliver our own Osman, too,' said Murphy. 'I think the risk to his life is serious and clear, even if we're only putting two and two together at this moment.' He looked at his watch. 'Me and Nige are on the one o'clock to Heathrow this afternoon for that meeting at Thames House tomorrow. I was thinking we'd do it as soon as we get there?'

Hope didn't hesitate. 'Do it,' he said.

'What about TIU? Do I tell them?'

'No. leave that to me. This is too sensitive.'

'Right you are, sir.'

'Kevin? Thanks.'

# 60.

BACK IN HIS office, Kevin Murphy tidied his desk and stuffed a few last minute items into his overnight case.

Then he looked at the clock on the wall.

*Probably in a lecture. But I might catch him.*

He dialled a number.

A young man answered.

'Hey, dad.'

His heart swelled, as it did whenever he heard Liam's voice.

His wee boy always reminded him of Mary.

Not that you could call a strapping nineteen-year-old university rower a wee boy any more.

'Hi, son,' he said. 'How's it going?'

'All good, dad. I got a first in that contract law essay I was telling you about, so my tutor was pleased with me.'

'Never in doubt, Liam,' said Murphy, smiling broadly to himself. 'Never in doubt.'

'Yourself?'

'Grand, son. Listen, I can't stay on long. I was just calling to say I'm away to England this afternoon on a wee bit of business. Back tomorrow night, but, just in case I forget, make sure you remember to call your granny tomorrow morning?'

'Don't worry dad, it's in my phone, so it is.'

'That's great. Listen, I cannat raise Siobhan. I've sent her a text, but can you remind her, too?'

'Aye, I know her head's in the clouds. How old is granny, just so's I don't sound stupid?'

'Eighty-two. I think. Might be eighty-three. Just say happy birthday.'

Liam Murphy chuckled down the phone line.

Just then, Nigel Johnson knocked and opened his door.

'Listen, Liam, big Johnno's here just now, so I'll have to be off. But I love you, son.'

'Love you too, dad. Safe flight.'

'See you when I get back. Be good. Not too much drinking.'

Liam chuckled again. 'Don't worry, dad, I'm sensible.'

'So you are, son, so you are. Right, I'm away.'

'Have a safe flight, dad. See yous.'

Murphy clicked the phone and – just for a moment – a vision of his late wife was in his mind's eye.

It had been tough these last few years, doing the work of two parents.

But it was worth it.

'Nige,' he said. 'Ready to go?'

'Aye,' said the detective sergeant. 'Got a bit more info on Dessie.'

'Go on?'

'The TIU are still at his flat but they've flashed something over about an address in England. The big daft bastard wrote it down in a notebook which they found by his bedside. He'd ripped that page out, but they've lifted it from the impression on the page underneath.'

'Oh, aye?'

'It's in Coventry. The local polis were round there an hour ago and the house was clean, but it's owned by an Irish fella who rents it out to a couple of Kosovans.'

'Kosovans, you say? Now, that's interesting.'

Kosovo had long been a source of arms to Republican terrorists – originally via the country's *Sigurimi* secret police, and then, in the post-Communist, wild west era, through the country's vicious and rapacious mafia.

'Isn't it just. Landlord's name is Mickey Delahunty. He's clean, but he has family connections.'

'Aye?'

'Among others, he had a cousin, Richie Delahunty, who was part of Saor Éire. Richie was shot dead by the Garda in Monaghan in 1974.'

'And Kosovans for tenants,' said Murphy, with a wry smile. 'I wonder, what would Dessie want with that address?'

'A weapon?'

'Certainly what I was thinking. Or some sort of safe house or operations base.'

Then a thought struck Murphy. 'Wait one, Nige,' he said. 'I had a look at Pat's known associates.' He opened his notebook. 'Yes,' he said. 'Here we are.'

He read the three names to Johnson.

'What do you think?'

'The name that stands out to me is Keogh. He was an armourer, after all. If anyone was dealing with Kosovans it'd have been him.'

'That's what I thought,' said Murphy. 'Give me two minutes, then I'll be ready.'

Johnson left, and Murphy called up Brian Keogh's intelligence file and CRO.

'Freckles,' he said to himself, under his breath. 'Have you been a naughty boy?'

He jotted down salient points as he read.

Mid-sixties. Reasonably brief criminal record. Minor stuff as a young man, and one serious offence of being caught with a weapon at a VCP in west Belfast. Fortunately for him, it had never been fired and thus couldn't be tied in to any killings; still, he'd served seven years in an H Block at the Maze for it.

If you went by his record, he'd learned his lesson from that – he'd not been arrested since, never mind convicted. But in fact the lesson he had learned was simply to be more careful – he had an intelligence file as long as a gorilla's arm.

His run as PIRA's Belfast armourer had been highly successful. In particular, he'd been part of the negotiations with Gaddafi's *Mukhabarat el-Jamahiriya* which had ended with the shipment of a hundred and fifty tonnes of Libyan weapons aboard four ships between September 1985 and October 1986. Semtex, air-to-air missiles, hand grenades, RPG launchers, flame-throwers, Dushkas, AK47s, a million rounds of ammunition... you name it, Freckles had helped to bring it in, along with several million dollars in cash. And when that source had dried up, he'd built up new relationships with gangsters in the Balkans who could supply more weaponry.

In 1996, with the Good Friday writing on the wall, sources said that he had moved caches of weapons to new locations, and had since allowed the Real IRA access to them on several occasions.

But he'd been extremely careful never to lay hands or even eyes on any of his contraband, and he lived an outwardly blameless life as a retired mechanic.

Murphy finished by making a quick note of Freckles' known addresses, associates, and haunts, closed the computer down, and picked up his bag.

Said to his secretary, 'That's me and Nigel away to the airport, then.'

And with that he was gone.

# 61.

AS IT HAPPENED, John Carr was at that moment sitting in his living room, drinking a morning cup of tea and half-watching Sky News, wondering what Oleg Kovalev was doing with the name that had been extracted from the men at the country estate in Sussex.

Oleg had called round early on Tuesday evening to confirm that the van had been dealt with, and the two Russians were now back in the Motherland.

As for the Ukrainians…

Well, Carr didn't want to know, but – hypothetically speaking – if Oleg happened to have an acquaintance who managed a crematorium, and who was comfortable in adding extra meat to the oven for a couple of hundred quid a pop, and if someone had turned up after hours, loaded a pair of body bags in through the back and straight onto the conveyor belt…

Carr had to agree that a long bake at 1,000 degrees Celsius would make it quite difficult for the authorities to recover any forensic evidence.

From Carr's flat, Oleg had gone straight to the airport to catch a flight to Moscow, connecting to Krasnodar, for a meeting with Mr Vasiliev.

Whatever it was he was up to now, Carr wanted as little to do with it as possible. Better to let the mad bastard get on with it himself – he certainly didn't need Carr's help, he had plenty of local lunatics he could call on first.

He was just about to switch the TV off when the picture on the screen changed, to show a middle-aged man in a T-shirt and jeans, and a big red caption which read ST HELENS MURDER: WITNESSES SOUGHT.

And when he saw that John Carr forgot all about Oleg.

'Jesus,' he said. '*Scouse.*'

# 62.

THE PHOTO OF MICK Parry had disappeared, to be replaced by a blonde reporter, standing in front of a police tape.

Several bouquets of flowers had been laid underneath it, against a stone wall.

'That's right, Kay,' the reporter was saying. 'Michael Parry had been out for a darts evening last night with friends at The Wheatsheaf pub in Mill Lane, just a few hundred yards from where I'm standing, and he was on his way home when someone – the police presume a man, or men – confronted him, and stabbed him twice. Why this happened the police have no idea, and they're appealing for witnesses – anyone who saw Mr Parry in The Wheatsheaf, or saw him walking home and having this confrontation – to get in touch with them in confidence. They particularly want to talk to a man they describe as being of muscular build, about six feet two inches tall, in his forties, with very short, blond hair, and speaking with a Northern Irish accent, who they think may be able to assist them.'

'What can you tell us about Mr Parry?' said the anchorwoman from the studio.

'Well, we're hearing that Michael Parry was a much-liked local man, a driver for the Parcelforce arm of the Royal Mail, a married man with two grown-up daughters who had recently...'

But John Carr was no longer listening.

His mind had wandered back two decades and more, to a young Scouse Parry, a lance-jack at Browning Barracks when Carr had first met him – moustache, like they all had back then, and big, and thickset. A regimental boxer, and a hard bastard, but fair by old school Para Reg NCO standards.

Scouse had been made a full screw at the same time as Carr had got his own first stripe, and they'd become good mates, with a lot of mutual respect.

Shared some rowdy times in Belfast.

And some busy times, too.

Carr thought back to patrols through city streets, and out in the cuds to the south, Scouse with his game face on.

Those joyriding kids on the Ballygomartin Road... Mick never had got the recognition he should have for risking his own skin to save the three of them.

And then there was that incident with the Caseys and Ciaran O'Brien, over in the Clonards. That had been a little dicey – the RMP had tried to suggest that Parry had been out of order there, and Carr vaguely recalled making a long statement to the SIB in that grey interview room at Knock Road, with the redcap sergeant who kept banging on about a delay in calling an ambulance.

Carr had played a very straight bat – not that his own conscience hadn't been entirely clear, anyway – and in the end it had gone nowhere.

Not least because Gerard Casey had been fucked from the moment that round cut through his arteries.

He looked back at the TV: what was it the reporter had said?

A big guy, forties, Northern Irish accent?

Couldn't be something from back then, surely?

The screen was now showing Mick Parry in a suit, carnation in his buttonhole, at his oldest daughter's wedding. Carr had been there, two years ago, at the Catholic Liverpool Metropolitan

Cathedral, and it had been a big old day – a reunion with half of C Coy going back to when Scouse had joined, and a fair few lads from the Regiment who had served with him before moving on. Carr could still remember the headache, one of very many he'd endured after various nights out with Mick Parry over the years; the two men had been very close in the Paras, and had stayed in touch after Carr passed Selection. They'd met up at least once or twice a year – usually at one of the regular 3 Para boxing evenings, or a seaside day on the piss – and often more.

He grinned, sadly. The last time, after a day at Haydock Park three or four months back, he'd crashed on Mick's sofa.

Sharon Parry had given them both a bollocking for…

*Christ.*

*Sharon.*

On the TV, the news had moved on from Mick Parry, and was now showing the talking head of the Prime Minister, Penelope Morgan, talking about some new terror threat, so Carr hit the remote, and reached for his mobile.

Switched it on – ignoring the immediate pinging of multiple text messages, all doubtless telling him the same thing – and scrolled through until he found Mick Parry's entry.

Dialled his home number.

It rang out for a long time, before a man picked up.

In the background, Carr could hear the sound of crying.

'Hello?' said the man, in a strong Scouse accent.

'Is that Bingo?' said Carr. 'We met at Sarah's wedding. John Carr. You might not remember me.'

'John, mate, of course I remember you,' said Brian 'Bingo' Parry, Mick's older brother. 'You're obviously calling because of…'

He tailed off.

'I just heard,' said Carr. 'It's terrible news. I'm so sorry, mate. What happened?'

'We don't really know yet,' said Bingo. 'He'd been to the pub

239

and someone attacked him on the way home. The bizzies think it was a mugging, like.'

'How's Sharon and the girls doing?'

'In pieces, mate. I'm here with my missus, and there's a lot of people been up to the house, so we're keeping them occupied.'

'Can I speak to Sharon?'

'She's gone for a lie down, John. I can wake her up if you want, but...'

'Nah, mate. Just tell them all I called, can you? I'll be up as soon as I can. You keep your chin up, eh, pal?'

'I am doing, mate. Thanks.'

Carr ended the call and started flicking through the text messages – all of which did indeed bring him the same, terrible news.

He got to the end...

...and saw that message again.

*'Did you get my text John? Do get in touch.'*

He scrolled up to the other, earlier message he had received from the same unidentified number.

*'Hello John. Please call me to discuss something that you need to know about.'*

He'd half-intended to call the number, just out of curiosity, but there were a lot of blasts in his past, and he didn't want to be in contact with them all.

And if the sender couldn't be arsed to tell him who he was...

But then.

*Mick Parry.*

Maybe it was worth making that call?

# 63.

THE MAN IN THE black jacket was walking along the seaweed-strewn beach at Portstewart with Pat Casey.

Casey had insisted on meeting somewhere out of the way, and it didn't get much more out of the way than a cold February morning, an hour north of Belfast into deepest, dampest County Coleraine.

The tide was out, but it was grey and blustery, and they had the sticky sand to themselves. The wind whipped their words away, and they were far enough from the A2 coast road for the passing traffic to be irrelevant, but, all the same, the Jacket kept his collar turned well up and a weather eye all about himself.

The stakes were very much higher than they had been when they had last met.

'Tell me again,' said Casey, his eyes burning with anger. 'Short version.'

'Basically, he got to Parry as he was walking back from the pub and did him there and then,' said Black Jacket. 'So far, so good. The bad news is that Parry managed to get a dig in as he went down, and Dessie's blood was all over him. They knew it was him before the sun rose.'

'I knew he should have used the gun,' hissed Casey.

'To be fair, like we said, that might have caused different problems. Midnight in the middle of St Helens... The gunshots, and all.'

'Jesus Christ,' said Casey, bitterly. 'What a balls-up. But they haven't found him yet?'

'Not yet.'

'Where is he now?'

'I don't know. No-one knows.'

'Has he not called Freckles?'

'If he had, would Freckles not have called you?'

That answer earned him a withering look from Casey.

'I mean, with the greatest of respect, obviously,' said Black Jacket, his voice full of contrition.

He decided he'd shut his gub for a wee while.

They trudged on through the soft sand.

It was hard going, and the Jacket was breathing hard and sweating, despite the cold.

Eventually, Casey stopped and turned to face the roiling sea.

'How long has he got before the Brit peelers pinch him?' he said.

Black Jacket looked at the angry water, narrowing his eyes against the salt air, watching the boiling waves spill onto the beach.

'Who knows?' he said. A lone seagull hovered on the gusting wind a few feet overhead, its dead, black eye looking him up and down. 'They could pick him up five minutes from now, or it could take five days. We have one thing in our favour. They'll know Dessie's pedigree, and they know Parry's ex-Army. They must be wondering if it's something to do with over here, but I doubt they've made the whole connection yet, so they don't know exactly what they're dealing with. They certainly don't want to rush into a big political shitstorm by talking about IRA men assassinating ex-soldiers on the mainland.'

Casey looked at him. 'So?'

'Well, they haven't named Dessie, and they haven't released pictures. That means the public aren't looking for him, which makes him harder to find. Obviously, within the police and the other agencies they'll have circulated him, and doubtless they'll be going through every bit of CCTV they can, visiting hotels, doing that sort of stuff. But it gives him a bit of breathing space.'

'Will I get a visit?'

'Why would you?'

'If the eejit talks when they find him.'

'Why would he talk? You can get to him in jail, if you have to. He's not frigging suicidal.'

Casey brushed his thick grey-black hair back from his forehead. 'What about the other one?' he said.

'Until we hear otherwise, I suppose we should assume the other one's still on.'

'But then they'll definitely make the link,' said Casey. 'I mean, I know the plod aren't that clever, but they didn't come down the Lagan in a bubble, neither. It wouldn't take a genius to look back at Parry's Army file, cross-ref it with the other fella's, and put two and two together. And where does that leave me?'

'Sure, it makes no difference,' said Black Jacket. 'Dessie's getting life for one murder, so two makes no odds to him. And, sure, the police will work out the link, right enough, but then they probably always would've. Doesn't mean it'll come back on you. Isn't Dessie an IRA man? Isn't it every IRA man's dream to kill an SAS man or a Para? Or both? He's just doing what comes naturally to him. They know fine well your brothers were involved way back in the original thing. But so what? They'll never be able to link Dessie to you unless someone who was at that meeting talks. Nobody will, so that's that.'

'I suppose there's the Kosovans in Coventry,' said Pat Casey. 'But they've been dealing with us for years. They know the form. They were asked to supply a clean gun, and I'm damned sure they wouldn't let it be traced back to them.'

They trudged on, heads down.

Then Black Jacket said, 'I hate to raise it, but there is another loose end.'

'Who's that?'

'Marie Hughes. The woman at Strandtown. She met you in the Beehive, did she not?'

Casey looked at him, a strange smile on his face.

'Don't you worry about her,' he said. 'She couldn't be trusted, so that's already been taken care of.'

Something in those words, and in the way he'd said them, sent a cold terror coursing through Black Jacket's body. He tried not to show it, but he felt like he had stared into the eyes of some ancient demon.

Overhead, the clouds somehow parted, and a weak sun shone on them for a few moments.

Pat Casey brightened. 'Ach,' he said, 'maybe you're right, and there's nothing to worry about. Have you time for a pint?'

# 64.

SEVERAL HUNDRED MILES away in Primrose Hill, the intercom at John Carr's flat buzzed.

He got up and loped over to the screen.

Two uniformed bobbies, one scratching his head, the other yawning.

For a moment, Carr's heart rate ticked up a beat or two.

*The Ukrainians?*

Then it dropped again.

*Nah. If it was something to do with that they'd be sending detectives and SC&O19, not a pair of woodentops.*

Not to mention, there was no way they could ever tie him in to it anyway.

*No idea what you want, but I think I'll give you a miss.*

He watched them as they buzzed again, had a quick conflab, and then one of them produced a card, scribbled something on it, and pushed it through the door. Then they put their hats back on and walked back to their car.

They'd be back if it was anything vital.

He looked at his watch.

Time to head to the gym.

It was as he was walking through to collect his kit that he saw his mobile, lying on the sofa.

He paused.

Pondered.

Finally, gave in to curiosity, and dialled his mystery texter.

After three or four rings, a man answered.

# 65.

THE DETECTIVE CHIEF SUPERINTENDENT in charge of Merseyside's hunt for Dessie Callaghan had spent the last hour on a conference call to MI5, his counterparts in the Police Service of Northern Ireland, West Mercia and Essex, and the Metropolitan Police's Counter Terrorist Command.

They had been trying to work up a strategy for capturing the elusive Provo.

It involved covertly watching John Carr's addresses in London and Hereford and the various addresses Dessie might be using in the North London Irish diaspora. He had a brother, an uncle and half a dozen friends of various closeness in Kilburn and Camden, and officers were on every one, with armed backup.

They agreed to maintain to the media the fiction that they didn't know the identity of Michael Parry's killer – the Met were taking instruction direct from the Home Office to that effect, with Downing Street worried about the effect on the fragile politics of Northern Ireland if it was revealed that the IRA was back in business carrying out mainland hits. A photofit had been produced and disseminated, ostensibly from eyewitness reports but in fact from Callaghan's numerous arrest photographs.

They discussed informing the Directorate of Special Forces, but the CTC counselled against it, for now. No need to call Hereford in: it was only one man, and if it all went noisy the police could surely handle that on their own.

And then the conference call ended.

The Merseyside D Supt sat back in his chair, looked idly at the framed Wales rugby shirt on the wall opposite, and sighed.

Michael Parry had been a decent family man, with a good record of service to his country: scrotes like Dessie Callaghan needed locking up, and the key chucking across the road into Salthouse Dock.

He was frustrated that their man was still outstanding.

Still, with the manpower and technical back-up now involved he would doubtless be picked up later that day.

Probably at that ex-SAS bloke's flat.

# 66.

DESSIE CALLAGHAN HAD passed another night of almost no sleep – the throbbing in his nose and upper jaw hurt like buggery, and only seemed to be getting worse – and he was starting to think he might have a broken cheekbone, too.

He tried to smile as he handed back his room key to the farmer's wife, but the best he could manage was a weird, twisted grimace.

'Toothache,' he said, as best he could, pointing to his cheek. 'D'you know where I can get some painkillers? Like a chemist, or something?'

'Oh, poor you,' she said, head on one side. 'I don't think there's a worse pain than toothache. I'd say Harlow's your best bet for painkillers. Down the drive, turn left, follow your nose. It's not far.'

She handed him the bill, and as he was digging in his pocket for some cash she said, 'You sound like you're from Northern Ireland?' she said. 'Underneath all that, I mean.'

Dessie looked at her face – her fat, ruddy-cheeked, *English* face – and briefly considered strangling her where she stood.

But then the farmer shouted through from the back – something about silage? – and he decided against. The farmer was a big old boy, and he didn't need the aggro.

'Uh huh,' he said, nodding.

'Yes, I thought so. Only, we know a beef man from near Ballymena.'

Dessie's hands contracted involuntarily into fists, and then relaxed. He nodded, and tried to smile. 'Really?' he said. 'Small world, eh? Right, I'll be off, then.'

He cursed himself all the way to the Mondeo, and all the way down the drive, and he was still going as he turned left onto the lane to Harlow.

Why in the living *fuck* had he not just stuck two rounds in Mick Fucking Parry from a safe distance? It wasn't a mistake he'd make again, that was for sure.

A short while later, as she was having a morning cuppa before going up to clean the guest bedroom, the farmer's wife turned on her TV and caught the BBC Breakfast news roundup.

Police had issued an artist's impression of the man they were seeking in connection with the murder of a Parcelforce delivery driver somewhere up north. It was 'based on eyewitness reports', they said, and showed a man – a man from Northern Ireland – whom they wanted to talk to. Blond and shaven-headed, broken nose, narrow eyes. Over six feet tall, the reporter was saying, and well-built with it.

Extremely dangerous, and not to be approached by members of the public, under any circumstances.

The farmer's wife put her hand to her throat, and put down her tea to avoid spilling it with her shaking.

No doubt about it: the man on the screen was the man who'd stood in front of her not fifteen minutes earlier.

It took her fully five minutes to stop shaking and recover her composure, and then to telephone Essex Police.

# 67.

BY THEN, DESSIE had spotted a little shopping plaza on the eastern edge of Harlow, with a branch of Boots nestling in the row of stores.

He parked up in a residential side street, well away from any CCTV.

Then, scarf pulled up around his face, a cap pulled down over his eyes, he half-jogged into the pedestrianised area.

Head down, hands thrust deep into the pockets of his coat, he headed for the pharmacy.

It was still early, and there were precious few shoppers around, but it wasn't like he had any fucking choice.

The place was empty apart from two people – a little Asian man in a white coat, who was fiddling with some display material, and a young bird who was replenishing various dispensary shelves with drugs.

*Drugs.*

The little Asian fella – the manager, Dessie assumed – stopped what he was doing and turned toward the Ulsterman.

'Can I help you?' he said.

'I want some painkillers,' said Dessie, gritting his teeth against the throbbing in his face. 'Something strong.'

'And do you have a prescription?' said the manager, blinking at him.

'Ah, for fuck's sake,' spat Dessie.

He walked forward and chinned the manager with a perfectly-executed uppercut. The man dropped like a stone, hitting himself on the counter on the way down.

'You,' said Dessie, turning to look at the girl. 'I want some painkillers. Strong stuff. Don't fuck me about.'

'What?' said the girl, losing his accent in her panic. 'I...'

'Don't fuck me about!' yelled Dessie. 'Painkillers! Now!'

'But I don't understand you!' yelled back the girl.

He was about to punch her, too, when a woman in her sixties, wearing a green mac, entered the shop behind him.

Dessie span round at the tinkle of the bell and shouted, 'Fuck off!'

She about-turned and fucked off.

And then, suddenly, the assistant put two-and-two together.

'Do you mean painkillers?' she said.

'Aye,' said Dessie, almost gratefully. 'Painkillers. Please.'

'What do you want? Paracetamol? Ibuprofen?'

'Stronger.'

'Wait there, please.'

'Quick!' shouted Dessie.

Working as though her life depended on it, the girl scrabbled along the shelves behind her, and turned round a few seconds later with two boxes of Tramadol.

'These are oral,' she said. 'They're extremely strong opiates, so make sure you only take...'

But Dessie cut her off, jabbing his forefinger into her face and cramming the pills into his pocket.

'No police,' he said.

Then he was gone.

As he left the shop, the girl collapsed, sobbing, to her knees.

Outside, the woman in the green mac was standing talking to a pair of security guards on the other side of the precinct.

Dessie heard her say, 'That's him!', and saw the guards start in his direction.

'Sir,' called one of them. 'Can you wait there, please? We want a word.'

Dessie ignored them, and walked away.

'You!' shouted the guard. 'Stop!'

They started running, and when Dessie heard their feet get near he turned around, calmly drew the Glock, and showed it to them.

His sheer nonchalance was bizarrely intimidating, and both men stopped dead in their tracks, turned, and sprinted back the way they'd come.

Dessie grinned and rounded the corner, out of sight, on the way to the Mondeo.

Armed police were at the scene in a matter of minutes, but by then he was long gone.

To London, everyone presumed.

# 68.

KEVIN MURPHY WALKED through into Heathrow Arrivals at a shade before 3pm and grinned broadly at John Carr.

The two men shook hands warmly, and Murphy gestured to the man by his side.

'This is Nigel Johnson,' he said. 'One of my guys. You can speak freely in front of him. I'd trust him with my life.'

Carr sized Johnson up: a big man with a square jaw, he looked like he'd been built at Harland and Wolff. They made cops tough in Belfast; they had to.

'Alright, mate,' he said, shaking his hand. 'Good to meet you.'

'John and I go way back,' said Murphy, to Johnson. 'I'd trust *him* with my life, as well. Have done, more than once. Remember Frankie Boyd, John? God rest his soul.'

'Aye,' said Carr.

They walked from the building, and once they were outside Murphy said to Johnson, 'Frank was my partner when I was first in the Branch. He got wind that a player called Kieran Devine was in a lot of trouble on the horses. Owed thirty thousand pounds to various people, and Frank thought it might be possible to turn him. So we called in John and his pals for protection, and arranged a meet. First meet went well, and Devine says he wants a second meeting, only we've to hand over ten grand to show goodwill on the part of the RUC. I drew the cash and we set off, but it was a trap. Soon as we turn into the car park to plot up, Devine and his pal Cian O'Hanlon open up on us.'

'Plan being to kill Kev and Frank and steal the money,' said Carr.

'One of the rounds hits poor old Frank in the head,' said Murphy. 'I stick it into reverse and pull out my weapon and empty it back at them. Pure fluke, I managed to hit O'Hanlon, but as I'm reversing I put the car up on a little concrete bollard. I'm sitting there, unable to move, wheels spinning, and Kieran Devine is running over with his AK47. I swear I thought I was a dead man. And Mary about to give birth to Siobhan.' He looked at Carr. 'And then this fella drives into the car park and rams Devine at 50mph.'

'That would do it,' said Nigel Johnson.

'Paralysed him from the waist down,' said Murphy. 'He was eventually strangled in his wheelchair in Long Kesh by his own pals. The story was they thought he was a tout, but I reckon it was mostly that they were angry that he'd not got clearance for the whole thing from the hierarchy.'

'We had some good results together over the years,' said Carr.

'Aye,' said Murphy. 'Tales I could tell.' He smiled. 'He's Siobhan's godfather, too, Nigel, though he's an awful godless man, and he doesn't see her as often as he should.'

Carr grinned, apologetically. 'How long's it been? I saw you last Christmas, didn't I?'

'Christmas before,' said Murphy. 'Time flies.'

'I'll get over in the next few months,' said Carr. 'That's a promise.' He looked at Murphy. 'So anyway, why the secret squirrel text messages? I thought it was some bird I'd got up the duff.'

Murphy laughed. 'Sorry about that. At that stage I just wanted to warn you about the witness coming forward, and I didn't think it would be very good for either of us if I used my own phone. All our call records are open, and Professional Standards would love to find a way to get rid of an old boy like me without paying me the pension.'

'Burner?' said Carr.

'Nothing so sophisticated,' said Murphy. 'Nigel, cover your ears. I pinched one from the property store.'

'I didn't hear that,' said Nigel Johnson.

'So what brings you over?' said Carr.

'We've a meeting with the boys at Thames House tomorrow morning.'

'Thames House?'

'Aye. MI5 have some old phone intercepts relating to a murder in the seventies. Every now and then we go through the charade of asking them to let us have the intercepts, and they go through the charade of pretending to consider our request.'

'Sounds familiar.'

'Nothing changes.'

'So where you staying?' said Carr, as they walked into the car park.

'They've booked us into a Premier Inn out Edgware way,' said Murphy. 'Miles from anywhere, but it's cheap. Budgets are tighter than our Siobhan's blooming jeans.'

'Cancel it. You can both kip at mine. I've got plenty of room. Save the PSNI a few quid.'

'No thanks,' said Murphy. 'Not without our sidearms. And you'd be better off in a hotel yourself, just now. This guy who killed your man Mick Parry yesterday? There's a good chance he's here for you, too.'

He fished into his inner pocket and pulled out an envelope. 'In fact, I need to give you this, formally.'

They'd arrived at Carr's new black Cayenne.

Nigel Johnson whistled appreciatively. 'Is this the Turbo S, is it?' he said.

Murphy chuckled. 'You're doing alright for yourself,' he said, with a grin. 'Unlike Nige, I'm not much of a car man, but I know a nice motor when I see one. What's this set you back?'

'About a year of your and my wages put together,' said Nigel Johnson.

'Nothing,' said Carr. 'Gift from my boss.'

'Gift?' said Murphy, his mouth dropping open.

'Performance-related bonus,' said Carr.

'My goodness. You're on a winner there, son.'

Carr pressed the button to open the tailgate and threw Murphy's bag inside, and then the three of them climbed into the vehicle.

Carr looked at the envelope Murphy had handed him. 'Osman Warning?' he said.

'Aye,' said Murphy. 'Speaking of which, have the Met been round?'

'I had a couple of uniforms knock on my door this morning. They stuck a card through asking me to call them. I guess that was probably it.' He stuffed the letter into his pocket. 'I've had more people try to kill me than you've had hot dinners, Kev,' he said, with a grin. 'And, by the looks of you, you've had more than a few of them.'

'Too many bacon butties at my desk,' said Murphy, ruefully. 'But I'd take it seriously, John.'

'Who is he?'

'Fella called Dessie Callaghan,' said Nigel Johnson, leaning forward in the back seat.

'Should I remember him?'

'Fringe player in your day,' said Murphy. 'He moved up later on. You'll definitely have seen the rascal here and about, but I doubt you'd ever have been tasked onto him.'

'Got a picture?'

Murphy turned his head. 'Have you got the file, Nige?'

Johnson opened his bag and handed a thin folder through to Kevin Murphy.

Murphy opened it, pulled out a large photograph, and handed it to Carr.

'Stands about six foot two, and weighs around ninety kilos,' he said. 'Your age.'

Carr propped the mugshot on the steering wheel and studied it, as he'd studied hundreds, probably thousands, before. His mind drifted back over the years he'd spent undercover in Belfast and elsewhere in the Province, first with the 3 Para COP, and then with the SAS and the Det. Like all operators, he'd spent long hours poring over photographs of key players, and had made it his business to memorise a couple of new names and faces every time he went out the door. By default, he'd developed an excellent memory for them, though there were so many that they tended to blend into one another.

But this one – nasty-looking as he was – didn't ring any bells.

'Nah,' he said, eventually. 'I don't recognise him. Looks handy enough.'

'He's a proper hard nut,' said Nigel Johnson. 'No doubt about that. Works the door at McKill's and the Vollie, and one or two other places.'

'What's his story?'

'Usual juvenile record. He was trying to make a go of it as a boxer, but he's just a big brawler so he kept walking onto punches. When that didn't work out, he fell in with Paddy Kilty and Johnny O'Gara... Big players in the nineties. You'd know them from your time?'

'Oh, yeah,' said Carr. 'Yes, I know those bastards, right enough.'

'He only really got started three or four years before the Good Friday Agreement, but he's killed three, that we know of.'

'Convicted?'

'He served time for the manslaughter of an off-duty constable who was kicked and punched to death outside the Duke of York,' said Kevin Murphy. 'The others... Well, they're still riddled with touts, like they always were, but no-one would come over, so we got nowhere.'

Carr nodded. 'So why's he come after Mick and me now?'

'We think it's to do with the deaths of Sean and Gerard Casey and that lunatic Ciaran O'Brien.'

Carr looked at him. 'Christ,' he said. 'That's years ago.'

'Aye,' said Murphy. He quickly ran through Marie Hughes' statement – and then her retraction – and then said, 'So that whole can of worms got opened up, and we reckon your names found their way to Pat Casey.'

'Dessie Callaghan's a fringe member of Casey's circle,' said Nigel Johnson. 'And his old man was a close pal of O'Brien's. So it all adds up.'

'It's too random for it not to be linked,' said Murphy.

John Carr committed the face of Dessie Callaghan to his memory, handed back the photo and turned the ignition key.

'So you think I should be worried?' he said, easing the Porsche out of the car park.

'We have reason to believe he could be armed, and he's a vicious bastard. He won't hesitate, and he won't come at you from the front.'

Carr nodded. 'What have you told the investigating officers?

'I left that to my boss. He was going to have a word with the TIU.'

'TIU?'

'Terrorist Investigations Unit. Part of Serious Crime. I know they're liaising over here with MI5 and the local police. The focus for now is on finding him. They'll worry later about why he did it.'

'You must have a leak,' said Carr, nudging the Cayenne forward in the stop-start traffic.

'Aye,' said Murphy. 'You know as well as I do the PSNI isn't the old RUC. The walls have ears, my friend.'

'So who knew our ID?'

'Me, obviously. Plus Nigel and one or two other members of our team. But I hand-picked them all myself and there's no way. Then you've the people who were at the meeting we had to discuss it. That's Gary Baxter from the Public Prosecution

Service, Charlie Hope, the Assistant Chief, and Conor Maguire, who's head of force PR.'

'Any of them?'

'I'd put my house on Baxter being straight,' said Murphy. 'And Hope is just a mainland copper who's biding his time till he can get a big job over here. Maguire, he'd be my guess, out of the three. Strong Republican ties going way back, and he doesn't even bother to hide his sympathies, either.'

Carr looked at him.

'Seriously,' said Murphy. 'We take anyone in these days. But all that said, I can't see him being so daft. Beyond that, who knows?'

'How about your end?' said Nigel Johnson, leaning forward.

'Everyone in battalion knew who'd shot them,' said Carr. 'I left for Selection a few weeks later, but I remember Scouse saying he never bought a drink till the end of the tour. Outside 3 Para it would have been restricted to a few SIB and senior ranks, and most of them are either dead or pissed in a bar somewhere. It'll be a big job, getting to the bottom of it.'

'It will.'

'Pat Casey was somebody back then, wasn't he? Wasn't he 2IC the Belfast Brigade?'

'He was, aye,' said Johnson. 'And *de facto* leader after Fergus lost his marbles.'

'Fergus lost his marbles, did he?'

'Alzheimer's,' said Murphy. 'They kept it quiet for a bit, but the game was up when he was caught sticking a bomb on his neighbour's car. He started out as a bomb-maker, of course, back in the early seventies.'

'Well, they do say that people with dementia live in the past,' said Carr.

'Aye,' said Johnson, stifling a giggle. 'They were having a row over a leylandii which was blocking out Fergus's Sky Sports signal. The ATO who disarmed it said it was perfectly constructed, mercury tilt switch and all, except for one small thing – he'd used his wee grandson's Play-Doh instead of C4.'

The three men erupted in laughter.

Eventually, Johnson said, 'Anyway, that was the end o' Fergus. But by then the second ceasefire was in force, so Pat never got the top job. He'd gone political, anyway. He's a member of the Assembly now, but he's not changed his spots. I'd think he was involved in the decision, for sure.'

'He wouldnae made the call to the shooter himself, though,' said Carr. 'He'd want some distance.'

'Aye,' said Murphy. 'It's a guessing game, and I'm just putting pieces together, but do you remember Freckles?'

Carr looked at him. 'Freckles? I know the name but I cannae call him to mind.'

'Ginger-haired fellow.'

'About two thirds of them had ginger hair.'

'Real name Brian Keogh. Married Róisín Cafferty.'

'Róisín the Machine?' said Carr, looking sideways. 'Diarmuid Cafferty's sister?'

'That's the one.'

'Yeah, I know Freckles, then,' said Carr. 'Armourer?'

'Aye. Responsible for scores of deaths, if he's responsible for one. Semi-retired now, of course, but still dabbling. He's a clever so-and-so, mind, so we've only pinched him the once, years back.'

'What makes you think it's him?'

Kevin Murphy swivelled in the leather seat to look at Nigel Johnson. 'Very close pals with Pat, for one thing,' he said. 'The rest is circumstantial, but strong. Have you that Coventry info, Nige?'

'It's in thon file,' said Johnson, nodding at the folder on Murphy's lap.

'Aye,' said Murphy, with a rueful shake of his head. 'Getting old.'

Murphy fished his reading specs from an inside pocket, opened the file and started reading.

When he'd finished, Carr said, 'Yes, that makes sense. An armourer like Freckles would have spent years dealing with the Kosovans, and this Delahunty guy must be a middleman. You reckon Freckles teed up Dessie and then gave him the address in Coventry?'

'I reckon so. Presumably so's he could go there to pick up a weapon. Heaven knows why he used a knife on Michael Parry. Maybe he...'

But then his mobile rang.

He looked at the screen.

Said, 'I'd better take this.'

Then, 'Kevin Murphy, hello?'

Carr heard a tinny voice on the other end.

'No, I'm in London for a couple of meetings,' said Murphy. He paused for a moment, and then said, 'Really? Tell me.'

He listened for a few moments, and then said, 'Okay, thanks for letting me know.'

He ended the call, and turned to look at Nigel Johnson.

'That body in the Turf Lodge a day or two back?' he said. 'It was Marie Hughes. They haven't formally identified her yet, but her sister reported her missing this morning.'

'That's the witness, is it?' said Carr. 'The woman from that night in the Clonards?'

'Aye. They tortured the poor lass and gave her the nutcracker. Dumped her half-naked in the Turf.'

'In the open?' said Carr.

'Pretty much bang in the centre of the estate. A van got burned out in Andy Town about the same time. No forensics, but they're assuming it's related.'

'Bastards,' said Carr, softly. 'Sick bastards.'

A sombre quiet descended on the car, and he pressed on through the stop-start rush hour traffic.

# 69.

OLEG KOVALEV LOOKED at the lights of some city far below and smiled to himself.

He'd had a productive twenty-four hours with Vitaly Vasiliev, the guy who'd put the £30k hit out on Konstantin Avilov.

Vasiliev was a sixty-year-old former Party boss from St Petersburg, who had climbed the greasy pole along with everyone else after the collapse of the USSR.

He had two reasons for wanting Avilov dead.

The first was that he had been promised an old Soviet tin mine in Kolyma, in far eastern Siberia, and had then watched impotently as the powers-that-be instead gave it to Avilov, in return for some favour or other.

It wasn't a particularly beautiful piece of real estate, and the mine – dug out of the freezing earth in the bad old days by starving political prisoners based at a number of Gulag camps around the town of Magadan – wasn't even working. But it had potential: Russian tin was making a comeback, and it had been estimated that this particular hole in the ground could produce upwards of twenty million dollars of the soft grey metal each year. It wasn't a king's ransom, but it was worth having, and he hated the fact that Avilov could afford to just leave it in the fucking ground.

The second reason was closer to home: Avilov had slept with

Vasiliev's wife two years earlier, and she had left him soon afterwards.

The mine – maybe you could forgive and forget the mine. The new Russia worked on patronage, and it was a big place; there were other baubles yet to be distributed.

But the wife? No, he couldn't forgive and forget the wife.

As soon as he learned of the failure of the hit he'd got out of town, taking a Georgian lingerie model away for a fortnight to a friend's villa at Dagomys, in Sochi. Hopefully, those Ukrainian fools would have better luck second time round; in the meantime, he would lie low.

But the friend had betrayed him to the FSB, the FSB had informed Oleg Kovalev, and Oleg had sent three very hard men down there to pay off his bodyguards and the lingerie model and make sure that Vasiliev went nowhere.

And then he had two choices.

Kill the fool, or disgrace him.

He chose the latter: better to let him spend the rest of his life dwelling on his stupidity in taking on a man with connections in the police, the security services, the presidential palace itself.

Which was why the fool was presently languishing in a Sochi police cell, awaiting transfer to Moscow, where he would be tried on charges of tax evasion and corruption and possession of drugs, child porn, and state secrets.

The verdict was not in doubt – Konstantin was friendly with a lot of judges – and Vasiliev would spend the rest of his life in a tiny cell in one of his country's grim and forbidding jails.

A much better warning to others who might think of crossing Avilov than a simple bullet in the back of the neck and a shallow grave somewhere.

Oleg smiled, sat back in his seat and sipped his scotch – not quite as good as Johnny's, but the best that a first class British Airways ticket could offer.

Konstantin was happy, the Ukrainians had been taught a lesson, and he'd even had a chance to visit the Bolshoi.

Forty thousand feet below, Europe slipped by at five hundred miles per hour.

# 70.

DESSIE HAD NO IDEA how close he had come to being nabbed, but he was keeping an ear on the radio news, and he had heard that the police had issued a photofit.

That mystified him, a bit. Some bullshit about a picture based on descriptions by eyewitnesses, when he was pretty sure there'd *been* no witnesses and it had been pitch fucking black anyway.

Gingerly, he felt his nose, which was still sore and crusted inside with dried blood.

They must have lifted his DNA from the fucking soldier's fist. That had to be it.

He cursed himself once again for not just slotting the fucker, and then he cursed the dickhead in the black jacket who'd got him into this in the first place.

He shook his head. He had other things to consider.

The Tramadol had taken the edge off the pain, enabling him to think about his plan.

Which hadn't changed.

He'd be making his way to Carr's flat and staking it out over-night.

If he saw the bastard, great.

If he didn't, he'd move off somewhere – he didn't want to attract

attention in daylight hours, so he'd get out into the countryside –
and then he'd come back and do it all again the following night.

Sooner or later, the murdering SAS bastard would show up,
and when that happened Dessie was going to torture him a while
and then shoot him in his fucking swede.

*I'll make sure you know it's coming*, he thought. *Get you begging.
Let you know that Dessie Callaghan's sending you to hell, on behalf of
Pat Casey, his murdered brothers, and the downtrodden people of Ireland.*

Everyone said the way to do it was straight in and out, no
messing about.

That was the correct way.

But how often did you get a chance like this?

A chance to make an SAS man beg?

He saw it all happening in his head, and he smiled, despite the
pain.

They'd have to write a whole new series of songs, just for him.

And paint a mural.

He could see it now: 'Dessie Callaghan, Volunteer, who carried
the fight to the SAS, behind enemy lines in England.'

Himself on a wall, twenty fucking foot tall, and looking like
a movie star.

His chances of getting away without a pinch were virtually nil,
now, but that mural, that would be sweet.

Very fucking sweet indeed.

# 71.

AT JUST BEFORE seven pm, John Carr, Kevin Murphy and Nigel Johnson walked through the door at the Namaaste curry house in Camden and found a table.

They ordered Cobras and food, and while they were waiting for the drinks to arrive Carr said, 'So, how's the kids? Liam must be in his second year now?'

'Aye,' said Murphy. 'He's going well. Knows more about the law than me, that's for sure.'

'No surprise,' said Carr. 'He always was a bright boy.'

'All from his ma,' said Nigel Johnson, with a grin.

Murphy chuckled and nodded. 'And Siobhan's just starting her masters up in Edinburgh.'

'I know,' said Carr. 'I do keep in touch wi' her, you know.'

The beers arrived and the three raised their glasses to each other.

'Aye,' said Kevin Murphy. 'She was very touched by the graduation present you sent over. Far too expensive, mind. She'd daren't wear it out the house.'

Carr had been invited to attend the ceremony, but work had intervened so he'd had a girl he knew pick out a white gold-and-diamond tennis bracelet for Siobhan and sent that over instead. It had been pricey, but he'd felt guilty at not seeing his goddaughter or her dad for the last year or more.

He took a long pull on his lager. 'Only seems like yesterday she was sitting on your knee in the front room, listening to our war stories,' he said.

His mind's eye conjured up a picture of a tousle-haired little girl with a big gap in her teeth, hanging on her father's every word as he and John Carr discussed some recent operation or other against PIRA.

'Aye,' said Murphy. 'Scary, isn't it?'

'And you're nearly finished yourself?'

'I'm out of there this summer, yep.'

'Plans?'

'Short term, I'm going to spend some time with my brother at his fishing operation in Lake Laberge in the Yukon. Longer term, I don't know. I've been talking to the RCMP about a bit of advisory work on gang crime, so I might stay out there. But if not... Well, they're always re-employing guys at Knock, so I'll probably end up working for this lump.'

He nodded towards Nigel Johnson, who grinned.

'What about yours?' said Murphy.

'Alice is in her first year of A levels,' said Carr. 'Still costing me an arm and a leg in bloody boarding school fees and clothes and gadgets and what-have-you. George is in the Paras hisself now.'

'My goodness. He was just a nipper when I last seen him.'

'Well, he's not a nipper any more. Thinking about going for Selection next year.'

'Hope he likes blisters.'

The waiter arrived with poppadums and chutney and the three men dived in.

'How's your love life?' said Murphy, as he ate.

'You know me,' said Carr. 'There's girls here and there, but I havenae the time for anything serious. I got all that out of the way with Stella. You?'

'Less complicated than yours. Would you believe, it's Mary's tenth anniversary soon?'

Murphy was silent for a moment or two, and again Carr's mind conjured up another image, this time of the policeman's wife. A pretty and vivacious nurse fifteen years her husband's junior, Mary had always been up for a drink and a laugh, and her death from an aggressive breast cancer at such a young age had been a terrible tragedy.

'Awful,' said Carr, soberly. 'Not surprised you haven't dipped your toe in the water since – you'd never have found anyone to compare.'

'Truer than you think,' said Murphy.

The food arrived, and as it was being dished up, the Detective Superintendent turned to Nigel Johnson. 'Nineteen years in an SAS Sabre Squadron, this one,' he said. 'Hereford groupies coming out of his ears.'

'Oh aye?' said Johnson.

'Nigel's a strict Presbyterian,' said Murphy, with a laugh. 'He'd not approve of that sort of thing.'

'I'm a man of the world, Murph,' said Johnson. 'So what do you do these days, John?'

'I'm in private security,' said Carr. 'Russian guy. I basically look after him while he's in London. Two weeks a month at most. Usually less. The pay's good. Normally a pretty quiet life. No dramas.'

'Normally?'

'Some guy tried to shoot him the other day. I took the pistol off him and put him in hospital, but he got off a couple of shots and killed a young woman.'

'Good lord,' said Murphy. 'Who was it?'

Carr's mind flashed back to the two Ukrainians, and the blood on the garage floor.

Kevin Murphy was an old friend, and he had vouched for DS

Johnson, but when all was said and done they were still police officers.

'Och, some random eastern European headcase,' he said. 'Why he wanted to kill Avilov I have no idea. Avilov's the kind of guy who upsets people everywhere he goes, and he goes a lot of places.' He cleared his throat. 'Anyway. This PIRA shit. I should take it seriously?'

Kevin Murphy paused, a forkful of chicken tikka masala in mid-air. 'The Republicans are not what they were,' he said. 'But then neither are we.'

Carr nodded. 'A couple of my mates work in training with the Special Reconnaissance Regiment. They've told me it's bad.'

'Special Branch and Five are all over the Islamic threat, so you can pretty much count them out. The Army's virtually gone. We're effectively on our own, and we don't have the manpower to deal with anything really big any more. The people we've lost are mostly the old-timers who knew how to fight the bastards, excuse my French. The muscle memory's all wasted away. We won't admit it, but we've conceded the streets in the obvious areas to the Republicans.'

'And Dessie Callaghan?'

'Every bit as bad as any of them ever were,' said Johnson, swallowing a forkful of vindaloo. 'You'd beat him in a fair fight, but he's a snidey so-and-so and it won't *be* a fair fight. Give him a chance and he'll take it.'

'Seriously, John,' said Murphy. 'Book yourself into a hotel. Why take the risk? He's bound to get lifted in the next few days, and then you can forget him. Look at your man, Parry.'

Carr ate in silence for a moment.

'Close friend, was he?' said Johnson.

'Aye,' said Carr. 'He was. The guy was a legend. Instructor when I joined 3 Para and, Jesus, he was a hard bastard. But fair. Brave, too. We stayed in touch after I moved on. He could easily have gone the same route, but he met his missus and had the brains to know when he was on to a good thing. Did his time and got out and then he was all about her and their girls.' He smiled. 'Not that he didn't still go off the rails now and then. Last saw him at the races a few months back. I've still got the hangover.'

# 72.

OVER THE YEARS, the men and women of the Provisional IRA had evolved sophisticated counter-surveillance skills.

They had done so partly by simple Darwinism – the stupid and the rash had ended up dead, or in jail – and partly with the help of experienced operators from various sympathetic governments and terrorist organisations around the world.

Dessie Callaghan had benefited from decades of accumulated wisdom, which was why he had stood off from Carr's flat for quite some time.

He was relatively confident that Carr was not at home – he had the top half of a large house at the foot of Primrose Hill, and the lights had been off since dusk had fallen three hours earlier – but he was also watching for signs of the police.

Even after a couple of hurried walk-bys – cap jammed down, scarf wrapped around his face against the chill night air – he'd seen nothing.

What he didn't know – what he couldn't have known – is that the Met and MI5 had a team in the area.

But unfortunately for them – and fortunately for Dessie Callaghan – they'd made an almighty cock-up.

Carr's flat was at No 12, but somewhere along the way, an extra '1' had been added to the surveillance briefing, and the Security

Service team leader responsible for the error had then gone off in a shift change.

So a dozen or more officers and agents were even now watching the wrong property, several hundred yards to the north and out of sight around a sweeping bend.

Dessie had spent some time pondering his options.

At 9pm – swallowing another Tramadol – he made a decision.

Police or no police, you just didn't get an opportunity to put an SAS notch on your gun barrel every day.

Time for action.

He walked up to the communal door of Carr's building like he owned the place, and rang the buzzer for the flat below.

# 73.

THERE WAS A BRIEF silence, and then a woman's voice answered.

'Hello?'

'It's John,' said Callaghan, standing to one side, away from the camera. 'From the upstairs flat?' Dessie could do a passable generic Scottish accent, and he was gambling on that and the distortion from the intercom speakers allowing him to get away with it. 'I've lost mah bluidy key. Any chance you could let me in?'

'Sure,' said the woman, and there was a buzz and a click.

Callaghan pushed at the door and it opened.

He stepped inside. Ahead of him were some stairs; to the left of the stairs was an internal door with a spyhole in it.

The door to the ground floor flat.

He walked towards it, stood to one side, and knocked.

Another momentary pause, and then the rattle of a key chain being undone.

The door opened.

A young woman – late twenties, big eyes, tousled blonde hair – was already talking.

'Do you want to wait here for the locksmith?' she said, 'because...'

And then she stopped, puzzled.

At the very moment she realised that the thickset skinhead with the broken nose standing in front of her was not John Carr, the thickset skinhead with the broken nose punched her hard in the face and knocked her to the floor.

And then Callaghan was inside the flat, slamming the door behind him, Glock in hand, aiming it first at the stunned and horrified woman, and then sweeping it around the interior hallway.

Finger over his lips to *shush* her.

A man appeared – the woman's boyfriend, husband, brother, who cared – and Callaghan stepped forward and cracked him on the temple with the butt of the pistol.

He went down like a sack of shit, and the woman started screaming.

Callaghan leapt on her and pushed her down onto the sofa, putting his hand over her mouth, cutting the sound off.

He waited like that for thirty seconds, all the time watching the unconscious man for signs of revival.

Eventually, the woman wide-eyed and gasping for oxygen through a bubbling nose, he hissed, 'Listen, if yous carry on doing that I'll have to kill you. But if you shut your gub I'll not hurt yous. Okay?'

She nodded, wide-eyed.

He released the pressure slightly; she gulped down air, but didn't scream.

'I'm serious,' he said. 'If you make one more sound I *will* fucking kill you, and I'll kill him, too. But if you play ball, yous're going to be okay. I've no argument with you, I don't want anything from you. Understand?'

She nodded again.

'Okay,' said Callaghan. 'I'm going to take away my hand now, and you're not going to say fuck all unless I tell you to.'

Nod.

He took away his hand.

The woman started crying gently.

Her right eye was starting to swell up, and there was a cut to her eyebrow.

'I want you to do three things,' said Callaghan. 'First, collect any mobile phones you have in the flat and bring them to me. Second, get some tape – Sellotape, masking tape, anything. The third is I want you get a plaster and some ice and sort out your eye. I'm sorry about that.'

Truth was he didn't give a shit about her eye, and he had no intention whatsoever of letting this woman and the unconscious man live any longer than was necessary. But he wanted to ask her some questions before he did what had to be done.

'What's the tape for?' said the woman.

Callaghan ignored her. 'What's your name?' he said.

'Daisy.'

'Him?'

'James.'

'Boyfriend?'

'Yes.'

'Pretty girl like you could do better than that,' he said, looking at her lasciviously. 'Anyway, I want the tape so's I can tape up James' hands and feet. When he wakes up properly he's going to be all over the frigging shop, and I'm going to need him to lie still and play nice.'

He looked at her face.

It was very pretty, but marked by fear.

He liked seeing fear in people's faces, and he especially liked seeing fear in the faces of pretty women.

But this fear needed controlling.

'Listen,' he said, 'if I wanted to kill either of yous I'd have done it, wouldn't I?'

At that moment James started to groan, and his eyes fluttered.

'Quick,' said Callaghan. 'Tape first, then phones.'

# 74.

THE CURRY HAD gone down well, and the three men had enjoyed their evening, Murphy and Carr telling tales from the old days and catching up, Johnson listening in.

'Fancy a nightcap somewhere?' said Carr, as he waved away Murphy's card and settled the bill. 'If you can call it a nightcap at nine o'clock.'

'Actually, I'm away up the road to have a late one with my brother,' said Nigel Johnson. 'He lives in Holloway, which isn't far away, is it?'

'Nah,' said Carr. 'Five or ten minutes. Do you want a lift?'

'Thanks,' said Johnson, 'but I'll get a cab. Actually, looking at the time I'd better get a wriggle on.' He stood up. 'John, it's been an education and a pleasure, and thanks for the curry. If you're ever over our way, next one's on me. Boss, I'll see you at breakfast.'

Handshakes all round, and the big sergeant strode from the restaurant.

'How about you, Kev?' said Carr.

'Ach, no, John,' said Murphy. 'Not as young as I once was, and I've a busy day ahead of me tomorrow. So I'll be away back to my hotel, if that's okay.'

'No problem. I might take your advice and book in somewhere myself.' He smiled. 'Not the Premier Inn at Edgware, though.'

'Sensible.'

'I must be getting old.'

'We both knew plenty who didn't get that chance,' said Murphy. 'So enjoy it.'

'I will, when it happens,' said Carr.

The policeman raised his glass in salute, and drained the last dregs of beer. 'It's been good,' he said. 'You must get over to see your goddaughter before I go to Canada.'

'Aye,' said Carr. 'I will.'

'Grand. Listen, where do I get a cab?'

'You'll not need a cab. I'll drive you. It's only twenty minutes up the road.'

Murphy argued the toss a little, but Carr insisted, so they left and headed for his Porsche Cayenne.

They chatted some more about the old days, and as Carr stopped at a set of lights a thought occurred to him. 'Hey, Kev,' he said. 'You still like your scotch, do you?'

'Aye, I do that.'

'I've got something for you back at my place,' he said, with a grin. He had several bottles left of a box of single malt from the Mess at Hereford, SAS label and all, and they made nice souvenirs. 'It's on the way.'

Murphy protested, but Carr waved him away and before long they had pulled into the Scot's street, and he was parking up near the flat.

'Wait one, John,' said Murphy, slipping into police mode. 'Let's just see if there's anything odd.'

They sat in the car for fully five minutes, but all they saw was the normal hustle and bustle of late evening in Primrose Hill.

Eventually, Carr said, 'Happy?'

'As I'll ever be,' said Murphy, and the two men got out.

# 75.

JAMES BALLARD WAS SITTING on the sofa, his feet and arms bound by half a large roll of Sellotape. He was also gagged. His eyes were open, but he had suffered a significant concussion and didn't have much idea where he was.

Daisy was also bound hand and foot. She had a sticking plaster over the small nick in her eyebrow, but she had not been gagged.

Callaghan was by the door, staring through the spyhole, and occasionally looking over at her.

'I want to ask you some questions about John upstairs,' said Callaghan, his eye focused on the communal front door. 'Is that okay?'

She nodded.

'But first I'm going to tell you something about him and me.' He paused for a moment, and tried to look as though he was dealing with unpleasant memories. 'John was married to my sister, and he beat her up. I mean, he *really* beat her up. So bad she lost her baby.'

Daisy looked horrified – the response he'd been hoping for.

If he could get her onside, it would make the whole process a lot easier.

'She's a mess. In the head, like. I've come to make him pay up for some treatment for her. Which is why I've brought this.' He lifted the Glock. 'To encourage him to get his wallet out.'

Daisy looked dubious. 'Why did you need to tie us up like this, then?' she said.

'If I'd asked if I could stand here by your door for an hour waiting for the bastard, what would you have said?'

She thought for a moment. 'I suppose you're right,' she said.

'How well do you know him?' said Callaghan.

She blushed, slightly. 'Not very,' she said. 'We bump into each other in the hallway sometimes.'

'What's he like?'

She looked over at James.

Then back at Dessie.

'I don't really know him,' she said. 'I've hardly spoken to him. But he seems friendly enough. Nothing special to look at.'

Dessie leered at her. 'You're fucking him, aren't ye?'

Daisy blushed again, this time properly. 'No,' she said. 'No, I'm not.'

Dessie laughed. 'Don't you fib to me, my girl. He's riding the arse off you, isn't he?' He chuckled, shaking his head. Then he was suddenly serious again. 'So where is he now?'

'I don't know,' said Daisy, trying to keep the embarrassment and anger and defiance out of her voice. 'Out, I suppose.'

'Where?'

'I don't know. Getting something to eat? At his girlfriend's? I don't know.'

'Has he a girlfriend?'

'Not a specific girlfriend,' said Daisy, shifting to ease the numbness in her legs. 'He has lots of different ones. I don't know any of their names.'

'Where might he have gone to eat?'

'There's so many restaurants. I don't know. I know he likes curry, if that helps.'

'Does he always stay here?'

Daisy thought for a moment. 'No, not every night. He's got a strange job. Something to do with security. He's away quite a bit.'

'For days at a time?'

'Sometimes.'

'When did you last see him?'

'This morning. He was going out for a run as I left for work.'

'Did he say he was going away?'

'No. But I'm only his neighbour. He doesn't tell me his movements.'

Callaghan looked at his watch. Just before nine-thirty. If Carr didn't come home tonight that presented him with a problem.

'So what do you do for a living, then, Dais?' he said, conversationally, eye back to the spyhole.

'I'm an estate agent,' she said, gabbling slightly in her eagerness to talk about something else. 'James is a barrister. Chancery law.'

'Ach aye, Chancery law.'

He hadn't a Scooby what Chancery law was.

'Yes, you know. Trusts, probate, that sort of thing.'

'Course I fucking know,' he spat. 'D'ye think I'm some sort of eejit?'

'No, no,' she said, trying to keep the desperation she felt out of her voice. There was a long silence, and then she said, 'I've just been given a big house to sell on Regent's Park Road. It's…'

Dessie zoned her out, humming the sad, lilting melody to *The End* by The Doors while he tried to work out how to play this.

His best hope of clipping Carr was to stay right where he was and wait until he *did* come back, whenever that was.

But what if the bastard didn't come back tonight?

He'd have to stay put.

So what did he do about Daisy and James?

He couldn't let them go into work tomorrow, and he wasn't going to trust them to call in sick.

If they didn't turn up for work, work was bound to ring them.

And when there was no answer – after a day, or maybe two – they'd send someone round.

Family or friends might come looking, too.

And eventually it would be the police knocking on the door, searching for a missing couple, and that was going to be awkward.

So…

'Can I get up, please?' said Daisy. 'I need to go to the loo.'

'No,' said Callaghan. 'I need to keep my eye on the front door.'

'Please?' said Daisy. 'I'll be quick.'

The gunman took a long look through the spyhole. *Better to keep the bitch onside for now,* he thought. *He's not going to come back in the next two minutes.*

'Quickly,' he said, striding across to her and helping her up.

'You'll need to cut the tape off my legs,' she said, apologetically. 'Otherwise, how can I…?'

He felt for his combat knife, and then realised he'd left it in the Mondeo.

'I need something to cut it,' he said.

'In the block on the kitchen work surface.'

Dessie crossed to the kitchen and switched on the light, and as he did so it crystallised in his mind.

Why was he trying to keep her onside?

Why was he even keeping them alive any longer?

He'd half been thinking of having a little fun with the girl, but the end game wasn't in doubt. He couldn't have them telling tales later, so they were getting offed.

Shame as it would be not to get to know Daisy a little better, the fact was she and the boyfriend were taking away his focus.

It was as he reached for the knife in the block – a smile just starting to play at the corner of his mouth – that he heard the lock on the main front door click open.

# 76.

JOHN CARR WAS a logical and sceptical man who liked to deal in hard facts and predictable outcomes, but his time at the sharpest end of the military had convinced him of the existence of something like a sixth sense.

It was very hard to define, and you weren't born with it, but you could learn it – usually through painful experience.

The best way he could explain it: it was the little voice in the back of your head that somehow told you which door the bad guys were hiding behind.

Trouble was, most people's heads were full of voices screaming that there were bad guys behind *every* door.

So the trick was to dial down the white noise and locate the signal.

And now, as he shut the front door behind him and followed Kevin Murphy forwards into the shared hallway, over the pizza leaflets and free newspapers, that familiar voice spoke to him.

Actually, it yelled.

From somewhere in the depths of his consciousness a thought exploded into his mind.

*He's here.*

*The fucker's here.*

Maybe it was the silence from Daisy's flat – the lights were on, but there was no TV, no music, no talking.

Maybe it was just plain old paranoia.

Or maybe it really was that elusive, indefinable extra sense.

But Carr knew it, as surely as he knew his own name.

He stood there, a few steps inside the hallway, holding his breath.

*Listening.*

And then, in front of them, he heard the click of the Yale lock to Daisy's door.

'Wait, Kevin,' he said.

But Murphy either didn't hear him, or misunderstood, and carried on into the hallway.

Then the door opened, and there was a man.

Big bastard.

Broad–shouldered.

Shaven head.

Busted nose.

Something black in his right hand.

*Pistol.*

*Dessie.*

Kevin Murphy saw him and reacted as brave men do, by launching himself immediately at Callaghan.

But he was older and slower than once he'd been, and although he closed the six feet between them quickly he was not quick enough.

Callaghan was able to raise the pistol and fire into the centre of the policeman's body mass at almost point-blank range.

One round went through Murphy's left arm and buried itself in the plasterwork of the hallway.

The second glanced off his sternum and ripped through his heart, stopping it instantly.

The last conscious thought Kevin Murphy had was a picture – dirty and fuzzy and slightly surreal, like a polaroid.

A family day out at Strangford Lough.

His children, aged about five and nine, holding their mother's hands in the golden sunshine, rippling water behind them.

Mary smiling at him, love in her eyes.

He experienced a sensation of great calm and happiness, and then he was gone.

But his dying momentum had driven him on, and now he barged into the shooter and knocked him down.

The pair of them sprawled on the floor just inside the downstairs apartment.

Although the dead weight of Kevin Murphy lay on top of him, Callaghan had a free shooting arm and a clear view of John Carr and of the front door.

Carr's sub-conscious mind had assessed the situation and evaluated his options before he even knew it himself.

Kevin Murphy was beyond help.

He couldn't stand where he was – Dessie Callaghan's eyes were fixed on him and the muzzle of the pistol was already moving off the floor.

He didn't have the time or space to get to the weapon before it was levelled at him.

And he couldn't go back out the way he'd come in, because that would give the shooter a clear view of his back.

He moved just as the pistol sounded again, the report deafening in this confined, empty space.

Dessie had snapped a shot, but the 9mm round whipped clear past Carr's legs, taking a chunk out of the wall and showering his feet in plaster and brick dust.

The Glock chambered a replacement round almost instantaneously, and Dessie's finger was snatching again.

But by now, driven by instinct, Carr was onto the stairs in front of him at an electric run.

Keys in hand.

His heart racing, but his mind icy.

Panicking got you killed, so he didn't panic. It was a simple equation.

Behind him, Dessie Callaghan had pushed Kevin Murphy's body off himself and as he was scrambling back to his feet he fired another un-aimed, opportunist shot after his target.

But it missed by even more, and now Carr bounced off the half-landing on the stairs and raced up the six steps to his own front door.

'You're a fucking dead man!' screamed Dessie, his voice an octave higher than normal through adrenalin, excitement, and fear.

Before the words had died away, Carr had his keys in the lock.

He heard Callaghan charging up the stairs as he opened the door.

He slammed it, but it bounced back and came to rest slightly ajar.

No time to go back.

Ran into his darkened bedroom and dived over the bed onto the floor opposite.

Reached under the bed.

Even former SAS NCOs are not allowed to keep automatic weapons in the UK, but they are allowed to own shotguns.

Carr had a very nice Beretta 687 EELL Classic – a beautifully-engraved, over-under twelve-bore which had been presented to him as a leaving gift from the lads in the Squadron when he'd finished as Sergeant Major.

He'd never expected to need it – other than for a bit of rough shooting, now and then – but his professional life had taught him to expect the unexpected, which was why he kept the Beretta loaded and lying under his bed, rather than locked away in the gun cabinet as the law dictated.

Better to fall foul of the cops than need a weapon and not have one.

He knew the Beretta was loaded, but he broke the barrel anyway.

In the dim streetlight streaming in through the window, he saw the brass heads of two cartridges, loaded one over the other.

Mammoth Magnum Lead. Double propellant, 12g, imported from the USA.

Lots and lots of stopping power.

He'd have preferred a few more shells, but two would have to do.

He snapped the weapon shut, slipped off the safety, then moved back to the bedroom doorway.

He got down on one knee, his body protected by the bedroom wall, and faced the main door.

The 7lb Beretta tight into his shoulder, he took careful aim along the length of the barrel.

His mind was clear and icy.

The tables were turned.

The weapon felt good in his hands.

His heart rate had now steadied.

He was back in his own world, playing the game of life and death, against Dessie Callaghan.

For one of them, life was now measured in seconds, not years, and Carr had plans for his old age.

He waited.

Counting.

Breathing, *Come on, you cunt.*

Ten seconds went by.

On the landing outside, Dessie had hesitated.

The first floor flat's front door was the breach – fondly known in the Regiment as the 'murder hole'.

It takes a special kind of man to step through a murder hole, and you can live or die by your actions.

John Carr had danced with that particular devil on many occasions, and the devil had always had his arse kicked.

That was because Carr knew what it took to breach successfully.

It took speed, aggression and surprise.

Dessie had lost surprise, and from the time it was taking him to come through that door it looked like he'd lost speed and aggression, too.

A creak.

That loose floorboard had annoyed Carr since he'd moved in, but DIY wasn't his strongpoint.

He'd never been happier about that than he was now.

Then a shadow disrupting the light at the base of the door

More hesitation.

The door started to open.

# 77.

BEFORE HIS RECENT encounters with Mick Parry and Kevin Murphy, Dessie Callaghan had killed four men, not the three for which the PSNI suspected him.

The RUC turncoat outside the Duke of York, Dessie had been part of a group which had seen its chance and taken it. Kicking that fucker's head in while hooting in joy had been a rare experience indeed.

Well worth every day of the sentence he'd served for it.

As for the others, in two of them he'd snuck up behind his victims and shot them in the backs of their heads, and in the other the fella had been lying in pieces in a puddle in Dunmurry, begging and crying like a girl.

The last thing he'd seen, this supposed OIRA hardman, had been big Dessie grinning down at him, finger squeezing the trigger.

They'd all been simple enough.

Dessie liked those odds just fine.

But it had suddenly occurred to him that when it came to entering and clearing rooms – particularly rooms containing nineteen-year veterans of the hated and feared SAS – he was some way out of his depth.

Things were not playing out the way he had expected.

He paused, his brain scrambled.

*Who the fuck is that guy I just shot?*

*Who knows.*

*Who cares.*

*I need to focus on this.*

Deep down, he wanted to turn around and go quietly down the stairs, and leave, and drive away, and never come back.

*But the shame.*

As against the respect.

The respect he'd earn from the other guys in the Vollie…

A vision in his head – himself, a Guinness in his hand, pressed there by an eager hanger-on, telling the bhoys once more how he'd gone right to the heart of the enemy to avenge his comrades.

Rod Stewart's voice entered his head, singing, *Going home, running home, down to Gasoline Alley where I started from.*

'Fuck off,' he said, aloud.

He felt the weight of the Glock in his hand.

*He's unarmed, Dessie,* he thought to himself. *Get a grip. The peelers could be here any minute. Let's get this show on the road.*

Imbued with a renewed confidence, he pushed open the door, raised the Glock, and moved forwards.

Unfortunately for Dessie, his expertise in this kind of thing was pretty much limited to what he'd seen in Hollywood movies.

He came through that door like the bald fucker in *Die Hard*, and, best will in the world, the bald fucker in *Die Hard* doesn't know what he's doing either.

Going through a door like that is a dance: there are steps you need to follow if you don't want to be caught wearing clown shoes.

The first step – the most basic rule of all – is that you move quickly to either side.

You get out of the doorway and clear the murder hole.

No-one had ever told Dessie that, and so he stood there, framing himself in the light from the hallway.

It cost him dear.

A split second after he appeared, Carr took aim low on the target, took up the first pressure on the trigger, and squeezed.

Dessie's mind registered a large flash from about fifteen feet away and the sensation of a giant sledgehammer smashing him in the balls.

Reflexively, his finger jerked the trigger of the Glock, the round ending up in the ceiling, as he was knocked halfway back through the doorway.

He found himself lying on the bright landing, his eyes temporarily blinded by the shotgun flash, the pistol knocked from his grasp.

Somewhere downstairs, he heard a woman scream, and then he felt an overwhelming pain in his groin.

Carr was up, out of the bedroom, into the hall and on top of Callaghan, almost before the wounded man had had time to work out what the hell had happened.

Keeping the Beretta trained on the IRA man's head, he checked for the Glock.

Saw it lying on the floor somewhere near Dessie's feet.

Slid it further away with his boot.

Not that Dessie had any use for it now. He was slowly curling up into the foetal position, both hands between his legs, and making a low, keening sound.

Carr placed the shotgun against the wall, leaned down, grabbed the gunman by his ears and dragged him bodily into the flat.

He switched on the lights.

He could see that Callaghan had already lost a fair bit of blood, and was turning pale.

His face was a rictus mask of shock and horror.

Carr punched him in the mouth.

'That's for ruining my carpet,' he said. 'And for Kevin Murphy.'

He punched him again, breaking his nose for the second time in a couple of days.

'And that's for Scouse.'

'Fuck!' said Dessie. 'Fucking mother of Christ!'

'She can't help you now, son,' said Carr.

Callaghan wailed.

'Who sent you?'

Callaghan mumbled something. Blood was pumping out across the floor, bright red from the femoral artery.

'Speak up!' said Carr. 'Who sent you?'

'Fuck off,' slurred Callaghan, teeth gritted, breathing hard.

Carr stood up and stamped down on his groin.

Callaghan screamed in agony.

'Your face looks swollen,' said Carr. 'Try this.'

He put his hands on the Irishman's face and pressed in as hard as he could. He could feel the parts of the broken cheekbone grating against each other.

Callaghan started crying, and then he passed out from the pain.

Carr slapped him and banged his head on the floor, and he came back round.

'Who sent you?' he said.

Weakened by loss of blood, Dessie Callaghan said something under his breath.

Carr put his head down closer to his mouth.

'Say again,' he said.

In that moment, Dessie realised that the pain was gone, and with it the fear.

In its place was a kind of calm.

He assumed that this must be because he was dying.

He smiled, somehow.

He had thrown the dice and lost, and that was how the game went.

But he was not going to go out begging for help.

'Pat Casey sent me,' he slurred. 'And there's plenty more where I come from. You're a dead man.'

He laughed, breaking into a rasping cough.

And then he propped himself up on an elbow and spat in Carr's face.

'You've actually got some balls,' said Carr, wiping the saliva away. 'Or you did have.'

Dessie sank back to the floor, muttering something.

'What's that?' said Carr.

'I said Crawfordsburn's a small place,' mumbled Dessie, with an evil smile. 'And your little girl's a pretty wee thing.'

'What do you mean?' said Carr, grabbing him by the throat. 'What the fuck do you mean?'

But at that moment Callaghan's eyes rolled back and he died.

Cursing him, Carr picked up the Beretta and the Glock, stepped over the dead man, and ran downstairs.

The girl in the flat below was sitting in her doorway, doing her best to cradle Kevin Murphy's greying head in her lap with her bound hands, and crying.

Carr knelt down, gently moved her hands, and felt for a pulse in his neck.

*Nothing.*

Turned Murphy's head to the light.

His eyes were open.

No reaction from his pupils.

'Oh shit,' said Carr. 'Kevin.'

*This is my fault.*

His head dropped, for a second, and then he pulled himself together.

'You alright, Daisy?' he said to the girl.

She looked at him, looked through him.

Almost catatonic.

294

'You're okay now. That guy upstairs... he's not going to bother us any more.'

He moved past her into her flat, found a knife, and cut her free. Then he did the same with her boyfriend, cradling their landline phone between his shoulder and ear and calling 999 as he did so.

Once he'd done that, he ran back upstairs to his flat, stepping over the prone corpse of Dessie Callaghan, and dialling another number.

It was picked up after three rings.

'Stella?' said Carr. 'It's me.'

'If it's about that ski trip, I...'

'No, it's not.' Carr was in his bedroom, and stripping out of his bloodied kit, and quick-changing, the phone held between shoulder and ear. 'Listen, love,' he said, pulling on a clean pair of jeans. 'Remember your neighbour? The old biddy who saw the guy in the blue car who was nosing about your house?'

'Rose? What about her?'

'You were right. He was RA. They've come over here for me, but they're looking at you and the kids as another way to get at me.'

'Oh, my God,' said Stella. 'What's happened? Are you alright?'

'I'm fine.' He was in the wardrobe, now, reaching for his grab bag, and checking that he had his phone, car-keys and wallet. In a few minutes, the police were going to be here and they'd be sealing off the building as a major crime scene, and he'd not be able to get back in. 'Never mind me, it's you three we need to think about. Pack a bag and get out of the house, right now. You and David both. Make sure you're not followed – you remember all the counter-surveillance stuff from before – and get yourself to a hotel. Somewhere a good way away. Call me and I'll pay. Tomorrow you both call in sick, and you stay sick until I tell you otherwise. Got that?'

'Why?' She was a tough girl, but she sounded shakey.

'Once the RA work out that your house has gone cold

they might try to pick you up at the Ulster. And if they can't locate you, they might try him. They follow him, they find you again.'

'But you and me's divorced. Why would they want to…?'

'Because they're evil bastards. Primarily, they'd want the kids. Especially George, if they find out.'

'Oh, God.'

'As soon as you're at the hotel, you need to call Alice and tell her she can't come over at the weekend like she was planning. Don't tell her why, no need to worry her. Make something up. George is in the States and then off to Kenya, so he's not a problem. I'll deal with him, anyway.'

'What about the police?'

'Don't say anything to them. You can't trust the PSNI.'

'Okay.'

'Got all that?'

'Aye.'

'Good girl. Now get that bag packed and get out of there.'

# 78.

THE POLICE AND paramedics were there not long afterwards, and, for the second time in the recent past, John Carr found himself sitting in an interview room talking to a pair of detectives.

They were as thorough as one would expect, but he told it pretty much as it happened, leaving out the fact that he'd kept a loaded shotgun under his bed. He knew the law, having been interviewed about many deaths in many different theatres: he showed them Kevin Murphy's Osman warning letter, told them about Mick Parry and stressed that he'd been in fear of his life.

'I'd just seen Kevin shot dead in front of me,' he said. 'This Callaghan guy was coming up the stairs after me. It was self-defence – I did what I had to do.'

The cops were happy enough with that.

They knew Carr's history, and they knew Callaghan's.

As far as they were concerned, the PIRA scumbag was just one more piece of human trash they didn't have to deal with.

The CPS duty lawyer agreed.

They released Carr, and he drove down to The Langham, where he'd booked himself into a junior suite – eight hundred quid a night, but Konstantin Avilov would pay.

He checked in, but he was wired and still full of adrenalin, so instead of heading to his room he made for the Artesian bar.

Despite the late hour it was reasonably busy, but he found a stool between a pair of women and a fat Arab, and ordered himself a large Glenmorangie.

He necked that in two swallows and ordered another, and, as the barman brought it over, the woman next to Carr turned to him.

'Well, you're thirsty,' she said, with a flirtatious smile.

She raised her martini to him by way of salute, and took a big slug.

She was American – Californian Valley Girl, Carr thought – mid-thirties, lightly tanned, and very good-looking.

And clearly pissed, or well on the way.

'I am,' said Carr.

'Makes two of us,' she said.

The woman on the other side leaned in and said something Carr didn't catch. Then she looked directly at him. 'So, I'm going to hit the sack,' she said. 'Nighty-night. You kids play nice.'

As she slipped off the stool and walked out, the first woman held out her hand. 'I'm Kelly,' she said. 'And you are…?'

'John,' he said, shaking her hand.

'John, huh?' said Kelly. She drained her martini and looked at Carr. 'So what does a girl have to do?'

He beckoned the barman over and got Kelly another martini, looking at her as he did so.

Good legs, nice clothes, silk blouse opened a button too low, and – by the way she was touching his knee – clearly interested.

'What brings you here, John?' she said.

'Business,' he said. 'You?'

'I'm a partner in a major US law firm,' she said. 'We're over here on a big merger and acquisition deal' – she slurred that slightly, Carr noticed – 'and it all got signed off today. So me and my friend Ellen were celebrating.' She took a good glug of the martini and looked at him meaningfully over the glass. 'This is my last night. Tomorrow I'm flying back to New York.'

She made a fluttering gesture with her free hand, the Cartier bracelet on her wrist glittering in the low light, and then let it rest back on his thigh.

Carr said nothing, just drank a little more whisky, enjoying the burn.

'How did you get that scar?' she said, looking at his chin.

'Long story,' he said.

'Uh huh. So, where are you from?' said Kelly. 'Your voice... Are you Irish?'

As she spoke, she wobbled slightly on her stool, and grabbed his forearm to steady herself.

'Oops,' she said, with a giggle. 'Pardon me.'

Carr looked down at her hand on his arm.

'Scottish,' he said.

'Well, I love your accent.' She removed the hand, took the olive out of her drink and popped it into her mouth, grinning at him. 'Bet you never heard that before.'

'Not often,' said Carr, with a smile of his own.

'And what line of business you in, John?'

'Security,' he said, drinking a little more whisky and looking into her eyes.

He could be in this bird's bed in two minutes, and inside her knickers in three, and he had a feeling it would be a thoroughly enjoyable experience. But...

It was as though she'd read his mind.

She threw back the dregs of the martini and slid off the stool.

'Security, huh?' she said. 'Well, I have an early flight. Maybe you could walk me to my room? You never know. I might need a big strong man to protect me.'

Carr looked into his scotch.

Then back at her.

She was certainly very fit.

'Here today, gone tomorrow, John,' she said, putting her hand on his left arm, and stroking his tricep.

He finished off the Glenmorangie, and stood up.

'Come on,' he said, looking down into her upturned eyes. 'Let's get you to bed.'

She led him to the lift, putting plenty into her walk.

'Fourth floor,' she said.

He pressed 4 and the car shot smoothly upwards.

A moment later, the bell pinged, and she stepped out. Taking his hand, she turned left and led him along the corridor to a room on the right.

He watched her open her purse and take out her keycard.

Put it into the slot.

The lock whirred, and she opened the door.

He could see a large bed, a black suitcase and various items of clothing on the floor and draped over a chair.

He hesitated.

'Okay, then,' she said, bending down to take off her heels. She looked up at him. 'Golly, you are big,' she said.

She grabbed him gently by the waistband of his jeans, to pull him into the room.

But he resisted.

'Listen, Kelly,' he said, 'I'm flattered. You're a beautiful girl. But I never like to take advantage of a lady when she's got the beer goggles on.'

She took her hand from his jeans and looked at him.

'Beer goggles?' she said.

'British expression. You've had a few, and you're not thinking with your brain. I wouldnae want you hating yourself in the morning.'

She smiled. 'My, my,' she said. 'An actual British gentleman. I thought they were like unicorns.'

'If you were around tomorrow I'd buy you dinner, and then who knows,' said Carr. 'But not like this.'

Kelly looked disappointed for a moment. Then she said, 'Wait here a second.'

He watched her walk into the room – wondering whether he wasn't making a big mistake – and over to the desk.

She bent over the desk, skirt tight, writing something.

Came back with it.

'If you're ever in New York,' she said, handing him a hotel letterhead with some scribble on it, 'look me up. I'd like to show you the town.'

He took the paper, folded it, and put it in his pocket.

'I'll do that,' he said. He bent down and pecked her on the forehead. 'You get yourself squared away, and have a safe flight tomorrow.'

He turned on his heel, walked back to the lift, and took it one floor higher.

Once in his suite, he dialled room service.

Ordered a burger and chips, fuck the fat and the carbs, a bottle of Evian, and a large Glenmorangie 25-year-old.

Rang back, made it two large Glenmorangies.

Rang back again, told them to bring the bottle.

While he waited for all that to show up, he unpacked his grab bag. His service life had drilled into him the importance of being able to get the fuck out of anywhere at a moment's notice, and so it contained spare toiletries, his passport, a thousand quid in cash, and a week's worth of kit. That amounted to seven pairs of Paul Smith socks and boxers, seven light blue Brooks Brothers shirts, two dark blue Hugo Boss sweaters and a dark blue White Stuff fleece, two pairs of Paul Smith jeans, a well-worn Triumph Bonneville waxed Barbour, and a pair of black Salomon Speedcross trainers.

He put it all away, neatly – something else the Army had drilled into him – and took a quick shower.

As he was stepping out, towel round his waist, there was a knock at the door.

He opened it, and a waitress pushed a trolley in with a large silver dome, a bottle of scotch and a bucketful of ice. Carr tipped her twenty quid, said thank you very much, pulled on his jeans and shirt, and sat down on the sofa in the suite's living room to eat and drink.

He clicked the TV on and flicked through the channels – late night news, cricket from somewhere hot, a film with Mel Gibson, a film with Keanu Reeves – and settled on an MTV channel with girls in bikinis gyrating around a pair of rappers.

Turned the volume down, ate his burger, drank his scotch, and watched the girls in the bikinis.

But all he was thinking about was Kevin Murphy.

What he was thinking was, *Poor bastard. My fault. We shouldn't have gone anywhere near my flat.*

He thought back to his first meeting with Murphy, way back in the early 1990s.

That business with Frank Boyd, and Kieran Devine and his mate, wasn't it?

Murphy had known that night that he owed his life to Carr, and, in turn, Carr had found the other man to be intelligent, honest, and trustworthy.

The relationship had quickly developed from there, and despite their different backgrounds and outlook they'd soon become close friends, to the point where Kevin had asked Carr to be godfather to little Siobhan when she'd come along.

Over the years, they'd spent many a night together in the policeman's house in Dunmurry, drinking Bushmills, putting the world to rights, and arguing good-naturedly about how to deal with the PIRA.

Carr was of the view that the Provos could be wiped out in an afternoon, if the politicians found the stones to order it. Murphy, a policeman first and last, had taken a less robust attitude, though in his heart of hearts he sometimes felt that the soldier was right.

There'd doubtless have been many nights in the future, too.

For it to all to end so suddenly …

*Didn't see that coming,* thought Carr.

Poor Siobhan and Liam.

He'd have to make contact with them and tell them that their dad's last evening had been good, that he'd been thinking and talking about them, and that he'd gone bravely, as he'd lived bravely.

Carr had seen too many good men die, in everything from freakish training accidents to the heat of mortal combat in Northern Ireland, in Sierra Leone, in Iraq, in Afghanistan, to let it affect him.

Or so he'd thought.

And yet he suddenly realised that he was bitter, and angry.

Mick Parry.

Kevin Murphy.

He'd never forget the military friends and comrades he'd lost, but they had accepted the risk, if not quite embraced it. They'd made a contract with death, and had been happy to do so.

But Mick Parry? No. He'd left all that behind. He was a van driver, for fuck's sake – a man about to walk his daughter down the aisle.

And Kevin Murphy? He'd been on the way to growing old, a widower who had devoted his career, his life, to keeping his streets and his community safe.

To have it all taken away by that worthless piece of shit…

It enraged Carr, to the point where the burger started to give him indigestion.

He put it to one side, half-eaten, angry at himself.

Angry at Dessie.

Angry at Freckles, whose bombs and guns had sent many men – and women and children – to their deaths in the name of a bullshit cause.

And angry – most of all – at Pat Casey.

Casey's brothers were murderers who had been righteously put down by men acting in self-defence. No right of vengeance arose from that.

Carr swallowed a big mouthful of scotch, and, as he did so, his mind went back to Callaghan's dying words.

*Crawfordsburn's a small place. And your little girl's a pretty wee thing. There's plenty more where I come from… You're a dead man.*

And he realised that Dessie was right.

Casey was a significant figure in the Republican movement.

The PSNI would get precisely nowhere, the Belfast *omerta* would see to that.

Probably wouldn't even nick him, and if they did he'd sit there with a Provo lawyer and a smile on his face, and say fuck all.

And then they'd let him go.

He knew John Carr's name, knew his address.

Knew his kids' home address, too.

*Plenty more where I come from.*

Carr could move to a new flat, sell the house in Hereford, run away and hide.

But eventually they'd find him – and, more importantly, he wasn't a man to run away and hide.

He hadn't wanted this fight – it had come looking for him.

But he was in it, and he had to win it.

It was just before 3am.

He polished off the half-tumbler of Glenmorangie and lay back on his bed.

He decided sleep was a good idea.

Not least because it might be in short supply in the coming days.

# 79.

CARR WAS BACK ON Pen y Fan twenty-five years earlier, struggling through Selection.

Scrambling up the scree in the pissing rain, bent double under his loaded bergen, blisters on his blisters, desperately fighting fatigue and burning lungs.

A few metres behind him, Geordie Skelton, blowing out of his arse, spitting and cursing and even giggling at the sheer hell of it.

That fucking racing snake Pete Squire half a mile ahead, gliding effortlessly over the rough terrain.

It was a dream Carr often had, and it was never pleasant – the endless hill sapping his energy and his spirits, and brutally smashing his hopes of passing the course, as his unconscious mind fought a hyper-realistic fear of failure.

His uncomfortable sleep in his strange hotel bed was interrupted at just after 7am by the sound of his mobile.

Head pounding from half a bottle of scotch, he looked at the screen.

A number he didn't recognise.

He answered anyway.

It was Nigel Johnson.

He sounded broken up.

He'd just left Charing Cross nick, where he'd been helping the murder squad detectives.

Carr agreed to meet him at the Riding House Café on Great Titchfield Street, a couple of minutes' walk away.

# 80.

NIGEL JOHNSON LOOKED a very different man from the curry house the night before.

He was a big guy, but he seemed suddenly weak and hunched and defeated.

Carr bought him a large Americano, and a tea for himself, and sat down.

'You okay, pal?' he said. 'You look like shite.'

'I just cannat fucking believe it,' said Johnson, shaking his head. 'I should have been there.'

'Then you'd be in the ground instead of Kevin,' said Carr. 'Or maybe with him. Trust me, I know. You can't think like that. It'll send you mad.'

There was a long silence, the detective blowing on his coffee.

Carr said, 'If it's any consolation, he died like a man.'

'What happened?'

'Dessie had taken the people below me hostage. We walked in, he come out with a weapon. Kevin was ahead of me, he saw him and went for him. Didn't hesitate. But...'

'Did he suffer?'

Carr clicked his fingers. 'Like that,' he said. 'He wouldnae felt a thing.'

'Dessie?'

'He chased me upstairs. Didn't know I had a shotgun.'

Johnson nodded.

Sipped his coffee.

Said, 'Ah shit. He was a good man. I *loved* him, you know?'

'Aye, I know. How long had you known him?'

'All my career, pretty much. Fifteen years. He knew my uncle, and when I joined up he took me under his wing.'

'*Knew* your uncle?'

'Aye. My uncle Georgie. My ma's only brother. He was a constable up at Dungiven – his da was in the Constabulary, too. The cowardly bastards killed him thirty years ago, near enough. Put a bomb under his car. My cousin Kathleen was with him. On her way to school, like. She lost a hand but survived, but my uncle...' He tailed off, had a swig of coffee and continued. 'Everything from the waist down was gone. He was in intensive care for three days, and then he...'

Carr waited a beat or two, then said, 'Did they ever get them?'

'Nah,' said Johnson. 'They knew who'd done it, right enough, but you know how it goes over there.'

'I do,' said Carr.

He looked at Johnson, trying to make a judgment about him.

Wondering whether he could trust the big policeman.

How much help he'd be.

*Fuck it. I've not done anything yet.*

*I can test the water.*

'Dessie's dead,' he said, 'but you know Pat Casey and his gang will walk away from this.'

'Aye. Probably.'

'How does that make you feel?'

'Angry.'

He looked it, too, thought Carr: his eyes were fathomless in a darkening face.

Irishmen were hard bastards, Carr knew, steeped in centuries of blood feuds, burning hatreds, and ceaseless war. Especially in the north. There was nothing quite like an Irishman with revenge on his mind, and he could see one in front of him now.

On the tip of his tongue was a question: *What would you think if I told you I'd like to get hold of Casey and his pals and fuck them up? I mean, really fuck them up?*

But then Johnson shrugged, and the anger softened into resignation.

'But that's the way it goes,' he said. 'If we start behaving like them, sure we're as bad as them. Right?'

# 81.

NIGEL JOHNSON LEFT at about 11am for his meeting at Thames House on Millbank.

He could have cancelled, but he was adamant that Kevin would have wanted him to carry on.

Once he'd gone, Carr made two calls.

The first was to an old friend from his days in the Regiment.

The second was to Oleg Kovalev.

They made an appointment for lunch at a very expensive restaurant in Mayfair – John's dad would have blown a mental gasket at the prices, and the food, but it was the big Russian's favourite place – and so it was that he found himself walking in there at a shade after one o'clock.

Oleg rose to greet him, a broad grin on his face.

'John!' he said. 'Is good to see you. Last time was not so pleasant.' An expression of regret settled over his features for a moment. 'Still, life goes on, yes?' He chuckled. 'For us, anyway. Sit.'

As they sat, a waitress appeared with water and menus.

Carr waited for her to leave, and then he said, 'So. What happened with the guy who ordered the hit?'

Kovalev picked up the menu and put on his Gucci reading spectacles. 'Let's just say, guy who ordered hit won't be ordering no more hits,' he said. 'Too busy watching his back for next fifty years in Russian jail.'

Carr winced. 'Rather him than me,' he said.

'I recommend miso blackened salmon,' said Oleg. 'Is beautiful. So, what this trouble you had yourself?'

'Some guy from the past tried to kill me,' said Carr, sipping his water. 'An IRA man. You know the IRA?'

'Of course,' said Kovalev, with a smile. 'We helped them out sometimes. Back in the day. You understand, John. When things was different.'

'Yeah, well,' said Carr, 'one of the people you guys helped out "back in the day" just killed two of my friends and tried to kill me.'

'I am sorry to hear that,' said Oleg. 'Genuine. Very sorry. You okay, though?'

Carr nodded. 'The Irish fella's not. I shot him in the balls.'

'Ouch,' said Kovalev, with a grin.

The waitress appeared, and took their orders.

Carr went for fillet, blue, despite the Russian's advice.

Then he said, 'So, is Konstantin back here next week?'

Oleg shook his head. 'No,' he said. 'Plan has changed. I just came to tidy up few loose ends. Konstantin is in New York right now, some business. I fly out there in couple of days, then we go to Aspen together for week of skiing. Boss was going to ask you to join us.'

'I can't,' said Carr.

'Oh?' said Oleg, surprised. 'Why is that?'

'Because I won't be around for a few days.'

'Vacation?'

'Not really,' said Carr. 'Business. Personal stuff.'

'How long?'

'A week. Maybe longer.'

'Konstantin will be sad about this,' said Kovalev. 'He just bought Aspen place. Fifteen million dollars. Beautiful skiing.'

'Another time, maybe,' said Carr.

The sommelier arrived with a bottle of La Mission Haut-Brion Rouge.

'As you requested, sir,' he said, showing it to the Russian.

'Thank you, Pierre,' said Oleg.

The sommelier poured, and the Russian tasted it and nodded. 'Very good year, 2011,' he said.

'I'll take your word for it,' said Carr. 'Far as I'm concerned, it's red or it's white.'

After the sommelier had poured two glasses and left, Oleg said, 'So, what is this personal business?'

Carr hesitated.

But not for long.

You didn't live the life he'd lived without being able to make a decision and carry it through, regardless of the consequences.

Oleg was cut from the same cloth.

He would understand, and Carr could trust him.

'I need to go over to Belfast,' said Carr. 'They won't stop until I'm dead, or they are. But I could do with your help.'

Oleg Kovalev spread his arms wide. 'John,' he said, 'you save my life. It's like Konstantin say. We are brothers. Whatever you want, if I can help you I help you.'

'There's a couple of things,' said Carr.

'I have all ears.'

Carr slid three items across the table – his iPhone, his keys, and a folded-up sheet of paper.

'First thing,' he said, 'is you delay your flight to join up with Konstantin for a few days.'

'Go on,' said Oleg.

'Second thing. My flat's closed off by the cops, but can you go up and sleep in my place in Hereford while I'm away? Use my car and phone. Do a couple of trips up and down the M5… That way, the phone looks like it's in my house every night, and the car's being picked up on ANPR during the day. Keep the visor down, wear my jacket, you'll be okay. And send a few texts to various people, including yourself. Don't take this personally,

312

but your English is shite. I mean, it's better than my Russian, but it's still shite. So I've written down a few messages on this sheet of paper, and who to send them to. They're all non-committal, won't involve getting into long conversations.'

'Very clever,' said Oleg. 'If police suspect you, they check your phone records.'

'I'll also need you to provide me with a physical alibi, so arrange a couple of business meetings for us. Out-of-the way places, where there's less CCTV. At night. Don't forget, you'll need someone else to drive *your* car and take *your* phone to make it believable.'

'Understood.'

'They're bound to look at me, and they'll do a cell site analysis. But if we're careful they may not have much else.' He paused. 'I just need to create a plausible alibi.'

Oleg sat back in his chair and swilled the heavy red wine around his glass, thoughtfully. 'So, no nightclubs, for a week. No fancy restaurants.' He raised his eyebrows. Then said, 'Okay. I can do this. I catch up on TV. What about your neighbours?'

'It's a big fuck-off house with a long drive and high hedges,' said Carr. 'No-one will see you.'

'Okay.'

'So you'll do all that?'

'Of course.'

'Thanks, Oleg. There's one other thing I need.'

# 82.

THREE HOURS LATER, in a quiet street in Brent Cross, at the foot of the M1, Carr opened the door of a black Audi A4 and slid into the passenger seat.

He took a moment to familiarise himself with the vehicle – cockpit drill, they called it, the instructors on his surveillance course.

He smiled to himself: some things you just couldn't shake.

Nearly three years old.

Nice dark colour.

Not too flash.

But four-wheel drive and a three-litre V6 engine, which would give him plenty of poke if needed.

He fished under the seat.

Found the key.

Pulled down the driver's visor.

A credit card, in a Russian name – Grigory Abramovich – with the PIN written on a Post-it note.

In the glovebox, a new burner mobile, and the log book and insurance cert for the car, which showed that the car was registered to an address in Watford in the same name.

He punched the stereo.

'Mr Abramovich' had left a CD in place, and paused on a specific track.

Adele.

*Skyfall.*

Carr shook his head and grinned.

'You cheeky bastard,' he said, to himself.

The Russian was a good man to know.

# 83.

GJERGJ LEKA HAD been in a bar in Coventry when his mobile rang.

Number withheld, but he took it anyway.

The only people calling him were people who wanted to do business, after all.

'Po?' he said, finger in his ear to block out the noise of the music. 'Yes?'

'It's Freckles,' said a voice. 'You sold something to my friend Mickey Delahunty, and he sent a man to collect it, yes?'

'Yes,' said Gjergj, his eye wandering left and following a young woman in a tight white dress. 'And?'

'The man he sent, it didn't work out well for him,' said Freckles.

'Oh?'

'It didn't work out well at all.'

Leka shrugged.

He got the Irishman's drift, but what business was it of his? This kind of thing went with the territory, after all.

'So?' he said.

'You need to be careful in case someone comes knocking on your door.'

'Someone, who?' said Leka, a note of derision in his voice. 'Police?'

'If you're lucky,' said Freckles.

'Ha!' said Leka. 'They already been. Asking questions. I did not say nothing to them. They find nothing. Don't worry, my friend.'

'When did they…'

But the girl in the white dress was back, and smiling at Gjergj Leka, and he killed the call there and then.

He was not a man to panic – not many Kosovan pimp-*cum*-gangsters are – and he wasn't very interested in what the stupid Irish had to say.

He was a hundred per cent confident that the Glock that he had passed on to Callaghan could not be traced back to him.

Its serial number had been ground off, and all original packaging destroyed.

It had never been fired before.

He had never handled it, nor the ammunition, without latex gloves.

The kind of people he dealt with, they would never tell the soft English police where they got hold of the things he sold them, and this particular one was dead anyway.

He held no stock at home: to all intents and purposes, he was just another hard-working Eastern European tradesman, who kept himself to himself, and had never got so much as a parking ticket.

So… pah.

Not my problemo.

Unfortunately, while Gjergj was a cruel and fearless man, he lacked imagination.

Specifically, he lacked the imagination to consider whether anyone other than the police might also come looking to talk to him.

That was why he was in bed, drunk and watching the TV, when John Carr let himself into the back of the terraced house in Coventry.

Carr had memorised the address when shown it by Kevin Murphy, and had been watching the house for several hours. It was always better to deal with one Kosovan than two, so he'd been happy to see Gjergj's girlfriend leave the house carrying an overnight bag, and happier still when she got in a taxi and left.

Off to earn her keep on the streets of the capital, by the looks of her.

The Yale lock had been easy to pick – Carr had been trained in the art during his time in Northern Ireland, and had covertly entered many houses and offices in his time – and now he stood in the kitchen, holding his breath and listening, allowing his eyes to grow accustomed to the dark.

Black clad, balaclava, thin leather gloves.

*Like the old days.*

Upstairs he could hear the muffled sounds of a television show, and regular guffaws from the Kosovan. The sink was piled high with unwashed dishes. The crusts from a takeaway pizza sat in a greasy open box on top of the fridge. There were empty bottles – Peja beer, vodka, cheap cider – littering the work surfaces.

*Let's hope he's pissed. Makes life easier.*

After five minutes, Carr slid into the living room.

A small black cat sat on the sofa and looked at him with mild interest.

Again, he waited and listened.

Nothing but the sounds of the TV and a laughing man.

At the bottom of the stairs, he paused again and reached around to his back, taking the extendable, hardened steel police baton from its pouch under his jacket.

He weighed it in his hands and slid it out carefully to its full length of eighteen inches, pulling on both ends to ensure that it was locked out.

Slowly, slowly, he started moving up the stairs, baton in his right hand, each step steady and controlled.

Enjoying the anticipation before the action, just as he had a hundred times – a thousand times – before, during his military service.

*Been a long time, John.*

At the top there were three doors.

Two – to the bathroom and the spare bedroom – were open, and the rooms themselves were clearly empty.

The third was shut.

He could hear the TV clearly now – some sort of reality show.

He took the door handle in his left hand and held the extendable ASP tightly in his right.

Then he opened the door quickly – and met Gjergj Leka coming the other way, on his way to the bog, one hand down his gaudy purple trackie bottoms.

No plan survives contact with the enemy, but at least Carr had a plan.

Whereas Leka was momentarily confused.

He stopped, his eyes wide and his mouth gaping.

Carr didn't hesitate, jabbing forwards with his left hand, fingers straight at Leka's throat, intending to incapacitate him.

But the Kosovan was no stranger to street-fighting, and had quickly recovered his wits.

He immediately dropped his chin, rendering the jab ineffective, and grabbed Carr's shoulders and pulled him close, trying to squeeze his arms shut and simultaneously to close down the distance between them to take the baton out of the equation.

He was ten years younger than Carr, and fit and strong, but Carr had three stones on his side, and a lifetime of combat from the backstreets of Niddrie to every war zone from Kosovo to Kabul.

He reacted on instinct.

Instead of trying to get free, he dropped the ASP and pushed forwards into Leka's body, using the momentum that he had created against him, and driving him across the room into the back wall with all his weight.

As he stumbled backwards, the Kosovan got one hand up around Carr's face, searching for his eyes.

Instead, he found his mouth.

Carr bit down as hard as he could, feeling the bones of the fingers crunch, and at the same time he put his right hand between Leka's legs and grabbed his balls.

He squeezed and pulled as hard as he could through the flimsy material of the tracksuit, maintaining the pressure, pulling viciously, ragging like a bull terrier on a rabbit.

Leka squealed and Carr immediately released his bite, knowing that the only thing that his opponent was worried about now was trying to free himself from the vice-like grip on his testicles.

As the Kosovan scrabbled for his wrists with his one good hand, Carr drew his head back and smashed it straight into the bridge of his nose.

That effectively put Leka's lights out, but as he slid down the wall Carr drove his right fist into the side of the semi-conscious man's head for good measure, swivelling his hips and putting every ounce of his shoulder into the blow.

Knocking him out cold.

The whole encounter had taken no more than eight or ten seconds, and – bar Leka's squealing – had been conducted in near silence.

Carr stood back, breathing heavily, and looked down.

Leka was groaning against the skirting board, eyes flickering, blood trickling from his nose and mouth.

# 84.

CARR GAGGED AND BOUND the Kosovan, turned the TV down and waited for him to wake up.

It didn't take long, and when he finally started to come round, Carr ripped off the tape.

The guy was still bollocksed – he didn't even yelp when the tape came off.

Carr got right up close to him, stared into his vacant eyes, and growled, 'I've come about that fucking gun you sold Dessie Callaghan.'

An innocent man wouldn't have known what the living fuck he was talking about, and it would have shown.

But Gjergj Leka was not an innocent man, and his reply – and his suddenly widened eyes – were all Carr needed.

'Oh, fuck,' said Leka, confused but just about together. 'Please! I give him...'

That was as far as he got.

He struggled, but Carr knelt across his chest and regagged him, and then dragged him downstairs, feet first, his head hitting every step with a hollow *thunk*.

There was a CCTV camera on the outside of the property, and it took Carr a matter of moments to trace its wiring to a small monitor in the kitchen. The monitor was linked to a hard-drive. He uncoupled it from the monitor and stuck it into his waistband.

Next, he made a quick but thorough search of the rest of the property until he was satisfied that there were no additional recording devices.

He looked at the semi-conscious Kosovan. Twelve stone? Thirteen, maybe? Nothing Carr couldn't manage. He pulled his balaclava up into a beanie, bent down and hoisted the groaning man onto his shoulder, and opened the front door. He poked his head out, ascertained that the dark, drizzly street was empty, and carried Gjergj to his car, where he opened the boot, dropped him inside, and slammed it shut.

Then he walked back to the house and went back up into the bedroom. He wanted it to look as though the target had left under his own steam; from the general state of him and the place, he didn't look the kind of guy to square his bed away before going out, so Carr left the covers where they were, picked up an iPhone from the bedside table, turned the TV off and went downstairs three steps at a time.

Pausing only to take a bunch of the keys which was hanging on a hook next to the front door, he left the house, closing the door behind him, and walked back to the Audi.

As he slid into the driver's seat, he looked at his watch.

The whole operation, from entering the house until now, had taken just over nine minutes.

He started the engine and drove south.

A minute or so later, the banging started.

Carr grinned to himself.

On the edge of the city, in a darkened street, he pulled over.

Got out.

Looked around.

No-one in sight.

He put a pin into the Kosovan's iPhone, removed the SIM card, and put it in his jacket pocket.

Dropped the phone to the floor and stamped on it, until it was completely destroyed.

Kicked the remnants into a drain.

Did precisely the same with the CCTV hard drive.

Got back in the car, turned round, and drove north.

Twenty miles into the journey, he wound down his window and flicked the SIM card out onto the road.

# 85.

TWO HOURS LATER, Carr crossed the Welsh border at Pontrilas, and entered the Brecon Beacons.

Almost immediately, he turned right towards Longtown.

Fifteen minutes later, a few miles along the winding, narrow road, and just back across the English border into Herefordshire, he took another right – this time, into a long private road. He drove on for a quarter of a mile, until he came to a pair of stone gateposts. He drove through them onto a sweeping, semi-circular gravel driveway, and halted at the steps to what could only be described as a small stately home – three stories high, and built from grey stone in the neo-classical Georgian style.

Its original owner had doubtless held balls and shoots for the local gentry there, in days of yore.

If there were any gentry left in these parts they were unlikely to mix with the current proprietor.

The year-old Land Rover Defender and the light behind the curtains in one of the downstairs rooms told him what he wanted to know.

He got out of the car and crunched across the gravel to the front door.

Three quiet knocks, and the door was opened by a man-mountain with a shaved head and a Bad Manners T-shirt.

'John,' said the Mountain. 'Good to see you, man.'

'Alright, Geordie,' said Carr, shaking the outstretched, shovel-like hand of Dave 'Geordie' Skelton, who pulled him close and gave him a bear hug.

'I've got that wee houseguest for you that I mentioned. Where's the best place to put him?'

'I've made his bed up in the stables over there,' said Geordie, nodding his head towards a low, brick building. 'I'll give you a hand.'

Together, the two men walked back to the Audi. Carr put on his balaclava and handed a second to Skelton – the Kosovan might have glimpsed his face as he was dumped in the car, but there was something disproportionately intimidating about masked men – and opened the boot.

He used the light from his phone to illuminate the interior.

Gjergj Leka stared back at him, his eyes wild and furious.

'Oh dear,' said Geordie. 'It looks like you've pissed yourself, mate.' Leka wasn't the biggest lump, and the big ex-SQMS reached in and dragged him out in one easy motion. 'Welcome to my humble abode. Let's get your head down for the night.'

Between them, they dragged the Kosovan into one of the stables.

In the centre of the uneven stone floor was a wooden pallet.

They dropped him onto the pallet and Carr held him down as Geordie lashed his legs to it, straight out in front of him, with plastic ties. Then they sat him up and pushed the pallet back towards the wall – though not too close. If he leaned back, he could touch it with his head, but that would put strain on his neck and shoulders. A classic stress position, and the start of the breaking-down process.

They stood back and looked at him. His eyes were wide and darting everywhere; clearly he was having a hard time working out how he'd got from his nice warm bed in Coventry to this place, wherever the hell it was.

Carr sat on his haunches and stared at Gjergj for a moment, and then he reached up and ripped the duct tape off his face, for the second time that evening.

This time, the Kosovan yelped, as stubble and the skin off his lips came away.

He started babbling in his native language, so Carr slapped him once across the face, hard.

He shut up and looked at Carr, his face a mixture of defiance and fear.

'Know who I am?' said Carr, eventually.

The Kosovan shook his head. 'Who gives a fuck?' he said.

Carr said nothing, but short-arm punched him in the centre of his grid.

Blood started flowing from his nose immediately.

The initiative regained, he started again. 'Know who I am?'

His eyes watering, Gjergj shook his head.

Some of the defiance gone.

'I'm supposed to be dead,' said Carr. 'The guy who was supposed tae kill me was going to do it with one of your guns. It didn't work out for him.'

The Kosovan shook his head. 'No.'

Carr nodded his, slowly. 'Yes.'

'But...'

'All I want to know is who sent him to you?'

'I don't know what you talking...'

Carr punched Leka in the face, harder this time, and felt his nose collapse

The Kosovan screeched, blood splashing onto his chest. 'You fucking *motherfuck*!' he shouted. 'I will fucking kill you and your family, I swear it!'

Carr laughed. 'Not you as well,' he said. 'Listen, pal, word of advice. Dinnae make promises you can't keep. As things stand, you're looking at a shallow grave in the woods somewhere. You might be able to talk yourself out of it, but I promise you one thing – you will not see tomorrow unless you tell me what I want to know.' He tweaked the man's bloodied nose, making him yelp. 'So you think about that for a wee while. I'm hank marvin, so I'm going to go inside, and my mate here's gonnae get me something to eat. Then I'll come back and you and me are going to have a proper chat.'

'I don't know what you talking,' said the Kosovan, again.

Carr sighed. 'Let's get a few things straight. I *know* you gave him the pistol. I *know* it was a Glock 17, brand new. I *know* what he paid you. He told me all this before he died. The one thing I don't know is who sent him. Whoever sent him put him in touch with you. So you're going to tell me who that was. And you *are* going to tell me. So you just stew on that for a bit.'

Geordie Skelton produced a hessian sack. Carr pulled it down over Leka's head and taped it tightly in place, checking that his hands and feet were securely bound. It takes a tough man to remain calm when his sight has gone and his breathing is restricted, and Geordie made it worse by turning to the iPhone attached to a pair of large Bose speakers on the floor of the stable.

The metallic thump of bass filled the air, loud enough to hurt Carr's ears.

'I hope you like this techno shite,' he shouted into Leka's ear, from an inch or two away. 'Personally, I don't.'

He patted the Kosovan's head and followed Skelton out of the stable, turning off the light off and leaving Gjergj to his own thoughts and demons.

'Still limping, you soft bastard,' said Carr, rolling his balaclava back up as they walked back across the yard.

'Fuck off,' said Skelton. 'If you'd shot that fucker on that job in Baghdad a bit quicker...'

Carr grinned. 'I was giving you a chance first,' he said, 'but you were too slow.'

They went into the house and down a long, red-flagged corridor to the kitchen.

'Grab a pew,' said Skelton, gesturing towards a large sofa next to a cream Aga. 'Drink?'

'Aye,' said Carr. He sat down on the sofa and watched Skelton rummage through a cupboard and take out a bottle of Scotch.

When he poured it, as ever, it was about three trebles in one glass.

'Christ,' said Carr. He took a sip. 'That's not bad,' he said, appreciatively.

'Japanese,' said Skelton. 'From Lidl. Hard to believe. Clever bastards, your Japs. Scoff-wise, chilli con carne is the best I can do for you, mate.'

'That'll be great,' said John. 'Home-made I assume?'

'Fuck off, Carr. What kind of bitch do you think I am?'

Carr chuckled. It turned to a cackle when Geordie opened his Smeg fridge. Skelton had fallen on his feet since leaving the Regiment, setting up a security business which he'd recently sold for many millions. He stank of money, but his short arms and deep pockets were legendary, and the extremely expensive refrigerator in his extremely expensive kitchen – designed by his then wife, who had soon become his ex-wife – was packed with Tesco own-brand value microwave meals.

Predominantly chilli con carne.

In fact, as far as Carr could see, *all* chilli con carne.

'You tight fucker,' he said. 'You never had any class, did you?'

'What?' said Geordie, innocently. 'I like chilli, and there was an offer on.'

Carr grinned and sipped his whisky as Skelton put a couple of chillis into a cheap microwave.

It pinged a minute or two later, and the Englishman handed a plate over.

'Come on then, man,' he said, as Carr started eating. 'What the fuck happened?'

Carr spent the next ten minutes outlining the events of the past couple of weeks.

After he'd finished, Geordie Skelton said, 'So that fucker supplied the weapon that the IRA used to kill an ex-Tom? And he's still alive *why*?'

'Do you remember Freckles?' said Carr. 'Real name Brian Keogh. Ginger hair. Armourer?'

'Aye, of course I do.'

'I'm ninety per cent certain that Freckles knows this Kosovan twat and put Callaghan into him. If I'm right on that it means Freckles is part of the hit. I need the Kosovan to confirm that for me. For bonus points, I'll get the name of any other contacts he has, and the location of his weapons cache, and pass it all to the Old Bill.'

'What then?'

'Then I'm going over there to sort the bastards out.'

'I meant what then for *him*.'

'I'll tell the cops where to find his weapons, and then I'll take him somewhere and cut the fucker loose.'

'You can't just let him go.'

'Why not? I don't need the heat, and he'll be a dead man walking. With the police all over his lock-up, there'll be a lot of nasty Kosovan bastards looking for him. Not to mention the Paddies.'

'That's a fair point,' said Geordie. He tipped back his whisky, with a bitter laugh. 'That's a very fucking fair point.'

Carr downed his drink, and wiped his mouth.

'Right then,' he said. 'Shall we see how good our friend's resistance-to-interrogation drills are?'

# 86.

NOT ALL THAT GREAT, was the answer.

In ordinary circles, Gjergj Leka would have stood out as a hard man.

He didn't impress Carr and Skelton all that much.

Mind you, he was tough enough that they didn't just kick the shit out of him.

Works with some people, not with everyone.

Carr was well-versed in the art of interrogation, and he knew that physical violence just gives some men something to resist.

A focus.

With those kinds of men, it's just counterproductive, and other, less messy ways work better. Carr and Skelton knew them intimately, having been trained to cope on the receiving end.

The first thing they did was turn on the light, click off the music, and remove the sack that was taped over Leka's head.

They wanted him to see what was happening.

They needed to get right inside his head.

Carr pulled his pallet round through ninety degrees and placed another one behind it, lashing them together with cable ties to create a flat platform.

'What you doing, friends?' said the Kosovan, nervously.

They said nothing, but forced him backwards and tied his

arms and wrists to the new pallet. Now he was lying down, and craning his head to watch.

Geordie Skelton walked outside and came back in with two breeze blocks, one under each massive arm. Carr lifted the foot end of the new platform, and Geordie slid the blocks under it. The Kosovan was now at an uncomfortable angle, the blood rushing to his head.

'What is this?' he said, a slight tremor in his voice. 'What the fuck is this?'

Geordie made a big show of filling two buckets of water from the tap in the stable and carrying them over to Carr.

Carr dipped a small hand towel into the water and started shaking it out.

Gjergj was struggling against his bonds in a way which made clear that he knew what was coming next.

'What the fuck you doing?' he was yelling. 'What the *fuck* you doing?'

Water-boarding will crack the bravest of men, and it only took two short periods – no more than ten seconds each – for the Kosovan to realise that he was in a hopeless position, at the mercy of these two crazy bastards.

Once he'd reached that conclusion, the dam broke and it all flooded out.

As with many such interrogations, once he started talking he couldn't stop, and in less than half an hour Carr knew that his weapons were stored in the attic of a rented house in a village not far from Coventry, and had the name and phone number of his contact in Coventry, the nickname of his paymaster in Belfast – it was indeed Freckles – and a lot more about his contacts in Eastern Europe.

He made meticulous notes, to be handed on to the right people at the appropriate time, until Gjergj was all talked out.

They knocked it on the head at 2am, and left the Kosovan

gangster well-secured and feeling very sorry for himself in the stable.

Back in the kitchen, Skelton poured the rest of the Japanese whiskey into Carr's glass, and dropped the empty into the recycling.

'I don't want all this,' said Carr. 'Especially if you've got none.'

But Geordie just looked at him and grinned.

Opened a cupboard door.

Performed a *ta-da* motion with his hand.

A dozen or more bottles, all the same.

A man of habits, Geordie.

'Your man out there in the stables,' said the big northerner, as he took one of the fresh bottles down. 'I wish we could have done that kind of thing when we were in. Fucking hell, it would have made life a lot easier.'

Carr nodded.

'Why don't you leave him with me?' said Skelton.

'You'll kill the bastard.'

'No, I won't. I'll dump him somewhere nice and quiet, well away from here. He probably doesn't know your name, but he certainly doesn't know mine. He doesn't know where he is. It'll take him a while to get home, and if he gets lucky and the Old Bill pick him up instead of the Kosovans then there's more distance between you and him.'

Carr thought for a moment.

'Sounds like a plan,' he said.

'So how you getting over there?' said Geordie, opening the second bottle and shooting a glug into his own glass. 'Birkenhead?'

'Nah,' said Carr. 'Cairnryan.'

'Lot further,' said Geordie. 'Six hours from here, and that's if the traffic's good.'

'True. But if I go from Liverpool it's eight hours on the boat instead of two. I'm going to want to stand out on deck, in the dark. I'd rather not do it all night.'

'Fair one.' Geordie poured himself a generous measure and settled down in his chair. 'Christ,' he said, 'we had some fun on them ferries.'

'We did that,' chuckled Carr.

Both men had travelled on them many times during their days in the Province with the Regiment, usually as part of a surveillance gig on some player who was heading over to the Mainland to chance his arm.

'Do you remember Dougie McHenry?'

'I certainly do.'

McHenry was a PIRA shooter who'd come over as part of a three-man team sometime in the early 1990s. It was a rough crossing, and unfortunately for him he was prone to seasickness.

He'd gone out on deck for a breath of fresh air, and never returned.

The *Belfast Telegraph* story the next day had told how the poor guy – a family man and well-known local charity worker, who was loved by all – must have fallen overboard.

And in a sense he had – helped by two plain-clothed SAS troopers who'd come up behind him, had a quick shufti around, and then hoiked the bastard over the rail.

'Remember what he said?' said Carr.

'I do, marra,' said Geordie, laughing. '"But I cannat swim ye bastards!" Poor old Dougie.'

'Famous last words.'

'His two gormless muckers walking round the boat looking for him,' said Geordie, shaking his head and wiping away a tear. 'Happy days. But Christ, we were naughty. If the Regiment had ever found out…' The big ex-soldier was silent for a few moments, and then he grew serious. 'Listen,' he said, 'why don't I come with you and watch your back? You're going to be very exposed over there. People keep telling me the Troubles are over, but you know better than that. Them bastards are still out there.'

'Thanks, mate,' said Carr. 'And if I was going to have anyone come with me it'd be you. You know that. Even with your gammy leg. But I can't drag you into this. In fact, you need to forget all about it.'

'You know it might go wrong?'

'I do. But when did that ever stop us?'

'What are you going to do about weapons?'

'I've got a plan.'

'And where are you going to stay? You don't want to show your face in a hotel, do you?'

'Got a plan for that, too.'

# 87.

BLACK JACKET AND PAT Casey were meeting again, with
Freckles along for the ride.

This time, with Dessie dead, they were being much more
careful.

Black Jacket had left home at 4am, at about the time Carr and
Skelton had finally put the whisky away.

He'd taken the A4 west to Fivemiletown and driving his sister-
in-law's car – he could no longer be sure that his own was clean.

What was normally a journey of an hour and a quarter had
taken twice as long because of the counter-surveillance measures
he was undertaking.

He'd driven halfway into Crocknagrally Forest in Tyrone before
parking up as deep in the undergrowth as he could, and he'd walked
the final two miles down a winding track, following the directions
which had been written on the inside of the Chinese takeaway
delivery leaflet slipped through his door the previous night.

It took him just over the border.

Casey and Freckles had spent the night visiting friends in
the Republic, and they approached the meeting point from
Knockatallon, sitting in the back of a borrowed van.

At just before 9am, Black Jacket climbed into the back of the
van and sat down opposite Casey.

'Are yous wearing a wire?' said Freckles.

'Oh, not this again,' said Black Jacket.

'He said, are yous wearing a wire?' said Casey.

'No.'

'Because if you are I'll have you skinned alive and salted like a fucking anchovy,' said Freckles.

'I thought you and my da' was pals?' said the Jacket, pleadingly. 'We go back, don't we?'

'*Are* you?'

'*No*. Why would I?'

'Men do stupid things.'

'I'm not wearing a wire. I'm on the same side as you.'

Casey looked at him, weighing him up. 'I think I'll have you checked first,' he said, eventually. 'And I hope you're telling me the truth.'

'Right,' said Black Jacket. 'Fine.'

The three of them stepped back out of the van, and a couple of men came round from the front.

'Strip,' said Casey.

'What?'

'You heard me.'

'This isn't necessary, Pat.'

'*Strip*.'

'Is *he* not having to?' said the Jacket, nodding at Freckles.

'He's the fucking armourer of the Belfast Brigade of the Provisional Irish Republican Army,' said Casey, through gritted teeth. 'So no, he isn't having to. Now, if you don't do as I fucking say right now…'

Black Jacket looked at him with a face like that of a spanked puppy. 'Alright, alright,' he grumbled.

Slowly, he removed all of his clothes, handing them to one of the two men, who felt everything carefully for batteries and wires.

He stood there in his pants and socks, looking in supplication from Casey to Freckles and back again.

'Everything,' he said, coldly. 'Shreddies as well.'

'Fuck's sake,' said Black Jacket, but he did as he was told and stood there, stark naked. 'Happy?' he said. 'Can I have my clothes back now?'

'They're clean, Pat,' said the man who had been checking. 'Well, considering,' he said, with a deep chuckle.

'Get dressed,' said Casey.

The Jacket hopped and stumbled his way back into his jeans and shirt, and was still doing up his laces as he sat back in the van.

'Can't be too careful,' said Pat Casey, by way of an apology. 'So what do the police know?'

'I'm working on it.'

'I thought we had volunteers in there? I thought we were *paying* people?'

'The investigation's all happening in England,' said Black Jacket. 'It's being split between the Met and Merseyside, with the counter terrorist people involved. MI5 too, I wouldn't be surprised. They're obviously linking the first soldier and John Carr, but all we're doing so far is helping out with background on Dessie. As far as I know, no-one's even mentioned you yet.'

'As far as you know?'

'I can't do better than that, can I?' He was almost pleading. 'I've got my ear to the ground.'

Casey looked at him, malevolently. 'Fucking Dessie,' he spat, bitterly. 'That fucking eejit. Send a boy to do a man's job, what do you expect. Got what he deserved. Mind you, it saved us the bother.'

'Will you send someone else?'

'No I will not send someone else. We got one, we'll have to make do with that.'

'Just be patient,' said the Jacket. 'Sooner or later they'll have to share more of what they know with our guys, because they'll want to dig up more on Dessie. When that happens, we'll be one step ahead.'

Casey snorted. 'First time for everything,' he said.

'Trust me,' said Black Jacket. 'Please.' He paused. Then said, hesitantly, 'One thing we don't know is whether Dessie told Carr anything.'

'If he'd told him anything, sure I'd have been pinched by now, wouldn't I?'

'Not necessarily.'

'Not necessarily?'

'I mean it could be worse than that.'

'Worse how?'

'I don't think he's the sort of guy to start telling the peelers what he knows. I think he's the sort of guy to come after you himself.'

Pat Casey was silent for a moment.

'I hadn't thought of that,' he said.

'If I can just say, Pat,' said Black Jacket, 'I think it would be a good idea to have a look at your own security. It never hurts to be prepared.'

Casey grunted. 'Has anyone told that halfwit Delahunty?'

'I rang him on Friday night, as soon as I heard,' said Freckles. 'And I spoke to the Kosovan straight after.'

'You rang him yourself? You didn't tell Mickey to speak to him?'

'You said it yourself – Mickey's a halfwit. I wouldn't use him for anything important. He's like my grandson, wit' the ADDHDD or whatever they call it. He cannat hold a thought in his head. I thought I'd better call Leka myself.'

'Will he say anything to anyone?'

'Gjergj? Not a chance. Sure, he wouldn't tell his mammy the time o' day. I've been dealing with him and his mates for twenty fucking years. I trust them like I trust you.'

# 88.

IN THE LATE MORNING, as Geordie made bacon sarnies and complained about his headache, Carr borrowed his laptop and did a little research.

He made copious notes until, satisfied, he closed the laptop.

Then he dialled a number on the burner mobile, being careful to block his own ID.

A girl answered.

'McGirks Lettings, Sonya speakin', how may I help you?'

'Morning, Sonya,' said Carr. 'I've just been told I'm being relocated to Belfast and I'm going to need a house. I wondered what properties you had on your books?'

'Oh, we've plenty. What are yous lookin' for, Mr...?'

'Miller. I'm bringing the family. I need a detached property with a decent garden and plenty of privacy. Within striking distance of the city.'

'That's grand. And what's your budget, there?'

'The company's paying, so I don't mind. It will need to be unfurnished, though. My wife will want to bring all of our own stuff.'

'Ach, I don't blame her. Much nicer to have your own bed and that, isn't it? So when exactly would you be looking to move in?'

'That's the thing. My first day at work there is on the third

Monday in March, but we'd want to get our furniture moved in over a couple of weekends. So I suppose a contract starting middle of next month?'

'Ooh, that *is* tight. You'll be needing somewhere that's already empty, then.'

*Already empty.*

The crucial part.

'Yes, I suppose we will.'

'Not a worry. We've a few places that fit your bill just now. Can you hold on a wee minute?'

Within five minutes, Carr had a list of five potential crash-pads and an appointment to view them with Sonya in a fortnight or so.

Geordie put a fat sandwich down in front of him.

'You always were a crafty bastard,' he said.

'You taught me everything I know,' said Carr.

He attacked the sandwich, went for a piss, and then gathered his kit.

Geordie shook his hand, looked him in the eye, and promised one more time not to kill the Kosovan.

And then Carr was in the Audi, down the farm track and away, game face on.

He was leaving himself plenty of time to get up to Scotland, time in the car which would help him to plan.

It helped to think of the whole thing in terms of a mission.

His objective was clear enough: to get to Pat Casey, Freckles, and their inside man in the PSNI, and neutralise them.

Logical thing was to start with Casey, whose identity he knew and whose movements he could discover, and work his way from there.

Carr wasn't sure yet how he was going to hit him, but one thing was for sure – there was no way he was going to walk the streets of Belfast without at least a pistol.

Geordie Skelton was right: if you believed the newspapers,

the Troubles were over, but the papers didn't know the half of it. True, PIRA was much diminished from its glory days, but there were various offshoots still active, and even those who had jacked it in... There were hundreds of men who would love the chance to take down an SAS man.

So, yes: he needed a weapon.

For personal protection, if nothing else.

He was sure Oleg could have helped him out, but it was just too risky to drive them over to Northern Ireland, what with random searches and sniffer dogs.

Which was why John Carr's mind was going back to a night twenty years earlier...

# 89.

## CLOWNEY STREET, WEST BELFAST
## EARLY HOURS, JUNE 27, 1996

01:00HRS ON A THURSDAY, in a muggy late June.

The junction of the Falls Road and Beechmount Avenue – known locally as RPG Avenue.

Coronation Street houses, with a rocket-propelled twist.

A dangerous, dangerous place in daylight hours – strangers stopped, searched and questioned by the local bhoys, and in serious trouble if they couldn't give the right answers.

People had been shot, nailed to floors, and beaten to death just for giving the wrong ones.

But now the street was quiet, with dawn still a couple of hours away.

Every man in a half-mile radius snoring in a drunken sleep, after the rare pleasure of watching those English bastards get kicked out of Euro 96 by Andreas Möller and his pals.

But something was afoot.

There were two or three unfamiliar vehicles cruising around, and something of an odd pattern in the traffic – not that the casual observer would have realised. In fact, a surveillance expert at the very top of his game wouldn't have put the pieces together, because the people involved were themselves the very best players around.

Presently, another car, a dark-coloured Vauxhall Cavalier, pulled over and two men got out.

Just a couple of mates who'd passed an evening together, and were now finishing the night and sloping off home to bed.

One, long-haired and slim, black Sisters of Mercy T-shirt, goatee, earring in each ear; the other broad and stocky, a fuller beard, dark jeans – not unlike Gerry Adams in appearance, now you mentioned it.

Both wearing black trainers and both looking like they needed a good wash.

One thing *neither* of them looked like was what they were.

Because they were both British soldiers, members of the Det.

Long days and nights spent operating in very close proximity to hardened terrorists, often alone, and with no immediate support.

Every single man – or woman – having put their hand up for this, well aware of the consequences of capture.

Not thinking too much about them, mind.

The front seat passenger leaned back in and spent a moment chatting casually with the driver. There was a chuckle, and a friendly slap of the shoulder, and then the Vauxhall departed back off along the Falls towards the city centre.

No-one saw the driver say, from the corner of his mouth, 'That's drop-off complete.'

The Gerry Adams lookalike – he was actually a six-year SAS veteran called John Carr, well into a secondment tour with the Det – looked at his mate.

Grinned, and – quietly, into his hidden mike – said, '19 radio check, toward RV1.'

*Rendezvous 1.*

A moment later, he and several others heard the response in hidden earpieces: 'All calls, this is Zero. 19 is towards RV1.'

The desk, acknowledging the call from the Operations centre,

343

miles away at a secret location on the south east side of the city – each phase of the operation being monitored there, at the Tasking and Co-ordinating Group at Knock, *and* by the hidden supporting team on the ground.

'Let's go, Steve,' said Carr.

They strolled down Beechmount like they hadn't a care in the world – though they kept to the shadows as much as possible, and their outward nonchalance hid minds that were working overtime.

Their senses only heightened once they'd turned left into Clowney Street, with its low ranks of brick-built terraces.

A full-ish moon, but a cloudy night, so no issues there.

The odd window was lit, though, and they were careful both to avoid the splash of illumination and to check for signs of life.

They walked silently on rubber soles, ears straining to hear any sound.

This was dangerous ground: enemy ground.

Truly, their lives were on the line.

But all was quiet.

Halfway down, they came to an alleyway which took you through to the next street, or left and right to the back-to-back gardens full of raggedy old sofas, rusty bikes and the occasional veg patch.

Whispering now, John Carr said, 'RV1 to FRV.'

FRV being the final rendezvous, the gate to the back yard of the target house.

'All calls, this is Zero, 19 RV1 to FRV,' said the desk, in his ear.

Down the alley.

Which was empty.

Left into the rat-run between the gardens.

Four gates down.

John Carr paused by the gate.

Heart rate slightly elevated.

Overhead, the clouds parted for a few fleeting moments, and he pressed himself against the wall to avoid the shadow cast by the two-thirds moon.

Whispered, 'At FRV.'

The moon vanished again, and both men waited in silence.

One minute.

Two minutes.

In the still night air, a distant car horn sounded and someone shouted something.

A few gardens away, restless chickens clucked in their coop.

Carr let his right hand drop to his waistband, and felt the reassuring presence of his Sig 226.

You never, *ever* wanted to fire a weapon in a place and time like this, because that meant things had gone to shit and your life was in extreme danger.

But it was better to have and not need than need and not have.

He put his hand around the pistol grip, and pulled it from his waistband.

Held it tight to his thigh.

Heart rate a little more elevated, now: this was an area of vulnerability.

This was not like a back alley in any other city in the UK. Here, in the heart of PIRA territory, if they were seen they were compromised.

And if they were compromised…

Carr looked at Steve.

Nodded.

Whispered, 'Towards entry point.'

The desk repeated the call.

He opened the latch on the gate – fortunately, it was recently greased – and stood to one side to let Steve pass.

Shut the gate.

Both men slipped across the courtyard.

A dozen silent steps and they were at the back door, in the shadow of the house itself.

Unseen.

They held their position and waited again.

Taking in the atmospherics.

The house was in darkness.

Two – no, three – doors down, a bedroom light was on.

But no-one looked out of the window, or any of the windows.

And why would they?

No-one had cause to suspect that this particular house would be of interest to the British Army, after all.

It was home to a Northern Ireland Electricity fitter and his lollipop lady wife, and – beyond a general dislike of prods and Brits – they had no connection to, or interest in, the 'armed struggle'.

*And yet.*

The biggest challenge for the Provisional IRA was in obtaining weapons; the second biggest was in hiding them away from prying eyes.

And by a very painful process of trial and error, they had become very creative.

Underground tunnels out in the southern wilds.

Waterproofed barrels in slurry pits.

Long-term caches laid in the foundations of new-build houses.

And others secreted in nondescript terraced houses in west Belfast.

With the knowledge of these locations kept to an extremely small circle, just two or three men, to avoid one arrest leading to the loss of everything.

The couple presently slumbering in the bedroom above John Carr's head were not long back from two weeks in Benidorm. Unbeknown to them, while they'd been sucking down sangria and giving themselves sunburn on the Costa Blanca, a brace of terrorists had entered their house and had hidden inside it a pistol and a long weapon, and a decent quantity of ammunition. There it would stay until such time as it was required; if and when that day arrived, the Northern Ireland Electricity fitter and the lollipop lady were in for a very great surprise indeed.

But if the owners of this house were completely oblivious to the existence of the weapons cache, others were not.

Army Intelligence had an exceptional source, a well-known Provo who went under the codename 'Catweazle'.

A key figure in the IRA infrastructure in the Beechmounts area, and a respected man amongst his peers, 'the Weasel' – as his handler liked to call him – was a man who, had he been a soldier of the Crown, would have been decorated for his sizeable contribution to the ongoing war against terrorism.

The Weasel had started out a true believer, and had never intended to help the Brits, whom he hated as much as the next man.

But we all have our weak points, and the Weasel's was in his personal proclivities.

It had happened late in the 1980s. He'd been driving to the bookie's with a smile on his face and a song in his heart, when, wouldn't you fucking know it, he'd been pulled over by the Army. What had at first appeared to be a minor ball-ache – though he'd miss the chance to get on the 3.50 – had quickly turned into something a lot more troubling.

The uniformed private who leaned in at his window was actually an intelligence officer working undercover – if you could get your head around that, and it had taken the Weasel long enough – and this had, in fact, been a pre-planned stop.

After a few moments' chat, the officer had reached inside his camo smock and handed over a slim file.

The contents of the file had left the Weasel drained of colour and feeling nauseated.

Four or five photographs of himself *in flagrante* with a young man in the public toilets at that park out at Mallusk.

High-resolution photographs, at that.

He was caught between marvelling at how the bastards had managed to take them, and wondering what would happen to him when the fellas found out. Homosexuality was frowned upon in his circle, to put it very mildly: the minimum he could expect was to be properly fucked up – like, a couple of weeks in hospital, and three months on crutches – and it might be a lot worse than that.

He was drowning in a sea of shite, and then the man from Army Intelligence had thrown him a rubber ring.

Working for the Army had not come easy, at first, but the money, and the protection, and the thrill of the risks he was running had all got mixed in together, and he had become extremely good.

Over the last few years, he'd helped to disrupt multiple operations against the security forces, leading to the recovery of numerous amounts of ammunition and weaponry, and the incarceration or death of several PIRA men.

Among the latter his own brother-in-law, who'd been shot like a dog by the SAS as he was about to fire an RPG7 into the rear of a police Hotspur on Fruithill Park.

Trouble was, the Weasel had been *too* successful.

Too many coincidences, too many times.

Too many botched operations where he'd been involved somewhere along the line.

He didn't know it, but the IRA's internal security team had been watching him closely, and – as John Carr and his oppo crouched by that back door at the rear of the house in Clowney Street – the Weasel had only a few days to live.

Not that that made any difference to the two Det men.

Steve was the entry man – trained to unlock locks and defeat alarms, he could have got you inside John Major's bog if required – and now he knelt down by the door, a set of picks in hand.

'At entry point, about to make entry.'

Repeated by the desk.

Steve made quick work of the mortice lock.

Behind them, a sudden noise – high-pitched, then a crash.

John Carr's heart skipped a beat.

A fucking cat, yowling, and then a bin lid.

'Entry complete.'

It had taken but a few seconds, and now they were inside the kitchen.

It smelled of fried food and air freshener.

Steve locked the kitchen door behind them, and both men stood there, pistols in hand.

Not moving.

Not even breathing.

Hearts thumping, listening for anything out of the ordinary.

If they had been set up – and it wasn't unknown – then this was when it would happen.

A minute went by.

Slowly, they exhaled and breathed.

Their eyes grew accustomed to the dark.

Two minutes.

Five minutes.

'About to conduct search,' whispered Carr, into his mike.

They moved quietly from the kitchen into the pitch-dark hallway.

The Weasel's intelligence was that the hide was under the floorboards in the cupboard under the stairs, but before they started looking they needed to clear the place, room-by-room.

So the next few minutes saw the two men creep through or into every room, until they found themselves back downstairs, having established that the only occupants were the fitter and his missus, and that both were deep in the land of nod.

There being no immediate threat, both pistols were put away and they got to work.

Steve took up a position with a view up the stairs, ready to whisper a warning if they stirred.

Carr opened the door to the cupboard and switched on a dim head torch.

'Thank fuck for that,' he said, under his breath. The small space was all but empty: a Hoover, an empty washing basket, a brush, and a stack of *Railway* magazines… Evidently, the man of the house was a trainspotter.

Carr took out a piece of paper and a pen and drew a quick orientation sketch, to show where everything was, and then began to remove the items.

Once everything was out, he felt along the top of the skirting board inside the cupboard.

Something gave on the section immediately to the right of the small door.

He pushed downwards, and the board popped up with a quiet *crack* which sounded to him like a rifle shot.

He waited a few moments.

No reaction from upstairs, so he prised out a two-foot section of skirting. That allowed him to remove the other two pieces and revealed that a new trapdoor had been created in the floor, with the hinges hidden by the skirting.

*Clever fuckers*, he thought. *Tidy work, too.*

He lifted the trap door and propped it back against the angle of the stairs.

In the low light from his head torch, he saw a black bag.

He reached down and…

A strangled *Psst*.

A noise from upstairs.

He clicked off the torch and then froze.

Out of the corner of his eye, he could see Steve pressed into the wall, Sig half-levelled, eyes up the stairs.

The sound of feet padding across the landing.

A bathroom door opening.

Silence for a few moments.

Liquid flowing.

Forever.

*Christ, he must have had a skinful.*

The bog flushing, muffled padding, a creak of bedsprings.

Silence.

Carr waited five minutes, maybe longer.

Then he clicked the torch back on, reached down and – very carefully, and slowly, to minimise the noise – retrieved the bag.

Opened it on the carpet.

There was a folded-up AKSU-74, and four magazines for the weapon, wrapped in a towel. Two pillowcases - one containing six twenty-round boxes of 7.62mm short rounds, the other a Browning 9mm Hi-Power automatic with three magazines and a hundred-odd loose rounds.

He confirmed the contents with the desk, and then began carefully photographing them, working methodically in the knowledge that the summer sun was on its way.

Eventually, job done, he replaced the weapons in the bag, and the bag in the hole, and put back the floor and the skirting.

Then – using his sketch – he replaced the contents of the under-stairs cupboard on top of the hide, and carefully shut the door.

Confirming his progress over the radio as he did so – 'Leaving target towards pick-up' – he crept back out to the kitchen, Steve following.

In a matter of moments they were through the door and out into the cool pre-dawn, and a minute later they had crossed the courtyard, and walked down the alleyway, and away.

The whole thing had taken almost exactly 180 minutes.

A few streets later, having conducted counter-surveillance, they were collected by a man driving a black work van.

Just two blokes heading off to start their day on a site some-where, as the first pink blush of dawn splashed across the sky.

# 90.

HE WAS NORTH of Stoke on the M6 by the time he had finished walking himself mentally through that night.

And, as he drove, Carr realised that the hairs on the back of his neck were on end.

The power of old memories.

For a moment there, he'd been back in that house, lifting those boards.

The reason he'd been revisiting that particular place in his mind was simple enough.

Three days after that late June operation, the Army source – the man codenamed Catweazle – had been taken from his bed by PIRA, gagged and hooded, and driven out of the city to Derry, well away from Belfast and those who knew him, under cover of darkness.

He'd been bundled from the car into a house on the Tullyalley Estate, and taken upstairs to a soundproofed room which was lined with plastic sheeting.

Never a good sign.

There, according to the intelligence, he'd spent the next five days being tortured to death in a metal chair which was bolted to the floor.

He was killed because the RA suspected – rightly, although

they weren't always right – that he'd been feeding information to the Brits.

During his torture, desperate to give his captors something, anything, to make them go easy on him, the Weasel had named several others as collaborators, including the two men who'd left the cache in Clowney Street.

With predictable and grisly results.

Once they'd killed Catweazle and the other two innocent unfortunates, the RA had written off those particular weapons as being compromised – they could never be sure that the security services were not watching the location – and too dangerous to retrieve. It was a no-brainer – they were not short of kit, thanks to Gaddafi and the Balkan connections. In any event, not too long after the raid the organisation had renewed its ceasefire, and then there hadn't been the need for them, anyway.

The only other way they'd have been removed, short of the householders accidentally finding them, was if the Det/SAS had been sent back in to Clowney Street to get them out. The Army never originated these jobs themselves, they had to be tasked, because the political and intelligence ramifications of such actions went well beyond the mere job in hand. The obvious choice for the job would have been himself and Steve, and – for the following eighteen months at least, before Carr transferred back to Hereford – that call had never come.

Why it hadn't come was anyone's guess, but it had been an extraordinarily delicate time, with the peace process motoring ahead and no-one remotely keen to rock any boats. Added to which, the TCG were always understaffed and overworked, with staff forever getting posted, or retiring, or dying, and its filing system – paper back then, and creaking at the seams – had been appalling, with files going missing on an almost weekly basis.

Crazy as it seemed, it was entirely possible that the whole lot was still *in situ*, and that only he and Steve remembered it had ever existed.

And Steve was a security man to the stars in Hollywood these days.

Only one way to find out.

And if the weapons *had* gone, then Carr would simply move on to one of a number of other possible locations.

# 91.

BY SEVEN THAT evening, John Carr had driven aboard the Stena *Superfast VIII*, parked up and made his way upstairs.

Baseball cap jammed down on his head, collar turned up, scarf on.

Heading straight out onto deck – cold as it was.

As he stood there, he tried to call Belfast to mind.

He'd not been there in more than a few years – the SAS had been pulled out in the early 2000s – but he'd spent what must have added up to years of his life in the place, and he quickly found that the mental map in his head was as good as it had ever been.

Allowing for a few demolitions, and new 'Peace Dividend' buildings here and there, he was confident he'd feel right at home.

It concerned him, a bit, that he'd be going in alone, with no back-up.

In the old days he'd always had a team around him.

Radios.

Helicopters.

Other soldiers watching his back, as he watched theirs.

But he'd always enjoyed a challenge.

And he had one thing in his favour.

Back then, he'd been a professional soldier, operating under the rules of engagement.

Constrained by them.

Now, not so much.

The people he was up against paid no heed to the rule of law; neither would he.

He hadn't asked for this shit: they had brought it to him and he was going to make them wish they hadn't.

Not long after he'd boarded, the throb of the huge diesels became more insistent, the screws began churning the black seawater, and the ferry moved slowly into the night.

And Carr turned his thoughts to killing Pat Casey.

The act itself would be easy enough.

The question was whether Carr wanted to spend the next thirty years of his life behind bars.

That basically came down to when and where and how the job got done.

The when and where parts of that equation were simple enough. Thanks to his political career, Casey's movements were easy to predict – he held regular surgeries, he appeared at public meetings, he travelled to and from Stormont.

What about the how?

Partly, that was dictated by what he was trying to achieve. Assassination is an art in itself. Sometimes you *want* the enemy to know their man has been hit – it's an act of terror. This was not one of those times. Carr wanted to kill Casey to avenge the deaths of Parry and Murphy, and end this, but he wasn't remotely interesting in sending any messages. He wanted the whole thing finished, and forgotten.

So ideally he'd make it look like an accident.

But to do that you need to get alongside your man, and Casey was bound to be protected.

If he couldn't make it look like an accident, what then?

A bomb? Carr was highly experienced in the manufacture and use of explosives, and it would have been a simple enough matter for him to improvise a small device, and make it look like it had been planted by some old Loyalist hand. But bombs were messy, and he couldn't guarantee that no innocents would be hurt. He also couldn't guarantee that he wouldn't start a whole new tit-for-tat war, and he definitely didn't want the heat that would follow such a dramatic assassination. Every piece of CCTV examined, every ANPR image of every car. Every spare PSNI body on overtime, spooks, maybe even his old Regiment... He'd prepared some sort of alibi, but he wanted to keep the odds as good as possible.

So a shoot, then? Assuming the pistol was still in place under the boards in Clowney Street, the actual killing would be a piece of piss. Pistols were always chancey – the short barrel makes accuracy a lottery, and he'd seen men miss a standing target at closer than ten feet in the heat of combat – but Carr had been one of the SAS's best shots. He knew he could do Pat Casey at twenty metres, maybe even twenty-five – though he was confident that he could get a lot closer than that at any one of a dozen locations, pretty much any day of his choosing. Just walk up to your man, pistol to the back of the head, single shot, good night Vienna.

Trouble was, then you were back to the heat that such a hit would bring. The shot would be heard if not all around the world then certainly in 10 Downing Street. The political noise, the press, the VCPs... All very bad news.

A knife? A 'robbery gone wrong' – the sort of thing they'd used against Mick Parry? It had a pleasant symmetry to it, but a knife meant close personal contact with the victim, which meant the possibility of DNA transfer in both directions. And then, walking down the street with a knife covered in blood...?

Pretty much the same went for strangling or clubbing Casey to death.

Carr stared at the black sea and pondered the problem almost all the way to the Northern Irish coast, and it was only as the ferry began to slow that he hit on the answer.

What if he could send everyone rushing off in another direction in the hunt for the killer?

*Misdirection.*

Carr smiled to himself.

It had a synchronicity which pleased him.

# 92.

HE DROVE OFF the ferry in Belfast and immediately headed south, to start looking at his list of 'rentals'.

He didn't stand out from the crowd, and he *knew* he didn't stand out from the crowd, and yet he couldn't shake off the feeling that he was being eyeballed from the moment he was off the ferry and onto the black tarmac.

Sure, it was probably paranoia. But paranoia had kept him and many of his friends alive over the years. The chances that any mates of Dessie Callaghan knew he was here had to be close to zero, but young men don't make old men if they don't consider the odds now and then.

So he took a circuitous route out of the city, doubling back several times through the Saturday evening traffic, and pulling over to the side of the road and stopping, just to check he wasn't being followed. It wouldn't defeat a trained and competent surveillance unit, of the sort his old mob could mount, or even the best the police could throw at you. But he was confident that the Provos had no such capability, and by the time he was heading to south Belfast on the A24 he was sure that he was not being followed.

The first two addresses on his list were impractical – both were jammed in close to neighbours, in well-lit estates – but the third was ideal.

A small former farmhouse on the edge of a golf course – the eighteen holes presumably cut out of what had once been the farmland – it had a longish drive and high hedges all around. And no alarm. The girl at McGirk's had assured him that the owner was prepared to fit one – and, at £1400 a month, so he should.

Carr could park his car in the streets nearby, approach on foot, and be almost certain that he'd remain unseen.

He went to the other two, just in case, but neither were as good as the little farmhouse.

So he headed back to that address and was inside in fifteen minutes.

Using what little ambient light made its way inside the building, he familiarised himself with the layout – though he'd be using only the upstairs toilet and one room to doss down in, he needed to know all the entry and exit points – and had a nice stroke of luck when he located a set of keys in an otherwise empty kitchen drawer. He could now lock the house up, and get in and out quicker and easier.

Most of all, he wanted there to be no obvious sign of his ever having been there. So he repeated a regular mantra to himself: *Leave nothing, wear gloves.*

Once he was satisfied that he could get out of the place quicker than anyone could get in, he lay down on the floor of his chosen room, head on his day sack, and tried to get a little sleep.

But his adrenalin levels were just too high, and eventually he gave up and lay there, waiting.

# 93.

JOHN CARR SLIPPED OUT of the farmhouse at just after 1am on the Sunday morning.

Waited in the shadows for a short while to see if anything stirred.

Nothing did, so he walked to the black Audi, got in, and drove off.

Found the Falls.

His guts tightening a little.

Every sense straining.

Unarmed, he felt highly vulnerable.

The streets seeming to shrink in on him.

Every alley, every privet hedge, every doorway hiding a possible threat.

He'd dealt with bad men and worse jobs in every continent, but nowhere felt like Belfast; he'd not set foot in the fucking place in a long time, but it still exerted a strange hold on him.

It was probably the weird disconnect between the outward appearance and the hidden reality.

In Baghdad, say, or Sangin, everything was alien, and it didn't seem all that odd that bad people wanted to kill you.

But Belfast could be any British city, with its Tescos and its pubs and its double yellow lines and bus stops and park benches – and, suddenly, a guy who looked like you, and spoke your language, and watched *Match of the Day*, and liked the same music, and drank the same lager, might seize his moment to shoot you, or bomb you, or stab you in the throat.

*Nothing personal, I just hate Brits.*

Yes, it was probably that disconnect, coupled with the legacy of his youth: Belfast had provided John Carr with his first experience of soldiering in the face of the enemy, his first taste of the business of death.

He had first gone there back in 1989 with 3 Para, on the tour when the incident that had started all of this had gone down, and he'd walked those streets on and off for the next decade or more.

Early on in DPM, with an SA80 at the ready, as part of many a Parachute Regiment patrol.

Later in civvies, with a pistol, working undercover with the Det, and with the SAS.

He'd spent more days and nights in this dirty, grey city than he could remember, or wanted to remember.

And when he wasn't staring at those graffitied walls and pacing that fag butt-Coke can-chip paper-and-dogshit-strewn asphalt, he'd been dug into hedges in cold, wet fields out somewhere in the green, empty, hateful cuds.

Always watching, listening, waiting.

People watching, listening, waiting for him, too.

He shook himself, turned into Clowney Street, past the hunger strikers' memorial, and the fading mural linking Ulster to the Catalans, PIRA to ETA.

Drove past the target house.

It looked to be in darkness.

*Promising.*

His instinct was to completely disassociate his car from the house, but this was not a military operation; he wanted it close, a lifeline for a quick exit from the area if things went wrong.

So he pulled into the first empty space at the intersection of Clowney Street and Ballymurphy Street.

Parked the car, locked it, and walked back down Clowney, and past the front door of the house.

He paused outside for a half-second – breaking every rule he'd been taught about surveillance, now – and saw no sign of life.

He continued down Clowney towards Beechmount Avenue.

Came to the alleyway which ran along behind the houses.

It was barred by a big, galvanised mesh fence and gate.

Seven foot tall, had to be.

Padlocked.

*Shit.*

*That wasn't here in 1996.*

He paused again, now.

Pulse hammering.

Same alleyway as all those years ago. But back then he'd had a Sig in his pants, Steve by his side, and a radio link to the TCG, and some of the finest fighting men the world has ever seen thirty seconds away.

Now, none of that.

He looked around himself. No-one in sight.

Over that fence and into that alley, and there was no turning back.

He almost walked away.

*Almost.*

Every challenge he'd set himself, he had met.

P Coy.

Selection.

Operations.

*Pull yourself together, John,* he thought. *Quitting's never been an option. You're not starting now.*

'Qui ose gagne,' he whispered.

Took a firm hold on one of the steel uprights and hoisted himself up and over in one smooth, fluid movement.

# 94.

HE ACTUALLY COULDN'T believe how easy it had been. Exact same lock, which was a piece of piss to pick.

All quiet upstairs.

The under-stairs cupboard had even less shite in it than it had last time.

He worked in complete darkness, by touch and from memory.

Holding his breath and gritting his teeth as he fiddled with the skirting.

Lifting the floorboards.

Groping under the floor.

He felt the bag, and – slowly, carefully, quietly – pulled it out.

He unzipped the bag and looked inside, using the lock screen from his mobile for light.

All still there, exactly as it had been left all those years ago.

He pulled out the AKSU-74: it felt good in his hands.

*Leave that where it is.*

*Get the Browning.*

He took out the pistol, and pulled the slide to the rear.

Placed it on the carpet.

Took out thirteen rounds and loaded the magazine, each metallic *snick* sounding like a handclap in the still darkness.

He picked up the pistol and gently inserted the magazine into the handle.

Allowed the slide to go forward under control, loading the weapon.

A light tap at the back to make sure it was fully home.

Dropped the magazine out and inserted another round into the top of the magazine and replaced it.

Fourteen rounds in total: the extra one doesn't sound like much until you hear the click of an empty weapon.

He put the Browning into his waistband, amazed at how different he felt now.

Then he hesitated.

*Who doesn't need an AK?*

*Fuck it, I'll take the lot.*

*In for a penny, in for a pound.*

With no need to photograph anything, and no need to worry if the householders woke up in the morning and wondered whether everything was exactly where it had been, he was back outside and walking back down the side alley fifteen minutes after entering it.

The reassuring weight of a loaded Browning Hi-Power tugged at his jeans, and the remaining rounds and magazines weighed down his coat pockets.

The AKSU and spare mags were in the bag over his shoulder.

He was trying and failing to keep the grin off of his face.

And then he turned the corner to the seven foot steel gate, and froze.

A few feet away, on the other side, two men – mid-twenties, both six foot tall and well-built.

Wearing T-shirts despite the cold, which was making clouds of their breath.

*Must be just coming back from a night out.*

*Shit.*

One of them about to turn a key in the padlock.

The other looking straight at John Carr through the mesh.

'Who the fuck are you, pal?' said the man, and his mate looked up from the padlock. 'And what's in your bag? Get your fucking arse over here, now.'

Carr said nothing.

Considered his options.

There were only two of them, and they were both shitfaced.

But he didn't fancy fighting two guys, shitfaced or not, in an alley in west Belfast.

He turned around, and calmly started walking in the opposite direction.

Behind him, the man shouted, 'You stop there, you fucking scrote. D'you know who I am?'

'Get the gate open, Gaz,' said the other man. 'The fucking robbing bastard's going to get away.'

Carr heard a curse as Gaz dropped the keys and fumbled for them on the floor.

He broke into a run, hoping against hope that the gate at the opposite entry to the alley would not be locked.

Just *knowing* that it would be.

Behind him, he heard the gate spring open and smack into the wall, and the slap of trainers on the damp ground echoing against the brick walls.

In the dim light of a streetlamp, he saw the other gate – chained and padlocked.

*Fuck.*

He gave himself three or four seconds until the first man was on him.

No way to get over it in that time.

Like it or not, he was going to have to fight.

Once you're committed it's all or nothing, and Carr was now focused on the violence that was about to happen.

He waited until the running man was nearly there, and then stopped abruptly, dropped down onto one knee, and bent his head.

At the same time, he released the bag in his left hand and drew the Browning from his waistband with the right.

In the dark, Gaz ran straight into Carr's back and went stumbling head over heels forwards, hitting the floor heavily and momentarily concussing himself.

Carr turned quickly, as the second man ran up, panting.

Not as fit as he looked.

*Good.*

The man stopped, briefly confused.

A low-level player in the Real IRA, he was used to getting what he wanted by intimidation.

What he wanted – and what he had been expecting to see – was Gaz kicking the shit out of the stranger.

But instead he saw the stranger standing in front of him, and no sign of Gaz.

And the stranger wasn't running any more.

He hesitated, and his hesitation was his undoing.

Carr moved quickly, driving his heel forward as hard as he could into the man's right knee, pushing all the way beyond the upright.

The knee joint is simply not designed for that movement and, under the pressure of all of Carr's weight, and his strength and aggression, it snapped.

The man collapsed, howling and vomiting up the kebab he had just eaten.

Carr turned.

Gaz had got back to his feet, and now he rushed towards Carr, swinging a haymaker at his head.

Carr ducked it, narrowly avoiding the blow, and stepped outwards and to the side, smashing the butt of the pistol into Gaz's temple.

He went down on one knee, stunned, and Carr brought the pistol down as hard as he could onto the top of his skull, fracturing it and knocking him out.

He fell silently forwards, smashing his face into the dirt.

The first man was still screaming, and lights were starting to come on in the houses in the immediate area.

Carr stepped forwards and stamped on his head, shutting him up.

Then he moved to one side, into the shadow of the wall, picked up the bag, and started to walk back in the original direction, the pistol in hand but close in to his thigh.

A garden gate opened to one side, and a man stepped into the alley.

He looked at Carr, looked at the pistol down by his side, and the two men lying prostrate on the alley floor.

He made the obvious assumption – that Carr was IRA, and the two men on the ground had been subject to a punishment beating, the poor fuckers – and nodded at Carr.

'Alright there, friend,' he said. 'I never saw nothing.'

He hurried back into the small courtyard of his house and disappeared.

Carr walked on, quickly, through the open gate at the end.

Smiling to himself, out into the street, and he was gone.

# 95.

THE KNOCK AT THE door was loud and firm, and Frances Delahunty heard it well above the sound of the lunchtime telly and the chatter from the grandchildren.

'Who's that now?' she said.

She wiped her hands on a tea towel and went to the door.

Through the obscure glass she could see two men.

*Jehovahs, probably*, she thought.

She opened the door, ready to tell them to piss off, but one of the men held up his hand.

Suited and booted, and holding something.

A card.

*A warrant card*.

'Mrs Delahunty?' he said. 'I'm Detective Sergeant Ross Vickery of West Midlands Police, and this is my colleague DC Grey. Is Michael Delahunty here, please?'

'Sure, he's not, no,' said Frances. 'He's away out for his pint.'

'Do you know where?'

'I do not.'

'Can we come in?'

'What's it about?' said Frances Delahunty. 'I've got family here.'

'Can we come in? It's freezing out here.'

'I suppose so,' she said, standing to one side. 'Come on through.'

She led the two detectives down the hallway and into the kitchen, her mental alarm bells ringing like Big Ben.

'So what's this about?' she said.

'When will Mr Delahunty be back?' said DS Vickery.

'Oh, in an hour,' she said. 'No more. He wouldn't miss his dinner.'

'And you don't know what pub he's in?'

'I wouldn't. He goes in them all.'

The two policemen exchanged looks.

'You and your husband own a few rental properties, is that right?' said Vickery.

'We do.'

'Can I ask you about a man who lives in one of your houses? A Kosovan gentleman, by the name of George, or Gjergj, Leka.'

'Well, there's a few houses,' said Frances Delahunty, trying hard to play dumb and keep her voice level.

She had no involvement in Mickey's PIRA work, but she knew very well what his Kosovan pal was about and inwardly she was cursing her husband. How many times had she told the daft fucker he was stupid to let a house out to the bastard? Let him find somewhere else to live.

Mickey had just laughed at her every time she'd mentioned it: sure, he was just Leka's landlord. There was no connection to himself if it all came on top, and the fella was guaranteed to pay his rent. What was she worrying about?

Well, maybe now he was about to find out.

'I can't say I know the name,' said Frances. 'Where's he live?'

'The Moorfield in Stoke Aldermoor.'

'Oh, aye, I know the one.'

'Mr Leka hasn't been seen for a day or two and his partner is most concerned about him. Apparently, it's very out of character.'

'And?' said Frances.

'And we want to find him. Can I ask, when was the last time you heard from Mr Leka?'

'Sure, I wouldn't even hardly know the fella.'

The police officer opened a document wallet and produced an A4 colour photograph of Leka. 'This is him,' he said. 'Does that help?'

'Let me get my reading specs,' said Frances. 'One second.'

She left them in the kitchen and walked into the living room.

Her daughter Emma was sitting on a rug, playing Lego with her young son.

'Call your daddy and tell him the polis is here for him,' hissed Frances, to Emma. 'Tell him they're asking about the Kosovan. Tell him the Kosovan's disappeared. Tell him my advice is to disappear himself.'

Emma nodded.

Frances picked up her reading glasses and returned to the kitchen.

Took the picture and peered at it for quite some time.

'No,' she said, eventually, turning her mouth down. 'Don't recognise him. But then, he's just a tenant. We've got twenty or thirty of them so...'

She tailed off for a moment.

'Look, I'm sorry, like, I'd love to help you, but I wouldn't know when I might have heard from him. They all pay by direct debit these days, out o' the housing, so it'd only be if we'd had a call for Mickey to go round to fix something. Even then, he usually sends one of the lads. I can have a look in our records and see what's in there, if you like?'

'Please,' said DC Grey.

Again, she left them standing in the kitchen and walked through to their little study, returning a few moments later with a large red hardback notebook.

On the cover was written in thick black felt-tip pen, 'TENANT BOOK'.

She put it on the kitchen table and looked at the detectives. 'We write everything down in here,' she said. 'In alphabetical order. Let's see.'

She quickly thumbed through the pages until she'd found the right one.

'Here,' she said. 'Okay, his tenancy started in July 2013. He's up to date wit' his rents. Mickey last went round in September to sort out a problem wit' the central heating boiler. We're holding a deposit for him. He came to us from a refugee hostel in Cheylesmore. We get quite a bit of business from the hostels. In trouble, is he?'

'We don't know,' said DS Vickery.

He didn't mention that someone had made an anonymous tip to West Midlands Police HQ early that morning, or that an hour ago officers had recovered two dozen brand new 9mm automatic pistols, six Skorpion machine pistols, a box of Russian military hand grenades, and some £40,000 in cash from the attic of a house in Meriden, a few miles west of the city.

Or that Leka's rented house was currently being gone through by forensics officers in white boiler suits, while his girlfriend sat in a cell at the city's main police station.

Or that her husband Mickey had been named as the PIRA connection to Leka, and that there were armed police in the street outside ready to nick him on sight.

'We'd just like to locate him. Which hostel was it, please?'

'The Carlton,' said Delahunty. 'It's in Poitiers Road. Just behind the community centre, there.'

'Yes,' said Grey. 'We know it. Thanks.'

Frances took off her reading specs and looked at the two policemen with a level gaze. 'Well,' she said, 'I'd like to help you fellas further, I really would, but I don't think I can.'

Vickery put the photograph back in the wallet. 'Can I ask,' he said. 'Do you or your husband have any friends in Meriden?'

'*Meriden?*'

'Yes.'

'No. Not that I know of. Why?'

'You don't own any property out that way?'

'No. Why?'

'Just wondering.'

'Are you aware of any criminality that Mr Leka might have been involved in?' said DC Grey.

Frances Delahunty tried to hide how flustered she felt. It wasn't easy, with both coppers now staring at her.

'No.'

'Specifically selling guns to people?'

'Guns? Oh my goodness, no. Listen, we run a tight ship. I'll get rid of him.'

'If we find him,' said Vickery. 'Do you mind if we sit and wait for Michael to come back home? We just want to ask him the same questions, really.'

'I suppose not. But I'm just doing dinner so you'll have to sit in the conservatory.'

She led them through to the back of the house, and as they sat down Ross Vickery's phone rang.

He listened for a moment or two.

Then he ended the call and – after Frances had left them alone – he turned to DC Grey and said, quietly, 'Leka's been picked up in Lincolnshire. Naked, battered to fuck, and bound and gagged in a ditch, apparently. They're on their way to collect him.'

# 96.

MICKEY DELAHUNTY HAD been drinking Draught Bass in the Town Wall Tavern in the city centre when the call came through from Emma.

He'd been in the middle of a story, with the lads all waiting for the punchline, but he just went pale, put his pint down, and left without a word.

His car was not far away, and he hurried to it, collar up, head down.

Then he thought better of it, and flagged a cab down.

Headed off towards the Foleshill area of Coventry, and St Joseph's, one of Coventry's bigger Irish clubs.

The cab dropped him five minutes later, and he hurried inside.

He walked through the bar, where a slack handful of middle-aged men were drinking and playing darts, and into the club secretary's office.

A fat man sat behind a desk, phone to his ear.

'Get off the phone, Belly,' said Delahunty, curtly.

'I've got to go,' said Belly, and put the receiver down.

'Give me a minute, would you?'

Belly left the office, head down.

Delahunty punched in a long number and waited.

After thirty seconds, he frowned and ended the call.

Frustrated, he punched in a new number.

Again, he waited.

This time, someone answered.

'It's me,' said Delahunty. 'Mick.'

'What is it?' said the voice on the other end.

'The fucking police are round my house,' he said. 'They're asking about me and the Kosovan. The Kosovan's disappeared, apparently.'

'Shit.'

'Shit's the word,' said Delahunty, sharply. 'First that dickhead you sent over, now this. I don't need this aggro.'

'Don't raise your fucking voice to me, Mickey,' said the man on the other end of the line. 'Know your place. The Kosovan's your responsibility. You need to find the fucker and deal with it.'

'Sorry, Freckles,' said Delahunty. 'But Jesus fucking Christ.'

'Why are they interested in you?'

'Fuck. I don't know. It's probably just to see if I can help them find the fucker.'

'I don't want the police talking to him and linking back to us.'

'No.'

'We certainly don't want that SAS fucker talking to him.'

'No,' said Delahunty. 'Shit. I'd not thought of that.'

'Like I said, Mickey, this is your responsibility. He's your man, on your patch. You need to sort this out. And if it comes on top for you, you take it like a man. Jail, whatever. You understand? You mention my name, or anyone else's, and you're a dead man. Understand? We can get to you anywhere, any time. Understand?'

Delahunty was silent.

'I said, *do you understand?*'

'I understand.'

'I've got to make a call or two of my own now.'

The phone went dead.

Mickey Delahunty stared at the receiver for a minute or more.

His reverie was interrupted by a knock at the door and Belly putting his head round it. 'Can I come back in now, Mick?' he said.

'No!' roared Delahunty. 'Get the fuck out!'

Belly beat a hasty retreat.

Delahunty pulled out his mobile phone and scrolled through several numbers. He picked up a biro and took various digits from each, combining them into a new number which he jotted onto a piece of paper. Then he dialled the number on the office phone.

After a few moments, another man answered.

A deep, guttural voice.

Eastern European.

'Yes?'

'It's me,' said Delahunty. 'We need to talk about your man, Leka.'

# 97.

FRECKLES HAD A FUNNY feeling that Leka had been taken by John Carr.

If he was right, he had to assume that Carr knew everything – the Kosovan wouldn't hold out for long just to protect a business relationship.

And Freckles had another funny feeling that Carr wouldn't take it lying down.

That was the trouble with the fucking SAS: they never knew when enough was enough.

Freckles hadn't stayed out of jail – or alive – all these years by being stupid or reckless, so he sat for quite some time, pondering.

He wasn't concerned for himself – if Carr came, surely he'd be coming for Casey – but he wanted to find a way to warn Pat that he might be in the picture.

He had to assume there might be people listening in, and so it was important to choose his words carefully.

He gave it some thought, and then he picked up his mobile and dialled.

Casey answered after a couple of rings.

'Pat, it's me,' said Freckles, conversationally. 'How're you doing?'

The mere fact that he was calling put the other man immediately on his guard, which helped.

'Not so bad, Freck,' said Casey. 'Yourself?'

'Very well. Are you at home?'

'No, I'm just round at my ma's, as it happens.'

'Give her my best, would you? Hey, listen, you know I was going to come round tonight? I can't. That thing with my lad turns out to be a bit of a problem, so I don't think it'd be a good idea to be at your house tonight.'

They'd made no such arrangement – in fact, Casey was due at a public meeting in the city between seven and nine – so he cottoned on quickly.

'Okay,' he said, guardedly. 'I hope everything's alright. With the lad.'

'Yeah, it'll all work out in the end. But I won't be at your house.'

'Shame. I was looking forward to it.'

'Yeah. I have a funny feeling our mutual friend might pay you a visit, though.'

'Really?'

Freckles could hear the sudden stress in Casey's voice.

'Well, it's possible,' he said. 'You never know.'

'True enough,' said Casey. 'I'll bear that in mind.'

Freckles hesitated, wondering whether to tell Pat Casey about the police and Mickey, but in the end he decided against. It wouldn't help him to know, and it could wait until they next met.

'Listen Pat. Look after yourself, yes?' he said.

'There was a long pause. Then Casey said, 'Aye. Well, I'll see yous when I see you.'

He put his phone down and stared at the wall.

He'd have to wait for a face-to-face with Freckles, but the message was pretty clear.

He dialled another number, and when the other person answered, said, 'It's me. I need to come down and stop at your place thenight.'

# 98.

ANY SOLDIER WILL tell you that hardest part of any operation is the waiting at the start line.

Doubts creep in, tension mounts, plans are questioned.

But John Carr had waited on too many start lines for too many signals to be affected by any of that.

He'd stripped and cleaned the Browning early on, and then he'd done the same with the AK, and he'd spent most of the rest of the day reading and dozing, keeping his adrenalin levels and heartbeat in check.

At eight o'clock, being careful to keep away from the windows, he stood up, collected his things, and left the farmhouse.

Pat Casey's wife had kicked him out three years earlier – his womanising having finally got too much after she caught him in the marital bed with his Stormont PA. The missus had kept the old house and Casey was living out on the western edge of the city in an executive home on a new-build estate.

Which was a win–win, for Carr.

He wanted his man alone; had he still been in west Belfast proper, where everyone lived on top of one another, and where suspicion and distrust of strangers was absorbed with mother's milk, then getting close to him would have been much harder.

By a quarter-past eight, Carr was out in the Audi, and driving past Casey's house.

It was in darkness, which he expected; Casey was scheduled to speak at some public meeting about education in the centre of the city.

Carr carried on past, parked in a parade of shops and walked back for another look.

Past the front, checking out the house and neighbours.

He was highly trained at the art of blending in and playing the Grey Man, and no-one paid him a mind, if they even noticed him. At just over six feet tall and weighing fifteen stones he was a big unit, but not so big as to draw attention. He was fitter and more muscular – a lot fitter and a lot more muscular – than most men of his age, but he was hiding that under a dark blue Hugo Boss jumper, a pair of jeans, and black Salomon running shoes.

*Pistol tucked into the front of his jeans, hidden by the top.*

Opposite Casey's house was a cut-through to the next street. The street lamp overhead was out, saving Carr the trouble of putting it out, so he walked into the alleyway and stood in the darkness for a few moments. Ideally, he'd have liked someone watching his back, but at least he'd hear the footsteps of anyone coming.

He stood light on his feet, ready to move on if anyone came.

But no-one did, and so he waited.

And waited.

Most people lack the patience for this kind of work. They get cold, and bored, and their feet start to hurt, and every little irritation is magnified, and the reasons to jack it in grow in number, and the voices in their heads keep telling them that they're wasting their time, and eventually they agree, and so they quit.

John Carr was not most people.

An hour went by.

Then two.

Occasionally, he had to move when people came through; he just walked the opposite way to them, purposefully, and recycled back to his observation point.

No movement at the house.

Still he waited.

# 99.

PAT CASEY WAS sitting on the stage at City Hall being lectured by a fat man about school meals for underprivileged children.

As a member of the Committee for Education at Stormont, this came with the territory, but he didn't mind admitting – to himself – that nights like this made him wonder whether going down the political route had been all that good an idea.

Yes, he got a salary and a pension, and some measure of respectability – though he'd never lacked for that in much of the city. He also got to sit inside the rooms where the key decisions were being made about the future of the Province. This was almost beyond price to the men who controlled him.

But, *Christ*, it was boring.

And on a bleeding *Sunday* night, of all nights.

Still, there was that curvy wee single mum sitting on the end of the second row who had been flirting with him. She'd suggested going for a drink afterwards, so as they could discuss her young son's special needs. Pat had reluctantly declined – Freckles' phone call had been unsettling, and he needed to get organised – but once this business was all done and dusted, the young mum would certainly be helping him with his *own* special needs.

He couldn't shake an uncomfortable sensation in the pit of his gut.

Clearly, Freckles had some intelligence about John Carr.

Maybe it was that the SAS man had crossed the Irish Sea, and was going to come calling.

He'd already put the word around among a few of the bhoys that they might be needed.

But he didn't know when, and he didn't know where.

He felt like prey and he didn't like that feeling at all. He was most unaccustomed to it.

He'd seen the surveillance photos of Carr, taken a few days ago in London, and he didn't like what he'd seen. He was a fit fucker, and broad and strong-looking. And his eyes... He'd been looking straight at the camera in one of the shots, and he looked ready to tear someone's head clean off.

What he'd look like staring at you with a gun in his hand... Casey shuddered involuntarily.

Maybe this whole fucking thing had been a bad idea?

Gerard and Sean were dead and buried, long ago.

Killing Parry and Carr wasn't going to bring them back.

But what was done was done. He sighed to himself, and tried to look like he was engrossed in the question of the allocation of free school meals to infant school children from deprived backgrounds.

All the while thinking about his contingency plan.

# 100.

CARR ALMOST MISSED him.

Two girls, arm-in-arm, giggling and gossiping, came bowling down the alleyway just before ten o'clock.

As with the few other people who had disturbed him, he quickly walked toward them, head down, and stood to one side as they drew level.

Most just passed by, but these two stopped, and looked at him.

'Sure, Robbie, what're ye doing out the night?' said one of the girls, flirtatiously. 'Does your wife know?'

'He'll be away up the Stag,' said the other girl, and they both cackled conspiratorially at that.

'Sorry, girls, but you've the wrong man,' said Carr, pushing past them, head down.

'You may not be Robbie, but you'll do for me, darlin',' called one of them, after him.

More cackles.

On the other side of the little gully, he carried on walking, to give the girls the chance to clear the area.

Then he circled back, crossing his fingers that Casey hadn't arrived and gone inside his house.

With a proper surveillance operation, this wouldn't have mattered, but he was one guy, with one set of eyeballs, and he had known from the start that it was going to take time, and would require luck and perseverance.

It was as he resumed his position just inside the alleyway that Pat Casey's car pulled onto his drive.

# 101.

THE THING CASEY missed most in the new era was the perks.

Sure, he'd never quite made it to the top – the old bastard had hung on, even when he'd gone doolally.

But there were still plenty of benefits which went with being 2IC of the Belfast Brigade of the Provisional IRA.

You got a taste of every bank robbery that happened, obviously.

You got a cut of everything that came across the border, too; he'd always had the latest TV, the latest gear for the kids, he'd never been short of booze or fags.

All FOC.

Rarely paid for a pint or a gallon of petrol.

And it might seem mundane, but best of all – apart from the regular supply of willing young women – had been the fact that he'd never had to drive anywhere.

It had felt like the absolute height of luxury to know that he could get steaming pished, any night of the week, and not have to worry about getting done for D&D.

Because the peelers would have loved that, alright.

If you couldn't get Al Capone for murder you got him on tax.

If you couldn't get Pat Casey for terrorism, you got him for littering, or parking tickets, or speeding, or anything.

Anything to make his life a little less comfortable.

The biggest embuggerance to the damned peace process had been in leaving behind a lot of those little treats.

He had at least to pay lip-service to democracy's bright new dawn, and to pretend that the old sectarian hatreds had been properly put away, and that the Republican paramilitary movement was no more. But he couldn't very well do that if he had a shaven-headed thug in a black jacket waiting outside for him everywhere he went. Everyone would have known what the *craic* was – even if they'd have believed he could afford a chauffeur on his Stormont wages.

So he'd got used to taking taxis – at least they were expensable, and he could always arrange one driven by one of the bhoys, current or past – or driving himself.

Well, all that was over now, and fuck what the voters thought.

After the meeting in Crock forest, the first thing he'd done was to get Paulie McMahon back on the job.

The cover story being Pat's back was playing up – he didn't want the Army Council asking any questions.

Paulie had been one of his closest associates for thirty or more years, and he was a great wheelman, a decent shot, and a genuine hardnut.

And it was Paulie who was at the wheel of the silver Volvo which now stopped on the drive of Pat Casey's house.

A loaded Taurus semi-automatic 9mm in the glovebox, for which he'd take the rap in the unlikely event that they got a tug.

In the darkened alleyway opposite, Carr frowned.

Held his breath.

His hand closing around the grip of the Browning at his waistband.

He had no intention of using the pistol, unless he absolutely had to, but it would help to persuade Casey to go along with him until it was too late to turn back.

Carr watched the Irishman get out of the passenger door and move away from the vehicle.

He grinned to himself: let him get settled in for the night, and then move in.

But then Casey stopped and returned to the Volvo.

Leaned in through the window as his driver handed him a phone.

Stood back up.

In the cold night air, Carr heard Casey say, 'No, don't worry, I've just come back to get my bag. I'll be here a minute, tops, and then I'm off to the farm. I cannat stay here, not till we know the situation.'

There was a pause while the other person spoke.

'No, I should have taken Maguire's advice. I don't like the fat bastard, but he's not stupid.'

Another pause.

'Okay, then, right yous are. I'll give you a bell when I get there.'

He threw the phone back into the car and hurried to his front door. The security light illuminated him as he fiddled with the lock and went inside.

Carr had two choices.

The first was to take Casey out here and now.

But the guy behind the wheel of the Volvo... he could be a government driver, or a legitimate high-end chauffeur. Carr didn't want to harm any innocents, and no-one who saw his face was living to tell the tale.

The second choice was to follow Casey.

He acted instantly, walking out of the alley like a man heading to the offie or the pub, and headed in the direction of the parade of shops, and his car.

He couldn't run, but it was cold enough that a brisk walk looked entirely natural.

He had to hope that he'd be quick enough to get back and tail the Volvo.

He wasn't.

He was only gone a couple of minutes, but as he drove back round to Pat Casey's street he saw that the driveway was empty.

He pressed on, hoping to catch him at a set of lights, or a junction, but there was no sign of the silver Volvo.

A couple of miles down the road, he pulled in to a layby, switched off the engine and closed his eyes.

*I'm off to the farm.*

He'd thoroughly researched his target, and Casey made a big thing of owning only one house, like the man of the people he was.

A friend's farm?

A relative's?

Had to be one or the other.

But where?

There were a thousand of the damned things within striking distance, plenty of them owned by Republicans.

Well, that made things harder, but not impossible.

Ultimately, if he couldn't discover the IRA man's whereabouts he could tail him from work.

But he was pretty sure he could find out from Conor Maguire.

*I should have taken Maguire's advice. I don't like the fat bastard, but he's not stupid.*

What was it Kevin Murphy had said?

*'Conor Maguire… head of force PR. He'd be my guess, out of the three. Strong Republican ties.'*

Not the most uncommon surname around these parts, but there was a good chance, wasn't there?

# 102.

OLEG KOVALEV SIPPED a very expensive brandy, mobile to his ear.

'Konstantin?' he said, in Russian. 'It's me. Listen, boss, I'd like to delay joining you for another day or two, if that's okay? I think our new brother may need a little assistance... No, it's just a feeling... Sure? Thank you. The Americans will look after you. Enjoy the snow, don't get too pissed, and I'll be with you very soon.'

Smiling, he ended that call and dialled another number.

Waited for the guy on the other end of his phone to pick up.

Eventually, he answered.

'*Finally*, Dmitri,' said Oleg. 'What kept you?'

'Sorry, boss,' said Dmitri Petrov. Sixteen years in the KGB, and now working for Oleg Kovalev and Konstantin Avilov. 'I was on the other line.'

'Okay. Now I have you. Where's my man?'

'Wait one second,' said Petrov.

Oleg heard the sound of a keyboard being tapped.

He could visualise Dmitri sitting at the desk in his flat in the Khamovniki district of Moscow.

Coffee in hand.

Three screens permanently on.

Everything humming with efficiency.

The guy was a machine.

'Ah, yes,' said Petrov. 'Here he is. Both he and the car are out to the west of Belfast, moving back in to the city centre. Now he's stopped.'

'Where's he staying overnight?'

Petrov gave him a rough address.

Oleg thought for a moment. Then he said, 'Listen, I want you to keep eyes on John 24/7. You'll need help, so get another couple of guys in. Don't tell them who he is, it's just somebody we're watching.'

'Okay, boss.'

'And I want you to set your system to send me updates – not grid references, street names – every fifteen minutes. His phone and his car. Night and day.'

'Got you.'

'Good man.'

'And this other man you want following, boss?'

'I'll call you with his follow details as soon as I can.'

'Okay.'

Oleg Kovalev ended the call and sat back in his chair, with his brandy. His window looked out onto Sloane Square, and for a few moments he watched shoppers and tourists and locals bustling to and fro outside.

'There may be troubles ahead,' he sang softly to himself, in English.

Knocked back the brandy. 'I hope you not getting yourself *too* much into troubles, Johnny,' he said.

But, just in case, it was time to book a flight to Belfast.

# 103.

CONOR MAGUIRE'S SLEEP had been fitful and plagued by nightmares for some days.

So he was snappy and irritable, at work and at home, and he'd been hitting the bottle hard to try and calm himself down.

Wife and kids getting it in the neck.

She'd tried to talk to him about whatever it was that was bothering him, but he'd brushed her off.

Not that he hadn't imagined the conversation with her many times.

*It's like this, love: for reasons best known to myself, I passed on the identities and addresses of two former British soldiers to the PIRA. One of the soldiers was then murdered. Then the other one, unfortunately, killed the hitman. Oh, I forgot to say – that second Brit soldier, he was a long-serving member of the SAS, so probably a bit of a handful. Now I think he might be on his way over here. What for? You know I'm not a betting man, but I should think it's to kill Pat Casey. And maybe to kill me, too… that's if the RA don't torture me to death for having the nerve to suggest the whole thing in the first place.*

Aye, Conor Maguire could imagine that conversation just fine, but he couldn't actually *have* it.

Which was why he was sitting in his armchair at home, staring into space, some crap on the telly.

Wife in the kitchen, putting away the shopping from her weekly trip to Sainsbury's.

Son upstairs on his PlayStation.

Daughter at the table doing her homework.

Everything normal.

On the surface.

He was trying to think his way out of this.

Coming up against dead end, after dead end, after dead end, like a rat in a maze.

The best he could hope for was that Carr didn't know his name, and that no-one would let on.

He was in way over his head, and he knew it.

He'd been happy to work for the Cause on the inside of the police – it earned him a little respect in the right bars, and, after all, it *was* the Cause – but there was a reason he'd resisted the lure of the PIRA.

That was that he was nobody's idea of a brave man, and could no more have shot someone or planted a bomb than flown in the air.

But organising fundraising events, offering moral support, providing information… that was a different matter.

It had all seemed a lot simpler a fortnight back, walking in to The Volunteer like the big *I Am*, with information that Freckles and the rest of them would have killed for.

He'd imagined himself as a Republican spy, doing the Lord's work behind enemy lines; he'd never be as celebrated as the gunman, but his contribution would surely be recognised in the right circles.

And then they'd gone and sent that fecking eejit, Dessie, and everything was going wrong.

He stood up, kissed his daughter on the head and walked into the kitchen.

'I'm away up the Glenowen for a jar,' he said.

'You alright, love?' said his wife.

He looked at her – sweet, naive, girl that she was.

Never a thought in her head about Brits and the Struggle and the sodding tricolour and a united fucking Ireland – she just worried about the kids and the mortgage and her job. She just tried to keep her husband happy.

And who was right, she or he?

'Aye, I'm alright.'

'You sure? You've been awful quiet and upset-looking these past few days.'

*It's like this, love: for reasons best known to myself, I passed on the identities and addresses of two former British soldiers to the PIRA...*

'Ach, work's just getting on top of me a bit. Don't worry, I'm fine.'

'Well, don't be too late, eh?'

'Sure, I'm driving so it's two pints, max.'

'Will I wait up?'

'You don't have to.'

'Okay, I might or I mightn't.'

He hugged her, pulled on his black jacket, and left.

# 104.

IT WAS A HALF-MILE drive to the Glenowen, where he could at least be sure of a Sunday evening chat with an old pal or two.

His mood lifted at the prospect.

He didn't notice the black Audi which was parked up fifty yards from his house, and which tailed him to the pub.

It carried on past, and then doubled back and parked several streets away.

# 105.

HE'D TAKEN A PUNT and had three pints – it wasn't too far, and the chances of getting pulled over and breathalysed were low, anyway – and his spirits had lifted a little by the time he left the boozer.

*Maybe he was worrying about nothing?*

If you thought about it, what did they actually *know*?

Okay, the Kosovan had disappeared.

But who said he hadn't gone on a bender, or hadn't shacked up with some other woman?

He tried to put himself in John Carr's position.

Why would he want to come to Belfast and take on the RA?

Surely he'd be more likely just to move to a new flat and hope it all went away?

He reached his car, zapped it, and got in.

Pulled on his seat belt.

Stuck the key in.

*Sure, that's what I'd do in his shoes. You'd have to be fucking mad to come over here and…*

That was when he heard the door open behind him, and sensed the weight in the car as a man from the shadows climbed into the back seat.

He felt something cold against his neck.

'Hello, Conor,' said a gravelly voice. 'My name's John Carr.'

'Oh, God.'

'This is a pistol. My finger's on the trigger, but I won't pull it if you do as I say. All I really want to do is talk to you. I know you're a family man. I'm not here for you. But I need your help.'

'Why should I believe you?'

'You're still alive, aren't you?'

Conor Maguire sat and trembled in silence.

'Now,' said Carr, 'I want you to drive out to Hannahstown. There's a little lane I know. We can chat there.'

Hands shaking, Maguire started the car, and turned left out of the pub car park.

A matter of minutes later, they were out in the Antrim countryside; after a mile or so, Carr said, 'Turn down there.'

A narrow, rutted track, hedges on either side.

Maguire hesitated.

'If you don't, I'll kill you,' said Carr. 'If you do, I won't.'

He did as he was told.

'Pull in there, engine and lights off,' said Carr. 'And keep your hands on the wheel where I can see them.'

Again, Maguire obeyed.

Carr lowered his window.

Black as your hat, except for the faint orange glow from the city behind them.

Cold air.

The ticking of the engine as it cooled.

Distant traffic.

Nothing nearby.

He waited a minute.

Then said, 'Why did you tell Pat Casey about me and Michael Parry?'

'I didn't.'

'Don't lie to me, Conor. Dessie Callaghan gave you up before I killed him.'

Maguire started crying, softly; it told Carr all he needed to know.

'Ugly fucker, Dessie,' said Carr. 'He didn't look any better with his bollocks blown off.'

He let Maguire snivel for a few moments.

Then he said, 'I just want to know why.'

'I don't know. It seemed like a good idea at the time. I didn't think he'd kill you.'

'If you lie to me we're really going to fall out.'

'Sorry.'

'You knew Casey would put a hit out, didn't you?'

Maguire nodded.

'Did you know Mick Parry had two daughters?'

'No.'

'One of them gets married in a couple of months. No dad to walk her down the aisle.'

Maguire started sobbing.

Carr waited for him to compose himself, and then said, 'I know Casey didnae put the hit out hisself. Too smart for that. I'm assuming it was Freckles?'

Maguire nodded.

'Real name Brian Keogh?'

'Yes.'

'I thought so. What does he look like these days?'

'My height. Pot belly. He used to have curly ginger hair, but he's going bald so he shaves it. His face is pink, like a… like a rat. Lots of freckles, obviously.'

'How old?'

'Sixties.'

'What does he wear?'

'Usual clothes. Jeans. A denim jacket. I don't know.'

'And where does he stay just now?'

'I don't know.'

'Come on, Conor, we're not playing games here. Don't lie to me. Because I know where *you* stay.'

'Honestly, I don't know. *Honestly* I don't. Somewhere in west Belfast, but I can't narrow it down. These guys, they don't advertise where they live. He'll not be on the electoral roll or the bills nor nothing.'

*True.*

'I can find out for you?' said Maguire, hopefully. 'Let you know tomorrow?'

Carr chuckled. 'The last man who took me for a fool wound up in rag order.'

'Sorry.'

'Okay, where does he drink?'

'He's in the Vollie most nights. On the Falls. And most dinner times, come to that.'

*Sounds about right*, thought Carr. *Pissheads, the lot of them.*

'What's The Volunteer like these days?' he said. 'Still full of players?'

'Not as many as used to get in. But there'll always be a few.'

'Will they search me?'

'I don't know. They might.'

'Okay. Do you have his phone number?'

'No.'

'Conor...'

'I mean, not *on* me,' said Maguire, frantically. 'I can't store it in my phone, can I? How would that look? Given who he is and where I work?'

'I need that number.'

'I'll have to call my wife.'

Carr thought for a moment.

Then said, 'Okay, you can call your wife. But be very careful what you say, unless you want her to hear you getting your brains shot out.'

'I will, honestly. Can I get my phone?'

'Carefully, and slowly, and remember I've got a gun at your head.'

Conor Maguire reached into his jacket pocket, pulled out his mobile, and scrolled down until he reached 'H'.

*HOME.*

Pressed the green button.

Waited for the connection.

In the dark silent night, Carr could hear it ring out.

Heard Maguire's wife answer.

'Hello?'

Tinny and distant, but clear enough.

'Hi sweetheart,' said Maguire. 'It's me.'

'Oh,' she said. 'Hi, love. Are yous on your way back?'

'Not just at the moment. Can you do me a favour, look in my little book and get me a number?'

'Surely. Wait a second.'

There was a pause while Maguire's wife went to locate the requisite book.

Then: 'Here we are, love. What number are yous wanting?'

'It's under N,' said Maguire. 'Should be down as Nicky. It's got a line through it, but you can still make it out.'

'Yes, got it.'

She read out the number, and Carr tapped it into his own phone as she did so.

'Is that it, love?' she said.

'Aye. It is.'

'Are yous okay? Only you sound a bit… funny?'

Car jammed the cold steel of the pistol harder into Maguire's neck.

'No,' he said. 'I'm fine. Don't worry about me. Give the kids a kiss for me.'

'The kids?' She sounded confused. 'Sure, it's gone ten. They're in bed, love.'

'Okay. Well, I've got to go. I'll see you later. I love you.'

She started replying, but Maguire had killed the call off.

He bowed his head, put his hands back on the wheel, and wept for a minute.

When he'd recovered, he said, over his shoulder, 'You're going to kill me, aren't you?'

'That depends on whether you fuck me about,' said Carr, calmly. 'Now...'

'Wait, wait,' said Maguire. 'That's not Freckles' number.'

'So you *are* fucking me about?'

'No,' he said, hastily. 'No, no, I swear. That's exactly why I'm telling you... Jesus, I cannat have an IRA armourer's phone number in my book, can I? I'm not that stupid. I've... I encoded it, a bit. Can you read me the number my wife read out?'

Carr read out the number.

'The dialling code?' said Maguire. 'The last digit should be a zero, not a nine. Then the number itself – take the middle two digits out and put them to the front.'

Carr did that, and read out the new number.

'Yes. That's it.'

Carr nodded in appreciation.

A little tradecraft.

In the dim light, he saw Conor Maguire's shoulders relax.

'I don't want you,' he said. 'I don't even really want Freckles. I want Casey. I went to his house, but he got away. Doing a runner, the coward. I overhead him saying he was away to some farm. Where would that be?'

'I don't know.'

'Why're you protecting him? Would *he* protect *you*?'

'No, he wouldn't,' said Maguire, bitterly. 'If I knew I'd tell you. I just don't know. I don't move in their circles. I see them out and about, but...'

Carr sat back and looked at the back of Maguire's head.

Thought long and hard.

He was wrestling with one question: Do I kill this fucker, or can I afford to let him go?

He'd been watching Maguire's house earlier that evening, and had seen his wife come home with two kids and a boot full of shopping.

Carr was not a heartless man, and he'd never even raised his hand to anyone who wasn't asking for it, much less killed them.

He had no desire to hurt an innocent woman or her children.

But the man sitting in the seat in front of him had started all of this.

He'd been hoping to engineer Carr's death.

And the odds were he'd been the one who'd identified Carr's own family, too.

Not to mention, could he trust Maguire not to alert Casey?

Could he trust him not to go to the police?

Fuck, it was tough.

'What's going on?' said Maguire, nervously, half turning his head.

'Eyes front,' snapped Carr. 'I'm wondering what to do with you.'

Thirty seconds later, he said, 'Okay. You left-handed or right-handed?'

'What? Left. Why?'

'And what's your favourite spirit?'

'What *is* this?'

'What spirit do you drink?'

'Whiskey or vodka.'

'Irish if it's whiskey?'

'Yes.'

'I guessed right. Now, I'm going to pass you through a half bottle of Jameson. When I pass it through, you're going to take your hands off the wheel just to unscrew it. Then you're going to put your right hand back on the wheel and you're going to use the left to put the bottle of whiskey to your mouth, and you're going to drink it.'

Maguire half-turned to look at him – the first time he'd done so. 'All of it?' he said.

'Aye.'

'That'll kill me.'

'It won't kill you, but it will put you to sleep. Half a bottle of whiskey'd knock a mule out, and by the time you wake up you'll not be sure if this was a dream or a nightmare, or what. In the meantime, I can take my leave knowing you'll not be following me or phoning no-one.'

'Really? That's it?'

The relief in his voice was palpable.

'No. If you call Casey or Freckles or anyone else, police included, you're a dead man. I know where you live, and I'm not working alone. Even if someone gets to me, you're not safe. Understood?'

'Yes, yes, understood. I'll not say nothing to no-one.'

'Right. Here you go.'

Maguire took the half bottle from Carr's gloved hand, and did as he was told.

It took him five minutes to finish the whole thing, and he was gagging by the end.

In the dim light, Carr watched the spirit take effect.

On top of three pints, it was quick and it was massive.

Inside ten minutes, Maguire was incapably drunk.

'Jeeessush,' he said, head lolling forward.

He mumbled incoherently for a few moments.

Carr got out of the car and opened the driver's door.

'Put your hands back on the steering wheel,' he said.

'Wha' the fuck?' slurred Maguire. 'Why?'

'I just want to secure you. I can't afford to have you wandering around drunk, Conor.'

Squinting, Maguire put his hands at ten to two.

Carr took two sets of plasticuffs from his pockets and quickly lashed Maguire's hands to the wheel, over the thick leather of his black jacket, tight enough to restrain him, but not to leave marks.

The Irishman hardly noticed.

Then Carr reached into his bag.

Took out a roll of cling film and started to wind it around Maguire's head and face.

He had completed three or four turns before the other man even realised what was happening.

Maguire started grunting and thrashing in panic, but Carr restrained him; it was easy enough, given his weakened, drunken state.

After sixty seconds, Maguire puked.

With his mouth sealed, he began drowning in his own vomit.

With that and the lack of oxygen, he was quickly unconscious.

Carr stood back from the car, and the smell of urine and faeces and vomit, and waited for nearly fifteen minutes, listening for any approaching wheels or feet.

Then he reached into his pocket and took out a Leatherman. He snipped both sets of plasticuffs and placed them in a carrier bag. He then slowly unwound the cling film and placed that into the same bag.

Placed the bag in his pocket.

Wound up the back window.

Made sure he'd left nothing behind.

Reclined Maguire's seat as far as it would go.

Put the empty Jameson bottle in his hand.

Closed his door.

Just another drunk who drove out here to drown his sorrows, fell asleep, and choked on his own puke.

Carr walked smartly away, keeping to the shadows.

Two miles to his own car.

He had not enjoyed his evening's work, and he felt truly sorry for Conor Maguire's family.

But it had had to be done.

By the time he reached the vehicle, John Carr had put it far to the back of his mind.

*Now for Freckles.*

# 106.

OLEG KOVALEV'S REDEYE flight landed in Belfast at just gone eight o'clock on the Monday morning.

He was never at his best early on, and he was glad to get out of the terminal so that he could suck down a Winston and breathe in some fresh diesel and kerosene fumes.

It reminded him of home.

He ground the butt of the cigarette into the pavement and climbed into a taxi.

And then he was on his way to the Europa.

The irony amused him; it was supposedly Europe's most-bombed hotel – though he suspected there were better contenders for that title in the Ukraine and the Balkans – and he'd almost certainly assisted the bombers during his KGB days.

But as he was whisked through the streets the smile slid off his face and was replaced by a thoughtful expression.

He knew John Carr well enough to know that Carr didn't want help.

When men like John Carr said *No, I'm going to do this on my own,* you were supposed to leave them to it.

But he also knew that even men like Carr could make mistakes, could misjudge the odds, could wind up in trouble.

He liked Carr, he owed Carr, and he was going to help Carr as best he could.

His plan was by no means foolproof.

First off, he couldn't follow Carr around. Carr was trained in counter-surveillance, and in Belfast he'd have his eyes out on stalks. Oleg was good, but it just wasn't possible for one man to trail a guy like that and not get made.

So he'd solved that with trackers in the car and phone he'd made available to him.

Trouble was, while he could see where Carr was heading, he couldn't see whether he was heading into an ambush.

He needed to find some way of tracking Pat Casey, and he was damned sure he'd be a tough nut to follow, too.

So he'd come up with a scheme, which – if it worked – would be very satisfying.

Oleg Kovalev was a serious *judoka*.

On the judo mat, you won by turning your opponent's strengths against him so that they became weaknesses.

He was confident he could exploit the weaknesses in Casey.

# 107.

PAULIE MCMAHON LEANED against the silver Volvo outside Stormont, inspecting his nails.

It was good to be back working for Pat, even if it was only short term, until this business with the Brit soldier blew over.

It got him out of the house, he enjoyed the banter, and Pat had promised to see him right.

True, it was a pain in the backside having to drive up and down between Stormont and the farm outside Camlough, where Pat was staying for a wee while.

Especially given that Pat insisted on taking the weirdest routes, and driving round every roundabout three times, and pulling all sorts of other stunts.

But even with all that it only took ninety minutes each way, give or take, and Pat had been very clear that he had to carry on with his Assembly work.

It was tough keeping everything hush-hush, too – sure, people knew he was driving for the big man, but Pat had been insistent that he told anyone who asked that it was on account of his bad back. No-one – but no-one – could know the real reason, or that Paulie was carrying. It was a pain in the arse, but, Jesus, five hundred quid a week was good money, and Pat had to have his reasons.

And it was only a brief visit today – a meeting at 10am, another at midday, and some internal Sinn Fein event after dinnertime. Unless there were any delays they'd be away at just after 3pm and Paulie could be back in Belfast by six-ish.

He was idly wondering about starting on his sarnies, when a guy walked up to him.

Stocky, short, greying hair.

A hard-looking bastard, but some sort of manbag over his shoulder and a camera round his neck, and a stupid grin on his fizzog.

*Tourist.*

'Excuse me,' said the guy, in some sort of thick foreign accent.

French?

German?

Paulie had no idea.

'I was just on tour of building and I find this on floor over there.'

He pointed into the middle distance.

Paulie looked down.

The guy was holding an iPhone.

Latest model.

'Aye?' said Paulie.

'Yes, I find this. I want to give to someone but now my wife she wait for me down there. I wonder, is possible I give to you, you give to someone?'

'Aye,' said Paulie. 'I'll hand it in to lost property for you.'

The man beamed at him. 'Very kind,' he said. 'Thank you very much. Now my wife...'

He shrugged and rolled his eyes, in a universal gesture which said: *I'd better get a move on, or else she'll have my guts for garters.*

Paulie nodded curtly, and the man hurried off in the direction of a coach.

If Paulie had bothered to watch him go he would have seen that the man didn't get on the coach but instead just disappeared

409

around the back of it. He might then have wondered why the man had chosen him, out of several drivers who were hanging around, to hand the phone to.

But all Paulie was thinking was, *This is an iPhone. Looks brand spankers, too. And the fucking thing's not even locked.*

He had no intention whatsoever of handing it in to any lost property department.

The only question in Paulie McMahon's mind was whether he was going to flog it for a hundred quid down the pub – he might even get two hundred for it – or give it to his missus for her birthday.

On the other side of the coach, Oleg Kovalev pulled a cap, a pair of shades and a dark jacket out of the bag, and crossed the road to observe the driver.

He was just in time to see the man slip the iPhone into his trouser pocket.

Oleg smiled.

'Khoroshiy mal'chik,' he said, under his breath.

# 108.

ONCE AGAIN, CARR had lain low during the hours of daylight.

He finally left his bolthole an hour after sundown, and headed into the city to buy a copy of the *Belfast Telegraph*.

Conor Maguire's untimely death was reported on an inside page, under the headline, *PSNI PR CHIEF FOUND DEAD.*

It wasn't a long piece, and it contained the line Carr was looking for.

*A post mortem will be carried out tomorrow, but at this stage police believe Mr Maguire's death was a tragic accident.*

That post mortem would show asphyxiation; with the alcohol and the vomit, the conclusion would be irresistible.

They'd waste some time trying to work out who 'Nicky' was, and why Maguire had called to get the number from his missus, but that was a blind alley and if it slowed them down then so much the better.

Carr turned west and headed for the Falls.

The Vollie was only a few minutes' drive away. The route took Carr past the Clonards, bringing back memories of that night almost thirty years earlier, and on past a dozen other streets which held personal significance for him.

Past the Davitts, where a grubby tricolour hung limp in the February night.

Past the Beehive, and the Red Devil opposite, and down past the West Belfast Sports and Social Club… places etched into his memory, where plenty of decent people were to be found, but among whom was a layer of the worst that mankind had to offer, men and women who sat and drank and plotted murder and misery.

His pulse was steady, and his mind was hyper-alert, but he could feel the hair on the back of his neck standing on end.

And then The Volunteer came into view.

Now Carr fought the urge to keep his foot down and drive on, and on.

*You've made your point.*

*They'll work out what happened to Maguire, even if the police don't.*

*You've scared them off.*

*Go home.*

But then he remembered the lads who'd died over here – from his own regiments, and others.

He remembered Kevin Murphy, and Scouse Parry, and their families, and poor Marie Hughes, and the countless others whose lives had been taken away by these bastards.

And he remembered Dessie Callaghan's dying words: *Plenty more where I come from. Crawfordsburn's a small place.*

He turned left down Donegall Road, pulled to the kerb and stopped next to a house with a thick privet hedge.

He couldn't go into The Volunteer with a pistol. There was every chance that there might be a few players inside, and if one of them decided to pat him down… He might take a few of them with him, but they'd get to him in the end, and he didn't fancy being beaten to death in a cellar somewhere. So he got out of the car, had a quick look around, and placed the Browning in the guts of the privet hedge with a gloved hand.

*Easily available if he found himself out in the open.*

He walked up towards the Falls Road, his heart beating a little quicker now, his mouth dry, and turned the corner.

The last time Carr had been into the Vollie had been in late 1994, a few years into his career in the Regiment.

He and another guy had gone into the place several times over a two-month period while imposing surveillance on some fucker whose name he couldn't remember.

It had been a very dicey operation.

Back then, the place had been heaving with players, and he could still taste the adrenalin and feel the trepidation – actually, call a spade a spade, the *fear* – he'd felt on walking through the door.

Carr and his oppo had needed to front it out more than once, and he'd been glad when the op had come to a premature end, as a result of the guy they were surveilling falling victim to an unhealthy concentration of lead in his skull after the UVF caught up with him outside his house one night.

And now, as he paused outside, looking up at the ornate front-age to the pub, he felt that same fear rise once again.

Back in 1994, he'd had a major team backing him – though, even then, he'd probably have been a dead man if compromised.

Sure, the modern-day RA were not quite the force they'd been.

But he felt very alone.

Still, he'd come this far, and he wasn't going home without achieving his objective.

He pulled on the brass handle to the big wooden door and walked in.

He hadn't known what to expect, but what he found was exactly what he'd expected.

There were flat screen TVs everywhere, now, and the fag machines were gone, and with them the fag smoke, but otherwise it hadn't changed much.

Same old high ceilings and dark wood panelling.

Same faded pictures of Republican heroes.

Same orange, white and green flags, and Gaelic writing on the posters.

Same crowd – or the sons and daughters of the same crowd, at least.

He pushed his way – carefully – through the early evening drinkers and stood at the bar.

Music playing, something mournful with the singer wishing he was in Carrickfergus.

The barman was over quickly enough, and Carr ordered a pint of Guinness.

As he sipped it, he scanned the crowd as casually as he could.

He couldn't remember Freckles' face. He'd spent a lot of time studying mugshots, but it was twenty years ago.

So, not ideal. But he did know a few things.

He knew his real name, Brian Keogh.

He knew he was looking for a guy with a pot belly, a pale face – freckles, obviously – and thinning ginger hair.

And he knew that he was a senior figure in the movement, so he was highly likely to be treated with respect by the normal punters – deferred to and given a wide berth, or surrounded by hangers-on, either or both could apply. What he wouldn't get was ignored, or pushed past, or dismissed.

There were maybe twenty people in the bar.

None of them fit the bill, but it was early.

Carr studied his pint, wondering if this was stupid.

He'd never known an IRA man yet who wasn't in love with the drink, but there were plenty of pubs and clubs this scumbag might use.

All he had was the say-so of Conor Maguire.

*He's in the Vollie most nights.*

A quarter of the way down his Guinness, he tapped the guy next to him on the arm.

'Where's the bogs, mate?' he said, although he knew very well where they were.

No point trying to change his accent or hide the fact that he was a stranger, people would realise soon enough.

He followed the man's directions to the gents', and stood there at the urinal.

Ears straining for any sound behind him.

Back then, this was where they'd come to suss you out.

Sure enough, he heard the noise of the door opening, and the music from the bar beyond getting temporarily louder.

A scuffle of feet, rubber soles squeaking on the old tile floor.

A guy, stocky, in a Gaelic football shirt, stood next to him.

Coughed, looked over.

Said, conversationally, 'Alright there, big man?'

Eyes a bit too firm.

Carr looked back at him, made sure to let his own eyes drift off.

Now was not the time to be confrontational.

'Aye, not so bad, mate,' he said. 'You?'

'Where you from, then?'

All friendly-like, but the fact that the question was asked at all told Carr all he needed to know.

Years ago, he had created and absorbed a detailed Army cover story which had him coming from Glasgow, but those details were hazy now, and Niddrie was ingrained in him. He could stand up to questioning about that area all night.

'I'm frae Niddrie,' he said, allowing his accent to thicken. 'In Edinburgh. How's aboot yoursel'?'

'I'm local,' said the man. 'So what brings you here, then?'

'Och, I met this bird online,' said Carr, with a wide grin. 'Bloody Tinder, eh? I swiped right, she swiped right, ye ken?'

'Aye?'

'Aye.'

'What's her name?'

'Angela. She works up at the hospital, like.'

Carr finished at the urinal, did up his fly, and turned round. For the first time, he noticed that they were not alone: another guy was leaning on the door, arms folded.

He felt his skin go cold: what if he'd somehow been made for who he was?

But as soon as it came it was gone. It was a while since he'd worked these streets, and if they'd recognised him he'd already be fighting for his life.

'Lives round here then, does she?' said Folded Arms. 'This Angela?'

'No, she lives out in… *Anderstown*, is it?'

'Andersonstown.'

'Aye, that's it. She lives out there and she dropped me off when she drove in to start her shift. Why're you asking?'

'Come over to visit her, then, did ye?'

'Aye, too fucking right ah did,' said Carr. 'She's a cracking wee lassie. Ah'm no' daft. I work on the rigs, like, and I had a week off, and nothing better tae do.' He made a gesture with his hands, as though he was cupping a pair of melons. 'Fuck me, the chebs on her,' he said. 'Mind, she can't half talk, like. She's gone off to work tonight and I'm glad o' the break. Fucking women, eh?'

And suddenly the tension was gone, both men laughing and raising their eyebrows in agreement.

The one who'd been standing next to Carr stuck out a hand. 'I'm Shane, pal,' he said, 'and this is Callum.'

Carr shook it. 'John,' he said. 'Good tae meet you fellas.'

'Got any ID, John?' said Shane.

'Not on me pal, no.'

He'd sanitised himself before leaving the mainland, and he'd been expecting this question.

'Not a credit card nor nothing?'

'I've only got cash. Mah missus reads mah fucking bank statements, like.'

He flashed a broad smile as he said it, but somehow the words sounded lame.

He kept the smile nice and confident, but he prepared himself for things to go bent. He was reasonably confident he could take these two out, especially if he struck first, but the noise, and the men in the bar beyond the door… Could he do Shane and Callum, and be out of the bogs, and then the bar, and then away, without being stopped and dragged down?

Truth was, he didn't know.

He kept his gaze level and steady, but he tensed his feet inside his trainers and slid his right foot back a few inches, ready to spring forward and nut the nearest guy.

Shane looked at Callum.

Callum grinned. 'Gone over the side, have ye?' he said. 'Ye dirty hooer, John.'

Shane looked back at Carr, and now he was smiling too.

'Your missus the jealous type, is she?' he said.

'Jealous? She'll cut mah baws off wi' a rusty hacksaw if she finds out,' said Carr.

The two men chuckled.

'I'd get rid, me,' said Shane, with a grin. 'So listen, we get a lot of undesirables in here, so we'd like to give yous a wee pat-down just to make sure that you're not somebody who wouldn't fit in.'

'No offence,' said Callum, 'but this is a Republican bar.'

'Aye,' said Carr. 'Ah'm no' daft. Ah seen all the pictures, like. I dinnae get the whole politics thing, but I'm a Hibee masel, if y'ken what ah mean.'

'Aye? We all have our faults,' said Shane. 'Celtic all the way for us.'

'Mah old man's team,' said Carr, opening his arms. 'Anyway, nae problem, guys. Ah've nothin' to hide, you just crack on.'

Shane performed a rudimentary search – but one which would have picked up the pistol, had he carried it.

Then he stood back, and smiled. 'Ach, you're okay, pal,' he said. 'Enjoy your night, eh?'

'Aye, ah will.'

The two men led him out of the toilet, and rejoined the crew they were drinking with.

Carr resumed his place at the bar. He didn't look round, but he knew they'd be nodding to one or two faces, letting them know that this stranger was alright.

Not that it meant he was safe.

He'd bought himself a little time, that was all: sooner or later someone a little more paranoid would take a longer look at him.

*About this nurse, then, big man...*

*So where are yous staying...*

*How come you've no fucking ID...*

He sipped his pint – it was what they'd expect him to do – and looked amiably about him.

No-one that looked like they might answer to 'Freckles'.

A guy came up and stood next to him.

'From Niddrie, are ye?' he said, holding out his empty pint pot for the barman.

'Aye.'

'Which street?'

'Why, who's asking, pal?'

A fine line, between confidence and aggression.

Get bolshy, you could be fucked up very quickly.

Show weakness or uncertainty, and it can all go very wrong equally quickly.

'Sure, *I'm* asking,' said the man, with a smile. 'I'm only being friendly. I know Niddrie. That's where my cousin lives.'

'Aye?'

'Aye. He lives on an estate where all the roads are called the same thing. Sure, I can't remember it. Funny-sounding name?'

Carr nodded. 'Niddrie Marischal, probably?' he said. 'I stay on Duddingston Road, overlooking the golf club. I work as a North Sea fitter, my middle name's Jim, and ma old man wears gorblimey trousers and he lives in a fucking council flat.' He smiled, broadly, openly. 'What's this, the fucking third degree? I only come in for a pint, not the Spanish Inquisition.'

*Confident.*

*Not aggressive.*

'No-one expects the Spanish Inquisition,' said the guy, with an equally broad smile. 'Niddrie Marischal, that's it. Real rabbit warren of a place. Bit of a shitehole, Niddrie.'

'Hey, that's ma home town you're slagging off,' said Carr, with a grin. 'But I cannae argue wi' you.'

The guy collected his pint, and punched Carr playfully on the shoulder. 'I'll see yous, big man,' he said.

Carr winked over his own Guinness, and concentrated on keeping his posture relaxed and his hand steady.

He felt as though every eye in the bar was on him; every sinew and muscle in his body was tight and coiled, every connection in his brain firing.

But he'd bought himself a little longer, and when he looked casually around himself he saw only people chatting, laughing, swilling drinks.

There were guys with their backs to him, though.

Could he be one of them?

He wondered.

Thought, *Just play it cool.*

Pulled out his mobile.

Dialled the number Conor Maguire had given him.

Casually looking round the bar to see if anyone picked up a phone.

Three rings.

Four rings.

No-one touched a phone.

And then the door burst open and in came a fat man with short, ginger hair, a pink, freckled face, and an expression of puzzled irritation.

Looking at a mobile phone.

And Carr recognised him straight away.

# 109.

BRIAN 'FRECKLES' KEOGH killed the call and put the phone back in his jacket, muttering about people he didn't know calling his personal fucking mobile.

John Carr pressed red, making a small show of leaving a quick message on some imaginary answer machine, but his mind was back in the nineties.

He'd seen this man on celluloid and in person many times before, the last time back in about 1995.

The IRA's 1994 Ceasefire had been in force, but there was a great deal of uncertainty as to how things would develop, so the Republicans had continued to amass arms and explosives.

The SAS and the RUC had targeted a number of importation routes and had made significant seizures, including a car boot full of Zastava rifles and machine guns, bought by Keogh and destined for various caches in and around Belfast.

The European connection and the driver of the car had been arrested, but Freckles – a clever man indeed – had been very careful, and there was no evidence to lay before a court.

Carr remembered photographing him outside a fish and chip shop on the Springfield Road – right up close, using a hidden camera – to provide an up-to-date image.

The intervening twenty years had added a good three stones

to his frame, and his ginger bog brush had died a death and was slowly sliding backwards off his head, but the freckles, and the eyes, and the cadence of the walk… Even in a bar, even older and fatter, his walk gave him away.

A slow, vulpine lope.

*Predatory.*

He looked at Carr, looked through him, and stood next to him at the bar.

Shoulder to shoulder.

Carr could smell aftershave, and cheap soap, and the brown leather of his jacket.

The barman literally broke off halfway through pouring someone else's drink and hustled over.

'Pint, Brian?'

'Aye,' said Freckles. 'And a chaser.'

He stood there waiting, hands spread on the mahogany bar.

Carr looked at the hands.

Fat and pink.

*How many men had they sent to their deaths?*

# 110.

CARR RECOVERED THE pistol and walked back up on to the Falls.

Surveillance in tight-knit areas is a difficult business. You can't sit around in a car drinking coffee and taking pictures with long lenses, unless you want to get yourself head-jobbed, because no-one sits in a car for very long and it gets you made. And you do everything you can to avoid target fixation. This is the biggest mistake anyone can make in this world: you're so tuned in to your man that you don't see the third parties watching *you*, and the next thing you know you're blown.

Blown *away* in west Belfast, more than likely.

So Carr stayed on foot, and tried to look like he belonged.

First thing he did was get himself a bag of chips and gravy from the Chinese takeaway just up from the bar.

He could hang around outside eating them and not look out of place for quite a while.

Not to mention, he was starving hungry.

He managed to eke the chips out for half an hour, and then he crossed over and wandered further up the Falls and did it all over again at a chippy.

Another half hour – this time, he didn't eat many of the chips – and still no sign of Freckles.

With few other options, he found a spot on the road where he could cover both the side entrance and front entrance of The Volunteer while standing back in the shadows and pretending to be making a phone call.

How long he could keep that going he didn't know, but it was all he had.

Carr spent the time productively, searching his memory.

Now that he'd seen Freckles in the flesh he recalled a lot more about him.

Could almost see the old files, hear the intelligence briefings.

Born in London to Irish parents, he'd moved with his family to Northern Ireland when he was a young teenager. Perhaps out of necessity – boys with English accents didn't get welcomed with open arms round this way back then – or perhaps simply because he enjoyed it, he had rapidly developed a reputation as a thug and a bully.

In his late teens he'd joined the RA, and was suspected of the hands-on murders of several people – Carr couldn't remember who, or how many, but that was not the point.

He'd really gone up in the world after marrying Róisín Cafferty, daughter of legendary gunman Coilm and sister of the revered – and very, very dead – bomber Diarmuid.

Róisín was a deeply evil woman in her own right, Carr remembered, and a significant terrorist.

She'd started out throwing dirty nappies and bricks onto the heads of soldiers walking past the Divis Flats, and tarring and feathering 'collaborators' – that being an elastic term which included anyone who so much as spoke to anyone they shouldn't. From there, she'd progressed through storing weapons and ammunition at her home, to procuring local girls to lure off-duty soldiers and RUC and UDR men to their deaths. According to intelligence reports, she'd taken part in several torture murders herself.

Including one which was very personal to John Carr.

Once Freckles was tied into the Caffertys, his position was all but unassailable, his authority almost unquestioned.

On the orders of his father-in-law, who had correctly identified his son-in-law as being brighter than the average, he'd been taken off 'active service' and put to work as an under-armourer. As time and the depredations of the Brits worked their magic, Freckles had moved up the tree, until he sat near its very top, armourer to the Belfast Brigade, and the best friend of and right-hand man to Pat Casey.

Carr shifted on his feet, and saw the door of The Volunteer swing open.

Freckles stepped into the street.

Had a quick look around, then started walking off heading east.

Carr turned on his heel and walked into Donegall Street, and waited.

Saw Freckles pass by on the other side of the Falls.

That familiar, loping gait.

Carr doubled back onto the Falls and fell in behind his quarry, on the opposite side of the road, about fifty metres behind.

As he did so, he kept his head down and his phone to his ear, laughing, and mouthing a conversation. Walking neither quickly nor slowly, every step and every swing of his arm shouting that he had every reason and every right to be there, he gradually gained on his target.

He was within twenty yards when Freckles suddenly crossed over.

Carr couldn't break stride, so his own walking momentum took him on so that they almost bumped into each other on the pavement.

'Watch where you're fucking going, pal,' said Freckles, but he just loped on down Fallswater Street.

Carr slowed, made a thing of gesticulating – the imaginary guy on the other end of his phone giving him some sort of directions

425

– and watched Freckles walk in through his front door, a few doors down.

*Bingo.*

Carried on along the Falls.

He knew this area like he'd grown up here, knew that Nansen Street was next, and that at the bottom was Iveagh Street, which took you back into Fallswater.

So he turned down Nansen.

Put the phone away.

Half way down, in the quiet dark, he knelt down by a van.

Took a small roll of black gaffer tape from his pocket.

Quickly tucked his trousers into his socks and taped them in place.

Put on a pair of gloves.

Taped his black shirt sleeves down over them.

Felt the pistol grip for reassurance.

Put his balaclava on like a beanie.

Carried on walking.

# III.

RÓISÍN KEOGH LOOKED up from the telly as Freckles came into the room.

'You're back early,' she said.

'Sure, there was no-one in,' he said, flatly. 'Is there anything to eat?'

'How should I know?' said his wife. 'Have a look in the bleeding fridge.'

'What do you mean, how should you know?' he said, the three or four beers and chasers he'd put down making him belligerent. 'You do the fucking shopping, don't you?'

'Ach, ballix to you,' said Róisín, angrily.

Freckles moved towards her.

'Don't you come another step closer,' she said. 'Not if you want to see the morning. I can pick up that phone now and have you sorted out, big as you think you are.'

He stopped.

It was true: his wife's family were nasty, and violent, and fiercely loyal.

'Ach, fuck you,' he spat.

'Not likely,' said Róisín, with a mocking smirk. She picked up her wine glass, downed it in one, and waved it at him. 'And you can get me another of these.'

She cackled as he went, muttering, into the kitchen.

And turned the television volume right up as he handed her the refilled glass.

Which was why they didn't hear the knock at the door, at first.

Outside, Carr, black balaclava now pulled down over his face, was looking up and down the street.

Thinking, *Come to the fucking door*, as he pressed himself into the doorway.

He knocked harder.

The sound of shouting and then a hall light clicked on.

*Shit.*

He'd have preferred darkness, but the cards were the cards.

He took the Browning from his waistband

Held it down between his legs.

There was a time when a man in Freckles' position would never have opened a door to anyone, but the war had been officially over for a long time, and the main threat – Loyalist hit squads – was all but gone.

He had grown fat and complacent.

The door opened.

*Freckles.*

'Who the fuck are you?' he said, staring at the black-clad figure in front of him. 'What...'

He got no further before Carr pushed him backwards with a gloved palm to the chest, brought up the pistol to his forehead and was into the house.

He closed the door behind him with his heel, eyes never leaving Freckles' eyes.

'Mother of God,' said Freckles, all the colour gone from his already pale face. 'This is it.'

Carr levelled the semi-automatic at his left eye, and walked him backwards, Freckles stumbling with the adrenalin rush which had left him uncoordinated.

Back, back.

Into the living room.

The telly on way too loud.

Róisín sitting on a green velour sofa, half-pint of wine halfway to her open mouth, staring.

Carr pushed Freckles down onto the sofa and stood in front of them both, Browning switching from one to the other.

'Who's this?' said Róisín.

'Who are you?' said Freckles. 'Can we talk about this?'

'We're going to talk, don't worry,' said Carr.

He looked beyond them into the kitchen.

Said, 'Both of you get on the fucking floor, face down, hands behind your heads.'

Freckles was on the floor remarkably nimbly for a man of his size and age.

'Do yous know who we fucking are, you eejit?' spat Róisín. 'You're a fucking dead man.'

Carr stepped forward and punched her square in the face, sending her wine glass flying.

Said, 'Get on the fucking floor.'

This time, Róisín did meekly as she was told, her nose streaming blood and snot.

Carr said, 'Hands behind your head. Now stay there, and do not move a fucking muscle.'

Went into the kitchen and came back out holding a knife.

Back in front of them.

Said to Freckles, 'Anyone else in this house?'

'No.'

'Kids?'

'No.'

'Because I'll fucking kill you and her and them if you're lying to me.'

'No, I swear. The kids left home years ago.'

429

Carr pointed at him. 'Just you. Get up, turn away from me, and lean against that wall, arms at full stretch.'

Freckles did as he was told.

'If you turn around I *will* kill you,' said Carr.

'I won't turn round.'

'Turn over and lie on your fucking back,' said Carr to Róisín.

Black eyes burning up at Carr with pure hatred, she did as instructed.

Carr looked down at her and rolled his balaclava up.

'Róisín "The Machine" Cafferty,' he said. 'As-was. I knew your brother.'

'Diarmuid?'

'That's the fella. Shame what happened to him.'

'He was a good man, a brave man.'

'If you think it's good and brave to blow up defenceless people. He killed a mother and her two kids in Strandtown, didn't he?'

'That bitch worked for the occupation forces of the British Army,' she said, defiantly. 'She deserved what she got.'

'She was a cookhouse *cleaner*,' said Carr, smiling. 'And her children? Did they deserve it, too?'

'Casualties of war.'

'Aye, that's one way of looking at it.' He looked over her shoulder. 'Don't you turn round, Freckles,' he said. 'I'm not playing games here, pal.'

'Oh, my,' said Freckles, a tremor in his voice.

Back to Róisín.

'Speaking of the occupation forces of the British Army,' said Carr. 'Do you remember a guy called Chris Murray?'

Her mouth said, 'No,' but her eyes said *Yes*.

'Aye, you do,' said Carr, nodding. 'I joined up with Chris, and we were in the same battalion. 3 Para. Lovely lad, he was. You'd have said he was too gentle to be a paratrooper, but he was a hell of a soldier. Only child, too, which made it worse for his folks. They were so proud of him.'

Róisín looked like she'd seen a ghost.

'Chris would be married with kids by now,' said Carr. 'Might even be a granddad. But none of that happened, did it? Because you got that tart from Turf Lodge to bring him down here on a promise, and then you gutted him alive, didn't you?'

'I never did nothing.'

'Och, I'm not saying you held the knife, Róisín, but you set the whole thing up, and you *watched*, didn't you?'

*Silence.*

Freckles started making a choking sound as his breathing rose.

'He was a brave man, Chris, but I bet he begged for mercy. Didn't he?'

'Aye,' said Róisín. 'He fucking did. He was…'

She got no further.

In one swift movement, Carr knelt down and rammed the knife through her neck.

It cut through her trachea and her spine.

Her eyes bulged in surprise as blood began bubbling from her mouth and nose.

Her mouth opened and closed wordlessly.

And then she died.

More mercy than she'd shown Chris Murray.

'What have you done?' said Freckles, half-turning his head.

'Keep your eyes on that fucking wall,' said Carr.

Covering Freckles with his pistol, he withdrew the knife from Róisín Keogh's throat.

Picked up her hands and made numerous defensive wounds on her palms and wrists.

Gave her one good puncture wound in the shoulder, and leant on her chest with his gloved hand to get her lifeless body to bleed a little.

Stood up.

Went to Freckles.

Pressed the gun behind his ear.

Whispered, 'I'm sure you've guessed, Freckles. I'm John Carr.'

Freckles' knees buckled slightly.

'Aye,' said Carr, with a chuckle. 'That's a bit shit for you, isn't it?'

'I didn't...'

'Wasting your breath, mate, I've heard it all before. Now's the time for listening.'

*Silence.*

'Good. Now, Róisín and me had a personal score, on account of my mate and all that. Funny thing is, I'd never have thought of settling it until you bastards decided to come after me. Big fucking mistake, eh?' He laughed. 'Anyway, it's different with you. I'm happy to let Róisín's old man and his connections deal with you.'

'Can I...?' said Freckles.

'No, you can't. What I'm going to do now is I'm going to pass you a knife. You're going to grip the knife nice and tight, for a count of three, and then you're going to drop it. Understood?'

Freckles nodded.

'Before we do that, you know who I am. I've put more men in the ground than you and your mates could dream of. Do as I say, and we'll just have a wee chat. But you try anything, and your brains are up that wall.'

'Okay,' said Freckles.

He was trembling.

Carr knew he would comply.

He did.

A few moments later, the bloodied knife hit the grubby carpet with a thud.

'Now,' said Carr. 'Please believe me when I say this. If you do not give me the answer I want to the next question, you're dead. Do you believe me?'

'I do, aye, I do, honestly I do.'

'Where is Pat Casey now?'

'At his uncle's farm near Camlough.'

'Where on the farm?'

'I believe it's an empty cottage near the farmhouse.'

'You sure?'

'I promise.'

Carr looked at him.

Decided he was telling the truth.

'What's the name of the farm?'

'Cairbre McKilty is the name of the uncle. I don't know the name of the farm, I'm sorry. Probably it would be McKilty's.'

'How many buildings are there?'

'I don't know, I've never been. Honestly.'

'What security has Casey got?'

'Four men.'

'How are they armed?'

'A couple of M16s and sidearms.'

'Does he have any vehicle other than that silver Volvo?'

'Not as far as I know.'

'Who's driving him?'

'Paulie McMahon.'

'How old?'

'My age. Fat and unfit.'

'Armed?'

'Yes. Nine millimetre Taurus. Pat wanted him to take the risk.'

'Okay,' said Carr, removing the pistol from Freckles' neck and watching the second hand on his watch crawl round to the vertical. 'You've been surprisingly helpful. I think it's only fair that I keep my side of the bargain, so…'

But as he spoke, in one swift motion, he brought the pistol round under Freckles' chin and pulled the trigger.

The crack of the shot was significant – though the carpet and the sofa and the curtains absorbed a lot of it, and much of the rest was masked by the volume of the TV, and contained within the thick brick walls – and the spray of blood and bone and brain matter up the wall dramatic.

Freckles hit the floor like a bolt-thrown bullock.

Working quickly, Carr made the weapon safe and knelt down beside him.

Placed the pistol grip into Freckles' lifeless hand.

Forefinger through the trigger guard.

Pressed it against the trigger.

Clicked the safety back off and placed the pistol on the floor a few feet away.

Carefully overturned a couple of chairs and a table with a lamp.

Went into the kitchen and threw some food and booze around.

Looked at his watch.

Sixty seconds had elapsed since he'd shot Freckles.

Went back into the living room and took a moment to look at the scene.

It wasn't perfect, but he knew from working alongside them that even the best and most experienced police officers will tend to take the obvious solution if it's offered to them on a plate.

Anyone coming in to this room would surely assume that Brian Keogh and his wife had had a violent, drunken argument, that Brian had stabbed Róisín, and that he had then turned a pistol on himself in remorse.

A proven IRA pistol, what was more, that had almost certainly been used in more than one shooting.

Shame to leave it there, but them's the breaks.

Being careful to leave nothing else behind, Carr walked into the kitchen.

*Ninety seconds.*

Out in the back garden.

Darkness.

Shut the door behind him.

Walked purposefully down the path.

Through the gate, into the entry.

Along the entry, back up the alleyway.

Stood in the shadows, ripped off the tape, put it in his pocket.

Took off the balaclava and gloves, too.

Walked back out onto Fallswater Street.

Just a fellow on his way out for a jar.

No sign of the police, yet – they weren't keen to rush in to this part of the city, where a call was quite likely to be false and designed to lure them into a murderous trap, and that was if they'd even *had* a call. Assuming anyone had heard the shot, they were very likely to be keeping their heads down, obeying the cast-iron Republican code of silence, which meant you didn't talk to the fucking traitor peelers, about anything, ever.

Especially when senior people in the RA were involved.

Turned right down Fallswater, and at the bottom he turned right into Iveagh Street.

*Keep walking, keep walking,* he told himself, trying to ignore the feeling of nakedness now that he'd no longer got the Browning. *No-one's looking for you. No-one knows who you are. Just keep walking.*

He passed Iveagh Parade, and then Iveagh Drive, and then hit a patch of waste ground.

Crossed that into La Salle Mews.

Where they'd once raided a house and found a player in bed with two girls, neither of whom were his missus.

Kept on into La Salle Drive, and then on into St James' Park.

*A distant siren – was that the Old Bill, maybe?*

He walked on, head down.

*I'm just a bloke heading up the Vollie for a pint.*

*Again.*

Turned right into Donegall Road.

Walked the length of that, back to the Falls.

Eight minutes and forty seconds since he'd sent Freckles on his way.

*There's the car.*

*Get in, nice and casual.*

And away.

# 112.

OLEG KOVALEV WAS lying on his hotel bed dozing when his mobile rang.

Dmitri Petrov, calling from Moscow.

'Da?' said Oleg.

'Your friend was in the Falls Road area earlier,' said Dmitri. 'Wandered around a little but basically went fixed there for about three hours.'

'I saw.'

'Interesting thing is, I've been monitoring the local police comms, as you asked me to, and two people have just been found dead in a house in that area. The police were called about fifteen minutes ago.'

'Is he still there?' said Oleg.

'No, he moved off in his vehicle twenty minutes ago.'

Oleg's mouth cracked into a smile. 'Who are the dead?'

'No formal ID yet, but the police believe they are a married couple, Brian and Róisín Keogh.'

'Do we know anything about these people?'

'I haven't looked at our own files yet, but the Belfast police chatter says they have very strong Republican connections. It sounds as though the male may have been an armourer for the IRA and the wife a senior member of the IRA, from a well-known IRA family.'

Oleg's smile widened. 'What are the police saying?'

'Officers at the scene think it's a domestic matter. Man stabbed woman several times, finally fatally, and then shot himself. They've recovered a handgun.'

'I see. And where is our friend now?'

'Back at his lying-up point.'

# 113.

CARR SPENT MOST of the next day eating and sleeping and building up his physical reserves.

He also took a trip to the Belfast Central Library, where he checked the newspaper for any report of Freckles' death.

It was being reported as a suspected domestic murder–suicide.

No-one else was sought.

Freckles was described as a 'respected member of the community' and his wife as 'a senior voice in Republican politics'.

Carr smiled. He doubted that Pat Casey would buy the domestic angle, but you never knew.

Then he logged onto a computer terminal and spent three or four hours using google maps to look at farms all over Northern Ireland.

When he'd finished that – and he must have looked at a couple of hundred – he spent half an hour trawling the web for livestock auctions, feedstuff providers and tractor dealerships.

Anything, basically, to produce the digital fingerprints of a man who was interested in agriculture generally.

A farm sales rep, maybe. Who cared?

The trick was to build a haystack.

The needle – that was the three or four minutes he had spent looking at the McKilty farm, and sketching its layout and approaches.

# 114.

CARR LEFT HIS hide at 3am, wiping everything down, just in case, and locking up as he went – he wouldn't be returning.

He was a little tired, but he'd spent years, decades, operating on little sleep, so that wasn't an issue.

Carrying the AK out to the Audi and then driving round with it, *that* was an issue.

There was nobody about, but, still, he walked out onto the pavement as though he'd lived there all his life.

People ignore confidence, it makes them feel comfortable; the human eye is drawn to weakness, and hesitancy, and unfamiliarity.

He strolled the few streets to his Audi, hefted the bag into the boot, and drove off.

He was taking a massive risk, now.

He'd disposed of the unneeded pistol rounds, but he still had a loaded AK47 and three mags in the back of the Audi.

His plan, if he happened to get pulled by the cops – it happens to everyone now and then, especially in the early hours, and you have to think ahead – was to let them look in through the window, and give them his fake name.

If that satisfied them, great, but if they asked him to get out of the car, or wanted to see in his boot, then he was out of there, foot to the floor, and abandoning the vehicle and losing the weapon ASAP.

If they ever caught up with him he'd be in bother, but not the kind of bother that came with ferrying automatic weapons around Belfast.

Camlough worried him, too.

There was a reason Casey had plotted up there, and the reason was that it was in the middle of South Armagh bandit country.

He was amongst friends.

In the darkest days of the Troubles, the British Army had been unable to move freely around the area, and the villages and fields around Camlough and nearby Bessbrook had been a killing ground, a hundred square kilometre butcher's block for soldiers.

Five klicks to the Irish border, it was riddled with Republicans and their sympathisers, and much more dangerous, in its own way, than Belfast.

In Belfast, as in any big city, people come and go, and you can blend in. Sure, you don't want to get caught speaking with a strange accent, or looking at the wrong person or building for too long, but if you know what you're doing you can generally stay one step ahead.

Not in Armagh. That place was brooding and claustrophobic, home to generations of rural folk, intermarried and intermingled and deeply suspicious of anyone they didn't know. You had no business there unless you had business there, and the regular Army went in something like company strength, or not at all.

Special Forces were different. They snuck in in small teams, under cover of the dark, digging in and observing and waiting.

Carr had done it many times, and it was how he intended to play it now.

An hour's drive to Camlough.

Abandon the vehicle in a little residential side street in the centre of the village – not ideal, but it would draw less attention there than if he tried to hide it – and tab half a mile across the fields to a little copse with a view of the farmhouse.

He ought to be in situ by dawn, and then he could lie up and observe Casey's departure.

The rest of his plan would depend on what he saw.

He smiled to himself as he drove.

# 115.

THE FARM WAS in the middle of nowhere, a good mile-and-a-half from any other habitation, and it sat in a shallow valley, with scrub to the front and a sizeable mountain rearing up behind it.

Carr was deep in the undergrowth at the southern edge of a short treeline well before dawn.

As the sun started to rise, he saw that the field between him and the McKilty farm was approximately eighty metres long, and about the same wide, hedged in on each side. A few bare, wind-bent trees and an old red tractor stood to the left of the house, which was built into a dip in the flat, brown earth. Off to the right was a long, low cattle byre, built out of breeze block, and a good fifty metres beyond that, pretty much in line with Carr's position, was a small stone cottage.

The farm was approached down a long track, a hundred metres at least, which led left-to-right from the road, which was itself a narrow, twisting country lane hemmed in underneath high hedges. The way Casey would return, Carr would be able to see him approaching from the village. He'd disappear into a dip for a moment or two, then turn right onto the track and be in plain view as he drove along past the main farmhouse to the little cottage.

There were lights on in both buildings, upstairs, and downstairs.

It was a working farm, and Carr had watched enough of them in his time to know that there could well be blokes out and about already, coming back from milking or doing whatever else it was that farmers did.

So he huddled low, rubbed dirt over his face, and dragged twigs and grass over himself.

And settled down to watch, focusing most of his attention on the cottage.

Around the time the dark sky began to turn grey, it started drizzling, but the tree canopy kept the worst of it off.

Tell the truth, Carr was loving it, anyway.

If he got wet, so much the better.

Filthy, ditto.

This was his kind of soldiering, and, much as he enjoyed poncing around London in a flash car and going to fancy restaurants with his boss, here he was in his element. He'd watched places like this for days and days, shitting in a bag, living off cold rations, waiting for his quarry. There was something primeval about it, the knowledge that he was here, within striking distance of his prey, while the prey was completely oblivious.

At about seven-thirty, a man in green overalls came out of the main farmhouse and disappeared round the back. A moment or two later he came out and headed off down the track in a red Toyota Hilux.

*The farmer, off out.*

There was no movement then until just after eight, when two men came out of the cottage and conducted a cursory sweep of the area around it. After a quick walkaround, they ambled down the track, and wandered around the main house, the cow shed and the big green barn. At this distance it was hard to be sure, but Carr put them both in their early thirties.

Neither looked very athletic.

Neither carrying long weapons, but Carr assumed they had pistols on them.

No more movement until they reappeared five minutes later, had a quiet conflab, and then walked back to the cottage and went inside.

*Sloppy*, he thought.

Four blokes wasn't enough to cover this place to start with – a dozen might have done it, with sentries posted in good observation points, and patrols out to a reasonable perimeter. But if four was all you had, you still needed more than the odd stroll around of a morning.

*Sloppy.*

Sloppy was good.

Sloppy made him happy.

At about a quarter past eight, he saw lights on the road from the village, and a few moments later the silver Volvo turned into the long farm track and started bouncing and juddering along it.

It drove past the farmhouse and stopped at the cottage.

A fat man got out.

Paulie McMahon, Carr assumed.

Walked to the door.

Knocked, waited, went in.

Carr reached into his daysack and took out a cereal bar.

Started eating it absently.

The front door opened and Paulie hurried out, followed by two men.

One of them scoping the lay of the land, the other bent over slightly.

Black, greying hair.

Specs.

*Pat Casey.*

*Keeping his head down.*

Casey got into the passenger side, Paulie the driver's side.

The minder leaned in, said something, and slapped the roof of the car to send them on their way.

After a five- or six-point turn, they were back off down the track.

They didn't spare the horses, either; Casey was clearly bricking it.

Carr grinned.

Looked at his watch.

*08.25hrs.*

As far as Carr had been able to discover, Casey had a 10.00hrs committee meeting which was expected to last until lunchtime.

After lunch he had a constituency surgery until 15:00.

That meant he'd be back at around 16:30hrs.

Carr finished the cereal bar, put the wrapper away, and picked at his teeth while he pondered his next move.

If the late and unlamented Freckles had been correct, there were four armed men here.

He wanted to be inside that cottage when Casey came back – he wasn't yet sure how he was going to deal with him, but if it was to involve gunfire that sound would be much better contained within four walls. The trouble with this was that it meant moving in daylight, which was less than ideal.

In terms of approaching the house undetected, he had two options.

The first was to move to his right and then cut down on the other side of a hedge bordering a field of sheep, which ran at right angles to the farm track and the front of the cottage. It wasn't perfect, but the hedge would at least give him cover from view until he got to within striking distance of the building.

But he had another plan, based on the exploits of the SAS of old.

He watched both the cottage and the farmhouse for another hour, and then made up his mind.

Slowly, Carr edged backwards into the copse.

Once he was sure that he was well-screened, he took a small bottle of water from his bag and used a little of it on his hands to clean his face.

Then, in a crouching walk, he headed back to the other side of the trees.

From there, he headed back to the lane and then back into the village.

He was at the Audi by not long after ten o'clock.

The little back road was all-but deserted, though he did catch the eye of an old biddy, who smiled at him when he winked at her.

Bag on the seat next to him, he started the engine and got on the move.

# 116.

IN THE SECOND WORLD WAR, the early Special Air Service had relied on daring and mobility and surprise to attack enemy forces which were often vastly superior in both numbers and firepower.

John Carr headed back to the farm, turned down the rutted track, and drove quickly to the enemy.

Past the farmhouse, stones skittering and clattering against a length of rusty corrugated iron, he arrived on the small concrete apron in front of the cottage, skidded to a halt, and debused.

Headed straight round the back of the cottage, keeping low.

What happened next was exactly what he had predicted would happen.

Two men burst from the cottage.

They headed for the black Audi, and peered inside.

*Nothing.*

By the time they looked up, Carr had circled the cottage and walked inside through the open door, AK in tight to his shoulder.

Adrenal glands pumping, every hair on his body standing on end, but he loved this shit, would have done it for nothing.

Would have *paid* to do it.

He cleared the room to the left, which was some sort of study.

Past the stairs and on through another door.

Swept the room with the muzzle of the assault rifle.

Terracotta floor, big old Rayburn stove, table and chairs.

The smell of frying.

Another man, just getting up from his chair, wiping his mouth.

On the table, half-eaten breakfasts, half-drunk mugs of tea, and an M16.

Which the guy was reaching for, startled eyes on Carr.

Mouth open, about to shout a warning.

Carr couldn't shoot him just yet – he didn't want to alert the bozos outside – but he covered the eight feet between himself and the guy in a heartbeat, kicked the table over, sent the M16 clattering to the floor, and clubbed him with the AK, knocking him spark out.

As he hit the floor, Carr stamped on his face to make sure.

In the same moment, he was already moving to the far side of the kitchen, where there was another door.

Which opened as he reached it.

A young guy, mid-twenties, doing up his trousers.

*A look of surprise on his face.*

Carr gave him something to be surprised about, reaching behind the guy's head and pulling it forward into his own forehead, which he thrust forward at speed.

It broke the man's nose and eye socket, and rendered him unconscious, too.

Two down, two to go.

He cleared the toilet, and turned to face the way he'd come in.

Sweeping the rifle sights across the door and round the rest of the room.

No other way in or out.

*Window.*

Outside, he saw movement.

He hit the floor, scrambled against the wall.

Waited.

Held his breath and listened.

He could hear talking outside, the two blokes shouting to each other.

*Have ye seen anything?*

*No.*

*D'ye think it's him?*

*How the fuck should I know?*

Carr had to stifle a laugh.

He hadn't felt this exhilarated, this alive, since he'd left the Regiment.

The two men outside had moved on, so Carr headed for the stairs.

Stairs are always tough.

You're going up.

Creaking.

Narrow.

He took them quickly.

Reached the top.

Three doors.

Took the left.

A bedroom.

*Clear.*

Kicked the middle door open.

A bathroom.

*Clear.*

Then a noise downstairs.

The two guys, coming back in.

*Bad timing.*

The first one headed straight past the bottom of the stairs into the kitchen.

Carr heard him shout, 'What the fuck?'

Then the second guy appeared and looked up the stairs.

He shouted something and raised his pistol.

*Bad move.*

Carr shot him in the head, the 7.62mm round painting the wall red.

The second guy shouted something panicky.

Stuck his pistol round the wall and fired blind.

Six or seven shots.

Carr was forced to jerk back.

And that's when he was clubbed on the head from behind.

# 117.

IT WAS VERY fucking hard to get the drop on John Carr –
no-one had ever managed it before – but that was what the fifth
guy had done.

*A fifth guy.*

Carr had known it was possible – that was why he'd been clearing the upstairs – and it was just a matter of unfortunate timing.

He'd been forced back by the pistol shots, his attention diverted,
and the guy had cleaned his clock from behind, with an iron of
all things.

He came-to in the cow shed, in a steel-tubed chair.

Naked, legs taped to the chair legs, wrists plasticuffed behind
him.

The mother of all headaches.

In his concussed state, it took Carr a few moments to find his
bearings.

Three men looking at him.

Young guy in a red lumberjack shirt. He was the fellow who'd
unloaded from the bottom of the stairs.

Then two blokes with badly busted-up faces – they didn't look
very happy.

The one he'd stamped on was wearing a pair of Nike trainers
and was missing three front teeth.

The lad he'd headbutted was in a yellow anorak. Big cut on the bridge of his nose, and little wads of bog roll up his nostrils.

Carr smiled and nodded at him, all friendly-like.

Then he realised that another man was standing in the doorway to the stone byre – big chin, greedy eyes and a cruel mouth. Long hair, and wearing a denim jacket and jeans.

Looked like a member of Status fucking Quo, thought Carr. Must have been your man with the iron.

Status Quo had a mobile phone jammed to his ear. 'Aye,' he was saying. 'He shot Bernard, the fucker. He was about to fucking shoot me and all, but I was too quick for him.'

Carr burst out laughing. 'He's fucking bullshitting you, Pat,' he called out, loudly.

One of the busted-up men – Nike Guy – stepped forward and slapped Carr across the side of his face.

Hard, with a real backlift to it.

It made his ears ring.

'Shut the fuck up,' said Nike Guy.

'Fuck you,' said Carr. 'Have we met before, pal? Yep. By the looks of you, I'd say we have.'

*Slap.*

*Ring.*

'There's a big empty chest freezer in the cottage,' Status Quo was saying, 'and we've put him in there for now. I was going to worry about his missus later. After we've sorted out this cunt.'

There was a pause, while he listened to whatever Pat Casey had to say on the other end.

'We can start now, if you like.'

Another pause.

'Nah, he's had a slap or two but that's it so far.'

Pause.

'You sure?' he said. Then, doubtfully, 'Okay, well, it's your call. So what time will yous be back?'

Casey said something.

'Okay,' said Status Quo. 'We'll see yous then.'

He clicked off the phone and turned to look at Carr.

'Shit drills there, pal,' said Carr, cheerfully. 'Casey's calls will be listened in to. You're all finished.'

'WhatsApp,' said Status Quo, equally cheerfully. 'End-to-end encryption, see? And it's free of charge, too. Fucking marvellous stuff, technology.'

He turned to the other men.

'Pat says we're to leave this fucker be till he gets back. He's very keen to watch every minute. Well, until he has to go back to Stormont tomorrow.' He laughed long and hard at that. Then he said, 'We're just to get the tools ready.'

Nike Guy grinned, toothlessly, and spat bloody saliva on to the stone floor of the byre. 'You're gonna love this,' he said to Carr. Then, to the young guy in the red lumberjack shirt, he said, 'Watch him while we go and sort them out.'

Lumberjack nodded.

The other three trooped out, and Carr sat in silence, looking at Lumberjack.

His mind racing.

Mostly he was wondering how the fuck he'd allowed himself to get into this position, but then he already knew the answer: if you will go clearing houses full of armed men on your own, this is a risk you run.

He parked that thought and started trying to work out the pecking order here.

He assumed the top man was Status Quo – he was clearly the oldest, he'd been on the phone to Casey, and he'd also been skiving off upstairs.

Had to be the boss.

Nike was 2IC – he'd dished out the order to Lumberjack to stick around and watch Carr.

Which made him the bottom of the pile, and Yellow Anorak No3.

Lumberjack looked to be about the same age as Yellow Anorak, maybe even younger.

Glock in his hand.

Carr smiled at him.

'That was some pretty good shooting back there,' he said. 'For a lad your age.'

The kid said nothing.

'You nearly fucking got me.'

Silence.

'That'd have been a notch on your belt, eh?'

Carr waited a beat, and then said, 'I see you're the strong, silent type.'

'Shut the fuck up.'

Carr sat quietly for a few moments. Then he said, 'I don't suppose there's any chance of a blanket or something? I'm freezing my baws off here.'

Lumberjack just stared at him.

Carr shrugged.

There was the noise of footsteps, and the three men re-entered the cowshed.

Status Quo was carrying a black wheel which was paying out an orange extension lead.

Nike Guy had an electric drill and a Black and Decker Jigsaw.

Yellow Anorak a car battery and jump leads.

'This looks like fun,' said Carr, brightly.

'You won't be laughing in a wee while,' said Nike Guy, bending down and plugging in the electric drill. He pressed the trigger, and listened to the whine. 'Not when you've had this fucker up your jap's eye. Mind, I might need a smaller bit.'

The others laughed.

455

'*He sends one of yours to the morgue, you drill his cock to bits,*' he said, in a passable pastiche of Sean Connery's speech in *The Untouchables*.

More laughter.

'Grand,' said Status Quo. 'Well, we'll just check you cannat go anywhere, and then we'll go back inside in the warm and leave you wit' Tomas here.'

Carr mentally scratched out 'Lumberjack' and replaced it in his mind with Tomas.

'Sorry, Tommy,' said the Quo. 'But that's always a young un's job.'

'Sure, I don't mind,' said Tomas Kelly. 'I'll happily watch the fucker.'

Something in the way he said it sounded like false bravado to Carr.

*A weakness?*

*Something to work on?*

# 118.

CARR SAID NOTHING but just bided his time for a good half hour.

Professional interrogators, torturers and guards have one golden rule, and it is this: never allow the subject to become 'human'.

This had been drummed into Carr on numerous resistance-to-interrogation courses during his career, the point being that if you can make the other guy see you as a person, it's a lot harder for him to hurt you.

Tomas was not by any stretch a professional at this game.

Added to which, he wasn't a hardened PIRA hand like they'd been in the old days. He couldn't be – the PIRA didn't offer its young guns the same opportunities any more.

What was he?

*Eighteen? Nineteen?*

Sitting there on the concrete floor, knees up, Glock at his feet.

Skinny little fucker.

He hadn't seen much pain, much less dealt it out.

'Tomas,' said Carr, laying on the Scots accent. 'I'm John, by the way.'

Tomas said nothing.

'Or should I say *Tommy*. Yeah. Listen, Tommy. You know they're going to torture me here, torture me and kill me?'

'Shut up.'

'They already killed another guy. Guy called Mick. Mick was a great bloke. Scouser, but Irish parents. You'd have liked him. You know he had a wife and two daughters?'

'Shut *up*.'

'Aye. Lovely girls, both of them. The youngest would be about your age. She gets married next month. Her dad'll no' be there, o' course. They buried him last week. Poor bastard. The funeral was very sad. Everyone was in floods o' tears, me included.'

As he spoke, Carr watched the young guard. He wouldn't meet his captive's eye.

'Are you close to *your* ma and pa, Tommy?'

'I don't want to talk to yous.'

'No, I understand that. I understand that. You're going to have to watch those guys drill through my knees in a few hours. You seem a decent young guy, so it cannae be pleasant for you.'

Silence.

Then, 'Mick was close to his daughters, Tommy, but they still killed him.' He jerked his head in the direction of the cottage. 'Your man Pat Casey had him killed over nothing.'

'He was a British soldier.'

'Aye, he *was*. Years ago. Just now he was a delivery driver for Parcelforce.' Carr chuckled and shook his head. 'And what the *fuck*? A British soldier? What is this, Tommy, the nineteen fucking seventies? The British arenae even *over* here the now. We're all supposed to be fucking pals, I thought.'

'You were a soldier as well.'

'Aye. Mind, I fucking *hated* it. Hated it, Tom. I only joined up because I was fucking unemployed. See, there was fuck-all to do round my way back when I was your age, and my dad, he says tae me, you get yoursel' a job, me and your mum arenae keepin' yous forever. So I admit it, I joined the Army. But it was the worst thing I ever done. All the top brass is English, right? Course they are. They hate the Scots just as much as they hate the Irish, like.

And the Welsh. It's us Celts against they English bastards, Tommy, I'll tell ye that.'

'You shoulda done something else.'

'I did, Tommy. I was only in five years, and got out soon as I could. Then I worked on the oil rigs, like. Couple of my best mates on the rigs was from Belfast, as it goes. You might know them, there was a fella called Gerry...'

'They said you was in the SAS.'

'They *what?*' said Carr, guffawing. 'The SA fucking *S*? Mate, I couldnae fucking *march* straight, let alone join that lot.'

Carr looked at the grey stone wall of the cowshed, and then at the concrete floor.

For a moment he imagined it being hosed down after... after...

He shook the thought off.

All this chat about the Army probably wasn't helping, so he changed tack.

'See, my mum, she had cancer. I watched her die, like. Which was rough.' He paused a beat. 'And I don't suppose I'll ever see my dad again, like. Not after today.'

At least that was true: his father had been dead twenty years.

'You should have thought of that,' said Tomas, 'before...'

'Before *what?* I havenae *done* nothing, Tommy. That's the crazy thing.'

'You just fucking killed Bernard.'

Ah. That was problematic.

Carr had been hoping to sweep that under the carpet.

'See, was he no' trying tae fucking' kill *me?*' he said. 'I come over here just tae fucking *talk* to Pat, and it all goes wrong like that. It wisnae *mah* fault. That's not very fair, Tommy.'

There was a long silence.

Carr concentrated on looking as weak and helpless as he could – which wasn't easy, he spent a fair bit of time in the gym – and watched Tomas surreptitiously.

The young Irishman stealing the occasional look of his own, out of the corner of his eye.

Carr was just about to try another gambit, when Nike Guy walked in.

'How're we doing?' he said, looking at Carr and grinning.

'Fine,' said Tomas.

'Good. Listen, me and the other boys're just going to nip up to the Heifer for a pint.' He winked at Carr. 'It's gonna be a long night.'

'Okay,' said Tomas.

'Let's just check his bindings,' said Nike Guy, and he got behind Carr and yanked his arms upwards.

It came close to dislocating Carr's shoulders, and he couldn't help but yelp.

'Yeah, they seem tight enough,' said Nike. 'Wouldn't want him getting away.'

He turned back to Tomas.

'Right, you've my mobile number, and you've Jacky's number, and you've the number of the bar. McKilty's under instructions to keep well away, so he's off ploughin' or fucking scatterin' or whatever farmers do. And the local polis has been warned off, and all. So you'll be fine.'

'Aye.'

Nike Guy turned back and crouched down in front of Carr. He opened his mouth; two of the teeth were completely missing, and one was a ragged stump. 'See these, big man,' he said. 'I'm gonna do this to you tonight, only I'm doing it to *all* o' your teeth, and I'm doin' it with pliers.'

And with a cackle he was gone.

Carr waited for the sound of a vehicle, and then he waited for it to recede.

Then he said, 'Listen, Tommy, can you do me one wee favour? Let me make one phone call?' In for a penny, in for a pound, and

Tomas didn't strike him as a rocket scientist. 'I want to ring my wife and say goodbye to her. My wife and my boy.'

'I cannat let you do that.'

'Sure, you can. He's the same age as you, my boy. Even looks a bit like you. You don't need to untie me. Just hold the phone to my ear.'

'No.'

'Please, Tommy. Just one call. One minute.'

'I said fucking *no.*'

Carr didn't push it any further.

*Try another tack.*

'So how long you been in the RA, then?'

No reply.

'I've got to be honest, Tommy, I always had a lot of respect for the RA. The Army did, generally. Very professional guys. Not like the Arabs and all that lot.'

'How would you know?' said Tomas, sharply. 'I thought you was out the Army after five years? There was no Arab terrorism then.'

*Not as dull as he looked.*

'Och, I'm talking about the PLO. Before your time.'

Tomas nodded. 'The Palestinians? Good people.'

Again, Carr was wrong-footed, and had forgotten the long links between the IRA and the various Palestine interest groups.

But it gave him an 'in'.

'Aye, you're dead right,' he said. 'Great people. They just want their homeland, you know? Just like you guys. Us Scots are the same. It's always the fucking English, isn't it?'

There was a long pause.

Then Tomas said, 'Aye.'

*A breakthrough.*

'Have you ever been, Tommy?' said Carr.

'Where?'

'To Palestine.'

461

'No.'

'You should. Put it on your list.'

'Aye.'

Silence.

Carr was keeping a mental clock running, trying to gauge how long he'd been in this chair.

Had to be closer to three hours than two, now.

That made it somewhere around one o'clock.

Four or five hours till Pat Casey showed up, but his chances of getting out of this predicament would decrease exponentially once the other three got back from the pub.

Not to mention, if they were pissed they could very well get started on him before Casey arrived.

He tried to work on the plasticuffs, but there was no movement there.

Fake something? A heart attack?

No. Tomas would just call the others back from the bar, and then...

His feet were taped tight to the chair legs. But the chair itself wasn't anything much. In the old days, when PIRA was properly set up for this, they'd had people on really solid chairs which were also bolted to the floor. But this was just a flimsy, tubular steel thing, the kind that you see in stacks in a village hall. Carr was pretty confident that he could stand up by brute force, and break it in the process. That wouldn't deal with his hands, and it would leave him less than mobile, but it was a start. If he could hobble over to the rough wall, maybe he could start to work on the plasticuffs.

But then what about young Tomas?

Sitting ten feet away with that Glock between his feet.

Well, life wasn't perfect and you played the cards you were dealt. He had to get cracking, or else he was going to be in a world of pain fairly soon; to be fair, it would be better to take one from the Glock anyway.

He closed his eyes and focused on building up a good reservoir of saliva in his mouth.

Then he focused on swishing it round, getting it nice and frothy.

After a few minutes, he said, 'Tommy, I feel a bit weird. My fucking chest...'

The teenager looked up at him.

Carr began mumbling incoherently, and half-closed his eyelids, rolling his eyes up to show the whites. He began to shake, and allowed some of the saliva to dribble from his mouth.

Hoping against hope that the kid would buy it.

That his animal fear of something happening to his prisoner before Pat Casey got here would override his higher brain.

Carr started groaning.

Then deliberately inhaled saliva, forcing an unmistakeably genuine choking fit, and slumping forwards, head down.

Tomas stood up.

Leaving the Glock on the floor.

Said, 'What the fuck...'

Walked over, hesitantly.

He bent down close to Carr.

Carr struck.

Using every ounce of his physical power, he stood up, partially collapsing and buckling the chair, and launched himself at the young Irishman.

The headbutt caught Tomas flush on the chin and knocked him over, stunned.

Carr's momentum hurled him over on top of the other man.

Face-to-face.

Eyeball to terrified eyeball.

He started butting and biting, screaming like a banshee as he did so to increase the sense of disorientation.

The teenager flailed away with fists, but his blows were weak and Carr hardly felt them.

463

Tomas should have rolled sideways, or even tried to get under Carr. But he'd never been in a fight to the death before, and so he did the natural thing, and wriggled back, desperate to get away.

Leaving his neck exposed.

Carr pounced.

Turning his head sideways, he managed to get his teeth around Tomas's throat, and now he bit down, hard.

Tomas half-squealed, half-gurgled, punching Carr frantically in the face.

Scratching at his eyes.

Carr tore at his neck, feeling the skin yield.

Salty metallic blood.

Bit into the windpipe.

Ripped from side to side, like a dog with a bone.

And in a matter of a minute or two it was all over.

He rolled off the dead man and took a moment or two to compose himself.

Spat blood and tissue across the byre.

Got onto his knees and shuffled towards the Glock.

Somehow managed to get a hand on it.

He couldn't aim it properly, but it was better than nothing.

He looked around the cowshed.

There was a stone manger at the other end.

He half-hopped, half-dragged himself to it, and turned around.

Felt for the rough edge, and starting rubbing the plastic tie against it.

Pistol gripped in his right hand.

Safety off.

One eye on the doorway.

Listening for a car.

It took him at least ten minutes to fray the black nylon to the point where it weakened enough.

He pulled his wrists apart and looked at them.

He'd taken half his skin off, too, and he was bleeding quite badly.

Did not feel a fucking thing.

He bent down, found the edge of the tape around his right leg, and ripped it off. Did the same with his left, and threw the chair into the corner of the shed.

Stood there, stark bollock naked, and laughed.

He checked the Glock.

A full mag, and it looked to have been well-maintained.

Went to the open doorway.

Quick peep.

No sign.

*Think, John.*

*Get into the house and get some kit on.*

*Then what?*

*See what other weapons there are and go looking for the fuckers?*

*No, wait for them to come back.*

Feeling very exposed, he ran from the stone barn to the cottage.

The door was unlocked.

He cleared the place quickly and efficiently – no saying that one of them hadn't decided to stay back – and it was empty.

Went back and propped the door open, the better to hear anyone approach.

Found his clothes – in a black bin bag, ready to be disposed of – and quickly got dressed.

Found the folding stock AK.

He'd fired two shots this morning, which meant he had twenty-eight left. No sign of the spare mags, but he wouldn't need them.

He could see the driveway through the kitchen window. It was dark inside the cottage, so he was confident they wouldn't see him.

So, keeping an eye on that window, he made himself a cup of tea and a jam sandwich.

Got rid of the taste of that young wanker's throat.

# 119.

THERE WAS NO clock in the kitchen, and they'd taken his watch off him, so he had to guess at the time.

His thinking was that it was about three when Status Quo, Nike Guy and Yellow Anorak appeared at the end of the drive, the three of them in a grey Merc Sprinter.

The van they'd have been burning his body in, twenty-four hours from now.

Or a lot longer than twenty-four hours, if he was unlucky.

Carr readied his weapons – he'd use the AK, for its stopping power, but he had the Glock in his trousers just in case.

Stood back from the open door, in the dark of the hallway, and waited.

The van stopped outside.

The sound of two doors slamming.

Feet crunching.

Ribald laughter.

Something about a barmaid.

'Ach, you fucking *know* I could've!'

*Getting closer.*

AK into the shoulder.

He could hear them talking now.

'...check on the fucker?'

'Aye, in a minute.'

'Sure, it looks like the door's open.'

'Aye, Tommy'll have gone inside for a piss.'

'Or a wank.'

*More laughter.*

'Them was the days,' said one of them.

'I'll beat the tar out of him if he is,' said another. Status Quo, Carr thought. 'You've to take this sort of thing fucking seriously. This guy's fucking dangerous, and...'

Three shapes filling the doorway.

Carr squeezed the trigger and gave them a dozen rounds.

At a range of a little over ten feet, the AK was devastating.

It near about took off Status Quo's head, and it smashed Yellow Anorak back out of the cottage like he'd been hit with a wrecking ball, which in a way he had − four rounds to the chest, each of them delivering over 2,000 joules of kinetic energy.

The third of the group, Nike Guy, had been at the back, and to one side, and whether through luck or astonishing reflexes, had moved even further out just as Carr open fired.

As a result, he'd taken only one round, in the top of his right shoulder.

Still, it had punched him backwards and onto the ground outside, and now Carr followed him and watched him scrambling to his feet, pissing blood, staring in shock.

Carr walked forwards, rifle at the ready.

Nike Guy stumbled backwards, hand up on his good arm.

Carr reached him and smashed the stock into his face, splitting his forehead open.

He went down again, and this time he stayed there.

'Get up,' said Carr.

'No.'

Carr grabbed him by his hair and dragged him towards the cowshed.

Inside, he released him and pointed the rifle at his head.

'Get *up*,' he said.

Slowly, the man stood.

'What's your name?'

'Declan Reilly.'

'That's my fucking watch on your wrist.'

'Eh?'

'My watch. On your wrist. See that's a Rolex, but it's not just any old Rolex. Special edition for the Regiment. You only get to wear one if you've served. When did you pass Selection?'

'Eh?'

'It's a simple question, Declan. When did you pass Selection?'

'I never.'

'Then you'd better give it back to me.'

Gritting his teeth through the pain in his shoulder, and wiping blood out of his eyes, Declan Reilly managed to unclasp the watch.

He passed it over, hand trembling.

'Sorry,' he said.

'Aye, Declan,' said Carr. 'I bet you are.' He kept the AK levelled at the injured man. 'Have you got a phone?' he said.

'Aye.'

'What is it?'

'iPhone.'

'I was hoping you'd say that. Contract?'

The IRA man raised his eyebrows in disbelief. 'Pay as you go,' he said.

'I was hoping you'd say that, too. Pass it me. No funny business.'

Reilly reached into his back pocket and handed over the iPhone, grimacing in discomfort.

'Thanks,' said Carr. 'What's the code?'

Declan Reilly hesitated, but when Carr prodded the barrel of the AK into his bleeding shoulder wound he gave him the digits.

Stepping back a pace or two to give himself a little extra space, Carr looked down at the phone and tapped in the code.

Opened the phone.

Went to 'Photos'.

Said, 'Fuck me, is this your sister?'

Then, 'Only kidding, Declan.'

Opened WhatsApp and stepped forward.

'I want you to record a couple of wee messages for me,' he said, handing over the phone and a piece of paper. 'I wrote them down earlier, just in case.'

Reilly looked down at the piece of paper and studied it.

Looked up at Carr and said, 'What's this for?'

'Never you mind,' said Carr. 'Just read them. Assuming you *can* fucking read.'

Reilly looked down. 'I have information about the death of Pat Casey and several others at the farm in Camlough,' he said, 'and about Casey's involvement in the death of Michael Parry, the former British soldier who…'

The speech continued for thirty seconds or so, Declan looking up now and then at Carr, Carr nodding encouragingly.

When he'd finished, he looked back at Carr.

'Is that it?' he said.

'That is it,' said Carr, with a grin, taking back the iPhone. 'Thank you, Declan, and goodnight.'

The muzzle flash illuminated the dark interior.

Declan Reilly hit the floor with a dead thud.

The smell of cordite filled the air.

John Carr smiled and breathed deeply through his nose.

He loved the smell of gunfire, and it had been a while.

# 120.

CARR TOOK THE piece of paper from Declan Reilly's dead hand, left the AK47 propped up by the open doorway and went outside.

The air was cool and the sky was grey, and he felt fucking fantastic.

He stood for a few moments, listening to the silence.

Looked at his watch, still warm from Reilly's wrist.

Just a wee bit before 4pm.

*Casey on his way.*

Leaving Tomas and Reilly where they were, he dragged the other bodies into the cottage.

Glock in hand, ran to the farmhouse.

No sign of the farmer.

*McKilty's under instructions to keep well away… he's off ploughin' or fucking scatterin' or whatever farmers do.*

Had a quick scout round.

Found the central heating tank.

Not far away, and an empty twenty-litre jerry can nearby.

He filled the jerry can with heating oil from the measuring bar.

Went into the barn first, dousing everything.

Then the house, top to bottom, every room.

None of his DNA to be left behind.

Saved a little for the Mercedes Sprinter van, into which he now climbed.

Then he sat down to wait.

# 121.

HEADLIGHTS PIERCED THE wintry gloaming at just after 17.30.

The silver Volvo, bouncing along the lengthy farm track.

Carr had counted the rounds in the AK.

Nine left.

Seventeen in the Glock.

More than enough.

He gripped the rifle and slid lower in his seat.

The Volvo ground to a halt in front of the cottage.

Carr watched it in the big Merc's wing mirror.

*No movement.*

Had they made him?

*No way.*

Maybe they'd called ahead to speak to one of their guys and were spooked by the lack of pick-up.

But in that case, why even drive to the farm?

Thirty seconds ticked by, and then the interior light came on as a door opened.

*A rear door, though.*

He looked closer.

*Oleg Kovalev.*

Holding a pistol, which was trained on the men in the front.

Carr cracked the door of the van.

*Careful, John. Let's not go spooking crazy Russians.*

'Oleg,' he called. 'It's me. In the grey van. I'm alone and I'm coming out, okay?'

'Slowly, John,' said Oleg. 'Walk to me.'

Carr hopped down.

Oleg backed and turned slightly, so that he could keep the two men in the Volvo in view, but see Carr out of his peripheral vision.

Flicked his eyes in the Scotsman's direction.

Turned his body back to the Volvo.

Said over his shoulder, 'Hi, Johnny. I bought you little present.'

He was grinning like a velociraptor.

'So I can see. What the fuck are you doing?'

'What you always say, John? Prior planning and preparation prevents performance?'

'Something like that.'

'So I plan and prepare to help you.'

Carr was at his side now, his own pistol pointing at the ground.

Kovalev opened the passenger door. 'Put fucking hands on you fucking heads!' he snapped.

Pat Casey and Paulie McMahon complied immediately.

Oleg shot Carr a glance. Took in a face which was cut and bruised and smeared in blood. 'If you don't mind me saying, Johnny, looks like you needed help.'

'Everything was under control.'

'If you say.'

As he said that, he backed away from the Volvo, pistol still levelled at the two men.

'Now, over to you, Johnny.'

Carr crouched down on his haunches.

Looked up at Casey.

'Hello, Pat,' he said. 'I believe you want to kill me?'

Casey looked at him, fingers interlocked behind his skull.

'I suppose it's no point me telling you I'm not who you think I am?' he said.

'Not really.'

'You think I'm a politician, but…'

Carr started laughing. 'A politician?' he said. 'You're a gangster and a murderer, legitimised by a corrupt peace process. Politicians don't send people to kill people.' He paused. 'Well, you know what I mean.'

'You think I'm a politician, but I'm a source, a source for MI5. I've been working for the British government for twenty years or more.'

Paulie McMahon had turned to look at his boss.

'Pat,' he said. 'You're a tout? Jesus. You cannat be fucking serious.'

'Shut up, Paulie,' said Casey. 'Call my handler. I can give you his codename and number.'

'Yes,' said Carr. 'Shut up, Paulie.'

He angled the Glock slightly and shot McMahon in the face.

Blood sprayed all over Pat Casey's right ear and cheek, but he didn't flinch.

'Call him,' said Casey, after a few moments. He wiped some of the blood and red matter away. 'He'll confirm it for you.'

'I'm not interested, Pat,' said Carr. 'Guys like you, you thought you could play both sides. We should have put you down like a dog when we shot your brothers.'

'You fucking bastard,' breathed Casey. But then he quickly softened his tone. 'I can pay you. What do you want?'

Carr chuckled and raised the Glock.

In that moment, Pat Casey was out of the door and away across the purple scrub, moving with a speed which was born of terror.

Oleg raised his pistol to shoot the fleeing man, but Carr smiled and held up a hand.

'No,' he said. 'Leave him. He's mine.'

Casey was slipping and sliding as he ran, and had not got far. His initial sprint had been based on adrenalin, but he was quickly out of breath, and slowing, and Carr caught up with him in fifty metres.

He tripped Casey from behind, and sent him sprawling onto the earth.

Casey got onto his knees, and started to cry.

'Please,' he said. 'Don't do it. I'll do anything. I know a lot of information that the British government would want. Murders, robberies, the Disappeared. I know the lot.'

'I thought you were a source, Pat?' said Carr, mockingly. 'Why haven't you handed that information over before now?'

'Oh, shit,' said Casey. 'I couldn't give it all… I needed…'

He tailed off, hopelessly.

Carr laughed. 'Pat,' he said, 'to tell you the truth I couldnae care less whether you're a tout, or not. This has fuck all to do with politics, or the Troubles. This is personal. You made it personal.' He levelled the pistol at Casey. 'This is for Mick and Kevin,' he said, and shot him once in the chest.

The round ripped through Casey's right lung and tore a hole out of his back, pushing him back down into the ploughed field, blood frothing from his mouth.

Carr listened to his laboured breathing for a moment, and then realised that he was better than this.

Killing a man was one thing; making him suffer unnecessarily was another.

He put a second round into Casey's head, and then bent to pick up the body.

Back at the track, Oleg said, 'John, let's go. We need to go.'

'Aye,' said Carr. 'I think that would be a good idea. Just give me a couple of minutes.'

# 122.

CAIRBRE MCKILTY HAD taken a call earlier on with strict instructions not to return to his farm before bedtime, and he knew better than to ask why.

His nephew was a bad, bad man, and those goons he had with him were thick and nasty.

Whatever they had planned, he didn't want to know.

So he'd gone over Tassagh way to his brother's farm for tea, and had hung around a while under the pretext of chatting about the state of agriculture.

Eventually, his brother had kicked him out – bedtime for dairy men is around eight o'clock, after all – and Cairbre finally turned into the track to the farm at gone nine.

He'd known, of course – the fire had lit the sky up for miles around, and as he'd got closer he'd realised it had to be his place – but still, the shock of seeing the cottage and the byre still well ablaze, with fire engines spraying water on the house...

It was upsetting, he didn't mind admitting that.

There were police there, too, peering into the smoking remains of a Volvo, at the body in the driver's seat.

And when it was safe to get into the ruins, and they found the rest of the bodies, there were questions galore for Cairbre McKilty.

Then he warned them that one of the dead men might well be Pat Casey.

As in, Member of the Legislative Assembly Pat Casey.

As in, speaking softly, Belfast PIRA 2IC Pat Casey.

After that, things had suddenly got a lot hotter.

By then, John Carr and Oleg Kovalev were long gone.

# 123.

THREE DAYS LATER, two telephone calls were made by an anonymous man with a Northern Irish accent.

He spoke slowly and haltingly, and he did not respond to any questions.

The first call, jotted down in shorthand by the startled reporter on the other end, was to the news desk of the *Belfast Evening Telegraph*, to inform the newspaper on behalf of the Real IRA that the late Patrick Casey had been a tout for the British, and that he and his associates had been executed for that capital crime by volunteers who had taken their confessions at the farm in Camlough.

The second was to the confidential Crimestoppers hotline.

That call was recorded automatically by the unmanned line.

It began, 'I have information about the death of Pat Casey and several others at the farm in Camlough, and Casey's involvement in the death of Michael Parry, the former British soldier who…'

# EPILOGUE

CARR WAS GETTING his kit together for a trip to the gym – he'd just got back from a visit to St Helens to see the widow of Mick Parry, to tell her, as far as he could, that justice had been served – when the buzzer went.

He was tempted to ignore it, but it went again, and then again, so he walked through to the kitchen.

The CCTV image was clear enough.

Two men.

Late forties, early fifties, he guessed, and well-dressed.

Then one of them peered up into the lens, and Carr looked closer.

'What do you want?' he murmured to himself, with a faint grin. He pressed the button. 'Come up, boss,' he said. 'First floor.'

He opened the door of his flat and went to put his gym bag away.

A moment later there was a tentative knock, and a voice he knew of old said, 'Hello, John? May we come in?'

'Well, the door's open, isn't it?' Carr called out. 'I'll be through in a sec.'

He stowed the bag in his wardrobe and walked out.

Guy de Vere was standing there – tall and slim as ever, in a grey suit and Para Reg tie.

The guy by his side was wearing a nice, old-fashioned pin-stripe.

Expensive shirt.

Pinkie ring.

Discreet silver watch.

Black shoes with a mirror shine.

Looked like a Guards officer, to Carr.

That, or a senior, old school spook.

'Hello, John,' said de Vere, holding out a hand. 'It's good to see you.' He grinned. 'I must say, you're in a better state than when I last saw you.'

'I am?' said Carr, momentarily wrong-footed.

'At my birthday bash in Fulham,' said de Vere. 'You and Evan Forrest were hammered.'

'Ah, right,' said Carr. 'Got you. I'd had a few...'

He felt himself flushing slightly, as an image of a naked Antonia de Vere jiggling and squealing in his shower forced its way into his head.

Mercifully, it dissolved as quickly as it had arrived.

Guy de Vere turned to the man next to him. 'John held my hand when I first joined the Parachute Regiment,' he said. 'And then we worked together at 22. He was one of my best guys there.' He chuckled. 'Mad John. The stories I could tell you.'

'Aye, well, never let the truth get in the way of a good story, Guy,' said Carr, with a smile.

'Terrible what happened to Mick Parry,' said de Vere. 'His wife and daughters... He was a good man.'

'He was,' said Carr. 'Top guy, Mick. You'll be at the funeral next week, I assume?'

'Of course,' said de Vere. 'I'll never forget that day in Belfast.'

'Me neither,' said Carr. 'Been on my mind a bit lately.' He looked at the other man. 'And you are?'

De Vere's eyes twinkled in amusement. 'John,' he said, 'can I introduce you to Justin Nicholls? Justin's a very good friend of mine, and a senior chap at MI6.'

'I'd never have guessed,' said Carr. 'Good to meet you, Justin.'

The two shook hands.

'Take a seat, gents. What are you drinking?'

'I don't think we should,' said Nicholls. 'We're expected at a JTAC meeting in about an hour.'

Carr ignored him. 'The Macallan do you, Guy?'

'Sounds good to me.'

Carr poured three large measures, passed them around, and then sat down opposite de Vere and Nicholls.

'I dinnae trust a man who won't have a drink with me, Justin,' he said.

'Fair enough,' said the MI6 man, taking a decent swig.

'So I assume this isn't a social visit?' said Carr.

Putting the glass down, Nicholls opened his briefcase with a solid click, pulled out a sheaf of papers, and put them on the coffee table in front of him.

He selected a photograph, put it on the table, and turned it to face Carr.

'Do you recognise this?' he said.

Carr looked at it.

It was a CCTV still showing him walking along the deck of the Stena *Superfast VIII*, on his way to Belfast.

Head down.

It wasn't clear.

But it was clear enough.

Carr swallowed a mouthful of Scotch and looked directly at Nicholls.

'Looks a wee bit like me,' he said. 'I can't remember being on any boats recently. Then again, I might have been. Busy life, I lead.'

He switched his gaze to de Vere, who merely smiled.

'How about these?' said Nicholls.

Several ANPR images of a black Audi.

Carr was visible – just about – behind the wheel in some of them.

'All taken from the roads around Patrick Casey's house or Brian Keogh's house,' said Nicholls. He pointed to one. 'Actually, this one is on the road to Camlough.'

Carr started to laugh. 'I haven't the faintest fucking idea what this is about, guys,' he said, 'but I do know that if you wanted to pin anything on me you wouldnae do it like this. So what d'you want?'

'I'd say you were about as good as it's possible to be for one man acting alone, John,' said Nicholls. 'Exceptional. Everything Guy said about you, I believe.'

Carr drank more scotch. 'Is that so?' he said. 'And?'

'You can probably imagine the shit that's been going down in Northern Ireland since your visit,' said Nicholls. 'The police aren't the brightest, but they're putting a lot of manpower into it. For the time being, they're buying the line that the whole thing was an internecine affair caused either by Casey taking it upon himself to kill Michael Parry, or by Casey's being a tout, or both.' He paused. 'He *was* a tout, by the way. Very strictly between us – you know I shouldn't be telling you. Been a valuable source for over twenty years.'

Carr shrugged. 'You've got others. And you'll not have to pay his pension.'

'The Chancellor of the Exchequer will be most grateful,' said Nicholls, drily. 'Anyway, a nice lot of confusion and misinformation sown there by someone. Give it another fortnight, though, and images like these, and who knows what will happen?' He paused. 'But don't worry,' he said. 'It's not going to court. We'll make sure of that.'

Carr nodded.

Knocked back his whisky.

Got up, replenished his glass, and came back.

Sat down and looked flatly at Justin Nicholls.

'Don't *worry*?' he said. 'Listen, pal, I lived with death for years. Many's the times I've got up in the morning and not known if I was going to see the sun go down. I've been in spots where my life expectancy was measured in seconds. I've had friends – good friends, close friends – shot dead next to me. I took a round in the chest in Baghdad myself. Body armour saved me, and I got up and carried on. I'm okay with all of that shite. I love it, truth be told. So I'm not worried, believe me. But I dinnae like being threatened. You know what happened to the last people who tried it. So you tell me: where is this fucking going?'

Guy de Vere held up a hand. 'John,' he said, 'Justin's not threatening you. Do you think I'd be here if he was? He's one of my oldest friends – you're another. We're on the same side, here.'

Carr sat back on his sofa.

Nicholls cleared his throat. 'I'm obviously going about this the wrong way, John,' he said. 'My apologies. My intention was just to show you what was out there. And I mean *was*. It's no longer out there – these images have been pulled off by us. They'll never reach the courts. You have nothing to be… concerned about.'

Carr looked at them both.

He'd known Guy de Vere since the posh bastard's first patrol – that fateful first patrol – back in Belfast twenty-five years ago.

A straighter guy he could not imagine; he trusted him implicitly.

'Okay,' said Carr. 'Apology accepted. But the question stands – what *are* you here for?'

'There have been a number of serious plots against targets in the UK and our overseas interests,' said de Vere. 'Some have been in the papers. Others haven't. We've just about coped so far, but at any given moment we might drop the ball in a major way. I can't tell you any more at this stage, but you know me, you know my background. I'm not a bullshitter, and I'm not bullshitting you now.'

'Okay,' said Carr. 'I wouldnae say you're not a bullshitter, but I get the general idea.'

'The government is paying lip service, but the economic situation is dire, the cuts will continue and we all know there are plenty of yes men who will give the politicians the cover they need.'

'Why are you telling me this?'

'What if I were to say that there's a group of individuals who want to do something about it?' said Nicholls. 'You're looking at two of them, but it doesn't matter who the others are. Take it from me that they sit in key positions within the government, MI5, MI6, other strategic organisations... you know the score.'

'The mythical deniable operations?' said Carr, with a broad grin. 'I thought you were from Six, not the CIA.' He chuckled. 'What were you thinking? An advert in the *Times* personal column? *Personnel wanted for dangerous overseas work, orphans preferred, family men need not apply?*' He shook his head. 'I'm surprised at you, Guy. You and I both know that all goes to shite the first moment someone gets caught or killed.'

'It's not quite like that, John,' said Nicholls. 'But you're on the right track. We aren't putting it in the *Times*. We're sitting in your drawing room.'

'You and I also both know that there are a lot of sensitive places to which we can't send UK servicemen for political reasons,' said de Vere. 'Or just because it would attract too much attention, or would take too long to do via the proper channels. But we can send contractors. The Americans have been doing it for years. They had a division's-worth of military contractors in Iraq.'

'Aye, and look how that turned out. How's your Blackwater shares doing these days?'

'We're not talking about that kind of thing,' said Nicholls. 'We're talking about a small outfit, sub-contracted through official channels, working in-country in a security role, or on fact-finding missions, or governmental outreach. It would vary. We need people who can go in, have a nose about, and take appropriate action. It might just be sending back intelligence. Or it might be laying the ground for the SAS or some other organisation to go in and do something official. Other times…'

Carr nodded.

Held up a hand.

Got up and wandered over to the large window.

Outside the sun was shining in the cold, blue sky.

Behind him, Nicholls continued. 'You'd be an employee of a company which is sub-contracted to another company, and that to another, and so on… The whole thing will be bounced around the world so many times no-one will ever track it back to us. But even if they did, your work would be perfectly respectable. It's just that, occasionally, you might be called upon to *defend* yourself. This is the real world. Shit happens. But self-defence is also perfectly legal. And I've just shown you what we can do to assist with… evidence.'

'What if it all goes to shit? What if I get killed or captured?'

'In the event of capture, we'd make the same efforts to recover you as we would any British citizen,' said de Vere. 'In the event of your death, your family would be well taken care of.'

In the street below, a young woman pushed a buggy containing a small child, a toddler tripping happily alongside, holding her hand.

Carr watched them go; his mind wandered back to a similar scene in Niddrie, forty years earlier.

Him and his own mum, toddling off down to the long-demolished library to take out some books, then on to the shops to get a *Commando* comic and some Findus fish fingers or a meat pie for his dad's tea.

Someone had to protect little boys and their mums from the wolves prowling out in the badlands, that much was true.

But he'd done his share of that.

More than his share.

He turned to face the other two.

'I'm flattered, fellas,' he said. 'I really am. A big part of me would like to get involved. But my life has moved on. I'm going to have to pass.'

Nicholls and de Vere looked at each other for a moment.

Then de Vere said, 'Will you at least think about it?'

'Never say never, Guy,' said Carr. 'But I'm not a man who changes his mind easily. You know that.'

'I do. You're a stubborn bastard.'

Both of the other men stood.

'Thanks for your time, John,' said Nicholls, extending his hand to shake that of Carr. 'You aren't the only man on our radar. We will be recruiting others. But I feel bound to say that I'm disappointed. Based on your background and on your... recent exploits. What you did took determination and courage, and, more importantly, you did it outside the law. A lot of men would have hesitated. But there it is.'

He reached down into his briefcase, and scribbled something on a piece of paper.

Clicked the briefcase shut, straightened up, and handed the paper to Carr.

'Can I give you this?' he said. 'It's my private mobile number. If you change your mind, please just contact me. Night or day.'

Carr nodded.

'And, of course, this conversation never happened, on either side. Those photographs will never see the light of day. And we'd be grateful if...'

'My lips are sealed,' said Carr.

'It's been too long, John,' said Guy de Vere, with a warm smile. 'Let's not leave it so long next time.'

John Carr shook his old boss's hand. 'You know where to find me, boss,' he said. 'I still like a drink, and it's still your round.'

# ACKNOWLEDGMENTS

Thanks to my wife, who keeps me on the straight and narrow.

Thanks also to my agent, Jonathan Lloyd, and all at Curtis Brown for their support and counsel; and to my editors, Nick Bates and Lucy Gilmour, and all at HarperCollins, for their hard work and dedication.

Finally, thanks to friends and former comrades from the Parachute Regiment and the 22nd Special Air Service Regiment who have helped me along the way.